## Praise for *New York Times* bestselling author Allison Leigh

"[Allison] Leigh has a natural ability to draw a reader into a story."

*—RT Book Reviews*

"Two endearing yet genuine characters along with a solid plot make this story hard to put down. A truly delightful read."

*—RT Book Reviews* on *Once Upon a Proposal*

"Her doubting heroine and true-believer hero are the ultimate yin and yang: their banter is perfect, and their chemistry is spectacular."

*—RT Book Reviews* on *Once Upon a Valentine*

# HOME ON THE RANCH:
# WYOMING
## VOLUME 2

**NEW YORK TIMES BESTSELLING AUTHOR**

# ALLISON
# LEIGH

**HARLEQUIN®** HOME ON THE RANCH

Recycling programs for this product may not exist in your area.

ISBN-13: 978-1-335-00504-5

First published as Home on the Ranch by Harlequin Books in 2004 and Just Friends? by Harlequin Books in 2007.

Home on the Ranch: Wyoming Volume 2
Copyright © 2017 by Harlequin Books S.A.

The publisher acknowledges the copyright holder of the individual works as follows:

Home on the Ranch
Copyright © 2004 by Allison Lee Davidson

Just Friends?
Copyright © 2007 by Allison Lee Davidson

This edition published by arrangement with Harlequin Books S.A.

For questions and comments about the quality of this book, please contact us at CustomerService@Harlequin.com.

**HARLEQUIN**®
™ www.Harlequin.com

**Printed in U.S.A.**

# CONTENTS

A frequent name on bestseller lists, **Allison Leigh**'s high point as a writer is hearing from readers that they laughed, cried or lost sleep while reading her books. She credits her family with great patience for the time she's parked at her computer, and for blessing her with the kind of love she wants her readers to share with the characters living in the pages of her books. Contact her at allisonleigh.com.

### Books by Allison Leigh

### Harlequin Special Edition

### *Return to the Double C*

*A Child Under His Tree*
*The BFF Bride*
*One Night in Weaver...*
*A Weaver Christmas Gift*
*A Weaver Beginning*
*A Weaver Vow*
*A Weaver Proposal*
*Courtney's Baby Plan*
*The Rancher's Dance*

### *Montana Mavericks: 20 Years in the Saddle!*

*Destined for the Maverick*

### *Men of the Double C*

*A Weaver Holiday Homecoming*
*A Weaver Baby*
*A Weaver Wedding*
*Wed in Wyoming*
*Sarah and the Sheriff*

### *The Fortunes of Texas: Welcome to Horseback Hollow*

*Fortune's Prince*

Visit the Author Profile page at Harlequin.com for more titles.

# HOME ON THE RANCH

# Chapter 1

"He is not an ogre."

Belle Day flicked her windshield wipers up to frenzied and tightened her grip around the steering wheel of her Jeep. She focused harder on the unfamiliar road, slowing even more to avoid the worst of the flooding, muddy ruts.

It wasn't the weather, or the road, or the unfamiliar drive that had her nerves in a noose, though. It was the person waiting at the end of the drive.

"He is *not* an ogre." Stupid talking to herself. She'd have to keep that to a minimum when she arrived. Not that she did it all the time.

Only when she was nervous.

Why had she agreed to this?

Her tire hit a dip her searching gaze had missed, and the vehicle rocked, the steering wheel jerking violently in her grip. She exhaled roughly and considered pulling over, but discarded the idea. The sooner she got to the Lazy-B, the sooner she could leave.

*Not exactly positive thinking, Belle. Why are you doing this?*

Her fingers tightened a little more on the wheel. "Lucy," she murmured. Because she wanted to help young Lucy Buchanan. Wanted to help her badly enough to put up with Lucy's father, Cage.

*Who was not an ogre.* Just because the therapist she was replacing had made enough complaints about her brief time here that they'd found a way through Weaver's grapevine didn't mean *her* experience would be similar.

*That's not the only reason.* She ignored the whispered thought. The road curved again, and she saw the hooked tree Cage had told her to watch for. Another quarter mile to go.

At least the ruts in the road were smoothing out and she stopped worrying so much about bouncing off into the ditch. The rain was still pouring down, though. Where the storm had come from after weeks of bone-dry weather, she had no idea. Maybe it had been specially ordered up to provide an auspicious beginning to her task.

She shook her head at the nonsense running through it, and slowed before the quarter-mile mark. It was raining and that was a good thing for a state that had been too dry for too long. She finally turned off the rutted road.

The gate that greeted her was firmly closed. She studied it for a moment, but of course the thing didn't magically open simply because she wished it.

She let out a long breath, pushed open the door and dashed into the rain. Her tennis shoes slid on the slick mud and she barely caught herself from landing on her butt. By the time she'd unhooked the wide, swinging gate, she was drenched. She drove through, then got out again and closed it. And then, because she couldn't possibly get *any* wetter unless she jumped in a river, she peered through the sheet of rain at Cage Buchanan's home.

It was hardly an impressive sight. Small. No frills. A porch ran across the front of the house, only partially softening the brick dwelling. But the place did look sturdy, as the rain sluiced from the roof, gushing out the gutter spouts.

She slicked back her hair and climbed into her Jeep once more to drive the rest of the way. She parked near the front of the house. Despite the weather, the door was open, but there was a wooden screen. She couldn't see much beyond it, though.

She grabbed her suitcase with one wet hand before shoving out of the Jeep, then darted up the narrow edge of porch steps not covered by a wheelchair ramp. A damp golden retriever sat up to greet her, thumping his tail a few times.

"You the guard dog?" Belle let the curious dog sniff her hand as she skimmed the soles of her shoes over the edge of one of the steps. The rain immediately turned the clumps of mud into brick-red rivulets that flowed down over the steps. Beneath the protection of the porch overhang, she wiped her face again, and flicked her hair behind her shoulders. Of all days not to put it in a ponytail. She couldn't have arrived looking more pathetic if she'd tried.

She knocked on the frame of the screen door, trying not to be obvious about peering inside and trying to pretend she wasn't shivering. Even sopping wet, she wasn't particularly cold. Which meant the shivers were mostly nerves and she hated that.

She knocked harder. The dog beside her gave a soft *woof.*

"Ms. Day!" A young, cheerful voice came from inside the door, then Belle saw Lucy wheel into view. "The door's open. Better leave Strudel outside, though."

"Strudel, huh?" Belle gave the dog a sympathetic pat. "Sorry, fella." She went inside, ignoring another rash of shivers that racked through her. It was a little harder to ignore Strudel's faint whine when she closed the screen on him, though.

She set her suitcase on the wood-planked floor, taking in the interior of the house with a quick glance. Old-fashioned furnishings dominated mostly by a fading cabbage rose print. An antique-looking upright piano sat against one wall, an older model TV against the other. The room was clean but not overly tidy, except for the complete lack of floor coverings. Not even a scatter rug to quiet the slow drip of water puddling around her.

She looked at the girl who was the reason for her waterlogged trek. "Your hair has grown." Too thin, she thought. And too pale. But Lucy's blue eyes sparkled and her golden hair gleamed.

Lucy dimpled and ran a hand down the braid that rested over her thin shoulder. "It's dry, too. Come on. We'll get you some towels." She turned her chair with practiced movements.

Belle quickly followed. Her tennis shoes gave out a wet squeak with each step. They were considerably louder than the soft turn of Lucy's wheelchair.

She glanced through to the kitchen when they passed it. Empty. More than a few dishes sat stacked in the white sink. The stove looked ancient but well preserved.

"This is my room." Lucy waved a hand as she turned her chair on a dime, stopping toward the end of the hall, unadorned except for a bookshelf weighted down with paperbacks. "Used to be Dad's, but we switched 'cause of the stairs." She smiled mischievously. "Now I have my own bathroom."

Belle's gaze drifted to the staircase. "And up there was your old room?"

"Yeah, but the bathroom's in the hall. Not the same. There's an empty room up there, though. You don't have to sleep, like, on the couch or nothing."

Belle smiled. "I know. Your dad told me I'd have my own room." She hoped the two upstairs rooms were at least at opposite ends of the hall.

She walked into Lucy's bedroom. It may have been temporarily assigned because of Lucy's situation, but it bore no sign that it had ever been anything but a twelve-year old girl's bedroom. There was pink…everywhere. Cage had even painted the walls pale pink. And in those rare places where there wasn't pink, there was purple. Shiny, glittery purple.

Hiding her thoughts, she winked cheerfully at Lucy and squished into the bathroom where the towels were—surprise, surprise—pink with purple stripes. As she bent over hurriedly scrubbing her hair between a towel to take the worst of the moisture out, she heard the roll of Lucy's chair. "Is your dad around?" She couldn't put off meeting with him forever, after all. He *was* employing her. He'd hired her to provide both the physical therapy his daughter needed following a horseback-riding accident several months ago, and the tutoring she needed to make up for the months of school she'd missed as a result.

Lucy didn't answer and she straightened, flinging the towel around her shoulders, turning. "Lucy? Oh."

Six plus feet of rangy muscle stood there, topped by sharply carved features, bronze hair that would be wavy if he let it grow beyond two inches and eyes so pale a blue they were vaguely heart stopping.

"I guess you are." She pushed her lips into a smile that, not surprisingly, Cage Buchanan didn't return. He'd hired her out of desperation, and they both knew it.

After all, he loathed the ground she walked.

"You drove out here in this weather."

Her smile stiffened even more. In fact, a sideways glance at the mirror over the sink told her the stretch of her lips didn't much qualify for even a stiff smile. "So it would seem." It was easier to look beyond him at Lucy, so that's what she did. "Sooner we get started, the better. Right Lucy?"

For the first time, Belle saw Lucy's expression darken. The girl's lips twisted and she looked away.

So, chalk one up for the efficiency of Weaver's grapevine again. Judging by the girl's expression, the rumor about Lucy's attitude toward her physical therapy was true.

Belle looked back at Cage. She knew he'd lived on the Lazy-B his entire life. Had been running it, so the stories went, since he'd been in short pants.

Yet she could count their encounters in person on one hand.

None of the occasions had been remotely pleasant.

Belle had had her first personal encounter with Cage before Lucy's accident over the issue of Lucy going on a school field trip to Chicago. Lucy had been the only kid in her class who hadn't been allowed to go on the weeklong trip. Belle—as the newest school employee—

had been drafted into chaperone service and had foolishly thought she'd be able to talk Cage into changing his mind.

She'd been wrong. He'd accused her of being interfering and flatly told her to stay out of his business.

It had not been pleasant.

Had she learned her lesson, though? Had she given up the need to *somehow* give something back to his family? No.

Which only added to her tangle of feelings where Cage Buchanan was concerned. Feelings that had existed long before she'd come to Weaver six months ago with great chunks of her life pretty much in tatters.

"Did you bring a suitcase?"

She nodded. "I, um, left it by the front door."

He inclined his head a few degrees and his gaze drifted impassively down her wet form. "I'll take it upstairs for you."

"I can—" But he'd already turned on his heel, walking away. Soundless, even though he was wearing scuffed cowboy boots with decidedly worn-down heels.

If she hadn't had a stepfamily full of men who walked with the same soundless gait, she'd have spent endless time wondering how he could move so quietly.

She looked back at Lucy and smiled. A real one. She'd enjoyed Lucy from the day they'd met half a year ago in the P.E. class Belle had been substitute teaching. And she'd be darned if she'd let her feelings toward the sweet girl be tainted by the past. "So, that's a lot of ribbons and trophies on that shelf over there." She gestured at the far wall and headed toward it, skirting the pink canopied bed. "Looks like you've been collecting them for a lot of years. What are they all for?"

"State Fair. 4-H." Lucy rolled her chair closer.

Belle plucked one small gold trophy off the shelf. "And this one?"

"Last year's talent contest."

Belle ran her finger over the brass plate affixed to the trophy base. "First place. I'm not surprised." Belle had still been in Cheyenne then with no plans whatsoever about coming to Weaver for any reason other than to visit her family. Her plans back then had involved planning her wedding and obtaining some seniority at the clinic.

So much for that.

"Won't be in the contest this year, that's for sure."

"Because you're not dancing at the moment?" Belle set the trophy back in its place. "You could sing." She ignored Lucy's soft snort. "Or play piano. I thought I remembered you telling me once that you took lessons."

"I did."

"But not now?"

Lucy shrugged. Her shoulders were impossibly thin. Everything about her screamed "delicate" but Belle knew the girl was made of pretty stern stuff.

"Yeah, I still take lessons. But it doesn't matter. If I can't dance then I don't want to be in the contest. It's stupid anyway. Just a bunch of schoolkids."

"I don't know about stupid," Belle countered easily. Most talented school kids from all over the state. "But we can focus on *next* year." She took the towel from her shoulders and folded it, then sat on top of it on the end of Lucy's bed. She leaned forward and touched the girl's knee. The wicked scar marring Lucy's skin was long and angry. "Don't look so down, kiddo. People can do amazing things when they really want. Remember, I've seen you in action. And I already think you're pretty amazing."

"Miss Day."

Belle jerked a little. Cage Buchanan was standing in the doorway again. She kept her smile in place, but it took some work. "You'd better start calling me Belle," she suggested, deliberately cheerful. "Both of you. Or I'm not going to realize you're talking to me."

"The students called you Miss Day during the school year," he countered smoothly.

"You're not a student, Cage." She pointedly used his name. More to prove that she could address the man directly than to disprove that whole ogre thing. The fact was, she knew he was deliberately focusing on her surname. And she knew why.

She was a Day. And he hated the Day family.

His eyes were impossible to read. Intensely blue but completely inscrutable. "I need a few minutes of your time. Then you can…settle in."

Belle hoped she imagined his hesitation before *settle*. Despite everything, she wasn't prepared to be sent out on her ear before she'd even had a session with Lucy. For one thing, she really wanted to help the girl. For another, her ego hadn't exactly recovered from its last professional blow.

She was aware of Lucy watching her, a worried expression on her face. And she absolutely did *not* want to worry the girl. It wasn't Lucy's problem that she had a…slight…problem with the girl's dad. "Sure." She rose, taking the towel with her. "Then I'll change into something dry, and you—" she gently tugged the end of Lucy's braid "—and I can get started."

The girl's expression was hardly a symphony of excitement. But she did eventually nod, and Belle was happy for that.

She squeaked across the floor in her wet sneakers

and, because Cage didn't look as if he would be moving anytime this century, she slipped past him into the hall. He was tall and he was broad and she absolutely did not touch him, yet she still tamped down hard on a shiver.

Darned nerves.

"Kitchen," he said.

Ogre, she thought, then mentally kicked herself. He was a victim of circumstances far more than she was. And he *had* painted his bedroom pink for Lucy, for heaven's sake. Was that the mark of an ogre?

She turned into the kitchen.

"Sit down."

There were three chairs around an old-fashioned table that—had it been in someone else's home—would have been delightfully retro. Here, it obviously was original, rather than a decorating statement. She sat down on one of the chairs and folded her hands together atop the table, waiting expectantly. If he wanted to send her home already, then he would just have to say so because *she* wasn't going to invite the words from him. She'd had enough of failure lately, thank you very much.

But in the game of staring, she realized all too quickly that he was a master. And she…was not.

So she bluffed. She lifted her eyebrows, doing the best imitation of her mother that she could summon, and said calmly, "Well?"

Interfering, Cage thought, eying her oval face. Interfering, annoyingly superior, and—even wet and bedraggled—too disturbing for his peace of mind.

But more than that, she'd managed to make him feel out of place. And Cage particularly didn't like that feeling.

But damned if that wasn't just the way he felt standing there in his own kitchen, looking at the skinny, wet woman sitting at the breakfast table where he'd grown up eating his mother's biscuits and sausage gravy. And it was nobody's fault but his own that Miss Belle Day— with her imperiously raised eyebrows and waist-length brown hair—was there at all.

He pulled out a chair, flipped it around and straddled it, then focused on the folder sitting on the table, rather than on Belle. This was about his daughter, and there wasn't much in this world he wouldn't do for Lucy. Including put up with a member of the Day family, who up until a few years ago had remained a comfortable distance away in Cheyenne.

If only she wasn't…disturbing. If only he hadn't felt that way from the day they'd met half a year ago.

Too many "if onlys." Particularly for a man who'd been baptized in the art of dealing with reality for more years than he could remember.

He flipped open the folder, reining in his thoughts. "Doctors' reports." He shoved a sheaf of papers toward her. "Notes from the last two PTs." Two different physical therapists. Two failures. He was running out of patience, which he'd already admitted to her two weeks ago when he'd flatly told her why the other two hadn't worked out; and he was definitely running out of money, which he had no intention of ever admitting to her.

He watched Belle's long fingers close over the papers as she drew them closer to read. He pinched the bridge of his nose before realizing he was even doing it. Maybe that's what came from having a headache for so many months now.

"Your last therapist—" Belle tilted her head, studying the writing, and a lock of tangled hair brushed the table, clinging wetly "—Annette Barrone. This was her schedule with Lucy?" She held up a report.

"Yeah."

She shook her head slightly and kept reading. "It's not a very aggressive plan."

"Lucy's only twelve."

Belle's gaze flicked up and met his, then flicked away. He wondered if she thought the same thing he'd thought. That Annette had been more interested in impressing her way into his bed than getting his daughter out of her wheelchair.

But she didn't comment on that. "Lucy's not an ordinary twelve-year-old, though," she murmured. The papers rustled in the silent kitchen as she turned one thin sheet to peruse the next. Her thumb tapped rhythmically against the corner of the folder.

"My daughter is not abnormal."

Her thumb paused. She looked up again. Her eyes, as rich a brown as the thick lashes that surrounded them, narrowed. "Of course she's not abnormal. I never suggested she was." She moistened her lips, then suddenly closed the folder and rested her slender forearms on top of it, leaning toward him across the table. "What I *am* saying is that Lucy is highly athletic. Her ballet dancing. Her riding. School sports. She is only twelve, yes. But she's still an athlete, and her therapy should reflect that, if there's to be any hope of a full recovery. That's what you want, right?" Her gaze never strayed from his.

He eyed her. "You're here."

She looked a little uneasy for a moment. "Right. Of course. You wouldn't keep hunting up therapists who are willing to come all the way out here to the Lazy-B on a lark. But my point is that you *could* just drive her into town for sessions a few times a week. She could even have her tutoring done in town. All of her teachers want to see her be able to start school again in the fall with her class, rather than falling behind." Her lips curved slightly. "The cost for the therapy would be considerably less if you went into town. You could have a therapist of your choice work with Lucy at the Weaver hospital. I know the place isn't entirely state of the art, but it's so new and the basics are there—"

"I'll worry about the cost." That faint smile of hers died at his interruption. "You're supposed to be good at what you do. Are you?"

Her expression tightened. "I'm going to help Lucy."

It wasn't exactly an answer. But Cage cared about two things. Lucy and the Lazy-B. He was damned if he'd admit how close he was to losing both. Like it or not, he needed Belle Day.

And he hoped his father wasn't rolling over in his grave that this woman was temporarily living on the ranch that had been in the Buchanan family for generations.

He stood, unable to stand sitting there for another minute. "Set whatever schedule you need. Your stuff is in the room upstairs at the end of the hall. Get yourself dry. I've got work to do."

He ignored her parted lips—as if she was about to speak—and strode out of the room.

The sooner Belle did what he hired her for and went on her way, the better. They didn't have to like each other. The only thing he cared about was that she help Lucy and prove that he could provide the best for his daughter.

Once Belle Day had done that, she could take her skinny, sexy body and interfering ways and stay the hell out of his life.

## Chapter 2

The rain continued the rest of the afternoon, finally slowing after dinner, which Belle and Lucy ate alone. Cage had shown his face briefly before then, but only to tell Lucy to heat up something from the fridge and not to wait on him. Belle had seen the shadow in Lucy's eyes at that, though the girl didn't give a hint to her father that she was disappointed. And it was that expression that kept haunting Belle later that evening after Lucy had gone to bed. Haunted her enough that she didn't close herself up in the guest room to avoid any chance encounter with Cage.

Instead, she hung around in the living room, knowing that sooner or later he would have to pass through the room in order to go upstairs. But, either she underestimated his intention to avoid her as much as possible, or he had enough bookkeeping to keep him busy for hours on end in his cramped little office beyond the stairs.

When she realized her nose was in danger of hitting the pages of the mystery she'd borrowed from the hallway shelf, she finally gave up and went upstairs. Walked past the bedroom that Cage had traded with his daughter. The door was open and she halted, took a step back, looking through the doorway. There was only the soft light from the hall to go by, but it was enough to see that the room was pink.

He hadn't painted over the walls in Lucy's original room as if she was never going to be able to return to it.

She chose to take that as a good sign. All too many people entered physical therapy without really believing they'd come out on the other side.

Though the room was pink, it still looked spare. All she could see from her vantage point was the bed with a dark-colored quilt tossed over the top, a dresser and a nightstand with a framed photograph sitting on it. The photo was angled toward the bed.

"Something interesting in there?"

She jerked and looked back to see Cage stepping up onto the landing. He looked as tired as she felt. "Pink," she said, feeling foolish.

His long fingers closed over the newel post at the head of the stairs. He had a ragged-looking bandage covering the tip of his index finger. She'd noticed it earlier. Had squelched the suggestion that she rewrap it for him, knowing it wouldn't be welcomed.

His eyebrows pulled together. "What?"

She gestured vaguely. "The walls. They're pink. I was just noticing that, I mean."

"Luce likes pink." His lashes hid his expression. "She's a girl."

"My sister likes pink." Belle winced inwardly. What an inane conversation.

"And you?"

"And I…what?" He probably thought she was an idiot. "Don't like pink?"

"No. No, pink is fine. But I'm more of a, um, a red girl."

His lips lifted humorlessly. "Pink before it's diluted. You fixed pizza."

She blinked a little at the abrupt shift. "Veggie pizza. There's some left in the refrigerator."

"I know. And I'm not paying you to play cook."

That derailed her for half a moment. But she rallied quickly. Anyone with two eyes in their head could see the Buchanans could use a helping hand. "I didn't mind and Lucy—"

"I mind."

She stiffened. Did he expect her to assure him it wouldn't happen again? "The whole wheat pizza and fresh vegetables, the fact that Lucy didn't want to eat that leftover roast beef you told her to eat, or the fact that *I* dared to use your kitchen? Any other rules I need to know about?"

Apparently, he didn't recognize that her facetious comment required no answer. "Stay away from the stables."

"Afraid a *Day* might hurt the horses? Why did you even bother talking me into taking this job?"

"The horse that threw Lucy is in the stable. I don't want her tempted to go there, and if you do, she'll want to, as well. And the only thing my daughter needs from you is your expertise."

"Which, by your tone, it would seem you doubt I possess. Again, it makes me wonder why you came to me, not once but twice, to get me to take on Lucy's case for the summer." The hallway seemed to be shrinking. Or maybe it was her irritation taking up more space as it grew.

"You have the right credentials."

"Just the wrong pedigree." Her flat statement hovered in the air between them.

Every angle of his sharp features tightened. "Is your room comfortable enough?"

"It's fine." She eyed him and wondered how a man she barely knew could be so intertwined in her life. "Sooner or later we might as well talk about it." His expression didn't change and she exhaled. "Cage, what happened was tragic, but it was a long time ago." She ought to know.

Finally, some life entered his flinty features, and his expression was so abruptly, fiercely alive that she actually took a step back, earning a bump of her elbow against the wall behind her.

"A *long* time ago?" His bronze hair seemed to ripple along with the coldness in his voice as he towered over her. "I'll mention that to my mother next time I visit her. Of course, she probably won't mind, since she barely remembers one day to the next."

Belle's stomach clenched. Not with fear, but sympathy and guilt. And she knew he'd never in a million years accept those sentiments from her, if he even believed she was capable of experiencing it.

She'd heard he was overbearing. But he believed she was the daughter of a devil.

She folded her hands together. Well, she'd been warned, hadn't she? "This was a bad idea. I shouldn't have come here. You…you should bring Lucy into Weaver. I will work with her there." She didn't officially have hospital privileges, but she had a few connections who could help arrange it, namely her stepsister-in-law, Dr. Rebecca Clay. And it didn't matter *where* Belle and Lucy did the tutoring.

"I want you here. I've told you that."

Belle pushed her fingers through her hair, raking it back from her face. "But, Cage. It just doesn't make any sense. Yes, I know it's a long drive to make every few days into town, but—"

His teeth flashed in a barely controlled grimace. "My daughter will have the best care there is. If that seems extravagant to you, I don't care. Now, are we going to have this—" he barely hesitated "—discussion every time we turn around? Because I'd prefer to see something more productive out of your presence here. God knows I'm paying you enough."

She sank her teeth into her tongue to keep from telling him what he could do with that particular compensation. Compensation they both knew was considerably less than she could have charged. "I'd like my time to be productive, too," she said honestly. "I have no desire to spend unnecessary time under your roof."

"Well, there's something we agree on, then."

Her fingers were curled so tightly against her palms that even her short nails were causing pain. "And here's something else we'd better agree on." She kept her voice low, in deference to Lucy sleeping downstairs. "Lucy doesn't need the added stress of knowing you detest me, so maybe you could work on summoning a little...well, *friendliness* is probably asking too much. But if Lucy senses that you don't trust me to do my best with her, then she's not going to, either, no matter *how* well she and I got along when she was in my P.E. class."

"I don't need you telling me what my daughter needs. I've been her only parent since she was born."

"And it's amazing that she's turned out as well as she has." She winced at the unkind words. "I'm sorry. That was—"

"True enough." He didn't look particularly offended. "She *is* amazing."

Belle nibbled the inside of her lip as thick silence settled over them. Should she have listened to her mother's warning that she was getting in over her head? Not because of the skill she would require to work with Lucy—as her therapist as well as a tutor—but because of who Lucy *was?*

Probably.

She sighed a little and pressed her palms together. "Lucy is a great kid, Cage. And I really do want to help her." That was the whole point of all this.

Mostly.

A muscle flexed in his jaw and his gaze slid sideways, as if he was trying to see the bedroom downstairs where his daughter slept. "If I believed you didn't, you wouldn't be here."

Which, apparently, was as much a concession as she was likely to get out of the man. For now, anyway. Fortunately, somewhere in her life she'd learned that a retreat didn't always signify defeat.

"Well. I guess I'll hit the sack." She was twenty-seven years old, but she still felt her face heat at the words. As if the man didn't know she'd be climbing into bed under his roof. She was such a head case. Better to focus on *the job*. The last time he'd come to her house—after she'd already refused Lucy's case once—he'd admitted that he'd fired Annette Barrone because of her overactive hormones. Belle had assured him that he had no worries from her on *that* score.

As if.

"I went over and checked out the barn earlier," she said evenly when neither one of them moved. "The setup is remarkable." And another indication of his devotion to his daughter. Every piece of equipment that she could have wished for had been there, and then some. The hospital in town should only be so lucky. "I rearranged things a little. If that's all right."

Now, his hooded gaze slid back over her face. And she refused to acknowledge that the shiver creeping up her spine had anything to do with his intensely blue gaze.

"Use your judgment."

She nodded. "Okay, then." The door to her bedroom was within arm's reach. Not at *all* at opposite ends of the hall from his. "Good night." She wished he would turn into his own bedroom. But he just stood there. And feeling idiotic, she unplastered her back from the wall behind her and went through the door, quickly shutting it behind her.

A moment later, she heard the squeak of a floorboard, and the close of another door.

Relief sagged through her. After changing into her pajamas, she crossed to the bed and sat on it, dragging her leather backpack-style purse up beside her. She rummaged through it until she found her cell phone and quickly dialed.

A moment later, her sister, Nikki, answered with no ceremony. "So, are you there?"

Belle propped the pillow behind her and scooted back against it. The iron-frame bed squeaked softly, as if to remind her that it had survived years and years of use. It was a vaguely comforting sound. "Yes." She kept her voice low. The house might be sturdy, but the walls were thin enough that she could hear the rush of the shower from the bathroom across the hall.

She stared hard at the log-cabin pattern of the quilt beneath her until the image *that* thought brought about faded. "The drive was hellacious in the rain."

"Well, we've heard Squire say often enough that Cage Buchanan doesn't like visitors, so there's not a lot of need for him to make sure the road is easy."

"I know." Squire Clay was their stepfather, having married their mother several years earlier. She tugged at her ear. "Anyway, I know it's late. You were probably already in bed."

"It's okay. I wouldn't have slept until I knew you hadn't been beheaded at the guy's front door."

"He's not *that* bad."

"Not bad to look at, maybe. I still can't believe you took this job. What do you hope to prove, anyway?"

"Nothing," Belle insisted. "It's just a job to fill the summer until—" *if* "—I come back to the clinic."

Nikki snorted softly. "Maybe. But I'm betting you think this is your last chance to prove to yourself that you're not a failure."

Belle winced. "Don't be ridiculous, Nik."

"Come on, Belle. What other reason would have finally made you agree to that man's request?"

"*That man* has a name."

Nikki's sudden silence was telling. That was the problem with having a twin. But Belle was not going to get into some deep discussion over her motivation in taking on this particular job. "Speaking of the clinic," she said deliberately. "How are things there?"

"Fine."

Now it was Belle's turn to remain silent.

"They still haven't hired anyone to replace you, if that's what you're worried about," Nikki finally said after a breathy huff.

"That's something, at least." And a bit of a minor miracle, given the number of patients the prestigious clinic handled. She still wasn't entirely sure it wasn't because of the position her sister held as administrative assistant to the boss that Belle had been put on a leave of absence rather than being dismissed.

"And I know you're wondering but won't ask," Nikki went on. "So I'll just tell you. Scott's only coming in once a week now."

She wasn't sure how she felt at the mention of him. A patient she hadn't managed to completely rehabilitate. Briefly a fiancé she shouldn't have completely trusted. "You've seen him?"

"Are you kidding? I hide out in my office. If I saw Scott Langtree in person, I'd be liable to kick him." Nikki paused for a moment and when she spoke, her voice was acid. "*She* comes with him, now, apparently. Has most of the staff in a snit because she's so arrogant. Not that I'm condoning what Scott did, but from what people around here are saying about his wife, it's no wonder the man was on the prowl for someone else."

Belle plucked at the point of a quilted star. "But you haven't seen her?"

"Nope. And I consider that a good thing. I'd have something to say to her, too, and then *I'd* have my tail in a sling at work, just like you."

Belle smiled faintly. Nikki was her champion and always had been. "Hardly like me. You'd never be stupid enough to fall for a guy who already had a wife."

"And you wouldn't have fallen for Scott, either, if he hadn't lied about being married," Nikki said after a moment. "Good grief, Belle. The man proposed to you and everything. It's not your fault that he left out the rather significant detail that he wasn't free to walk another aisle."

"I caused a scandal there."

"Scott created the scandal," Nikki countered rapidly, "and it was half a year ago, yet you're still punishing yourself."

Belle wanted to deny it, but couldn't. Her relationship with Scott Langtree *had* caused a scandal. One large enough to create the urgent need for Belle to take a leave of absence until the furor died down. But it wasn't even the scandal that weighed on Belle so much as the things Scott had told her in the end.

Things she didn't want to dwell on. Things like being a failure on every front. Personal. Professional. Things that a secret part of her feared could be true.

"So," she sat up a little straighter, determined. "Other than…that…how are things going at work? Did you get that raise you wanted?"

"Um. No. Not yet."

"Did you *ask* for it?"

"No. But—"

"But nothing. Nik, you stand up for me all the time. You've got to stand up for yourself, too. Alex would be lost without you, and it's high time he started realizing it. I swear, it would serve the man right if *you* quit." But she knew Nikki wasn't likely to do that. Alexander Reed ran the Huffington Sports Clinic, including its various locations around the country. He had degrees up the whazoo, and was a business marvel, according to Nikki.

Belle just found the man intimidating as all get-out, but had still worked her tail off to get a position there.

A position she *was* going back to, she assured herself inwardly.

"So, what's he like? Cage, I mean. As ornery as everyone says?"

Belle accepted Nikki's abrupt change of topic. Alex was too sensitive a subject for her sister to discuss for long. "He is not an ogre," she recited softly.

Nikki laughed a little. "Keep telling yourself that, Annabelle."

Belle smiled. "It's late. Get some sleep. I'll talk to you later."

"Watch your back," Nikki said, and hung up.

Belle thumbed off her phone and set it on the nightstand. She didn't need to watch her back where Cage Buchanan was concerned. But that didn't mean she would be foolish enough to let down her guard, either.

The bed squeaked again when she lay down and yanked the quilt up over her. Even though the day hadn't been filled with much physical activity, she was exhausted. But as soon as her head hit the pillow, her eyes simply refused to shut, and she lay there long into the night, puzzling over the man who slept on the other side of the bedroom wall.

When he heard the soft creak of bedsprings for the hundredth time, Cage tossed aside the book he was reading and glared at the wall between the two bedrooms. Even sleeping, the woman was an irritant, and as soon as she was busy for the day, he was going to oil her bedsprings.

The last thing he needed night after night was to hear the sound of that woman's slightest movement in the bed that was so old it had been ancient even when he'd used it as a kid.

He hadn't noticed the squeaks before. Not with either therapist. Hattie McDonald with her militant aversion to smiles and her equally strong dislike for the remoteness of his ranch, nor Annette Barrone who'd made it clear she'd rather be sleeping in his room, anyway.

He climbed out of bed—fortunately a newer model than the one next door—and pulled on his jeans. He'd never been prone to sleeplessness until six months ago when he'd gotten the first letter from Lucy's mother. A helluva way to kick off the New Year. She wanted to see her daughter, she'd claimed. A daughter she'd never even wanted to have in the first place. He'd put her off, not believing her threat that she'd enlist her parents if he didn't comply. When he'd known Sandi, she'd wanted nothing to do with her parents beyond spending her tidy trust fund in any manner sure to earn their dismay.

Only she hadn't been bluffing. And it was a lot harder to ignore the demand for access to Lucy when it came from Sandi's parents. Particularly when it was backed up by their family attorneys.

Then came Lucy's accident several weeks later and his insomnia had only gotten worse. In the past week, with Belle Day's arrival pending, it was a rare night if he got more than an hour or two of sleep at a stretch. It was pretty damn frustrating.

He'd given up coffee, counted sheep and even drunk some god-awful tea that Emmy Johannson—one of the few people he tolerated in Weaver—had suggested. Nothing had worked.

And now he could add Belle Day's bed-creaking presence to his nightly irritations.

Barefoot, he left his bedroom. He could no more not glare at her closed door than he could get a full night's sleep these days.

He went downstairs, automatically stepping around the treads that had their own squeak, and looked in on Lucy. She'd kicked off her blankets again and he went inside, carefully smoothing them back in place. She sighed and turned on her side, tucking her hands together beneath her cheek in the same way she'd done since she was only months old.

There were times it seemed like twelve minutes hadn't passed since then, much less twelve years. Yet here she was, on the eve of becoming a teenager.

That was the problem with baby girls.

They grew up and started thinking they weren't their dad's baby girl anymore.

He left her room, leaving the door ajar so he could hear if she cried out in her sleep. Since she'd been thrown off that damn horse he should have sent back to her grandparents the day it arrived, she'd been plagued in her sleep almost as much as Cage.

He didn't need any light to guide him as he went through the house. The place was as familiar to him as his own face. Nearly the only thing that had changed since his childhood was the bed he'd just left behind and, if he'd had any foresight of the financial hit he would soon be taking with all manner of legal and medical costs, he wouldn't have bought the thing last year at all.

He went out on the front porch where the air still carried the damp from the rain even though it had finally ceased. It was more than a little chilly, but he barely noticed as he sat down on the oversize rocking chair his mother had once loved.

If the room at the care center would have had space for it, he'd have moved it there for her years ago. There wasn't much she hadn't done sitting in the chair here on this very porch. She'd shelled peas, knitted sweaters and argued good-naturedly with Cage's father when he and Cage came in after a long day.

But her room, while comfortable enough, wasn't that spacious.

And the one time he'd brought her back to the Lazy-B, she hadn't remembered the chair any more than she remembered him.

He leaned back, propping his feet on the rail, and stared out into the darkness. Strudel soon appeared beside him, apparently forgiving Cage for his banishment after dining on yet another pair of Cage's boots. He scratched the dog's head for a minute, then Strudel heaved a sigh and flopped down on the porch. In seconds, the rambunctious pup was snoring.

Lucky dog.

There were a lot of things Cage wished for in his life. But right then, the thing at the top of the list was sleep. He'd nearly achieved it when he heard a short, sharp scream.

Lucy.

He bolted out of the chair, leaving it rocking crazily behind him as he went inside. And he slammed right into the slender body hurtling around the staircase.

He caught Belle's shoulders, keeping her from flying five feet backward from the impact. "Lucy—" Her voice was breathless. Probably because he'd knocked the wind clean out of her.

"She sometimes has nightmares since the accident." He realized his fingers were still pressing into her taut flesh and abruptly let go. His eyes, accustomed to the darkness, picked up the pale oval of her face, the faint sheen of her skin. A lot of skin, it seemed. She was wearing loose shorts and some strappy little top that betrayed the fact she wasn't skinny everywhere.

He deliberately stepped around her and went into Lucy's room. But his daughter was already quiet again. Still sleeping, as if nothing had disturbed her at all.

He raked his fingers through his hair, pressed the heels of his palms to his eyes. God, he was tired. Then he felt a light touch on his back and nearly jumped out of his skin. He turned, pulling Lucy's door nearly closed again. "What?"

His harsh whisper sent Belle backward almost as surely as their collision had.

"Sorry." Her voice was hushed. "I thought…" He felt her shrug more than saw it. "Nothing."

He pinched the bridge of his nose. He could smell her, rainwater fresh. The sooner she went back to bed, the better. He wasn't interested in what she thought. Or how she smelled. Or why she couldn't keep still for five minutes straight in that old bed. "You thought what?" he asked wearily. He wished the moon were shining a little less brightly through the picture window in the living room, because with each passing second, he could see her even more clearly. Definitely not *all* skinny.

She tugged up the narrow strap of her pajama top and hugged her arms to herself. "Nothing. It doesn't matter."

"Fine. Then go to bed."

She laughed—little more than a breath. "You sound like my dad used to."

He knew it was an innocent enough comment, aimed at the order he'd automatically given. Knowing it, though, didn't keep him from reacting. Before he could say something that might send her straight for the decrepit Jeep she'd arrived in—and away from any possibility of helping his daughter—he stepped around her and headed upstairs.

"Cage—"

He didn't want to hear anything she had to say. She'd said the magic word, sure to remind him just who she was, and to what lengths he'd been driven for his daughter's sake.

Dad.

"Just go to bed, Belle," he said, without looking back.

# Chapter 3

Belle propped her hands on her hips and counted off a slow inhale and an even slower exhale. It was far too beautiful a morning, all promising with the golden sunrise, to let annoyance ruin it already. "Cage, I need to go over a few things with you about Lucy. I wanted to last night, but we never got to it."

His long legs barely paused as he passed her in the kitchen and headed out the back door of the house. "I've got a water tank that needs fixing." His tone was abrupt, as if he begrudged providing even that small bit of information.

Clearly, that somewhat approachable man she'd encountered in the middle of the night was banished again.

She hurried after him, letting the screen door slap shut noisily after her. She darted down the brick steps and jogged to keep up with him. She raised her voice. "Lucy told me yesterday that you haven't worked with her on any of the exercises she's supposed to do on her own."

He stopped short. Tilted his head back for a moment, then slowly turned to face her. The shadow cast by his dark brown cowboy hat guarded the expression in his blue eyes, but even across the yards, she could feel the man's impatience. "I can't be in two places at once, Miss Day."

She mentally stiffened her spine at his exaggerated patience. So much for his one slip of calling her Belle the night before. "I'm aware of that, *Cage.* But you hired me to help Lucy, and—"

"I didn't hire you to lecture me on my ability to parent my own daughter."

Her lips parted. "I wasn't suggesting—"

His eyebrow rose, making him look even more sardonic than usual. "Weren't you?"

"No!"

"You weren't so reticent before Lucy's accident when you accused me of being unreasonable where she's concerned 'cause I wouldn't let her go on that godforsaken field trip to Chicago."

She glanced back at the house where Lucy still slept. The truth was, she *had* thought he was being unreasonable. But that was half a year ago and there were more important things on the agenda than eliciting his approval for a simple school field trip. "Look, maybe we should just talk about…things." She'd thought so all along, but hadn't had the courage to do so. Hadn't had much of an opportunity, either, given their brief conversations about Lucy where Cage had firmly kept control.

His expression hadn't changed. "You're here for one reason only, Miss Day. It'd be better all around if you'd remember it."

Her jaw tightened uncomfortably. "I'm not the enemy, all right?"

His expression went from impatient to stony.

Her hands fell back to her sides. "I see. I *am* the enemy." Of course. Resulting from long-past history neither could change.

"If you need something that strictly pertains to Lucy—whether it's her therapy or her schoolwork—I have no doubt you'll let me know. Other than that—"

"—stay out of your hair?" Her tone was acid.

"That's one way to put it." He slapped the leather gloves he held against his palm. "Excuse me." He turned on his heel and strode away.

Belle stuck her tongue out at his back, and returned to the house. She yanked open the aging avocado-green refrigerator door. Maybe it was wrong of her, but she took great delight in making breakfast out of a leftover slice of pizza.

For Lucy, however, she set out an assortment of supplements on the counter, and then prepared a real breakfast. After peeking in the girl's bedroom to see that she was still sleeping, Belle pushed her feet into her running shoes and went back outside.

Even though the sky was clear, the dawn air still felt moist from the previous day, as she set off in a slow jog. Well beyond the simple brick house stood the sizable barn, doors open. She didn't want to wonder if Cage was in there. She wondered anyway, quickening her pace and then had to tell herself that she was being a ninny. The man ran a ranch. If he was in his barn, so what? Better there than in the house, bugging her and Lucy. Might present a problem when she and Lucy went to the barn to use the equipment, though.

She didn't doubt that he wanted the best for Lucy,

which she certainly couldn't fault. Nevertheless, she'd never met a more antisocial man in her life. But, then, she'd been warned well enough before she took on this job, so complaining about it now was only so much wasted energy.

She figured she'd run a good hour by the time she returned to the house. She darted up the brick steps and went in through the front door, peeling out of her sweatshirt as she went. Surely the bathroom wouldn't still hold the lingering scent of Cage's soap by now.

The bathroom was no longer steamy, true. But she still took the fastest shower in her life before changing into fresh workout clothes. Then she went and woke Lucy. While the girl was dressing—something she didn't need assistance for—Belle wandered around the cozy living room.

She peered again at the silver-framed black-and-white photos hanging above the fireplace mantel. Cage's parents. And a young Cage. She sighed faintly as she studied the Buchanan family. She knew only too well that he'd been a teenager when he'd lost his father, and for all intents, his mother, as well. She ran her fingernail lightly over the image of the solemn-looking little boy. Were there any photos of him smiling?

*Did* Cage Buchanan ever smile? Ever laugh?

"Hey, Belle. I'm fixing waffles for breakfast. You know the fruity kind with whipped cream? Those frozen waffles are really good that way. Like dessert."

Belle looked back to see Lucy rolling her chair into the kitchen. She headed after her, and hid a smile at Lucy's disgruntled "Oh." Obviously, she'd seen the breakfast that Belle had already set out for her. There would be *no* frozen waffles.

She stepped around Lucy's narrow chair, tugging

lightly on her gilded braid along the way. "It'll be good, I promise."

"Dad calls breakfasts like this 'sticks and weeds.'"

At that, Belle laughed softly. "Well, these sticks and weeds are a lot better for you than just a frozen waffle out of a box. It's a bran mix. And the strawberries on top are plenty sweet already without adding cream or sugar. But I could fix you eggs if you'd rather." She refused to wonder what Cage had eaten.

Lucy's perfectly shaped nose wrinkled. "Eggs. Gross."

"Yeah," Belle agreed. "I used to think so, too. But they're good for you, and there are lots of ways to fix them. So, what'll it be?"

Lucy eyed the table for a moment. Then she shrugged, and started to wheel forward. Belle casually stepped in her path and held out her hands expectantly.

And she waited.

And waited.

Finally, Lucy put her hands in Belle's. And she stood, her weight fully concentrated on her uninjured leg.

Belle winked cheerfully. Lucy wasn't the first patient she'd ever had, and certainly not the first who was leery of leaving the safety net, no matter how much they wanted to. But there was absolutely no reason why Lucy should still be depending entirely on the chair. "Stiff?"

Lucy nodded. There was a white line around her tight lips. Belle supported her as she twisted around and sat at the table. Then she tucked the wheelchair out of the way and sat down across from Lucy.

"Aren't you having any twigs?"

"Ate earlier. Not everyone sleeps in until noon."

Lucy rolled her eyes. "Yeah, right." She picked up the spoon and jabbed at her food. Gave an experimental taste. When the girl gave a surprised "hmm" and took another taste, Belle busied herself by filling a few water bottles and putting away the dishes they'd used and washed the night before as well as the stack that had already been there. She refused to feel guilty about it, either. It wasn't as if she was stealing the Buchanan family silver. She was just washing some crockery.

Lucy was nearly finished with her breakfast before she spoke again. "Did you see my dad this morning?"

"Yes, for a few minutes." Belle folded the dish towel and left it on the counter next to the sink. "He was heading out to fix a water tank."

"Oh." Lucy passed over her dishes.

Belle took them and set them in the sink. She flipped on the faucet to rinse them and glanced at Lucy. "Were you hoping for something different?"

Lucy shrugged but couldn't quite hide her diffidence. "He works the Lazy-B mostly by himself, you know."

Belle did know. She also knew that he hired on hands as needed, and that he usually didn't much want to admit to needing anything.

The man gave *loner* new meaning.

"I know." She smiled gently and moved the chair back around for Lucy. "Come on. It's beautiful outside. Let's go for a little walk."

"No exercises yet?"

Lucy looked so hopeful that Belle had to smile as she helped the girl back into her chair. She crouched in front of her. "I'll tell you a secret," she confided lightly. "Exercise comes in all sorts of forms. Sometimes you don't even know you're doing it." She grazed her fingertips over Lucy's injured leg. "So. What do you say? A walk?"

Lucy nodded. Satisfied, Belle rose and handed Lucy

a bottle of water, took one for herself and they headed out the front of the house, where Lucy's ramp was located.

Before long, Belle had to push the chair for Lucy because of the soft ground. The morning was delightfully quiet, broken only by the song of birds flirting in the tall cottonwoods that circled the house.

They walked all the way down the road to the gate then headed back again. "Do you like living on a ranch?"

Lucy lifted her shoulder, her fingers trailing up and down her braid. "It's okay, I guess. I used to spend part of the week in town. During the school year. Dad pays my friend Anya Johannson's mom for my board for part of the week. She teaches me piano and takes me to my dance lessons after school and stuff. Well, that's what we used to do." She tossed her braid behind her back.

They were within sight of the large red barn before Lucy spoke again. "You grew up in Cheyenne. Right?"

"Yup. Until I took the job at your school last year, and when I went away to school, I'd always lived in Cheyenne. My sister, Nikki, still does. And my mother's been living at the Double-C Ranch since she married Squire Clay a while back."

"Were your parents divorced?"

"No. My dad died just before Nikki and I turned sixteen."

"Does she look like you? Nikki?"

Belle grinned. "Nah. She's the pretty one. Likes to shop for real clothes, not just jeans and workout gear. She looks like our mom. Auburn hair, an actual *figure*."

Lucy made a face, looking down at herself. She plucked the loose fabric of her pink T-shirt. "Yeah, well,

I'm never gonna get…you know…boobs, either." Lucy's pale cheeks turned red. "Not that you don't, uh—"

Belle laughed. "It's okay. I do. But believe me, my sister got the larger helping in the chest department. And you're only twelve. You've got oodles of time yet."

"I'm gonna be thirteen next month."

Belle renewed her grasp on the handles of the chair, pushing it harder over the gravel road. "Why sound so glum about it? Are you going to have a party?"

"And do what?" Lucy thumped her hands on her chair.

"Who needs to *do* anything? You're going to be thirteen. I remember when Nik and I turned thirteen. We sat around with our friends and talked boys and makeup and music, and ate pizza and popcorn and had a blast."

"Doesn't matter. Dad's not going to let me have a party, anyway."

"Has he said that?" She would be upbeat if it killed her. "It never hurts to just ask. What's the worst that could happen? That he'd say no? You've already decided that, anyway. And he might surprise you." Whatever she'd seen or heard about Cage, the man was admittedly doing back flips for his daughter. What was one small party?

"He doesn't want me to do anything," Lucy insisted flatly. "Ever since my accident, he's been—" she shook her head, and fell silent.

"Worried about you, perhaps?" Belle maneuvered Lucy's chair through the opened barn door.

Lucy didn't respond to that. But she did respond to the changes Belle had made inside the barn. Most particularly the portable sound system she immediately flicked on. Banging music sounded out and Belle looked past Lucy's slack jaw as she handed her a sizable stack of CDs. "Hope there's something you like in there. I brought a little of everything."

Lucy flipped through the cases. Pulled one out. "Dad would like this."

Belle glanced over. Beatles. Drat. Her own personal favorite. "Anything *you* like?"

"Classics." Lucy shrugged diffidently. "Weird, huh?"

She felt as if she'd hit a treasure chest when she leaned over to flip down several more CDs in Lucy's lap and the girl laughed delightedly. "Beethoven. Pachelbel. Rachmaninoff. A little of everything."

Belle took the stack and set it on a crate next to the portable boom box. She slid in a CD and the strains of Mozart soared right up to the rafters.

Cage could hear the music a mile away. It was loud enough to scare his prized heifers out of breeding for another two seasons, and certainly loud enough to put his daughter in hearing aids before her next birthday. He wanted to race hell-bent for leather to the barn the way Strudel was, but he kept his pace even for Rory's sake. He was walking the horse back to the stable, hoping Rory's lame leg wouldn't require more than some TLC and rest. He knew the vet would come if he called, but it sat wrong in Cage's belly to keep looking at the balance of his bill with the man, knowing he wouldn't have it paid off anytime soon.

Naturally, the music grew even louder the closer he got to the barn and it showed no sign of abating even after he'd tended to Rory. He strode inside, only to stop short at the sight of Belle and Lucy. His daughter was lying on the incline bench. Not an unusual sight. But she was laughing, her head thrown back, blond hair streaming down her thin back, her face wreathed in smiles.

And Belle was laughing, too. She sat on the floor in front of the bench, her legs stretched into a position he thought only Olympic gymnasts could obtain, and she was leaning forward so far her torso was nearly resting on the blue mat beneath her. The position drew the tight black shirt she wore well above her waist, and for way too long, he couldn't look away from that stretch of lithe, feminine muscle.

Neither his daughter nor Belle noticed him and he felt like an outsider all over again. He liked it no more now than he had the previous day.

Then Belle turned her head, resting her cheek on the mat, and looked at him.

Not so unaware, after all.

"Come on in," she said. And even though she hadn't lifted her voice above the music, he still heard her. Her brown gaze was soft. Open.

She didn't even flinch when Strudel bounded over to her, snuffling at her face before hastily jumping over her to gleefully greet Lucy.

Safer to look at the slice of Belle's ivory back that showed below the shirt than those dark eyes. Maybe.

He deliberately strode to the boom box and turned down the volume. "Trying to make yourselves deaf?"

Lucy rolled her eyes. "It wasn't *that* loud."

He wished for the days when she hadn't yet learned to roll her eyes at him. "I'm going in to get your lunch."

"Belle already did."

At Lucy's blithe statement, Belle pushed herself up and drew her legs together, wriggling her red-painted toes. He saw a glint on one toe. She wore a toe ring. Figures.

"We left a plate for you," she said, apparently trusting that he wouldn't lecture her about her "place" in front of Lucy.

In that, she was correct. For now, at least. He eyed her for a moment. "Then I'll go down to get the mail."

Lucy ignored him as she flopped back on the slanted bench. Belle's gaze went from him to Lucy and back again. "If you have some time this afternoon, maybe Lucy could show you a few of the new exercises we've been working on."

He nodded and resettled his hat as he left. In the seconds before someone—his daughter probably—turned up the volume of the music again, he heard Lucy's flat statement. "He won't show. He never does."

It was an exaggeration, but that didn't stop the words from cutting. But he was only one man. As he'd told Belle, he couldn't do it all. Keep the Lazy-B going and spend hours with his daughter when he'd already hired a therapist for her for that very purpose. He whistled sharply and Strudel scrambled out of the barn, racing after him. The dog might have promise, after all.

He drove the truck down to get the mail. There was a cluster of boxes belonging to the half-dozen folks living out his direction. His place was the farthest out, though. The box was five miles from the house. Usually, he swung by on Rory. Not today.

Back in the house, he dumped the mail and the morning paper on the kitchen table and yanked open the refrigerator door. Sure enough. A foil-wrapped plate sat inside. The woman made pizza with whole wheat. Whole wheat? He wasn't even aware that he'd had any in his house. Either she'd brought it in her suitcase, which was entirely possible since she had no qualms about thinking she knew best where his family was concerned, or the stuff had been lurking in his cupboards courtesy of Emmy Johannson, who periodically brought groceries out for him.

God only knew what lurked on that plate under the foil. He ignored it and made himself a roast-beef sandwich, instead. He was standing at the counter eating it when he saw Belle through the window over the sink striding up to the rear of the house. He turned a page of the newspaper and continued reading. Something about a chili cook-off.

It wasn't engrossing stuff, but it was better than watching Belle. The woman had a way of moving and it was just better off, all around, if he didn't look too close. He didn't like her, or her family, and she was there only out of his own desperation. So he needed to get over the fact that she turned him on and he needed to do it yesterday.

The screen rattled as Belle pulled it open and popped into the kitchen. His gaze slid sideways to her feet. Scuffed white tennis shoes—a different pair than the wet blue ones the day before—now hid the red-painted toes and the toe ring. He looked back at the newspaper and finished off the sandwich.

Only Belle didn't move along to the bathroom, or to do whatever it was she'd come in the house to do. She stood there, her arms folded across her chest, skinny hip cocked.

He swallowed. Finished the glass of milk he was drinking.

She still hadn't moved.

He sighed. Folded the newspaper back along its creases. Crossed to the table to flip through the mail. Too many bills, circulars advertising some singles' matchmaking network, an expensive-looking envelope with an all too familiar embossed return address.

He folded the envelope in half and shoved it in his back pocket. "What is it now?"

"I noticed that Lucy is still depending exclusively on her wheelchair."

The one remaining nerve not gone tight at the sight of the envelope now residing next to his butt joined the knotted rest. He opened a cupboard and grabbed the bottle of aspirin that had been full only a few weeks ago. He shook out a few, the rattle of pills inside the plastic sounding as sharp as his voice. "And?" He shut the cupboard door again only to find her extending a condensing bottle of water toward him.

"And it concerns me, because it's encouraging her to keep favoring her injury."

"She's not supposed to use her leg, yet." He swallowed the aspirin.

"She's not supposed to use it completely," Belle countered. "But she should have been up on crutches weeks ago, yet since I've been here—"

"Twenty-four hours now?"

"—I haven't even *seen* a pair of crutches. She does have them, doesn't she?"

Cage strode over to the tall, narrow closet at the end of the kitchen and snapped open the door. Inside, along with a broom and the vacuum cleaner, stood a shining new pair of crutches. "Satisfied?"

Her lips tightened. She flipped her long ponytail behind her shoulder and brushed past him to remove the crutches. He looked down at her, clutching the things to her chest. The top of her head didn't reach his chin. In fact, she wasn't much taller than Luce.

The realization didn't make Belle seem younger to him. It only made his daughter seem older.

He pushed the closet door shut and moved across

the room. "She says that she still hurts too much to use 'em."

Belle nodded. "I understand, believe me. But getting on her feet with these is a major component of her recovery. And the longer we wait, the more it's going to hurt. You're going to have to get over trying to protect her, Cage. Her recuperation is *not* going to be pleasant all the time, but she does have to work through it before it'll get better." Her hand reached out and caught his forearm, squeezing in emphasis. "And it *will* get better." Then, seeming to realize that she was touching him, she quickly pulled back.

"Easy advice," he said flatly. "You ever watch *your* child trying to straighten or bend a leg that doesn't want to do either despite two separate surgeries that should have helped it? To steel yourself against the pleading in her eyes when she looks at you wanting permission to…just…stop?" If he'd expected her to look shocked at his unaccustomed outburst, he was wrong. Shock would've been better, though, than the expression softening her eyes. It was easier to take when she figured he avoided Lucy's sessions because of the never ending needs of the Lazy-B.

"I haven't watched *my* child," she said. "Since I've never even had one, that would be difficult." Then she suddenly lifted her foot onto one of the kitchen chairs and whipped the stretchy black pants that flared over her shoes up past her knee. The scar was old. Faded. It snaked down from beyond the folds of her pants on the inside of her taut thigh, circled her knee and disappeared down her calf. "But I have dealt with it myself."

The water and aspirin he'd just chugged mixed uncomfortably with his lunch. Lucy's healing surgical scars were bad. But when they healed, he knew they would look far better than Belle's.

"Not pretty," Belle murmured, and pulled her pant leg back down. "My hip doesn't look quite so bad."

"What happened?"

It was hard to believe it, but her brown eyes looked even darker. "I thought you knew."

"I suppose that's why you went into physical therapy," he surmised grudgingly.

"Yes." She sucked in one corner of her soft lip for a moment. Her expression was oddly still. "I was with my dad that night, Cage. The night of the accident."

He'd been wrong. His nerves *could* get tighter. "I didn't know you'd been hurt." He couldn't have known since her family had been living in Cheyenne at the time.

She studied the crutches she held. "I was lying down in the back seat. I didn't have on my seat belt, which my dad didn't know. When…it…happened, I was thrown from the car. Metal and flesh and bone. Don't mix well usually." She lifted her shoulder slightly. "Which is something you know only too well, I'm afraid. I'm sorry. I thought you knew," she said again then fell silent.

She looked miserable. And damned if he could convince himself it was an act, though he wanted to.

"Look, Cage, it's not too late for me to go. I know Lucy knows about the accident between our parents and she doesn't seem to hold it against my family. But everyone warned me this would be just one constant reminder after another." Her gaze whispered over him, then went back to the crutches. "I can hold my own against those opinions." Her voice was vaguely hoarse. "But if your feeling the same way gets in the path of Lucy's progress then my efforts here will be for nothing. Are…are you sure you want me to stay?"

No. He stared out the window. Lucy was sitting in her chair just outside the barn, Strudel half in her lap while they played tug with a stick. "Lucy still needs help." His voice came from somewhere deep inside him.

He heard Belle sigh a little. "I could talk to the people I worked with at Huffington. Maybe I could find someone willing to—"

"No." He couldn't afford to bring someone else out to the ranch, to pay their full salary. Belle had been willing to agree for less than half what she deserved, and he knew it was only because of her fondness for his daughter. Something he'd deliberately capitalized on. The fact that she'd be able to provide the tutoring Lucy needed was even more of a bonus. "You came to help Lucy. I expect you to hold to your word."

"All right," she said after a long moment. She tucked her arm through the center of the crutches and carried them to the door. Then paused. "I'm really sorry your father didn't survive the accident, Cage."

"So am I," he said stiffly. He'd lost both his parents that night, even though his mother had technically survived. Apparently, the only one to escape unscathed that winter night nearly fourteen years ago had been the man who'd caused the accident in the first place.

Belle's father.

And even though he'd died a few years later, Belle was, after all, still his daughter.

# Chapter 4

"I want to go with you."

Cage shook his head, ignoring Lucy's mutinous demand. "Not this time, Luce."

"Why not? I want to see Grandma."

He wished Belle wasn't standing at the kitchen sink washing up the pans she'd used to prepare Lucy's breakfast. He wished she'd stop doing things he wasn't paying her to do. She'd been under his roof for three days. He'd already warned her to stop dusting the shelves and mopping floors. They may have needed it, but when he'd come upon her doing the chores, he'd lit into her. More than necessary, he knew, but seeing her so at home in his house bugged him no end. He didn't want her being helpful. Not unless it was on his terms. "I'll take you to see her another time."

"When?"

"A few weeks."

Lucy's lips thinned. "I haven't seen her all summer."

"And nothing's changed." Her eyes widened a little at his sharp tone. He stifled a sigh. Before Lucy's fall, they'd gone every weekend. "Maybe this weekend. When Miss Day is off."

The prospect seemed enough to satisfy his daughter. "Miss Day's day off," Lucy quipped. Her lips tilted at the corners, thoroughly amused with herself and he felt his own lips twitch.

God, he loved the kid. "Yeah."

"Don't make fun of my name," Belle said lightly over the clink of dishes in the sink. "I grew up hearing every pun you could ever think of."

"Day isn't bad," Lucy countered. "You oughta hear what people used to call my dad."

Belle leaned her hip against the counter as she turned to look at them. The towel in her hand slowed over the plate she was drying. "Oh?"

"Yeah, Cage isn't his *real* name, you know. Who would name their kid *that?*"

Cage caught his daughter's gaze, lifting his eyebrow in only a partially mock warning. "Did you make your bed?"

Lucy laughed. But she took the hint and didn't pursue the topic of Cage's first name. She lifted her arms and he automatically started to reach for her to transfer her from the chair at the table to her wheelchair. But he caught Belle's look.

How to protect someone in the long run by causing them pain now? He felt the humor sparked by his daughter drain away and instead of lifting her, he handed her the crutches that were leaning against the wall.

"Dad." Lucy pouted.

"Lucy," Belle prompted gently. "We've talked about this."

He supposed that wasn't surprising. If she'd taken him to task about the crutches, she'd probably done the same with his daughter. Understanding the reasons was one thing. Liking it another.

Lucy took the crutches. Belle set down the towel and helped the girl to her feet. With the crutches tucked beneath her arms, Lucy looked at Cage. "She told me not to pout around you 'cause you were too much of a marshmallow to hold out against me." Then she shot Belle a look before awkwardly swinging out of the kitchen.

Belle's cheeks were pink and she quickly turned back to the dishes.

Cage filled a coffee mug with the fragrant stuff she'd made earlier, damning the consequences, and watched her for a moment. She was wearing another pair of those thin, long pants. Jazz pants, he knew, because he'd had to buy some for Lucy for something her dance class had done last winter.

Today, Belle's pants were as red as a tomato. She wore a sleeveless top in the same color that hugged her torso and zipped all the way up to her throat.

She'd have been about Lucy's age when the accident happened. How long had it taken her to recover from *her* injuries?

He abruptly finished off his coffee. Learning that she'd been hurt in the same accident as his parents didn't change anything. Gus Day had killed his father on a stretch of highway outside of Cheyenne, pure and simple. He sat the emptied mug down with a thunk. "Marshmallow?"

"She wasn't supposed to tell you that."

"She's still young. She hasn't learned the art of discretion."

"She's learned a lot of other things. If you're worried that going with you to Cheyenne today will be too taxing, don't. She's up to the trip."

He'd told Belle and Lucy that he was making the drive when they'd both stopped in surprise at finding him in the kitchen that morning instead of already out for the day as he usually was. "It's business," he said again. True enough in a sense. Personal business. The kind he wasn't inclined to share, not even with Lucy. Not until he was forced to. "I probably won't be back until late."

Belle didn't look happy.

"I told you that I can have Emmy Johannson come over to watch her."

"And I told you that would be ridiculous since I'm staying here anyway. You want to have the argument you've been spoiling for now that Lucy's out of range?" She shot him a look, her eyebrows arched, and when he said nothing, she deliberately dried another plate. Short of yanking it out of her hands there wasn't much he could do about it. "I'm not going to twiddle my thumbs between sessions and lessons, Cage, but that wasn't what I was trying to get at anyway. Has it occurred to you that maybe Lucy wants to be where *you* are?"

"She wants to see my mother. And this discussion is over." Maybe he couldn't keep her from washing the damn dishes, but he didn't have to listen to advice unrelated to Lucy's rehabilitation.

Belle shrugged and focused on the dishes again, seeming not to turn one hair of her thick brown ponytail at his decree. But her lashes guarded her eyes. And he damned all over again the turn of events that had prompted him to bring her into this house.

A timely reminder of why he was going to Cheyenne in the first place.

He rose and grabbed his hat off the hook. "Luce has my cell-phone number," he said as he strode from the room. He thought he heard her murmur "drive carefully" after him, but couldn't be sure.

Lucy was in her bathroom when he hunted her down to tell her he was leaving. He rapped on the door. "Behave yourself," he said through the wood.

She yanked open the door, leaning heavily on her crutches. "What else is there to do," she asked tartly. "You won't let me go near the horses anymore."

"When I'm sure you're not going to go near *that* horse, I'll consider it."

"You're *never* going to let me ride Satin again, are you?"

It was an old refrain and one he didn't want to be pulled into singing. "Make sure you feed Strudel," he said. "And do the exercises on your own that Miss Day says you're supposed to be doing.

"I hate doing them. They hurt. And they're boring." Her face was mutinous. An expression that had been too frequent of late.

"I'm sorry they hurt, but I don't care if they're boring," he said mildly. "They're necessary."

Her jaw worked. Her eyes rolled. Then all the fight drained out of her and she gave him a beseeching look. "How come you won't let me go with you today?"

Dammit, he *was* a marshmallow where she was concerned. But not this time. "You got a problem hanging around here with Miss Day?"

Lucy rolled her eyes again. "Jeez, Dad. Her name is

Belle. And *no* I don't have a problem with her. Not like *you* do, anyway."

"I don't have a problem with Miss Day."

"Right. That's why you watch her like you do. You oughta just ask her out on a date or something."

"I do not want to date Miss Day," he assured evenly and gently tugged the end of her braid as he leaned down to kiss her forehead. "Behave."

She grimaced. "Like there's anything else you'd let me do? Say 'hi' to Grandma for me."

He nodded as he headed out. If he did go by the care center, he'd pass on the greeting, but he knew there would be no reciprocation, which was the very reason why he would *never* want to date Miss Day.

"Have you ever been in love, Belle?"

The question came out of the blue and Belle looked up from Lucy's leg. "Is the cramp gone?"

Lucy nodded, gingerly flexing her toes.

It was evening and they were back in the barn again. Cage hadn't yet returned from Cheyenne.

"So, have you?"

Belle leaned back and grabbed a hand towel, wiping the remains of oil she'd been using from her palms. "Yes."

"With who?"

Belle flicked Lucy with the end of the towel and rolled to her feet. The CD had ended and she exchanged it for another. "Howie Bloom," she said.

"Howie?" Lucy echoed.

"We were in second grade together. I thought he was the perfect man. He, however, thought Nikki was the perfect woman."

"They liked each other?"

"Nikki told him to take a hike. She'd never have poached on what I considered my territory."

"I wish I had a sister," Lucy grumbled dramatically. She flopped back on the blue mats, flinging her arms wide, before slowly moving them up and down. If she'd been in the snow, she would have been making snow angels. Belle wondered if the girl even knew she was partially moving her legs—both of them—as well, and decided not to point it out. It wasn't the first time she'd noticed Lucy unconsciously using her injured leg.

"Instead, I'm all alone," Lucy lamented. "With dad. I think he needs a woman. Then mebbe he wouldn't be on my case all the time."

Belle sank her teeth into her tongue for a moment and when the urge to snort passed, she chanced speaking. "If your dad wants to be with someone, I'm sure nothing would stop him." It seemed a safe enough response. And Lord knew the man was attractive. For a grouch.

"I s'pose. He could'a dated Anya's mom. They were in school together when they were little. But she got engaged to Mr. Pope. Dad's way hotter than he is."

Larry Pope was a teacher at the high school. A perfectly nice man, what little Belle knew of him. She seriously doubted anyone in Weaver muttered *ogre* behind his back. But he wasn't in the same hemisphere of hot that Cage Buchanan occupied.

Which was neither here nor there, Belle reminded herself.

"Then Anya and I would be sisters. But Dad never looked at Mrs. Johannson like…you know."

"And Anya is away visiting her dad?"

Lucy nodded. "'Til next month." She exhaled, sounding utterly dejected.

Belle pushed to her feet and held out her hands.

"Come on. Let's go make popcorn and watch movies." Lucy had a sizable collection of videotapes in her bedroom from which to choose. Maybe one of them would provide enough distraction that she'd stop wondering what kind of woman Cage did look at like *you know*.

Cage could see the blue-tinted glow through the living-room windows as he finally drove up to the house that night. Television was on. It was after midnight.

He parked near the back of the house. Sat there in the dark, listening to the tick of his cooling engine. Unlike the bluish light coming from the window at the front of the house, the light he could see from the upstairs one looked golden. Either Belle had fallen asleep with the light on, or she was still awake. Probably the reason for that blue glow downstairs.

He blew out a long breath and grabbed the manila envelope that had been his companion on the long drive up from Cheyenne and headed inside. His trip had been successful only in giving him some breathing room.

Hopefully.

The aroma of buttery popcorn met him. Two bowls—one empty, one nearly so—sat on the table.

He hadn't stopped for dinner before driving back and grabbed a handful from the remains. Lightly doused with Parmesan cheese. Lucy's doing, he figured. Kid liked the stuff on everything.

The low murmur of voices and familiar music from the television kept the house from being entirely silent. He went into the living room. Lucy, tangled up with her favorite pink blanket, was sprawled over most of the couch. And Belle, as well, since her legs were tossed over Belle's lap.

His daughter didn't budge as he walked in the room. She was asleep.

"Did your trip go well?" Belle's voice was soft.

He finally let himself look at her. Only long enough to see that she was wrapped in a bulky white robe that was falling open at the base of her long neck. "It went. City seems to get busier every time I drive down there. You probably can't wait to get back there, I suppose."

"That's the plan," she agreed evenly.

He eyed her for a moment. She hadn't said anything, but she had to think his place was stuck somewhere two decades past.

God. What a mood he was in. "How long's Luce been asleep?"

"Since Ariel got her legs."

He glanced at the television. Judging by the stack of videos on top of it, he knew this movie hadn't been the first they'd watched. *The Little Mermaid* might not be recent, but it'd been Lucy's favorite Disney flick since the day she first saw it. "She hasn't made it through that video without falling asleep since she was five."

"Didn't hurt that she worked pretty hard today."

"You told me you'd be doing all the same exercises she does, right alongside her."

"Yes. But I'm not working at a disadvantage the way she currently is."

Memories of Lucy growing up battled for space in his mind against memories from his own youth. He'd believed none of the Days had been affected by the accident. God knew, Gus Day had never said a word of it during the few times he'd tried contacting Cage afterward. Now, he knew Belle had been hurt, as well. He dropped his envelope on the ancient coffee table and leaned over the couch.

Belle sucked in her breath, unable to prevent the reaction when he moved so suddenly. But he gave no notice. Simply slid his arms under his daughter, hands impersonally skimming Belle's thighs in the process, before lifting Lucy's limp form easily against his chest. She swallowed and tried not to be obvious about clutching the comforting folds of her robe together over her legs. She needn't have worried what Cage would think, however, since he was already carrying his daughter down the hall toward her bedroom, the pink blanket trailing around his long legs.

She'd seen his expression one too many times when he looked at his daughter. Naked devotion.

On the television, Sebastian was beseeching the prince to kiss the girl, and Belle hit the remote, stopping the singing crab midnote. She was tidying up the scattered napkins and loose kernels of popped corn from the coffee table when Cage returned. "Did she wake up?"

He shook his head and closed his long fingers over his envelope before she could move it out of her way. "Except for the nightmares, it takes something cataclysmic to wake her up in the middle of the night."

She wasn't sure if it was censure she heard in his voice, or not. But they hadn't discussed Lucy's bedtime, so she could honestly say she hadn't deliberately flaunted his rules. She also could honestly say that standing there with him in the hushed light of the snowy television screen seemed suddenly, abruptly, far too personal. As he was fond of pointing out, she was there to do a job. Wondering what in the package—with its embossed return address for an attorney in Cheyenne—was responsible for the tense muscle flexing in his jaw wasn't part of that job.

"Well. It *is* the middle of the night." She lifted her

cupped hands a little. "I'll just throw this stuff away." But he was pretty much blocking the way to the kitchen because there was little room to maneuver between the couch and table. She pressed her lips together for a moment, awkwardly waiting for him to shift aside. When he finally did, she hurried past him and dropped her handful of trash in the garbage can beneath the kitchen sink. She rinsed and dried her hands, then remembered the bowls on the table and started for them. But Cage beat her to it, handing her only the empty one even as he shoved his other hand in the leftovers.

"Luce didn't put so much parmesan on her popcorn this time," he murmured before popping some into his mouth. "It's still edible for once."

Belle pushed her lips into a smile. Maybe he was oblivious to the fact that she was wearing her robe, but she was not. And the popcorn he was devouring hadn't been Lucy's, it had been hers. "Yes. Well. Good night." Gloria Day had drilled manners into her daughters, prompting the polite words when her most immediate desire was to simply run up to the safety of her bedroom. He, however, didn't return the sentiment and she thought he wouldn't as she headed into the hall.

"Belle."

Why did he only know her name when his home was bathed in midnight shadows? She caught her hand around the door jamb. "Yes?"

"Thanks for watching Luce today."

It really was the very last thing she might have expected from him. Surprise softened her for a moment until she gathered herself. "You're welcome."

He nodded once, and that seemed to be the end of it. Of course, he was plowing through the remains of her popcorn as if he were starving. "Did you eat dinner?"

He'd leaned one hip against the counter, cradling the popcorn bowl against his stomach. "This is fine." Which was no answer at all.

"There are leftovers in the fridge."

Information that didn't seem to fill him with glee.

"I made some hamburger-casserole thing," she added. "Didn't have a name, but Lucy said it was one of her favorites. The recipe was in the recipe box in your cupboard." It had taken her a while to gather her nerves to even open the little metal box that was crammed with yellowed newsprint recipes as well as neatly hand-printed recipe cards. It was in keeping with the other aging, but homey, touches the house still possessed.

"That was my mother's recipe box."

Exactly what Belle had assumed, and why she'd hesitated. "I hope you don't mind. Anyway, that's what I fixed. It has hamburger and carrots and potatoes and—"

"Yeah." He set aside the bowl and watched her, his hooded expression too shadowed to read. "My mother used to fix it for us. It was my father's favorite, too."

And wasn't that a handy way to put a stop to their awkward conversation? "There's plenty left for you," she said and continued down the hallway to the staircase.

Upstairs in the bedroom, she felt an urge to call her sister, but didn't. Just because she was having a hard time sleeping under Cage Buchanan's roof didn't mean she needed to share the problem by interrupting Nikki's sleep, as well.

She tossed her robe over the wooden chair in the corner and climbed into bed before snapping off the lamp sitting on the nightstand. Every time she closed her eyes, though, she saw Cage in her mind's eye. Striding toward the house, lean hipped and long legged in worn jeans, his cowboy hat set on his bronzy head at a no-nonsense angle. Wolfing popcorn. Carrying his daughter.

She scooched down the bed. Scrunched up her pillow this way and that. Turned from one side onto her other.

Then sat bolt upright when she heard the brisk knock on her door. "Yes?" Oh, stupid, Belle. She should have gotten up and put on the robe. Instead, she sat there in bed, tangled in sheet and quilt while the bedroom door opened and Cage appeared.

She couldn't summon so much as a coherent thought or word as he entered the room, walking right across to her.

Then he suddenly knelt, one hand braced on the mattress only inches from her bare knee. The mattress dipped and the springs gave out a loud moan.

For some reason, she felt as if they'd been caught doing something…intimate.

"What—" Finally her tongue loosened. "What are you doing?" But his head just kept going lower.

She leaned over, grabbing the sheet up against her chest, flinging it more fully over her leg to see him actually slipping beneath the high-set bed. "Looking for the boogeyman?"

He had a small can in his hand, she realized. "You creak." His voice was muffled.

"Only in the mornings when I first get out of bed," she muttered.

She heard a soft spraying sound, followed by a hint of an oily scent. Then he was pushing out from beneath the bed again, and levering himself to his feet. "The bedsprings."

"I noticed."

He headed to the door. "So did I."

A statement that was disturbing only because it made her wonder what he was doing on his side of the wall that he could hear *her* bedsprings creaking. Did he listen for her as closely as she listened for him, hoping to avoid running into him? Bad enough to know she hid out in this very room early every morning until the sounds of him moving around in his room, then showering in the bathroom, were long gone.

He stopped at the door and glanced back. The light from the hallway spilled around his broad shoulders. "And, so you know, you don't have to keep hiding the scars on your leg."

She blinked.

"If Luce sees that you're self-conscious about yours, she's going to be the same way about hers," he continued abruptly. Then he closed the door.

Belle flopped back on the bed. The bedsprings gave one halfhearted creak, then were silent.

Of course. His only concern was Lucy.

## Chapter 5

"Did you ask your dad yet about having a birthday party?"

Lucy shook her head, apparently too intent on painting her toenails—pink, of course—to answer. They were taking a break from studying and Lucy was sitting on the floor in her bedroom, leaning over with the polish brush.

"Why not?" Belle tucked the tip of her tongue between her teeth watching the way Lucy compensated for her injured knee. Lucy was unusually limber, which in general was a plus, but occasionally—when she would ordinarily be forced to make her leg try harder—she could work around it. Which was something she nearly always did. Even though she'd made faces and grumbled about their actual therapy sessions in the five days since they'd begun, she hadn't been completely obstreperous, which Belle had initially feared. What interested Belle even more, though, was the fact that when she was just going through her ordinary day Lucy accomplished ever so much more. Unconsciously.

Lucy still hadn't answered her question, though. "Hey there." She leaned over, looking into Lucy's absorbed face. "Why haven't you asked him, yet? You said yesterday that you were going to." And the day before that, and the day before that.

"He won't let me have any boys come and if no boys come, then none of the girls will want to come, either."

"Do *you* want boys to come?" Belle idly plucked a bottle of clear polish out of Lucy's collection and shook it a few times before unscrewing the top.

"Anya's gonna want Ryan to come."

Belle flattened her hand on the top of a teen magazine and began stroking the clear polish over her fingernails. Ryan, she knew, was Ryan Clay. Her nephew by virtue of her mother's marriage into the Clay family. "Okay, so I know what Anya wants, but what about you?"

Lucy straightened, and lifted one shoulder as she put the cap back on her polish and tossed it back in the pretty, lacquered box that contained her modest assortment of polishes. "I dunno."

Belle switched hands to paint the rest of her nails. "My old boss used to call me *bulldog,*" she murmured. "Because I don't give up very easily. So why don't you just tell me what's really holding you back on having a party? Otherwise, I'll just have to keep asking."

"Bulldog?" Lucy looked skeptical. "You're making that up."

"I can call Nikki and she'll tell you I'm not. She's Mr. Reed's assistant, and he tends to give everyone a nickname."

"How come you don't still work there?"

"Oh, I'll be going back," Belle assured her with a blitheness she was far from feeling. "I'm sort of on vacation."

"So, you won't be at my school next year?"

Belle shook her head.

"Then how can you tell me we'll work on something other than dancing for the talent contest?"

"We've got the rest of summer vacation to figure it out for you."

"But then you'll be leaving."

Belle heard loneliness underlying Lucy's matter-of-fact tone. And why wouldn't she be lonely? Living on a remote ranch. No company other than a dog, a television and videos, a horse she wasn't supposed to go around and a father who worked from sunup to sundown. Other than the day he'd gone to Cheyenne, Cage had been noticeably absent around the house.

He'd even stopped complaining that Belle was cooking meals for his daughter, and had stopped coming in, himself, to make sure Lucy had lunch. "Yes," she finally answered honestly. "I'll be leaving. Because you're going to be running circles around me by then and you won't need me anymore. But we'll still be friends, sweetie. You can call me anytime."

"Do you and Nikki live together in Cheyenne?"

"Lord, no. I love my sister, but we'd drive each other mad in two days flat. We're only a few blocks away from each other, though. She has this beautiful town house that she's been decorating herself. I have an apartment that is completely standard issue. Well, I *had* an apartment." She hadn't renewed her lease when it expired, because she'd been in Weaver, by then. Instead, with the help of Nikki and some friends, she'd moved her few personal items of furniture into the little house in Weaver where she was staying. "I'll have to find a new place to live when I go back there." She smiled, determined to cheer the solemn look from Lucy's face. "Maybe your dad will let you come and visit me there, even."

"Really?"

"Of course."

But Lucy's sharply hopeful moment was brief. "Dad won't let me, anyway."

Belle stopped fanning her hands and tested the polish. Dry. "Enough of that. Your dad seems pretty willing to do back flips for you."

"He won't let me go see my grandparents."

"He said he would think about taking you to Cheyenne to visit your grandmother this weekend."

"My other grandparents. The Oldham side." Lucy dropped the lid back on the lacquered box and lifted it onto her legs. Her hand smoothed over the fine surface. "My grandmother sent this to me a few months ago. Dad nearly had a cow."

"Maybe he's not comfortable with his little girl being old enough to wear nail polish. Dads can be that way sometimes." Hers certainly had been.

"That's what *he* said."

"Well. There you go." Belle's mind was busy, turning over the notion of Lucy's maternal grandparents. The only thing the rumor mill had produced on them was that they were wealthy. "Have they invited you to visit or something?"

Lucy shook her head. "Not really. I just—we've talked a couple times on the phone. Dad doesn't know, though."

Belle wished Lucy hadn't imparted that little tidbit, but the girl was continuing. "They live in Chicago. They're the ones who sent me Satin, too."

The horse that had thrown Lucy.

"Isn't Chicago where that performing-arts school you were interested in is located?"

"Yeah." Lucy leaned her head back against the foot of her bed. "Guess it didn't matter that Dad wouldn't let me go on that field trip there. Even if I could have gotten to visit the school during one of the free days, they wouldn't want me like this."

"Satin hadn't thrown you yet when the field trip was scheduled. Even so, it doesn't mean the school wouldn't want you when you *are* ready again," Belle pointed out.

Lucy just shrugged again. Then she set aside the lacquered box and turned, pulling herself up onto the bed. She grabbed the crutches propped beside her and braced her weight against them to push to her feet. "Even if I earned a scholarship, he wouldn't let me go." She slowly clumped out of the bedroom.

This is what she got for becoming personally involved with a patient, Belle thought, watching the girl leave. Instead of just being concerned with rehabilitating a body, she began wanting to fix everything else, too. And while she didn't know whether or not Lucy would be better served by going to a private school so far away from home, she *did* know that Lucy was uncommonly talented.

She slid back into her shoes, grabbed Lucy's discarded tennies, too, and went after her. "Come on," she said when she found Lucy leaning against the kitchen counter, staring out the window. "We've explored all over the Lazy-B this past week except for one place." She waved Lucy's shoes. "Sit and put these on."

"There's only one place we haven't gone."

"Right. The stables."

"Dad doesn't think I should go down there."

Belle nodded. "Unsupervised," she improvised, remembering Cage's words. But Lucy's mood had been in the dumps long enough and Belle was tired of trying to catch Cage to talk to him about her observations where his daughter was concerned. Including her suspicion that Lucy's reluctant attitude toward her recovery was somehow related to the horse that had thrown her. "His point is that he doesn't want you trying to ride yet, and I agree with him. Your muscles are nowhere near ready for the strain of a horse's girth. But visiting is not riding. And you've got more horses than just Satin, right?"

Lucy looked vaguely skeptical, which didn't do a lot for Belle's tinge of uncertainty. But it was the middle of the afternoon. If Cage's habit held, he wouldn't make an appearance until it was nearly dark. It wasn't that Belle intended to get away with something. She'd let Cage know, after the fact, that they'd visited the horses, and that doing so had lifted Lucy's spirits. If he had a quarrel with *that,* she'd deal with it.

She was suddenly impatient to get going before she lost her nerve, and crouched down to tie Lucy's shoes, herself. And when that was done, she brought out the wheelchair that was mostly stored in the corner of the kitchen these days. "You can ride this time." The stables were considerably farther out from the house than the barn was. "Bring the crutches, though."

Lucy looked relieved to shift into the chair. She propped the long crutches against the metal footrest and her shoulder, and they went out through the front, to use the ramp.

The summer afternoon was hot, and Belle was perspiring by the time she'd pushed Lucy all the way to the stables. "Too bad you don't have a swimming hole around here," she said as they entered the shade of the stable. "We could use a little cooling off." She doubted that Cage would grant Belle permission to take his daughter out to the ranch her mother lived on with Squire. The Double-C had a great swimming hole.

Maybe she'd look into driving Lucy into Braden. The town was some distance from Weaver, but there was a public pool there. And swimming would be good for Lucy's leg.

"That's Rory," Lucy pointed out as they passed an SUV parked in the space of what would be two stalls and came to the first horse. "He's older 'n I am."

The big buckskin stuck his head over the rail, nudging at Lucy's outstretched hand. "I should have brought carrots." She braced the rubber tips of her crutches against the hard-packed earth that formed the aisle between the stalls and stood. Belle stepped around the chair and slowly walked down one side of the aisle with Lucy. At each stall, they stopped. Lucy greeted the horses as if they were long-lost friends.

It was practically heartbreaking.

Then they got to the last stall in the row.

Satin, Belle immediately knew. Aptly named because she'd never seen a more beautiful black. It was as if Black Beauty had stepped right out of the pages of the classic novel. "Oh…my," she murmured. She'd been around horses her entire life as a pleasure rider, but she'd never seen such a magnificent animal.

Lucy was hanging back slightly but as soon as she realized that Belle noticed, she tossed her head and continued forward as if her hesitation had never happened at all. "Satin Finish," Lucy said. "He's seventeen hands. Sired out of Knotty Wood. He was a Triple-Crown winner."

Belle started. "A *racehorse?*"

"Satin's never raced, though." Lucy started to reach for the horse, but stayed the movement, never quite touching him.

What on earth was a horse bred like that doing on a working cattle ranch? Belle found it unfathomable. "He's quite a gift. Is he being ridden at all?"

"No, and he's not going to be."

The deep voice was flat. But the fury in it was unmistakable, and Belle nearly jumped right out of her skin. She was faintly aware of Lucy reacting similarly as they both whirled around, feeling caught and guilty as sin, in the face of Cage's towering disapproval.

It wasn't directed at his daughter, though. His fiercely blue gaze rested on Lucy for only a moment, obviously seeing that she was perfectly fine, before settling on Belle. "What…the…hell…do you think you are doing?"

She very nearly quailed. She'd known she was taking a chance on angering him. But Lucy's recovery mattered more. She clasped her hands together behind her back. She could feel Satin's huffing breath at the nape of her neck. "I asked Lucy to introduce me to her friends here in the stable."

"Lucy, go wait for me in the truck."

"But—"

*"Go."*

The girl sidled along the row until she passed her father, then she quickly swung herself down the aisle to the dusty brown pickup truck Belle could see parked at the end.

Belle started, watching the girl's movements. The moment they heard the click of the truck door closing,

Cage stepped toward Belle and she nervously took a step back, only to feel the iron rails of the stall press against her shoulder. Satin began nibbling at her ponytail.

She shifted, quickly pulling her hair out of the reach of temptation. She was undoubtedly safer with the horse's attention, though, than with Cage's.

"The first day you came here," he said, his voice deadly quiet. "What about our conversation that day did you not understand?"

"I'm not a horse thief." The stab at lessening the tension failed miserably.

"You'd be better off at the moment if you were. You could steal *that*—" he jerked his chin toward Satin "—and I'd applaud you all the way to the state line."

Belle stiffened her spine. "So what are you going to do? Glare and stride around all heavy booted and macho? For heaven's sake, Cage, did you even notice what Lucy did a few minutes ago?"

"I *noticed* she was ten inches away from that spawn of a horse," he snapped. "He's unpredictable. I don't need to worry about something else taking my daughter away from me, too."

"She put weight on her foot!" Her hands clenched. Unclenched. "What do you mean, *too?*"

He glared at her, his jaw flexing. "Satan—"

"—Satin."

"*—Satan,*" he repeated, "threw her once. She's a good rider, and she could have been killed."

"But she wasn't," Belle reminded him slowly. "And if you hate the horse so much—think he's such a danger even when he's not being ridden—why is he still here?"

He turned away from her as if he couldn't stand the

sight of her. "Lucy would hate me more than I hate that horse if I got rid of him."

His admission was so raw it tore at her. She pressed her lips together for a moment, scrambling for the objectivity that she was supposed to have. "Lucy says that she wants to get better. But something is holding her back during her sessions, Cage."

"And your answer to that is tempting her back onto that horse."

*That horse* nickered softly and tossed his head, brushing hard enough against Belle's shoulder to make her stumble forward. She caught herself before she knocked right into Cage. "I wasn't doing anything of the sort," Belle defended. "And Lucy doesn't want to get *on* Satin, anyway."

"She bugs me about it constantly."

"Then it's an act!"

"You can't tell that."

"I can," she assured evenly, "as easily as I can see that she's deliberately holding herself back in our sessions. And if you weren't so intent on avoiding me, I'd have talked to you about all this already!"

His expression was plain. He didn't believe her.

Frustration churned inside her. "You'd see it, Cage, if you took more than five minutes out of your day to spend with her. I know why you avoid me, but to avoid Lucy, too, is ridiculous. When you and I first met, I thought you were just a stubborn dad who wasn't ready to let his child go off on a field trip so far away from home."

"That field trip to Chicago was planned a year in advance, and Lucy knew all along I wasn't going to let her go." He leaned over her. "You were interfering then and you're interfering now."

"Well, maybe you *need* some interfering around here! You know, half the population of Weaver considers you an ogre, but I didn't want to believe it. Goodness knows, the people around here have known you a lot longer than I have. So maybe they're more accurate than I am! As far as I'm concerned, keeping the stable off limits to Lucy because you're jealous of a horse given to her by her grandparents isn't overprotective or stubborn. It's cruel."

She brushed past him, knowing the words shouldn't have left her lips, but there was no way to retract them. Instead, they lingered there, silently following as she strode out of the shadows into the lengthening afternoon light.

He'd fire her now, for sure. And maybe that was just fine with her.

But she stopped, seeing Lucy sitting in the truck, her young features pinched into worried lines.

Belle veered back toward the vehicle, propping her hands on the opened window. "Don't worry," she said huskily. "It's me your dad is angry with, not you."

"He better not fire you," Lucy said, throwing her arms around Belle's neck. "I'll hate him forever if he does!"

Belle smoothed her hand down Lucy's gilded head. "You're not going to hate him." She'd once told her father she'd hated him, with devastating results. "And he hasn't fired me." Yet. She didn't even dare look over her shoulder to see if he was bearing down on her to deliver that very coup de grâce. But, of course, she had to.

She looked back.

Cage was still standing by Satin's stall, his hands braced against the top rail, his head lowered. Strudel danced around his legs for a moment, but he didn't even seem to notice, and eventually the dog skittered away from Satin's vicinity to jump at a woven blanket hanging off a high hook.

Belle pressed her cheek against Lucy's blond head and closed her eyes, but Cage's image was seared into her mind, as clear as a painting.

*Man at end of rope* it was titled. And it made her heart simply ache.

"It'll be okay," she murmured to Lucy. If she had more guts, she'd approach Cage. Apologize. Try to make amends. Again. Either he'd fire her or he wouldn't, and that would be the end of it.

He still hadn't moved.

And she wasn't brave enough, after all, to take a dose of his bitterness, no matter how deserved. "I'm going to drive back into town," she told Lucy. It was a few hours earlier than she would have left for her weekend off, but just then, the idea seemed prudent.

Lucy caught her hands. "Are you going to come back?"

She forced a smile. "Monday through Friday. That's the deal."

She looked back again at Cage. Belle simply had to believe that things *would* work out.

For all of them.

# *Chapter 6*

She was out in her yard, hunched over a lawn mower.

Cage parked across the street next to the sidewalk bordering Weaver Park and the school and cut the engine. He unhooked his sunglasses from the rearview mirror and slid them on. But his gaze didn't waver from Belle Day puttering about in her small front yard.

Annoying. Interfering. Too sexy for such a scrawny thing. He'd expected those things when he'd hired her, because he'd thought those things from the first day they'd met when she'd cornered him about that damn field trip.

So, he'd expected all that. Been prepared for all that. Been ready to have the daughter of a man he'd hated for longer than his adult life living under his roof because he was beyond desperate to prove to a passel of lawyers that nobody—not even two people rich enough to buy heaven—could provide a better home for his daughter than he could.

He *hadn't* been ready for his daughter to become

the woman's champion. Hadn't been ready for Lucy's tearful accusations—when he'd discovered her actually doing her small exercises on her own without him having to get on her case about it—that he'd scared off Belle Day for good. Damn sure hadn't expected to come after the woman, two days later hat in hand.

She was sitting on the grass now, banging at the mower. The metallic noise rang out, sounding out of place in the morning air.

He got out of his truck and crossed the empty street. Down a few doors, a trio of kids played in a picket-fenced yard. The other direction, a teenage boy was slopping a sudsy rag over a shining red car.

He couldn't ever remember feeling as young as they looked. Or as young as Belle looked, for that matter, though he knew she was only a few years younger than he was.

Maybe that's what a man got for inheriting an adult's responsibilities when he was sixteen.

He rolled the sleeves of his shirt farther up his arms as he stepped up on the sidewalk. He could hear Belle muttering colorful curses under her breath. It was almost amusing. "What's the problem?"

She jerked, craning her head around. A tangle of emotions crossed her face. "Won't start." She turned back to the mower. The ends of her ponytail flirted with the faint breeze, dancing around the waist of her faded jeans.

Cage walked around to the other side. Splotches of black grease covered her hands. A few more clangs rang out courtesy of her banging. "That helping?" His voice was dry.

She angled him a look as she tugged up the halter strap of her red bikini top. "Does it look like it? What are you doing here?" Her chin set and she looked back down at the engine. She had a smudge of grease on her collarbone, now. "As if I can't guess."

He bent his knees, hunkering down next to the mower. Better to look at the engine. He slid the wrench out of her unresisting fingers. Just because he was there didn't mean the words weren't sitting in his throat fit to choke him. "I brought Luce into town. She's at Emmy Johansson's."

"Stored there all safe and sound where I can't lead her down danger's path?" She grabbed the wrench back from him. "You're all dressed up. You're going to get greasy."

A clean gray shirt and black jeans was dressed up? She must really think he was a hick. "Luce told me you weren't going to let her ride."

"I told you that, too." She unwound her crossed legs and knelt, leaning over the mower as she strained to remove the housing.

God. He had a straight view down her lithe torso and she had no clue whatsoever. Her nipples were as hard as—

He looked across the street to the park.

She huffed and sat back down on her butt, stretching out her legs. "This is hopeless."

Hopeless was getting the branded image of her breasts out of his head. "She also implied you wouldn't be back on Monday. Give me the wrench."

She eyed him. "Is that the newest euphemism for telling someone to go…soak your head?"

"I heard that Colby's has an open-mike night on Saturdays," he said blandly. "You can try out the stand-up comedy there."

She flipped up the wrench like a one-fingered salute. "And take away your spotlight?"

"Funny." He didn't go to Colby's and they both knew it. Next to Ruby's Diner, Colby's was the best stop for buffalo wings, beer and gossip. He preferred beef, didn't drink beer or anything else alcoholic and couldn't abide wagging tongues. He grabbed the wrench. Studied the mower for a moment then easily unfastened the housing and set it aside.

"Show-off," Belle muttered.

"You're welcome."

She snatched the wrench back once more. "If you've come to fire me, just get it done and over with. As you can see—" she waved her hand beyond the mower to her slightly overgrown grass "—I have things to do." She tugged at the halter strap again and leaned over the mower. She stuck her fingers here and there, poking and plucking and he knew she didn't have a single clue what she was doing.

Irritation rippled along his spine. "I didn't come to fire you. I told you what Lucy said. I came to make sure you didn't quit on me. Don't stick your finger in there." He pushed her hands out of the way, but she didn't move so easily. And now, his hands were as greasy as hers.

She swatted at him. "It's *my* mower!"

He closed his fingers around hers. "So I should just sit here and let you ruin the chances of ever fixing it?"

Her eyebrows peaked. Their fingers felt glued together by the sticky grease.

Heat collected at the base of his spine, shooting right up it, threatening his sanity. He let her go.

She sat back, her wrists propped on her knees, gooey fingers splayed. "Well." Her voice was a little husky. "There's a concept."

"My daughter is not a bloody lawn mower. And you need a new spark plug."

"I *know* your daughter isn't yard equipment." She shook her head, looking disgusted. "So, you came because you're afraid I'm a quitter."

"Are you?"

"I don't quit on people I care about," she said after a moment.

"Admirable. What about Lucy?"

She huffed. "I care about *her.*"

"And not me."

Her eyebrows rose again over brown eyes that looked too vulnerable for comfort. "Wouldn't that be the height of folly? It really must have frosted your cookies when Days began moving to your neck of the woods, instead of staying nice and faraway in Cheyenne. Do you loathe the Clays, too, since Squire had the bad form to marry my mother?"

"Does that mean you're in Weaver permanently?" She started to reach for the housing, but he beat her to it, mostly out of pity for the equipment. In seconds, the mower was assembled.

"No," she said fervently. "Believe me, I cannot *wait* to go back to my job at the clinic in Cheyenne. If you didn't live out on the Lazy-B like some hermit, you'd probably know that. As a topic for gossip, I'm as much fair game as anyone else who lives here." She stood and started to grab the mower, but stopped, looking beyond him with a grimace. "Oh, great."

"Problems, Belle?" A cheerful female voice assaulted them.

Cage looked over and saw Brenda Wyatt practically skipping down the sidewalk, she was in such a hurry to get the latest scoop. "Speaking of gossip," he muttered under his breath.

"Nothing major," Belle assured the woman, ignoring him.

"Anything I can help with?" Brenda stopped shy of stepping on the grass, her eyes curious and sharp as a hungry bird.

"Not unless your husband has a spare spark plug for this thing." Belle nudged the mower with her tennis shoe.

"Well, I'll just go and see." Brenda's gaze rested on Cage for a moment. He could practically see the speculation turning inside her head. Then she smiled again, and hurried back toward her picketed yard.

"Now she's gonna feel compelled to come back, you know."

Belle's smile was mocking. "So? Nobody's asking you to stay. Consider your brief presence here your good deed for the day. It'll provide hours and hours of entertainment for Brenda."

"Is this what it's gonna be like now if you come back to the Lazy-B?" He still had some doubts that she'd return, because she hadn't actually said she would. "Open warfare?"

"You're the one who declared it, Cage."

"Thought you wanted to maintain some civility for Lucy's sake."

"All I was trying to do was help. That's all I've ever wanted to do. But you've either treated me like a leper or a liar. I'm sorry for the past, Cage. More than you can possibly know. Maybe you think you're being disloyal to your father's memory, or to your mother, by employing the enemy. But your father is gone and your daughter is very much here. I *want* to help."

"You think I don't know that?" He nearly choked to

keep his voice down. Brenda was jogging back down the sidewalk, waving something in her hand.

"Here you go," she said gaily, trotting up to them. She dropped the small box in Belle's hand.

"Thanks, Brenda. I'll replace this for you as soon as I can get over to the hardware store."

Brenda nodded. "Sure. Sure. Whenever." Her gaze bounced eagerly between Cage and Belle. "So, how is young Lucy doing? Such a terrible, terrible tragedy."

"Good grief, Brenda. Lucy's not paralyzed," Belle countered.

Brenda's smile stiffened. "Well, of course she isn't. And it's so nice of Cage to give you a job, too, after all that—" she waved her hand "—messiness you had in Cheyenne."

Save him from catty women. He took the box and pulled out the spark plug, kneeling down to replace it. "Isn't that your youngest crossing the street, Brenda?" He knew it was because she brought her trio of brats to every school meeting he'd ever had to attend.

She turned around. "Timothy Wyatt," she yelled, dashing after the boy. "You get out of the street this instant!"

"Nothing quiet about living down the street from the Wyatts," Belle murmured.

"Wouldn't think so." When the spark plug was in place, Cage rose. He primed the engine, then grabbed the cord and gave it one good pull. The engine turned over and ran, smooth as butter.

Belle's hands closed over the handle. "Thanks. I, um, well you should go on inside and wash your hands at least. So you don't get grease all over you the way I have."

Looking at her various splotches of grease only meant letting his gaze wander back to the vicinity of her bikini top. Not a good idea. He nodded and headed up the narrow, flower-lined walk while Belle busily pushed her mower over the postage-stamp-size lawn.

Inside, the house was small. Newer than his place, but much smaller, and that was saying something. When he'd come here to ask her in person to take the job, he'd stood on the little porch. Both times. He hadn't wanted to go inside her house any more than she'd been prepared to invite him inside.

He'd thought then, and he thought so now, that the small house was hardly the kind of place where he'd have expected Gus Day's daughter to live. The man had been the most prominent attorney in Cheyenne.

He went into the kitchen—a straight shot through the small living room—and washed up at the sink there. She had little pots of daisies sitting in the window next to a small round oak table. Photographs were stuck all over the refrigerator door with funky magnets.

He didn't particularly want to see all the mementos of her family. Her friends. He looked, anyway.

There were no photographs of her father that he could see. Just her with students he recognized from the school. With kids of all ages, many who were members of the Clay family. Several with a woman who looked a lot like Belle, except for their coloring. Probably the sister.

He leaned closer to one photo. Belle, grinning from ear to ear, a mortarboard on her head and a diploma clutched in her hand. She looked young and carefree. Not much different then she usually looked now.

He'd finally gotten his college degree when he'd been twenty-five. Five years ago now.

He straightened and headed back out, just as she was coming in. Bits of grass clung to the legs of her jeans and he stopped short when she suddenly leaned over, whipping them down her legs, kicking them free to leave on the porch. "Get the grease off?"

He was long past the teenage kid who'd been struck dumb by the seductive efforts of an older blonde, but right then Cage felt just as poleaxed by Belle as he'd been by his first experience with any woman. Only now he knew how high the cost could be.

"Cage?"

The rest of her bathing suit—cut like snug boxers—was modest by current standards. But it still showed enough.

She glanced down at herself, grimacing. "Sorry. I should have warned you." She walked past him to the kitchen.

He could probably span her waist with his two hands. The swells of her breasts—the pink-tipped visions he wouldn't be getting out of his head anytime soon—would fit the palms of his hands. And her hips...

He heard the rush of water when she turned on the faucet and shifted sideways a little. He could see her vigorously scrubbing her hands and arms with soapy water. When she was done and dry, she grabbed a long-sleeved white shirt off the coat rack by the back door and slipped into it. The tails hung around her knees. It was obviously a man's shirt.

"Warned me?" Whose shirt was it?

"The scars. Well, you've seen a little of them already."

Right. Scars. They were there all right. But it wasn't the scars that had made his jeans so damn tight he could hardly move without making the problem obvious. "How long did it take you to recover?"

She flipped her ponytail free of the collar and padded into the living room, not looking at him.

Good thing.

"I'll let you know when I'm finished." She was leaning over, busily stacking together the magazines scattered over the top of the iron-and-glass coffee table. The shirt crept up the back of her insanely perfect thighs.

Was she doing it deliberately?

He ran his hand around his neck. He was driving Lucy down to visit his mother that afternoon. Even thinking about his daughter and his mother didn't alleviate the knot inside him.

Belle straightened and turned, her faint smile rueful. "Almost two years, actually. Recuperating put me behind a grade in junior high school. Hopefully, if we get Lucy's test scores high enough, she won't have to deal with being held back. I had to work with a tutor, too. In high school. All three years, to make up time. So my twin sister wouldn't graduate ahead of me."

He'd had enough reminders of her family. "Do you always strip off in front of strange men?"

Her dark lashes dipped for a moment, then she eyed him with wide eyes. "Why, yes, I do, Cage. I thought you knew that about me." She propped her hand on her hip, but her face was red. "And are you still going to keep calling me Miss Day even now that we know each other so well? Having seen me in my bathing suit, the way you have, that is. Why, we just might have to get married for the scandal of it all."

"You've got a smart mouth."

"The better to eat you with, Goldilocks," she muttered, turning away.

He nearly choked, but she was oblivious.

"I'm allergic to grass, okay? And my jeans were covered with it." She didn't look at him as she returned to the kitchen once more. Apparently, her bravado went only so far.

He followed. "Then why mow your own grass if you're allergic?"

"Well, who *else* would be doing it?"

"Hire someone."

She gave him a cross look. "I could say the same to you, then you would have some *time* to give to your daughter when she needs you. What *is* your real name, anyway?"

"What?"

"Cage isn't your real name, right?"

"No."

"Kind of an odd nickname."

"So?"

"So…how'd you get it? I'm sort of surprised it's not *rock,* because sometimes you act as if you're living under one."

"Calling me a snake?"

Her expression stilled for a moment. "No, actually. I've met one of *those.* Was engaged to him, actually."

Despite Cage's aversion to gossip, he'd heard the brunt of Belle's story. Was the former fiancé the owner of the shirt? Dammit. He didn't want to wonder. He damn sure refused to care.

"I paced," he said abruptly. Anything was better than thinking about how Belle came by the shirt she wore with such casual sexiness.

She looked blank.

"When I was a kid and indoors, I paced. Back and forth like I was in a cage."

"Ah." She yanked open the refrigerator and pulled out two longnecks. Extended one to him.

He shook his head.

"Seriously?"

"I don't drink."

She shrugged and put the beer back, then came out with bottles of water, instead. She handed him his, then leaned her shoulders against the fridge, opening her water. She tilted her head back and drank deeply, then capped the bottle again, resting it against her abdomen. "So, you like being outside better than inside, ergo, *Cage.* The pacing thing, by the way, seems to be something you got over. I've never seen a man who could be so still as you are. And you don't drink. What else is there about you that the Weaver grapevine hasn't already published? Ah. How ironic. Back to the beginning, again. Your real name."

"It's…unique." His voice was clipped. He strongly considered dumping the cold water over his head. Nearly anything would be preferable to the unacceptable thoughts running through his head.

Her eyebrows rose. "You're actually giving a hint? I'm amazed. Something unique. Unique for the English language? For a man? What?"

"Are you going to be at the Lazy-B tomorrow morning, or not?"

Her eyes narrowed in consideration. She tapped her finger against her water bottle, drawing his gaze for too long a moment. Then, her finger stilled midtap, and her cheeks colored, her gaze flicking to his, then away.

So, she wasn't as unaware as she'd seemed.

If it were anyone other than her, he'd do what nature intended. He'd step up to her, press her back flat against that photo-strewn refrigerator, kiss her until neither one of them knew their own names—real or nick—and tug away that bathing-suit top to see if her nipples tasted as sweet as he feared.

And she still hadn't given him an answer. "Miss Day?"

"One condition," she said after a moment.

"What?" He wasn't agreeing until he knew what sort of string she was dangling.

"Well, maybe more than one."

His molars were nearly grinding together. "What?"

"Not treating me like the enemy is probably more than I can expect. But you can at least stop acting like I'm some schoolmarm and call me *Belle*. You don't freak out if we visit…*visit*…the stable. *And* you suggest to Lucy that she have a birthday party."

"A party?" He eyed her. "Lucy doesn't want a party."

Belle *tsked*. "You may be able to spot a faulty spark plug, Cage, but *I* can recognize a lonely girl when I see one. Besides, she and I have talked about it. She wants a party but she figures you'll refuse to allow it."

"If she wants a party, fine."

"With boys?" Her eyebrows rose a little.

"What?"

"Loosen up, *Dad*," she said evenly. "Your daughter is a teenager, and teenagers do generally have some interest in the opposite sex, if you can remember."

He remembered all right. He remembered where his thoughts had been when he'd been thirteen-fourteen-going-on twenty. "I remember what teenagers do with the opposite sex." Same damn thing he inconveniently thought of nearly every time he set eyes on *Miss* Belle Day. "I remember what I was doing when I was barely seventeen. Conceiving Lucy."

Belle's lashes lowered for a moment and when she looked up again, he knew that statement hadn't been some big revelation for her. Of course not. She may have lived in Weaver for only six months, but that would be long enough for a town where gossip vied with ranching as the number-one occupation. "I seriously doubt you were just out sowing your oats," she said after a moment. "Your dad had died. Your mom was critically injured. You had the responsibility of the ranch on your shoulders. You were alone, and you probably needed someone. Badly, I'd imagine."

He'd had responsibility for the ranch since he'd been younger than that. "I had a hard-on for a sexy blonde I saw dancing at a rodeo," he said flatly. Understanding, sympathy or anything of that ilk were not things he wanted from Belle. "Fortunately, I've learned how to ignore wanting things that aren't good for me."

She flushed, obviously realizing where the pointed comment was directed. Too bad he could see the way that rosy color drifted down her throat, to her chest. Because it made him wonder how far the blush went.

She set aside the water bottle and clutched the shirt together with both hands. "Well. Anyway. Your daughter and her friends are more interested in holding hands and getting up the nerve to dance with a boy than…anything else. You agree and I'll be there tomorrow morning."

"She can have a party."

"And?" Her eyebrows rose expectantly.

His jaw felt tight. "You can visit the horses, but I'd appreciate it if you'd wait until I could be there, too." It was the most reasonable he could be.

She inclined her head. "And?"

And. Always another *and.* "And if I'd had a schoolmarm who looked like you, I wouldn't have been ditching classes to sleep with a wannabe dancer named Sandi Oldham." He reached out and brushed his thumb over her soft lips, watching her eyes flare. "Believe me, Miss Day. Some things are better left alone."

# Chapter 7

Belle's second drive out to the Lazy-B was accomplished without a deluge of rain. ·

Instead, she had to deal with a deluge of nervousness that put her misgivings on the first trip to shame.

The drive took much less time, courtesy of the dry roads, as well as her familiarity with the route. So, it wasn't even lunchtime when she closed the gate behind her and drove up to the brick house.

Strudel was again lying on the porch, but he popped up and scrambled down the steps to greet her when she climbed out of her Jeep. She laughed a little, scrubbing his neck as he jumped up on her. "What'd you eat this time that got you banished from the house?"

The dog panted and rolled his eyes in joy.

"Strudel." Cage's voice from the porch wasn't loud, but the command was unmistakable. "Get off the woman."

The dog went back down on all fours. Danced around

in circles. Belle ducked back into the Jeep to grab her suitcase. She felt some sympathy for the dog. There was enough adrenaline jolting through her system that she could have run in mindless circles, too.

She hadn't really expected to see Cage just yet. Running even a small ranch offered enough tasks to keep ten men busy, much less one. But he *was* there, and she'd have to suck it up. Just because she'd spent the rest of the previous day and night preoccupied with the things he'd said…the way he'd *looked* at her…

She realized she was still standing there with her rear hanging out of her old Jeep. Hardly conveying a composed demeanor. She yanked out the suitcase and closed the door. Cage had moved down the steps and was heading her way.

"Where's Lucy?" A nice touch of brightness in her voice. Not too shrill. Not too desperate. First order of business with the girl was to find out why she'd implied to her dad that Belle was prepared to quit.

"Talking to Anya on the phone about the birthday party. You were right."

Hallelujah. One good deed accomplished. Though she was surprised that he so easily acknowledged it. She hastily surrendered her suitcase when he reached for it. Easier than fighting over the thing.

He looked amused, as if he recognized her scrambled thoughts. A disturbing idea. She reached back inside her vehicle. "I nearly ran into the mailman on the road here," she said. "Thought I'd save you a trip."

If she hadn't imagined the glint of humor in those eyes that rivaled the sky for color, it disappeared when she held up the bundled newspaper and envelopes. He silently took the mail and turned back to the house.

Belle sighed at the slap of the wooden screen behind him. "Why, it was my pleasure, Cage. You're *so* welcome." She followed him up the steps where the ramp still blocked half the width. If she did her job well enough, he'd be able to dismantle it for good. Once inside the house, she heard Cage's footsteps overhead and knew he was putting her suitcase in her room.

Lucy was sprawled on her bed in her downstairs room, the phone apparently glued to her ear. She waved and smiled widely when Belle stuck her head through the doorway. She pressed the phone to her shoulder. "You're back!"

"Yes," Belle said arching her eyebrows. "Apparently, that's some big surprise."

The girl had the grace to look somewhat chagrined. "Well, now you know my dad really wants you."

Belle tucked her tongue between her teeth for a moment. She knew what Lucy meant, though the words suggested something quite different. "Finish your call," she suggested. "Then we'll get down to business."

Lucy grimaced. "You're not, like, going to take it out on me by making me do some really hideous exercises or something, are you?"

Belle smiled wickedly.

Lucy groaned. When Belle turned back to the staircase, she heard Lucy giggling into the phone again, though. Obviously, she wasn't too fearful of Belle's retribution.

She dashed up the staircase. Sure enough, Cage had put her suitcase on the foot of the bed, and she unpacked again, as quickly as she had the previous week. After all, her clothes took up no more space now than they had then.

She closed the door long enough to exchange her jeans for Capri tights that she covered with a loose pair of shorts, then put on her tennis shoes again and went back downstairs. Cage was in his office. She could see a wedge of his shoulder through the doorway.

Fortunately, the clump of Lucy's crutches coming along the wood floor put the kibosh on any notion she might have been entertaining of going toward that office. What would she have said, anyway?

They were who they were and never the twain would meet.

A shiver danced down her spine and she looked up at the ceiling. Maybe the place was developing a draft.

Right. Blame your nerves on phantom drafts. That's a sane thing to do.

"Belle?" Lucy was standing nearby watching her. "Something wrong?"

Belle shook her head. Then did a double take. "Good grief. You're wearing...blue."

"And you're wearing yellow. Call the newspapers. Come on. Just don't torture me too bad, okay?"

There were already filled water bottles in the refrigerator. Belle hid a smile at that. The prep work had to have been Lucy's doing, because she just couldn't envision Cage taking the time to fill water bottles. She grabbed two, and they walked outside, crossing to the barn. They'd only made it halfway when Strudel came tearing after them. He ran to the barn, then back, barking gleefully.

"That dog needs antidepressants," Belle said as she pushed open the barn door.

Lucy laughed. "Dad found him on the side of the highway last winter. He's a happy dog."

"So I see." It should have been harder to envision cranky Cage stopping to rescue some cold, shivering puppy. But it wasn't hard, and the image burned bright in her mind.

Then Lucy flipped on the boom box that Belle had left there. Debussy soared out, startling the images from Belle's head.

Good thing.

Belle dragged the blue mats into place, then Lucy dropped her crutches and inched to the floor, balancing her awkward position with no small amount of grace.

"You're going to dance on the stages of New York one day," Belle murmured. "Specially if you work as hard on your recovery as I know you can."

Lucy flushed. But she looked pleased by the idea. "My mom is a dancer. Did you know that?"

"Yes."

"That's why she's not here, you know. Because she went to Europe to be a dancer."

Belle knew what it was like to strive for a career, but privately, she couldn't imagine leaving behind her own child. "Do you hear from her?"

"I've got copies of programs from her shows," Lucy said, not exactly answering as she reclined again. She lifted her uninjured knee up to her chest, then slowly straightened it, her toes pointed, knee nearly resting on her nose.

A program was not a phone call or a letter, Belle thought. And because she was too curious about the role that Sandi Oldham played in the Buchanans' life, she kicked off her shoes.

"All right," she said briskly. "Let's get you warmed up. We have a lot to accomplish today. After we're done in here, you have a history test to pass."

Lucy groaned.

Standing just outside the barn door, Cage watched Belle and his daughter. Even Strudel sat quietly for once, leaning heavily against Cage's leg, occasionally slapping the dusty ground with his feathered tail. Lucy started out muttering and outright complaining about every single movement Belle put her through. But he never noticed a single sign of impatience in Belle. She was calm, encouraging, humorous. No matter what Lucy threw her way, she maneuvered his daughter into accomplishing whatever task she'd set out.

And eventually, Lucy was grinning as often as she was groaning.

Even though he had a million and one things that needed tending, Cage stayed there, out of sight, for the entire session. Only when Belle was helping Lucy get her leg situated in the whirlpool afterward did he finally turn away.

Belle might be a Day, she might be a pure source of frustration for his peace of mind, but where Lucy was concerned, Cage felt as if he'd finally done something right.

There was no way a judge could come along now and say that *anyone* could provide better for his own daughter.

Cage's satisfaction lasted well into the next week. And when it ended, it wasn't even because of Belle Day. It was because of his daughter.

He watched her from the door of his office. Watched her long enough to know she hadn't just gone in there for a piece of paper or some such thing. Not that he'd really believed it, given the fact it was nearly midnight.

He leaned his shoulder against the doorjamb. "Who were you calling?" His voice was mild, but she nearly jumped right out of her skin, casting him a guilty look that made his insides tighten.

"Nobody."

He pointedly looked at the telephone situated two inches away from her twitching fingers. "Is that their first or last name?"

She glared at him for a tense moment. Then her face crumpled and she burst into tears and snatched her crutches, racing past him. A few seconds later, she slammed her bedroom door behind her.

He let out an exasperated sigh. The kid had been moody as all get-out for days. He strode after her, only to find she'd locked the door. He rapped on it. "Luce. Unlock it."

"Leave me alone!"

"Who were you talking to on the phone?"

"I *said* leave me alone!" Her muffled voice rose.

He knocked harder. "Open the damn door."

"Cage?" Belle darted down the stairs, peering at him over the banister. "What's wrong?"

"Nothing that concerns you."

She straightened so fast her hair danced around the shoulders of her white robe. "Pardon me." She pivoted on the stairs, going up even faster than she'd come down. Which was saying something.

He jiggled the knob. "Unlock it, Luce, or I will."

The door yanked inward. Lucy glared at him. She was sitting in her chair. "I don't want to talk to *you*. I wanna talk to Belle."

Sixty-three inches of not-so-little girl knew how to pack a punch. He eyed her for a long moment. She eyed him right back. God help him, she was the spitting image of the woman who'd borne her, but he knew she got her attitude straight from him. "Who were you talking to on the phone?" If it was the Oldhams, he was going to have the bloody phone disconnected.

"I don't have to tell you!"

He lifted his eyebrow. "Oh?"

She exhaled loudly. If she could have managed it, he was pretty sure she would have stomped her feet. Instead, she wheeled her chair sharply away from the doorway. "I wanna talk to Belle." Her voice was thick with tears again.

He shoveled his fingers through his hair. "She's your physical therapist," he said flatly. "And it's the middle of the night."

"She's also my *friend*."

While he was only Lucy's dad. And no matter how much he needed to keep Belle Day firmly in one slot, she kept slipping out of it.

He watched Lucy surreptitiously swipe her cheeks. Dammit.

He went upstairs. Stared at another closed door for a long moment. Then knocked.

Belle opened it so fast, he wondered if she'd been standing there waiting for the opportunity to gloat. Only he couldn't detect any complacency in her expression. She just looked soft. From the top of her rippling brown hair to the tender toes peeking out beneath her long robe.

He was being punished for something, surely. Why else would he be surrounded by females he didn't know how to handle?

"Lucy wants to talk to you."

She tightened the belt of her robe, clearly hesitating.

"What are you waiting for? Yes or no?"

Her soft eyes cooled. "I'm waiting to see if you keel over, because I'm sure you must be choking on coming up here to pass that on."

"If you don't want to go down, say so."

"Given my continued presence under your roof each week, I'd think it would be clear by now that I'd do just about anything for Lucy."

"And nothing for me."

Her eyebrow rose and even though he could practically tuck her in his pocket, she managed to look down her nose at him. "As if you'd accept…anything." Her lips twisted a little and she planted her hand in the center of his chest, pushing until he moved out of the way.

When he did, she slid past him, a wisp nearly smothered in white terrycloth and topped by wavy brown hair.

He followed her downstairs. Told himself he imagined the oddly sympathetic look in her eyes in the moment before Lucy shut the door. Females on the inside.

Him on the outside.

He scrubbed his hand down his face and returned to his office. His desk was a jumble of papers, books and a hackamore he was repairing. The telephone sat smack in the middle of it all.

Who had she been calling? If it were just her friend, Anya, Luce would simply have told him. He'd have been irritated that she was up so late—and on a long-distance phone call, yet—but hardly enough to inspire that reaction. He rounded the desk and sat down. Leaned back in his chair.

Across from him, pinned to the wall, were all of Lucy's school photographs. But he didn't need the pictures to remember every single moment. The missing teeth. The crooked ponytails. The grins.

"Are you all right?"

His gaze slid to the doorway. Belle stood there. Arms crossed, hands disappearing up the opposite sleeves of her robe.

"She called the Oldhams, didn't she?"

Belle looked startled. "Her grandparents, you mean?"

"What did she tell you?"

"Don't bark at me. The only thing I know about her grandparents are that they've sent her some gifts. Dance programs of her mother's."

"Gifts including that horse." That horse that Belle insisted on letting Lucy visit. He'd gone with them once. Been frustrated as all hell to see that Belle had been right about something else. Lucy might talk a fast game about wanting back on Satin, but she was definitely afraid.

He looked up at Belle, sidetracked a little by the gleam on her lips when she moistened them. "Yes," she admitted. "Lucy...mentioned it."

He propped his elbows on his desk, crinkling letters and invoices. "Then what *did* she tell you?"

She looked down the hallway for a moment then stepped more fully into the confines of his office. There was no chair for her to sit. "She didn't tell me she'd called her grandparents tonight."

Which didn't mean that Lucy hadn't made the call. She thought he didn't know about the other times she'd called. "Then what's she going on about?" Having to voice the question stuck in his craw big-time.

"We, um, we need to go into town tomorrow."

"For cake mix and candles already?"

Her cheeks were pink. "Well. We could do that."

"I find it hard to believe she's going berserk at midnight over a cake she doesn't even need for weeks yet. It's not like she's going to be troubled over picking a color for the frosting. It'll be pink. Or pink."

"She's not upset about her cake."

"Then what?" He pushed away from his desk only there was no room to pace in the small room. Not unless he wanted to go near Belle, and he didn't want to do that.

Because getting *near* wasn't remotely as close as he wanted to be. And knowing it just pissed him off even more.

"There's something else you need to know." Belle was looking anywhere but at him. "Lucy didn't even want to tell you, but I said she really needed to."

His neck tightened warningly. "What?" His voice was harsh and Belle took a step back.

"Nothing bad," she assured quickly.

"Nothing bad that has her sneaking in my office to use the phone when she's supposed to be sleeping? If she wasn't calling her grandparents, who the hell was she calling?"

"Evan Taggart."

He stared. "What?"

"Who," Belle murmured. "But she didn't get hold of him, anyway, because his parents answered the phone and said it was too late to talk."

"At least Drew Taggart has some sense," he muttered. "So she was upset because she couldn't talk to some little kid."

"Evan's in her grade, Cage. She…likes…him. I think the Taggarts have been out of town on vacation or something. She was making sure he knew he was invited to her party."

He absorbed that.

"But that's not the real problem."

"Then what the hell is?"

"Would you calm down?" She moistened her lips. "Seriously, this is nothing for you to be wigging out over and—"

He grabbed her shoulders. "What…is…it?"

Her lashes lowered. "Well, actually, Lucy got her first period tonight. She's too embarrassed to tell you. And that's why we need to go to town tomorrow. Because I wasn't exactly prepared for this, either."

He sat down on the edge of his desk. "What?"

She tugged her belt tighter. "Judging by your expression, I think you heard me just fine."

"She's only twelve!"

Belle quickly pushed his office door closed even

though she knew the barrier wouldn't completely buffer Cage's raised voice. "You want to argue Mother Nature with me? She's all but thirteen, and regardless of *what* her age is, this is happening." She almost felt sorry for him. He looked positively shell-shocked. But sympathy didn't quite douse the sting of being put in her place by him.

"Your daughter is growing up, Cage, and you better start getting used to the idea, or you're going to be dealing with a lot of episodes just as pleasant as this one! The poor thing is being ruled by hormones right now."

He was silent for a moment. Then he held out his hands, cupped palms turned upward. "When she was born I could hold her right here in the palms of my hands. She was that small." His fingers curled and he dropped his fists. "Lucy's always been able to talk to me."

So much for holding on to her indignation.

She impulsively caught his hands in hers, smoothing out his fingers from those tense fists. "This isn't about you, Cage. It's about her. She's no more used to the things that are going on inside her—emotionally and physically—than you are."

His lashes lifted and his eyes met hers. She was abruptly aware that holding his hands wasn't just a matter of trying to extend comfort.

It felt intimate.

It felt addictive.

She started to pull away. But his thumbs pressed over her fingertips, holding them in place. She could feel the calloused ridges as he slowly brushed over her fingers, grazing over her knuckles.

Her lips parted, yet her breathing had stalled.

They were so close she could easily pick out the black ring surrounding his blue, blue irises. Could have counted each black lash that comprised the thick smudged-coal lashes he'd passed on to his daughter. Could have touched the nearly invisible scar on his chin just below the curve of his lower lip.

She realized she was leaning in, and shock jerked her back, hands and eyes and traitorous hormones and all. Was she no better than Annette Barrone?

He wrapped his hands around the edge of his desk on either side of his hips. "Put whatever you need in town on my account," he said after a moment. His voice was low.

She nodded and started backing out of the office. Bumped into the door that she'd closed. Heat stung her cheeks as she fumbled for the knob. Thankfully, the door opened. Escape was near.

"Belle."

She really felt safer when he called her *Miss Day*. Did he know how close she'd come to leaning forward those last few inches and pressing her lips to his? "Yes?" Lord, she hoped not. Her humiliation would be complete.

"Thank you."

Her knees threatened to dissolve right there. She nodded quickly and poured herself out of his office.

She hoped to heaven that he couldn't see the way she had to wait until she stopped shaking at the foot of the stairs before climbing them. She hoped to heaven that when she did go up the stairs, she'd remember somewhere along the way that Cage Buchanan was off limits.

He blamed her father for the accident that stole his parents. He didn't know—couldn't possibly—that it was Belle's fault that she and her father had been out at all on that icy road that long-ago night.

## Chapter 8

Cage saw her coming. There was no mistaking the sheaf of brown hair streaming back from her as she leaned low over the horse, seeming to race with the wind. Belle was quite a sight. Three weeks had passed since that night in his office. Three weeks of relative peace and quiet. Except for the nights, spent wakeful and alert with her only a room away.

He propped his wrists over the end of the posthole digger and watched her closing the distance between them. Anticipation tangled with wariness and it wasn't a combination he particularly welcomed.

At least she wasn't foolish enough to be riding that satanic horse. No matter how well Lucy was doing after working with Belle all this time, he'd have still probably fired Belle for it.

The horse was a line he wouldn't let anyone cross.

He leaned the digger against the truck and shoved

his wire clippers back in his toolbox, then sat on the opened tailgate and chugged down a half a bottle of water, waiting.

Because sure as God made little green apples, he knew that Belle Day was gunning for him.

He heard the hooves pound and wouldn't allow himself the luxury of looking away as she neared, slowly reining in the animal. She looked fragile as she dismounted, but he knew only too well that she was nothing but muscle and nerve under those body-skimming clothes she wore.

She flipped the reins around the side-view mirror of the truck then lifted her hand, shading her eyes from the noonday sun as she looked at him. "As usual, you're a hard man to track down. Gone before breakfast. Back after dinner."

"Where's Lucy?"

"Emmy Johannson brought Anya out to visit now that she's back from visiting her father. They're eating lunch right now. Emmy's going to give Lucy a piano lesson, too."

"Then what's wrong?" He pulled a fence post out of the truck bed and shoved it into the hole he'd already dug, then pushed at it with his boot, aligning it. "And why didn't you drive?"

She propped her hands on her narrow hips and tilted her head. Her long hair flowed over her shoulder and her eyes glanced at him, then away. It had been that way for days. Weeks. Looking, but not looking.

Wanting but not touching. At least on his part, anyhow.

He kicked the post again.

"I'm not unfamiliar with horses," she countered. "I've been riding all my life. And I wasn't foolish enough to ride Satin. Though I did notice you're letting him run at least."

He hated the horse because of what he stood for and how it had hurt his daughter. But he wasn't cruel enough to keep the animal penned in a stall forever. He pushed the post once more, still not satisfied with the way it stood. "I'd have preferred you ask me, first."

She huffed a little then walked around him. "Fine. I will, next time." She grabbed the heavy post beneath his hands and put her shoulder against it, nudging it in his direction. "Centered?"

He narrowed his eyes, studying the top of her dark head for a moment. "Yeah." He made quick work out of filling the hole again then quickly fastened the barbed wire back in place when she moved out of the way.

She flipped her long ponytail behind her shoulders and pulled a long, thin envelope out from behind her. He barely glanced at the envelope, distracted by the wedge of skin she displayed when she'd flipped up her shirt to pull out the envelope tucked against her spine beneath it. "This looked important. A courier brought it out."

His stomach clenched as she extended the envelope.

He slowly took it. Eyed the embossed return address.

"Do you want to talk about it?" Her voice was surprisingly diffident.

"No." He folded the envelope in half then pushed it in his back pocket. If he had to read a letter that he was another step closer to losing custody of his baby, he damn sure didn't want to do it while Belle Day was standing there to witness it.

But she just stood there, though, hands clutched together. "Is there anything I can do?"

"No." Not unless she had about fifty grand lying around unused. He figured it would cost at least that much to get Sandi to back off. Either the money would go in her pocket, or the lawyer's. He turned back to the truck. Hoisted the next pole over his shoulder and moved down to the next hole.

"Cage, if you have some legal problem, my family might—"

"No." He didn't like feeling as if he'd kicked a calf when she paled a little and pressed her soft lips together. But he didn't have it in him just then to apologize.

"Well, then do you think—"

"Dammit to hell, Belle, I said no."

She winced. "You don't even know what I was going to ask!"

He exhaled roughly. Shoved the post into the ground with a vengeance. "I don't want your help. God knows I don't want your family's help. I don't want anything." Except her body. A problem which was becoming more evident by the minute. "Satisfied?"

"The Clays are having a party," she said stiffly. "They wanted me to extend the invitation to you and Lucy."

He looked up into the sky. He'd never had much against Squire Clay or his sons. The boys had been ahead of him a few years, but they knew each other passably. Didn't mean he wanted to sit down with tea and cookies across the table from Squire's wife, Gloria Day.

There was probably a special place in Hades for him, but he just couldn't look at the woman without thinking about his own mother, and what Gloria's husband had done to her. Call him a miserable puke, but there it was.

"What's the party for?"

Her brown eyes widened a little. Surprised that he'd bothered to ask, no doubt. "Angeline's birthday. She's

Daniel and Maggie's oldest. The party is a week after Lucy's, actually."

He'd seen the girl. Dusky skinned. Pretty as a picture. All he knew about her was that her natural parents were dead and Daniel and Maggie had adopted her a long time ago. "Take Lucy."

"Really?"

He *really* wished she'd go on her way. The letter was burning a hole in his butt. "If she wants to go."

"Well." She brushed her hands together, obviously surprised. "This is wonderful. We'll be swimming. The Double-C has a great swimming hole, you see, and—"

"—and I don't have time to stand around shooting the breeze," he said flatly. "So why don't you go back and tend to what I *am* paying you for?"

Her chin lifted a little. "Keep up with the ogre routine, Cage. One of these days you'll have it perfected and maybe even you will forget it's an act." She strode over to the truck and snatched the reins. With a move he admired whether he wanted to or not, she slid onto the horse's back. In a flash, they were racing away.

When she was out of sight, he let his eyes rove over the land around him. When he'd inherited it, the Lazy-B hadn't been much more than a chunk of dirt from which his father had scratched out a meager living.

Now, it was prime. As was his stock. Prime enough that he knew he could get a decent price if he asked. God knew, he'd gotten more than a few offers over the years, specially from the Clays who ran the biggest operation in the entire state.

Problem was, Cage didn't want to sell.

But he didn't want to lose his daughter more.

He pulled out the letter and looked at the envelope.

Delivered by a courier this time. Was that a polite word for a process server? He didn't know.

He went over to the truck. Sat down on the ground beside it in the shade and was glad there was no one but the birds sailing overhead to know his hands were shaking as he tore open the envelope.

The letter was brief. The missive unmistakable.

Sandi hadn't been bluffing. The Oldhams wanted Lucy in their family fold. And Sandi was using her parents' significant wealth to make it happen. He hadn't buckled to her, so she'd sicced her parents on him instead. And now their personal requests to see their granddaughter—denied by him—had become a legal challenge. For custody.

He leaned his head back against the truck and closed his eyes. And there was no way the attorney he'd been able to afford would be up to fighting the half-dozen attorneys the Oldhams had pitted against him. Even if he sold the ranch to pay an attorney of that caliber, there was little chance he'd win.

They were the Oldhams of Chicago. Bank president. Society matron. Old money, older reputation. Everything that Sandi had shunned when she'd been twenty years old. Everything she'd warned him about when she'd convinced him that telling her parents she was pregnant would be their biggest mistake. And back then he'd been more interested in keeping Sandi from doing something stupid to end her pregnancy than to argue the issue of informing *her* parents about the baby.

Obviously, it suited Sandi now to have her parents on her side. He pinched the bridge of his nose, fleeting ideas of taking his daughter and getting the hell out of Dodge hovering in his mind.

But he'd never been a runner. If he had been, he'd

have run hard and fast from the responsibilities of a ranch and a child when he'd still been pretty much a kid himself.

He thumped his head back against the truck.

Lucy deserved more. She deserved every single privilege that came with being the only Oldham grandchild.

But lying down without a fight just wasn't something he could do.

"Cage?"

He pushed to his feet and pushed the papers into the envelope as he looked across the truck. Belle was back and he'd been too preoccupied to hear. "What?" He slammed down the lid of the toolbox, the envelope safely inside. If she asked him again about it, he was going to rip something apart.

Her hand was shading her eyes. "What were you doing? Hiding?"

No matter what, the idea had appeal. Take Lucy. Hide. Try and forget the turmoil caused by various members of the Day family. "Forget something?" She couldn't have made it to the house and all the way back again in the amount of time that had passed.

She slid off Dexter's back and tied him loosely, again, to the truck's side mirror. "Figured Lucy wouldn't be finished with her lesson yet. And she needs some time to just hang with Anya, anyway. Are there more gloves in that toolbox?"

"Why?"

She shrugged and walked to the truck bed herself. "Because I don't want to get blisters."

He stepped in her path before she could flip open the toolbox. "Caused by...what?"

She pointedly looked at the posts stacked lengthwise in the bed.

"I don't want your help." Her body? That was something entirely different.

God. He needed to get out of Weaver more often. There were plenty of women he knew around the state who were more than happy to spend a few recreational hours with him. Women who didn't want or expect anything more than what he was willing to share. Intelligent, independent, warm women, who never thought to—or wanted to—interfere in his life.

"Yes. You've made that abundantly clear," Belle said evenly. "The gloves?"

He frowned down at her, but she didn't come close to taking the hint. She just looked up at him, head tilted to one side, eyes squinting in the sunlight that turned her dark brown eyes to amber-stained glass. "You need a hat," he muttered.

"Well, it so happens that I don't have one of those, either." She lifted her shoulder, barely covered by the narrow strap of a snug gray shirt. "Just so you know, if I *do* get blisters, it's going to be hard for me to work out Lucy's muscle spasms, but—"

He nudged her aside and flipped up the toolbox, blindly grabbing a pair of leather gloves. He slammed the lid back down and slapped them in her hand. Then shoved his own bloody hat onto her head. "You're a pain in the ass, you know that?"

"I believe you've expressed that sentiment, as well, even if you haven't used those particular words." She nudged back the hat so it wasn't covering her eyes. It was too big for her.

But damned if she didn't look cute.

Bloody hell.

He yanked on his own gloves and reached for the posthole digger. Pushed it at her. "Know how to use one of those?" Maybe it would shut her up. Keep her from looking at him with those big brown eyes.

She rolled her eyes. A habit picked up from Lucy? "Yes," she drawled.

About as well as she knew how to fix her lawn mower, he figured. He shouldered a heavy post and headed away from the truck. She hurried after him. Five minutes, he calculated, and she'd be all too ready to go back to the sanctuary of the house.

Only five minutes passed and she showed no sign of stopping. Even though the ground was harder than stone and the muscles in her arms were standing out as she struggled.

He swiped his sweaty forehead with his arm. "Give me that."

"I can do it." Her voice was gritty.

"Maybe," he allowed blandly, "but why would you want to?"

She tossed her head, her tied-back hair rippling. "God only knows," she muttered. She wrapped her fingers freshly around the long wooden handles. "Maybe because I still haven't gotten over needing to prove that I can." She lifted the digger and slammed it back into the earth. The sharp edges of the shovel finally bit. "Ha!" She pulled apart the handles, catching a small amount of dirt between the blades, then dropped it to one side.

There was such satisfaction in her sudden grin that Cage stepped back and let her work. Sweat was dripping from her forehead by the time she'd dug the hole deep enough for the post and tossed aside the digger.

"You gonna plant the post, too?" His voice was dry.

She shook her head, leaning over, arms braced on her thighs. "Wouldn't want you to start feeling wimpy," she said breathlessly. "Oh, God. Now that's some serious work, isn't it? No wonder you never have to touch the weights in the barn." She straightened, only to tear off her shirt and wipe her face with it.

He nearly swallowed his tongue, though the sport bra she wore was made of some thick gray stuff that was about as erotic as wool socks.

He had an unbidden vision of Belle wearing nothing *but* wool socks.

He shoved the post in place, backfilling the hole. "Now that you've played at manual labor, mebbe you could get back to your *real* work?" And leave him alone with his frustrating visions, fueled by the memory that wouldn't die even after all this time of her perfectly formed breasts.

She pulled off his cowboy hat and lifted her hair from her neck, stretching a little. "Everybody needs to play now and then," she said, her eyes slanting toward him. "Even you."

He grunted and turned away from the post. More importantly, he turned away from the sight of her, stretching like some sort of lithe cat. "Consider this my back nine."

"Do you golf?"

He looked at her.

Her lips twisted ruefully. "Suppose it's hard to golf, when there's no course around here."

"Suppose it's hard to golf when there's no time," he corrected.

"Do you even *know* how to play golf?"

"Do you?"

She shook her head.

He smiled a little despite himself and headed for the truck. Dexter had his nose buried in the grass, and didn't even lift his head when Cage passed him.

"You didn't answer." Belle said, following him.

"Observant of you."

"Afraid I might bandy about the news of your golfing prowess around Weaver?"

He spotted the tool chest in his truck bed and the brief spate of humor shriveled.

"Go back to the house, Miss Day," he said flatly, and plucked his hat out of her fingers. "Playtime is over."

She blinked a little. "Maybe if you *indulged* in some playtime, you'd start sleeping at night." She grabbed up Dexter's reins and smoothly swung up into the saddle.

As she rode away, he thought he heard her mutter. "Ogre."

## Chapter 9

"Range of motion remains severely limited despite marked increase in muscle tone and—" Belle stopped writing when she heard the scream.

Another nightmare. The third since the afternoon Belle had ridden out to see Cage.

She pushed back from the kitchen chair, concern propelling her down the hall even though she knew in her head that Cage would beat her to Lucy's room. Sure enough, he was striding into his old bedroom, and in the half light, she watched him sit on the side of Lucy's bed.

She hovered there for a moment, then turned back to the kitchen and her notes. She sat down, staring at the report that she made out each week charting Lucy's progress. But her mind was still stuck on the picture of Cage with his daughter.

She'd seen him helping Lucy with her exercises a few days earlier. And had hidden out of sight, so as not to interrupt the moment. And, maybe, to absorb the knot of emotion the sight had caused inside her.

She pressed her lips together now, as unsettled as she had been then, and hurriedly shut the file folder.

She needed to talk to her sister. She and Nikki had been missing each other's phone calls for too many days now.

Her cell phone was upstairs in her room, but when she headed for the stairs, the sight of Cage standing in Lucy's doorway stopped her in her tracks.

"She's asking for you."

Belle paused, trying to read his expression. Should she refuse? Make some attempt at sliding back into the professional role she was supposed to be occupying?

She nodded silently and headed toward Lucy's room. Who was she trying to kid? Her professionalism where this family was concerned was nonexistent.

She slipped past Cage into the bedroom, casting him a quick look.

His face was hard.

She ducked her head again and crossed over to Lucy's bed, sitting in the same spot that Cage had. Lucy's hair was tumbled, her face glistening with sweat. Belle snatched a tissue from the box on the nightstand and pressed it to Lucy's forehead. "What's wrong?" Lucy shifted, looking past Belle.

She looked back to see Cage watching from the hall. At their attention, he turned on his heel and went into his office. The door shut after him.

Softly, quietly. Controlled.

Belle chewed the inside of her lip and focused once more on Lucy. "Are you sick or something?" They'd already survived last month's first-period episode. Lucy, fortunately, had adjusted quickly enough.

Belle wasn't sure she could say the same of Lucy's father.

"I have a charley horse in my leg."

"Same place as before?" If the nightmares were frequent, the muscle spasms were more so. Nearly every day the girl had been plagued with muscle spasms in her calf. Lucy nodded and Belle pushed aside the bedding, reaching for Lucy's leg. She gently began massaging, and determined immediately that if Lucy'd *had* a charley horse, it was long gone. She kept working her fingers into the muscle, though. "Another bad dream?"

Lucy made a noncommittal sound, remembering to offer a wince now and then in honor of her phantom cramp.

"Want to talk about it?"

Lucy merely turned her cheek into her pillow.

"I used to have a recurring nightmare." Belle shifted so she was sitting more comfortably, and continued working Lucy's leg. "From when I was hurt."

"In the accident where my Grandma was hurt?"

"Yes."

"It was pretty bad, huh."

It took no effort at all for Belle to recall the excruciating details. Which she didn't want to do. "Yes. Anyway, I was in the hospital for weeks, too. Like you were after Satin threw you. Fortunately, I didn't need surgery like you did."

"How old were you?"

"Thirteen. I had nightmares for a long time after that."

Lucy's face was a canvas of shadows.

"I didn't dream about the accident, though. I kept dreaming that everyone I knew and cared about was walking. On a street, in a store. The places changed sometimes. But they were walking. And I couldn't keep up. Couldn't make myself take one single step no matter how hard I tried. I couldn't run, much less walk, after them. I couldn't walk *with* them." Her fingers slowed. "Of course, when I was awake, I knew that my family and my friends weren't leaving me behind, but when I was asleep?" She shook her head.

"But they stopped. The nightmares. Right?"

"Yes, they stopped."

Lucy looked at her. "When?"

"When I started talking about them." She waited a moment, hoping Lucy would heed the hint. But the girl remained silent. "Charley horse gone now?"

Lucy nodded.

"Good." She tucked the covers back in place and headed for the door. "G'night, sweetie."

"Belle? Could you—"

She stepped back to the bedside. "Could I what?" she prompted gently.

"StayuntilIgotosleep?" The words came out in a rush.

Belle's heart squeezed. "You bet." She pulled up the small pink chair that was crammed in the corner and sat beside the bed.

Lucy scooted further down her pillow and turned on her side, facing Belle. "Are you going to be here for my birthday party?" Her voice was little more than a whisper.

"If you want me to be."

Lucy nodded. She closed her eyes.

In minutes, she was asleep again.

Belle sat there a while longer, her thoughts tangled. When it seemed clear that Lucy was sleeping soundly, she quietly moved the chair back to the corner and left the room, pulling the door partially closed.

Cage's office, when she peeked around the doorway, was empty. But she didn't have to look far to find him. It was the middle of the night. Naturally, he would be sitting out on the porch, his long legs stretched out in front of him, his eyes staring into the dark.

She pushed open the screen to see him more clearly, but didn't go out. "Lucy's asleep again." Her heart ached a little, because she knew it had to sting that his daughter had turned to her again. "It's not my imagination that her nightmares are coming more often, is it?"

The shake of his head was slow in coming.

"Have you—" Lord, she didn't want him berating her for being interfering again "—um, have you told her physician that she's plagued with them?"

His gaze slid her way. Unreadable. He nodded. Shifted, crossing his boots at the ankle. The pose ought to have been casual. Relaxed.

Belle knew better. She also knew better than to probe for the reasons causing *his* habitual sleeplessness.

"She also asked if I'd stick around for her birthday party." Better to get that out now. The party was scheduled for Friday night, after Belle would have ordinarily left for the weekend.

"Damn straight," he murmured. "It was your idea in the first place. Least you can do is play chaperone."

She absorbed that, alternately glad that she wasn't going to have to butt heads with him over the matter, and unnerved that she didn't.

"Then you can kiss her wounds when the party is a bust," he added darkly.

"It's not going to be a bust."

"There's no room for a bunch of kids in this house."

"We'll figure it out. Maybe use the barn."

He shot her a look.

"I'm serious. Crepe-paper streamers and balloons. Plenty of soda and munchies. It'll be fine. In fact, it was Lucy's idea. She mentioned it earlier this week. We've already bought the decorations and stuff. We'll just put it all up in the barn instead of the house."

Cage ran his hand through his hair, finally showing some emotion. Chagrin. "Might as well. *This* place is a mess."

Belle chewed the inside of her lip. She was not going to be charmed by the dusky color running under his sharp cheekbones. If he hadn't been so ornery about her helping with some of the household tasks, the house *wouldn't* be quite as unkempt as it was. "Hard for one person to do everything," she said pointedly. Running the B. Raising a daughter on his own. Taking care of their sturdy, little brick home.

Cage hadn't responded—either to agree or disagree. And standing there in the doorway was making her feel out of place. She started to turn back inside.

"What if nobody comes?"

His gruff comment jangled in her head for a tight moment before her brain engaged her tongue. Instead of stepping inside, she stepped outside the screen door, her fingers holding the door long enough to let it close without a sound. "That won't happen, Cage," she assured quietly. "They are Lucy's friends."

"Their parents aren't mine."

She swallowed, pressing her lips together for a moment. She watched the bevy of moths beat themselves against the glow of the porch light. "Only because you won't let them be. The only reason people speculate so much about you is because you hold yourself apart from them."

"I don't like everyone knowing my business."

"This is a small community. That's bound to happen no matter what you like or don't like. And if you weren't so…standoffish—" She waited a beat at that, sure he'd cut her off. But he didn't. "Maybe people would surprise you. Maybe they'd accept your need for privacy more if you were more accepting of them." Which, even to her, sounded convoluted.

Disregarding the wisdom she was not displaying, she crossed the porch and sat on the low rail, facing him. The night air was cool on her bare arms but she knew if she went in for a sweater, the moment would be lost. "In any case, despite the fact that you hold others at a distance, Lucy hasn't. People in Weaver care about what happens to her, and they'll want to celebrate with her, too. Everyone who was invited accepted weeks ago. You can't really think that they'd blow her off now right before the party."

He looked far from convinced. "It's late. You should be in bed."

Her cheeks warmed, despite the cool night air. "You get up even earlier than I do. I don't know how you do it, frankly. I was still up so I could finish my report and get it in the mail to Lucy's orthopedist. Otherwise I'd be sawing logs by now."

"Lucky you." He leaned his head back against the chair, watching her from beneath lowered lids. "Did she tell you what her nightmare is about?"

Those thin slices of blue—pale even in the subdued porch light—were unsettling and she looked down at her stockinged feet. Two inches from his boots.

She curled her toes down against the wood porch and shook her head. "She'll talk when she's ready, I imagine. Same way she puts effort into her therapy only when she's ready."

"She's been doing her exercises on her own on the weekends."

"I know. I can tell when we work together each Monday. She's still not making the progress I would have hoped." Belle wasn't sure what made her admit that to him. It wasn't that Lucy wasn't progressing at all.

"And what did you hope for? To have her dancing on her toes by Thanksgiving?" He sat forward suddenly, elbows on knees, fingers raking through his hair.

If she lifted her hand, she'd be touching the bronzed strands springing back from his forehead. She pressed her fingertips harder against the wooden rail beneath her. "Maybe not by Thanksgiving," she admitted. "Now, Christmas?" She shrugged, smiling a little, even though they both knew Belle would be long gone before either holiday.

"She's on crutches. Not walking on her own entirely, but given what the doctor told us after the accident— that she might not walk that well again, ever—I think it's pretty amazing." Then he glanced up at her, the corners of his lips turning up.

The surprise of that half smile had her nearly falling backward off the rail. She jerked a little and he shot out his hand, grabbing hers. "Thanks." She hoped he'd blame her breathlessness on being startled.

"I don't need you breaking your neck on top of everything else," he muttered.

So much for him nearly smiling. She wiggled her fingers, drawing attention to his continued hold and he released her.

Her wrists still felt surrounded by a ring of warmth as she scooted past him toward the door. Asking him what caused *his* sleeplessness would be pointless. Foolish.

She still wondered.

A lot.

She opened the door and quickly went inside. "Good night, Cage."

Not until she was nearly at the foot of the staircase did she hear his quiet reply. "Good night, Belle."

She tightened her grip on the banister and forced her feet to the first riser. And the next. It was frightening how hard it was to continue when everything inside her was tugging on her to go back out there. To keep poking and prodding as if *she* could break through his barriers.

Crazy. That's what she was.

She passed Cage's room, carefully averting her eyes from looking inside, and went in her own room. She'd barely climbed into bed—which had been squeaking again for a solid month despite Cage's efforts shortly after she'd arrived—when her cell phone gave a soft squawk.

She grabbed it off the nightstand. "Nik?"

"I've been calling you for hours."

Something inside her went on full alert. "What's wrong?"

"Who said anything's wrong?" Nikki's voice was tight. "I've left you a half-dozen messages."

Belle flopped on her back, covering her eyes with her hand. "I'm sorry. I should have tried harder to reach you. Oh, God, Nik. I don't know what I'm doing here. Why I thought I could…make up somehow for the past."

"Scott's been released."

Her thoughts floundered. "What? Oh. Well, good. Then his wife won't be making the staff there miserable."

Nikki was silent for a long moment. "Okay, catch me up here, Belle. When you said make up for the past, I thought you meant proving to yourself that you had what it took to be a good therapist. After Scott blamed you because he wasn't ever going to be able to get back to football—"

"Scott hasn't even been the last thing on my mind," she murmured truthfully. And it was a relief to know it. "I wanted...I very nearly...I wanted to kiss him, Nikki. Taste him. Breathe him in. More than once now."

"Scott...oh, no." Dismay colored her sister's voice. "Please tell me you're not talking about Cage Buchanan."

"Okay, I'll tell you that," Belle whispered after a long moment. "But I'd be lying." She waited for Nikki to say all the things that were running through her own mind.

Don't get personally involved with patients or their families.

Don't get personally involved with a man who loathes your parentage.

Don't get personally involved period, end of story.

Nikki said none of them. She merely sighed. "Oh, Belle."

And with that soft, sympathetic murmur, tears stung Belle's eyes. "He's a good man, Nik. And he loves his daughter so much it is heartbreaking and beautiful all at the same time."

"What are you going to do about it?"

Her fingers plucked at the quilt. Had Cage's mother made it? Was quilting just one more thing that had been amputated from her existence the night of the car accident? "There's nothing *to* do. He didn't hire me out of personal interest, after all." Far from it. "I'm here because of Lucy. I just need to focus on her and everything will be fine."

The words rang a little too hollow, and Belle was grateful that her sister refrained from observing it. "So, why the half-dozen messages to call you back, anyway?"

"I quit."

The words made no sense at first. "What? Oh, hell's bells." She sat forward on the bed, pressing the phone tighter to her ear. "Why? Alex refused to give you the raise you deserve, didn't he? Is he out of his tiny little mind?"

"I never asked for the raise." Nikki's voice sounded thick and Belle realized her sister had been crying. She felt like a selfish witch for not having immediately noticed.

"Then why? You love your job." She heard Nikki sigh shakily and her nerves tightened. "Nik? What's really going on here?"

"This is harder to tell than I thought it would be."

"Nikki, you're scaring me. What?"

"I'm…um…I'm pregnant."

Belle blinked, staring blindly at her fingers that were clenching a handful of quilt.

"Belle?"

She scrambled. "Since when? Are you feeling okay? Have you been to the doctor?"

"Almost six weeks ago. Yes. And yes."

"Six weeks…God, Nik, I didn't even know you were involved with someone."

Her sister made a watery sound. "Well, that's just it, isn't it. I'm *not* involved."

"Then how—"

"The usual way."

Belle swallowed. Her sister didn't indulge in casual sex any more than Belle did. "I'm coming down to see you."

"No. You have a job there."

"Then I'll come on the weekend. Don't try to put me off, Nicole. I'm not going to rest until I've seen you in person. Have you told Mom?"

"No. And you better not, either."

"She's going to have to know sooner or later. Angel's party is a week from Saturday. You're going to the ranch for it, aren't you? Mom's going to know something is up."

"I'll deal with next week…next week. Look, Belle. We're not sixteen years old anymore. I just…need some time before I tell her."

Belle chewed her lip. Her sister had always been the one with straight As in school. Who'd never taken a single step off the line of excellence and responsibility. It was Belle who'd been the one to bumble through life. Not Nikki. "What about the father?" She pushed at her temples. "And why quit your job now? You're going to need your medical benefits…unless, do you already have someplace else you're going to?"

"No."

"Then why quit? I can't believe Alex let you go after all this time. Does he know? Is that why he allowed you to leave? There are laws, Nikki—"

"The only one who knows is you. I needed to tell someone or I was going to go mad."

"I have a million questions, you know."

"I know. Can we just deal with them another day?"

"Yes." Her sister was pregnant. And Belle hadn't felt a hint of it. "You're sure you're feeling okay?"

"Tired. Otherwise, fine."

"And you're done talking for now," Belle surmised.

"Yes."

Her eyes stung. "I love you, you know. No matter what goes on. You're going to be a great mother."

Nikki's soft laugh was watery, but it was a laugh. "You'll be a great aunt."

"I'm coming down this weekend," Belle reminded, half warning, half reassuring.

"G'night, Annabelle." Her sister hung up.

Belle stared at the small phone in her hand for a moment, then tossed it aside. She pushed off the bed, and left the room, her mind too busy to rest.

The house was dark now, Cage's bedroom door closed. She let herself out the kitchen door and was halfway to the barn before she realized she hadn't put on her shoes. Her soles prickled, but she didn't turn back.

Inside the barn, she blindly stuck a CD in the sound system, turned it down from Lucy's preferred roar, and dragged out a floor mat. An hour later, she was still at it. Two hours later, her muscles were screaming and her hair was clinging to her sweaty face and neck. Her mind was still teeming, but at least she'd managed to numb the questions into submission. She blew out a long breath and dropped down onto the incline bench, closing her eyes.

Maybe she'd just sleep right there.

"Get 'em worked out?"

Numb enough not to be startled when Cage spoke. She looked at him. "What?"

"The demons," he said.

Not in a dozen workouts. "I thought you'd finally gone to bed." Maybe he had. He wore an untucked white T-shirt now with his jeans, instead of the chambray shirt from before. "Don't you *ever* sleep?"

He ambled closer. Handed her a small towel off the stack she'd kept handy since she'd come to the ranch. "This is usual for me. Not for you."

She took the towel and pressed the white terry cloth to her face. She'd sit up just as soon as she had the energy. "My sister quit her job." She winced behind the towel, wishing she'd kept her mouth shut. But she supposed it was better than blurting out Nikki's *other* news.

"She works at the same place you did, doesn't she?"

"Huffington." Belle dropped her arms, the towel

clutched in one hand. Cage was standing near the foot of the bench. "She was the boss's right hand, in fact."

"Afraid that means you're not going to be welcomed back to the clinic with open arms when your...leave... is over?"

Forget aching, tired muscles. She popped off the bench. "No. The thought hadn't even occurred to me," she snapped. "Not that I expect you to believe that I—a *Day*—could be concerned about something outside of myself." She brushed past him, hating the way her voice shook. But his arm shot out, his hand wrapping around her arm.

"I'm sorry."

She shivered. Wanting badly to blame it on the night air drifting over her sweaty body. Knowing it was just as much because of the gruff tone in his voice and the way his knuckles were pressing against the side of her breast.

She tugged away from his hold, that wasn't really a hold at all when he let go of her so easily and she was grateful she hadn't betrayed the way he made her feel.

Without looking at him, she walked over to the sound system. Flipped the power, cutting off Paul McCartney midnote.

"I'm sorry, too," she whispered.

About so many things.

She walked out, leaving Cage standing there in the barn, surrounded by weights and mats and bars and balls, all procured with the intention of helping Lucy walk and run and dance again.

Just then, however, it felt to Belle as if she and Cage were the ones in need of walking lessons.

## Chapter 10

"What are they doing in there? I've only been gone ten minutes."

Belle looked up at Cage and shot out her arm, barring him from barreling into the barn. "They're dancing," she said, taking an extra step to keep her balance. She didn't have to keep her voice lowered. There was no possible way the kids inside the barn would hear a word they said outside the barn. The music was too loud.

"I don't *want* them dancing."

A sputter of laughter escaped before she could prevent it. "Don't be such a grouch." Belle wrapped her hands around his forearm, digging in her heels. "You agreed to this," she reminded.

The lights from inside the barn were dim, but the moon was full and bright. Easily clear enough to see his expression as he looked from her hands to his arm. Belle hastily released him and circled her fingers against her palms. For days now, she'd managed to keep her thoughts right where they belonged.

At least she had while she'd been awake.

Sleep? That was a whole other kettle of tuna.

"Just peek in then," she allowed. "See for yourself."

He angled his head so he could see through the open barn door without drawing attention to himself.

Belle chewed the inside of her lip, waiting. She knew what he'd see.

And she knew the moment he *did* see, for his hand suddenly flattened against the weathered red wood and he exhaled slowly.

His newly turned teenage daughter was dancing with a boy. Crutches and all.

"That's Drew Taggart's boy."

She swallowed, an image of Cage's face so close to hers flashing through her mind. "Yes."

"He's got his arms around her."

"Well," Belle smiled gently, "in a manner of speaking, he does." The truth was, Evan Taggart looked as if he was half-afraid to touch Lucy and Lucy looked as if she was equally unsure of the entire process. But they were surrounded by fifteen other couples in exactly the same situation and nobody was making a move to change it. "She was afraid everyone would dance except her." She leaned her shoulder against the wall, watching. "I think they're doing pretty well considering she's still using her crutches."

Cage shifted, moving behind her. A shiver danced down her spine that she couldn't hope to blame on anything other than him. He propped his hand above her head and leaned closer, obviously trying to follow Lucy and Evan's lurching progress around the balloon-bedecked interior.

She felt surrounded by him.

And because it wasn't entirely unpleasant—well, not at all unpleasant if she was honest with herself—she focused harder on the kids. She'd agreed to help chaperone this shindig. She couldn't very well do that when she was preoccupied by the wall of warm, male chest heating her back.

She felt parched but her trusty water bottle was empty, and she was afraid if she stuck her head in amongst the dancers to get another drink, the boys and girls would retreat again to their opposite corners the way they'd been for the first hour.

"Thirteen," Cage murmured. "I guess I blinked."

"They do grow up fast. Every time I turn around my nieces and nephews have grown a foot." She glanced up at him, only to find his focus not on his daughter, but on her. She forgot about being amused right along with the art of breathing.

For days she'd worked so hard at forgetting…things. And now, all that hard work was for naught. "Arnold," she blurted.

His gaze didn't seem to stray from her lips. "What?"

"Your name." A naughty breeze skipped over them, splaying her hair across her cheek.

He caught the strands, brushing them back. "I told you. It's unique."

Arnold wasn't the current rage, but it wasn't unique. She cast her mind about, but coherence was annoyingly elusive. "How long is it?" Why did he still have a lock of her hair between his fingers?

His eyebrows rose. "Excuse me?"

She turned, facing him. Putting some necessary space between them. Shoving her hair behind her shoulders. "Letters. Syllables."

"Six. Two."

Easily as tall as some of her stepbrothers. Tall enough that she could wear heels and press her lips against the curve of his brown, corded throat.

Her face went hot and she hoped to heaven that the moonlight wasn't bright enough to reveal that. "Six letters," she murmured. "Two syllables." Though she'd bet his height *was* right around six-two.

"You're shivering."

"No, I'm not." She quickly turned back around, looking inside the barn. The music had changed. Most of the couples still danced. Not Evan and Lucy. But the boy was handing Lucy a cup of soda, his expression verging on adoring.

"You are." Cage's hand cupped her shoulder.

Belle closed her eyes for a moment. "It's the breeze," she lied.

He didn't reply. But he lowered his hand. And she heard the scrape of his boots on the gravel and turned to see him walking toward the house.

She blinked. Well. Okay. So her imagination was running riot again.

She turned back to watch the goings-on inside the barn. As Murphy's Law often proved, just when the boys and girls were starting to really have fun, it would be nearly time for them to leave. The boys, at least. The girls were staying for an overnight.

She tilted her watch to the light. Less than an hour and the rides would start arriving. Even with carpooling, there were several cars needed. Given the surprising occurrence of a party being held on the Lazy-B, the adults who'd brought their sons and daughters had admirably contained their curiosity. But she'd bet her paycheck that once they were back in town, the phone lines started buzzing.

"Here."

She nearly jumped out of her skin. Cage had returned. And he was tossing a plaid wool jacket over her shoulders.

Gads. It smelled like new-mown hay and fresh air with a dollop of coffee. It smelled like *him*. She clutched the collar with both hands, keeping it from sliding off her shoulders. "Thanks." The thing did nothing for her shivers, however. And the faint twist of his lips implied that he knew it.

Particularly when he scooped her hair free of the jacket and let it drift over her shoulders. "You don't wear your hair loose very often."

She hurriedly turned back to watch the youths. "No." It came out more of a croak, and she felt her face heat. "It gets in the way." That was better. A little less amphibian.

"Why not cut it?"

She shrugged. The slick lining of the jacket slid over her bare shoulders. Proving that she really was losing her mind. It was an ageless woolen jacket with a crinkling, polyester lining, for God's sake. Not seductive lingerie. "Lazy, I guess." She shoved her arms through the sleeves. The cuffs hung well below her fingertips. She probably looked like a clown. Hardly seductive.

Which she wasn't aiming for anyway. Right?

"You, lazy? That what gets you outta bed to jog around this place nearly every morning?"

How could the man be aware of things occurring when he was out doing the rancher thing? She marshaled her thoughts with some difficulty. "Easier to pull it back in a ponytail than mess with some shorter style. And the weight keeps the waves more or less controllable."

"Ever had it cut?"

"Of course." She had it trimmed regularly. "Never more than an inch or two, though. Cage—" She turned to face him, only to find whatever she'd planned to say flying right out of her head.

He'd sifted his fingers through the long ends of her hair. "Whose shirt was it?"

"Hmm?"

"The shirt you put on that weekend I came to your house." His fingers trailed along her jaw. Came perilously close to her lips.

Her mind was five steps behind the times. "Umm, I don't—"

"Hell with it," he murmured. His hand slid behind her head, cupping her nape, tilting her head back.

Belle froze, disbelief warring with anticipation. She wasn't sure which would win out, but it didn't matter, because Cage lowered his head and pressed his lips against hers and her senses simply exploded.

Her hands were pressed against his chest. She could feel his heavy heartbeat. She knew there were good reasons she should be pushing him away. Knew it.

She just couldn't manage to put her finger on one of those reasons right at the moment.

And then she stopped worrying about it altogether as the taste of him overwhelmed everything else.

Somehow, his arms had circled her, beneath the jacket. Her thin shirt was no barrier against his fingertips, which strolled up and down her spine. She shivered again.

"You're not cold." She felt his murmur against her lips.

"No."

The moment she answered, he took advantage, his tongue finding hers. Her knees dissolved. Had she ever felt a kiss down to her toes? Beyond? She arched against him, arms snaking around his shoulders, fingers seeking the shape of his head. Her muscles liquefied even while white-hot energy blasted through her.

Her head fell back as his mouth dragged over her jaw. Found her neck. Overhead, the stars whirled. Pounding music throbbed in the air, vibrating through their bodies.

This was not effective chaperoning, she thought hazily. "Cage—"

His mouth covered hers again, swallowing her half-hearted stab at sensibility. And when he finally did lift his head, she gave a soft moan of protest.

He made a rough sound and pressed her head to his shoulder. "This is a bad idea."

She nodded. Her fingers were knotted in his chambray shirt as surely as his fingers were tangled in her hair.

He muttered an oath. Tipped her head back. She didn't know what to say. Then he swore softly again. Pressed a hard kiss to her lips, before deliberately stepping away.

She swayed a little.

"I don't have time for this." His voice was quiet. Rough.

And even though his expression was as ragged as his voice, the words stung. "You kissed *me,*" she reminded. "I wasn't chasing after you."

His gaze angled her way. "Did I say you were?"

"You—" No. He hadn't said that. But she'd been accused of chasing after Scott—which she hadn't been—but the humiliating memory of it lived on. And there was still the tacit warning he'd given her when he'd told her why Lucy's last therapist had been sent on her way.

"No." She raked back her hair, dismayed to see her hands were shaking.

Giggles gave them a very slim warning before a gaggle of girls darted out of the barn. They nearly skidded to a halt as they spied Belle and Cage. "Oh, good." Anya Johannson was the tallest of the three. "Lucy wants to cut her cake now. Is that okay?"

Belle couldn't prevent her quick glance at Cage. "Sure." She found a smile from somewhere and pinned it on her face, answering when he seemed to have no inclination to do so. "Good idea, actually," she went on, glancing at her watch as she followed the girls inside. "The boys will be leaving soon." And come morning, as soon as she could, she'd be leaving, as well, for the weekend.

She had a date to buttonhole her sister for some answers. She'd talked to Nikki on the phone twice since her sister had dropped the news. Nikki had been frustratingly closemouthed. She'd even warned Belle not to come see her.

Fat chance.

Cage followed her into the barn. He lit the candles on the cake and the kids sang. Lucy blew. Belle cut. Kids ate. The barn was filled with chatter and laughter. The time passed quickly enough, before the first headlights bounced over the ground outside the barn announcing the arrival of the first ride. But it seemed to Belle that the minutes crept because every ticking moment of them she was excruciatingly conscious of Cage's presence.

He didn't have time for "this." Did he honestly think that *she* did?

After what seemed an eternity, he disappeared along with the last of the departing boys, leaving Belle to deal with getting the girls settled. No small task. But she finally got the girls staying behind bedded down snug as bugs in Lucy's bedroom. They easily covered every spare inch of floor and bed space. When she finally closed the door on their whispers and giggles, she was vaguely surprised that some of them hadn't decided to bunk in the shower.

She was in the kitchen, trying to restore some order when Cage reappeared. She ignored him and continued tying up the trash bag that bulged with discarded plates and cups. She started to take it outside, but he silently took the bag from her and went out himself. When he came back, her hands were buried in soapy bubbles, the sleeves of the jacket rolled up to her elbows.

"When I asked you to stick around for the party I didn't mean you had to pull maid duty."

"When it comes to my pitching in around here you've made your feelings abundantly clear." She rinsed a pretty glass bowl that was probably older than she was and carefully set it down on the towel she'd spread on the counter.

"Yet you continue doing whatever you want." He scooped up the last few pretzels in a bowl before she could dump them out and plunge the bowl into the hot, soapy water.

"Yes, well, maybe I think you have enough to deal with without having to wash a few dishes."

"I don't need anyone's pity."

"Fortunately you don't have it." Her voice was stiff. "Nobody would be so stupid as to offer it, believe me. So why don't you go sit out on the porch again. Do whatever it is that you do when most normal people are sleeping."

He crunched through the pretzels. Deliberately set her aside then picked up the stack of remaining dishes and shoved them in the sink, splashing suds over his arms and chest.

He looked so much like a boy having a tantrum that she couldn't help the bubble of laughter that rose most inappropriately in her.

He glared at her.

She bit her lip, composing herself, and picked up a clean dish towel. Began drying the dishes. After a moment, she heard him sigh. "Lucy looked like she was having a great time." His voice wasn't quite grudging.

"Yes." She opened an overhead cupboard and began stacking the dishes inside. But when she would have dragged over a chair to reach the highest shelf, Cage took the glassware from her and did it himself.

It was positively domestic.

Utterly surreal.

"How long were you and Lucy's mother married?" She nearly chewed off her tongue, cursing her lack of discretion.

He pulled the stopper in the sink and watched the bubbles gurgle down the drain. "Why?" His voice was tight.

"Curiosity," she admitted huskily. She knew what the man tasted like now and her curiosity could no longer be contained.

He was silent for a long moment. Then seemed to shrug off his reticence. "We were together, more or less—usually less—for about seven months. She never lived here at the ranch."

Belle frowned. So little time. She wanted more details, but she'd already asked questions she shouldn't have. "You were really young," she observed instead.

"Old enough to get a marriage license. Sandi was nearly twenty-one."

Older than he was, then. She tried to picture him as a teenage groom. Had he been reluctant? Insistent? Blinded by love for the woman who was carrying his child—a child who would be living, breathing family for a boy who'd lost so much?

She folded the towel he'd discarded into neat thirds. Then thirds again. "You don't sound as if you're still nursing a broken heart. That's what some people say, you know. To explain why you don't date anyone from town."

He snorted softly. "Some people. Suppose you believe everything you read, too."

She shook her head, all too aware that he hadn't actually denied it. "How'd you meet?"

He turned around, crossing his arms over his chest, an action that only made him seem even broader. The man was both mother and father to his child, and she'd never met anyone more masculine.

She quickly unfolded the towel. It would never dry with those tight folds. He was watching her, and she hastily draped it over the oven handle.

"Want to make sure there's no hidden wife in the wings when we end up in bed together?"

She went still, emotions bolting through her. Foolish of her to assume that *her* personal business had remained personal. After all, if Brenda Wyatt knew about the debacle with Scott Langtree, then she'd have undoubtedly informed the rest of the Weaver population. Which apparently included even a reclusive rancher who was, himself, the brunt of considerable conjecture.

"I guess you've listened to your own share of gossip. And, just for the record, you and I are *not* going to end up in bed together."

He lifted an eyebrow, his gaze dropping to her lips.

She flushed, heat streaking through her with the tenacity of a forest fire. "I don't sleep with men I don't love." She didn't care if she sounded prissy or not. She was old enough to know what she did and did not want. Wasn't she? And meaningless sex was not something she'd ever wanted to indulge in.

*Only it wouldn't be meaningless, would it?*

"Did you love him, then? The guy of the white shirt? Keep it as a memento before you decided he was a snake?"

"You're really preoccupied with that shirt," she murmured, trying to banish the whispering thought of meaningless versus meaningful. "If you must know, I think my stepbrother Tristan left it behind a long time ago when he and Hope were dating. It's her house, you know."

"There's not much else that's sexier than a woman wearing a man's shirt and little else. But no man wants to see a woman *he* wants wearing another man's shirt."

Well, that was blunt. The man went for days, *weeks,* without hardly saying a word, and in one evening he'd kissed her silly *and* admitted to wanting her.

She snatched up a bottle of water. Fiddled with the cap. Put the bottle back on the table for fear she'd just spill it over herself.

"Must be inconvenient to want something you despise," she murmured. And wished like fury that she didn't want, so badly, for him to deny it. She wasn't supposed to care how he felt about her. She was only supposed to get Lucy back on track, and maybe, just maybe regain some of her professional confidence in the process.

*That's not all you want.*

She ignored the little voice.

Cage still hadn't responded and she felt something foolish inside her wilt.

Exactly what she deserved for getting too involved with her patients.

*Cage isn't your patient.*

A muffled shriek of laughter startled her. The girls, of course.

She brushed her hands down her thighs. "Well. Good night, Cage. Try to get some sleep for once."

He remained silent. Big surprise.

But she felt his gaze on her as she left the kitchen and padded up the stairs.

It wasn't until she closed herself in the relative safety and solitude of the bedroom next to Cage's that she realized she was still wearing his jacket.

She lifted the worn wool close to her nose and closed her eyes, inhaling the faint scent of him while impossible images danced in her mind.

The truth was, it would be a miracle if any of them slept at all that night.

# Chapter 11

"Got a problem?"

Belle pressed her forehead to the steering wheel for a moment. She'd gotten up early, knowing Lucy and her pals would still be sleeping, and hoping Cage would have been doing the same.

Foolish of her to think that of a man who never seemed to sleep.

She looked sideways at him through the opened window and dropped her hand away from the key. She'd been trying—and failing—to get the Jeep started. The engine kept dying. "What gave it away?"

The corner of his lip lifted and her stomach gave a funny little dip. She quickly looked down, but the sight of his long fingers absently brushing through Strudel's ruff was no less disturbing.

"Pop the hood." He gestured toward the front of her vehicle and the unbuttoned denim shirt he wore rippled, baring a slice of chest. "I'll take a look," he prompted when she just sat there like a ninny. The sideways look he cast her had her stomach dancing again. "Unless you've got a wrench handy somewhere and plan to attack the engine yourself with it?"

"So funny." She flexed her fingers, blocking out the insistent and too fresh memory from the night before, and pulled the lever to release the truck's hood.

She'd feel better—about everything—once she saw her sister. She drummed her fingers on the steering wheel for a moment, then climbed out and went around to stand by him. She braced herself for Strudel's loving assault, but Cage said a quiet word that had the dog settling on his haunches.

She looked under the hood, managing not to skitter away when he shifted, closing the distance between them. But he merely reached into the engine.

She watched him fiddle with this, tinker with that.

She could have been staring into noodle soup for all the sense it made to her.

Then he straightened. His fingers were covered with black smudges. "Try it again."

She blindly climbed behind the wheel once more. Automatically turned the key as she'd done a million times before. Thank goodness for habits because the sight of his chest, up close, was still occupying her retinas.

The engine started, spat a little then settled in with a purr.

"How does he do that?" she asked no one in particular. "Thanks," she said loudly.

He shut the hood and brushed his hands together, watching her through the windshield. "You should get it into the mechanic soon," he warned. Then the corners of his lips quirked up a little.

For a moment she simply forgot how to breathe.

Then he waved and headed back to the house. Strudel bounded after him.

Belle sank into her seat, her breath coming out of her with a little *whoosh.* She was actually trembling.

Her purse suddenly chirped and she nearly jumped out of her skin. She grabbed the thing from the passenger seat where she'd dumped it, and dug inside for the ringing cell phone. She barely had the presence of mind to look at the displayed number.

It was her mother.

Belle swallowed and quickly pushed the phone back into the depths of the purse where it continued squawking.

Guilt congealing in her stomach, she eyed the purse, then quickly shoved it behind the seat and turned up the volume on the radio until she could no longer hear the summons.

Giving the brick house another last look, she pulled the Jeep around and drove away. The sooner she got to Cheyenne to see her sister, the better.

A nice plan.

She still believed it had a chance of working, too, even when—two hours later—she was at her little house in Weaver, trying to figure out how to borrow a car because her Jeep was still sitting on the side of the highway where it had given out.

Handy that one of her stepbrothers was the sheriff. Sawyer had driven her the rest of the way to town and assured her that he'd have the Jeep towed in for repairs. Even more fortunate that he'd received a call and hadn't had time to stick around and chat when he'd dropped her off at her place.

It had been easy to love her stepfamily. They'd all welcomed her and Nikki with open hearts when Gloria married Squire. But she wasn't ignorant of their ways, particularly the men.

Steamrollers, all of them.

But none of them had anything on Gloria. She'd wrapped them all, to a one, around her finger without so much as turning a hair. And even though there were plenty of Clays around who would lend Belle a vehicle so she could drive to Cheyenne, there was no way she could count on that information not getting back to Gloria. And given the fact that Belle hadn't been back to Cheyenne in months, she knew her mother would be suspicious about Belle's urgency in getting there, now.

Weaver didn't possess anything so convenient as a car-rental agency, either.

She tried calling Nikki, hoping she could convince her sister to drive *to* Weaver, but her sister wasn't answering *her* phone, either. Probably hiding out from it, much the same way Belle was.

Hoping she wasn't creating a bigger mess, she quickly dialed the Lazy-B. And much later that afternoon, Belle sat alongside Cage as they drove to Cheyenne.

Too bad Lucy had fallen asleep. She'd chattered nonstop for a solid hour before succumbing to the after-effects of her birthday party. And Belle could only stare out the window at the scenery whizzing past for so long when it did nothing to keep her thoughts safely occupied.

She glanced back at Lucy, sprawled on the rear seat

of Cage's SUV. Deliberately waking the girl so she'd start gibber jabbering again would be selfish.

She faced forward. "Thanks again," she murmured. "For letting me hitch along with you." Even though Cage had begun taking Lucy again on the visits to see his mother, she still felt presumptuous. And warily surprised that Cage had readily offered to drive to Weaver and pick her up before making their trip. It would be evening before they arrived. "I guess I really lucked out in catching you and Lucy before you left."

His sideways glance touched on her and it was like being physically dipped in something warm. Something intoxicating.

"We weren't planning to go this week," he said after a moment. "We'd barely started getting Lucy's friends rousted out of their sleeping bags when you called."

She stared. "Then…why?"

"Obviously you're anxious to get there. And Luce always likes visiting my mother at the care center."

She absorbed that. Kept waiting for some dark comment, some grimace, some *something* from him to remind her of the reasons his mother was in the care center in the first place.

But there was nothing at all conveying that in his expression.

There was nothing but a long, slow look from eyes that should have been too pale to have the singeing effect they did.

She swallowed, and trained her own gaze front and center, straight out over the hood of the vehicle. "I see." But she didn't. Not really. "Well. Thank you."

"You're welcome." His tone was dry.

She looked back at Lucy. "*She's* not used to so little sleep at night."

"Wouldn't matter if she'd slept twelve hours." He smoothly passed a slow-moving semi. "For driving company, she's a bust." His lip quirked. "She passes out as soon as she hears the sound of the tires on the highway. Always has."

Oh, Lord. She was staring at the slashing little dimple that had appeared in his lean cheek. She blindly began fumbling in her purse. "Guess she finds it a soothing sound."

"Guess so. When she was a baby, I could get her to sleep sometimes by strapping her in her car seat and driving down to the gate. You mining for gold in there?"

She closed her hand over an object and pulled it out, relieved to see it was something useful. "Just these." She shook the little tin, making the mints inside rattle softly. "Want one?"

"Is that a hint?"

She flushed. The man tasted better than any mint. "No."

He chuckled softly and held out his palm.

She dropped a mint in it, and popped one in her own mouth then put the tin back in her purse. As a distraction it had been much too brief.

"Did you have to drive her around a lot?" She sounded a little frantic, and swallowed. "To get her to sleep, I mean," she added much more calmly.

"Enough."

Which only made her wonder more how he'd managed at such a young age. "You didn't have any help with her?"

"There was an insurance settlement," he said after a moment. "Eventually, anyway. It came through about the time Lucy was born. Got my mother settled in the care center. Hired a few hands for a while. High-school kids who needed to earn some extra cash."

"*You* were a high-school kid," she murmured.

"Honey, I was born old."

Honey. Nearly every male in the entire state called women that. It meant nothing.

It…meant…nothing. Any minute now, he'd start calling her *Miss Day* in that stubborn way he had.

"You're not old," she dismissed.

"Why? Because you're less than a handful of years younger than me?"

He was teasing her. She scrambled through the surprise of that. "I'm certainly not about to think I'm on the cusp of being old," she said lightly. "Besides. I think *old* is more a state of mind."

"Spoken with the blitheness of someone who hasn't had her child look at her with rolling eyes."

Belle smiled and glanced back at Lucy. Sound, still. "She *is* pretty great."

"Despite me," he murmured.

She flushed again remembering her statement—a serious statement—to that very effect. She turned a little in the seat, facing him. "I still don't understand why you wouldn't let her go on that field trip, Cage." Her voice was low. "If it was a matter of cost—"

"It wasn't." His voice had gone flat as the look he gave her.

She nodded, even though she didn't necessarily believe him.

"I didn't want her in Chicago."

She tugged at her ear. "What are you going to do the next time a field trip comes up? Each class tries to take a cultural trip each year. They're often out of state."

"As long as it's not Chicago."

"Because of her grandparents, or because it's where that private school she's interested in is located?" She straightened in her seat again, certain he wouldn't respond to that.

"Take your pick," he said in a low voice. "I'm not going to lose my daughter to either one."

Her lips parted, but no words came for a long moment. "You could never lose Lucy, Cage. She loves you too much."

But his lips twisted and he said no more.

The sun was setting by the time they hit the outskirts of Cheyenne. Belle pointed out the directions to Nikki's place.

He stopped at the curb in front of the town house. "Looks dark."

Truer words. There wasn't a single light burning from the windows of Nikki's home. Even the porch was stone-cold black.

Lucy, awake since they'd hit town, hung her head over the seat. "Was she expecting you?"

"She knew I was coming. She's probably just out getting a bite for dinner." Belle smiled with more certainty than she felt. "Don't worry. I have a key." She grabbed up her purse and pushed open the door with more haste than was dignified. There was nothing about the trip that hadn't been disturbing. Not sitting alongside Cage. Not listening to the things he'd said. Not speculating about the things he hadn't. She slid off the high seat. "Thanks again for the lift."

"Wait."

She halted long enough to see Cage scribbling on the back of a small piece of paper he pulled from the console.

"Here." He held out the note. "That's where we stay when we're in town and my cell-phone number. Call."

It was more an order than a request and her spine stiffened. "I appreciate the ride, but really, Nikki's car is in *much* better shape than mine. I'll be back at the Lazy-B on Monday as usual."

"Oh, please, Belle. Drive back with us tomorrow. She could even come with us to have supper, right, Dad?" Lucy smiled hopefully.

Despite Cage's knowing expression, Belle couldn't make herself disappoint the girl entirely. She plucked the note from his fingers. "It's really not necessary," she assured. And probably not wise. Being cooped up again in such close quarters. And Lucy wouldn't be much of a chaperone, given Cage's warning that the girl hit the *z's* on any road trip.

"Then we'll wait with you."

"Excuse me?"

Cage's face was set. "You heard me." He turned off the engine.

She made a soft sound, not sure whether she was charmed or exasperated. "It's not as if you're dropping me on some dangerous street corner. This is my sister's home in a perfectly respectable neighborhood."

"Humor me."

She tossed up her hands. "Fine. Whatever. I'll *call*."

"Good." He started the vehicle once more. "We'll wait until you get inside."

Obviously, arguing would be pointless, so she headed up the geranium-lined walk, digging through her purse again. Fortunately, Nikki's house key *was* still on Belle's key chain, and she fumbled only a little in the dark before pushing open the door and stepping inside. She flipped on the porch light and waved at the idling vehicle.

He didn't drive away until she'd closed the door.

Belle leaned back against it, listening to the soft rumble of the departing truck. Then she flipped another switch and warm light pooled through the entry from the two buffet lamps Nikki had situated on a narrow foyer table. Even though she knew her sister wasn't there, she still walked through the place, upstairs and down, calling her sister's name.

There was a folded note on the kitchen table with Belle's name written on it. She dumped her purse and Cage's note on the table, picked up Nikki's and read.

"If you're here, then you didn't listen, and I love you anyway. I'm okay, but I'm not ready to talk about any of this yet. I'll see you at Angel's birthday party. Love, Nik."

"Well, fudgebuckets." She dropped the note and it fluttered to the tabletop, rustling the scrap of paper that Cage had insisted she take. The hotel name and phone number were written in bold, slashing strokes.

No nonsense. That was Cage Buchanan.

She wandered back into the living room and threw herself down on her sister's squishy couch. That day's newspaper was sitting on the coffee table. Proof that Nikki hadn't been hiding out for too long.

She sat forward and pulled the paper closer. Flipped it open to the classified section and ran her eye down the rental listings.

Several in the right area of town, conveniently located nearby the clinic. Decent rent. Good space.

She flipped the paper over, folding it in half.

Perfectly decent rentals and not a one of them held any appeal.

Or maybe it was the fact that moving back to Cheyenne—as she'd always planned to do—was no longer as appealing as it had once been. Because every time she contemplated it, her mind got stuck over a sturdy little brick house and the bronze-haired man who lived there.

"Oh, Nikki," she murmured. "What kind of messes are we getting ourselves into?"

She went back into the kitchen to use the phone there, and dialed the number Cage had left. She nearly lost her nerve as it rang. But on the third, he answered.

"Hi," she greeted. "You guys still up for some supper?" *Say no. Say yes. Better yet, just shoot me now and put me out of this insane misery.*

"Find your sister?"

She crossed her fingers childishly. "Yes. Well, no, just a little crossing of our wires. So…have you fed Lucy, yet?" She could hear the girl in the background, asking Cage if it was Belle on the line.

"In the thirty minutes since we dropped you off?" He sounded amused.

Only thirty minutes? It seemed longer. She tucked a loose strand of hair behind her ear. "I'll take that as a no. If you, um, want to come back here, I can throw something together."

"No." His answer came a little too fast and some of her nervousness dissolved in favor of humor. She cooked regularly for Lucy, but she knew there wasn't much of anything that she'd left that Cage had tried. He'd labeled her cooking as inedible from the get-go and hadn't changed his opinion since. "I mean, Lucy's begging for pizza. I imagine if you flash those Bambi-brown eyes of yours at the cook, he'll make you some wheat-vegetarian thing."

Bambi eyes? She glanced in the window-fronted cabinet above the counter. And shook herself when she realized what she was doing. "All right, but I'm paying. Hey—" she was prepared for his immediate protest, and spoke over it. "It's the least I can do, given the chauffeur job you took on."

"Then breakfast is on me before the return trip," he said after a moment.

Her imagination went riot. Oatmeal and raisins, she thought desperately, trying to counter it. A useless endeavor, it seemed, since her imagination was most definitely in the driver's seat.

"Belle?"

"What?"

"I said we'd be there in twenty minutes." His voice was dry and she had a terrifying suspicion that he was perfectly aware of the reason for her distraction.

"Right," she said briskly. "I'll be ready."

She hung up and sat there in the kitchen. Then, realizing how time was ticking, she darted upstairs. Nikki had been moaning over Belle's lack of interest in fashion for years. If her sister weren't so stubborn, she'd undoubtedly have enjoyed the sight of Belle rummaging through her closet.

With a bare five minutes to spare, she stood in front of Nikki's mirror. Cowardice accosted her. She rarely wore dresses and she'd never filled out one the way her sister did. But before she could change back into her jeans and T-shirt, the doorbell rang.

Her nervous system went into hyperdrive. She looked longingly at her jeans.

The doorbell rang again.

She could almost hear Nikki's musical laughter in her head.

"I'm ready," she called out, clattering in the unfamiliar heels down the steps, the skirt of the floaty sundress flying around her ankles.

She skidded to a stop on the tile at the door and blew out a deep breath. She'd be composed if it killed her.

Then she opened the door and silently blessed Nikki and her well-endowed closet when Cage's eyes sharpened, taking her in from head to toe, a look so encompassing that it made her skin feel too snug.

It was *not* a bad feeling. At all.

"I'm ready," she said again.

She just wasn't quite ready to admit to herself what she was ready for.

## Chapter 12

"So. You do eat junk food." Cage watched Belle across the red-and-white checked tablecloth. The jar in the center of the table glowed from the lit candle inside it. The place was redolent with the smell of sausages, onions and garlic.

Nirvana.

And there Belle sat, looking like some fairy-tale fantasy with her long, waving hair providing the dark cloak around that surprising dress. Innocence and seduction all rolled into one intoxicating woman who was eating her wedge of pizza—the real kind, not some bastardized "healthy" version of it—backward. From the crust to the tip. Licking cheese from her fingertips. Gustily working her way through a healthy helping of pepperoni, black olive and mushroom.

She'd raised her eyebrows at his comment, a mischievous dimple flirting from her smooth cheek. "Call the health-food police," she challenged.

Lucy's elbows were propped on the table, her chin on her hands. "Belle's cooking is good, too, Dad," she said loyally.

"That's all right, Lucy," Belle assured her easily. "Your dad doesn't have to try my cooking. Some people are afraid of—"

"Eating birdseed?"

"—trying something new," she finished, her eyes laughing.

"I'd sooner eat Rory's oats."

Belle smiled, obviously not offended. "Might be good for you," she suggested blandly, and lifted the remains of her pizza slice.

He watched her work her way toward the tip. Given the presence of his daughter, he tried to pretend that Belle's obvious relish of her food was not turning him on. "Why start with the crust?"

She glanced from the remaining wedge, little more than a glob of gooey cheese on her fingertips, to him. "Saving the best for last," she said, as if it ought to have been obvious.

His mind, and his damn body, took a left turn at that, right down horny lane. What other kind of "bests" would Belle savor right up to the end?

He grabbed his iced tea and chugged the remaining half glass.

Belle was eyeing his plate where an untouched slice still sat. "You weren't very hungry?"

There was hunger and there was hunger. And he was damn near starved. "Guess not."

"Whenever I take more than I can eat, Dad tells me my eyes were bigger than my stomach."

"Well, right now, your eyes look in danger of falling asleep." Belle finished off her pizza slice, her own lashes drooping. But it wasn't tiredness on her face.

It was an expression of utter bliss.

Cage pushed back from the table. "I'll be back." He ignored the surprised looks—in duplicate—they gave him and headed toward the front of the crowded, cozy pizza joint, maneuvering his way through the line of people waiting for a table, and escaped out the front door.

He hauled in a long breath of cool, evening air, willing his body back under control. If he'd been a drinking man, he'd have found the nearest bottle of single malt and admired the curves of that.

But he didn't drink. There'd already been one Buchanan who'd done more than enough of that. And even though Cage knew his dad's habit hadn't contributed to his death, there'd been plenty of times it had contributed to Cage taking over the reins of the Lazy-B while his dad *was* alive.

He moved out of the way for a family to get to the door and walked along the sidewalk bordering the restaurant. Through one of the windows, he could see Lucy and Belle at the table, dark head and light, angled together companionably. The waiter stopped by the table and Belle smiled up at the kid.

Jesus.

He let out a harsh breath, walking farther, around the corner of the building and away from that winsome sight only to stop short.

Everything hot inside him froze, stone-cold at the sight of the woman standing there, eyeing him with considerably less shock than he felt.

Thirteen years—minus about six days—had passed since he'd laid eyes on Sandi Oldham. Then, her hair had been a wild mane around her shoulders, her cheeks smudged with running mascara. Not because she'd just handed over their baby to him for good, but because her credit-card limit had been reached and she wasn't able to buy the plane ticket to get her to Brazil where there was some dance troupe she wanted to get hooked up with.

Now, her gold hair was pulled back in a sophisticated-looking twist at the back of her head, and her face was cruelly perfect.

"What'd you do," he asked after a moment. "Hire someone to follow us?"

Her eyes flickered, and he knew he was right.

He also knew he had a piece of legalese that said she had no right to be around the child she'd borne but had never mothered. He turned on his heel, but she jogged on treacherous heels until she stood in his path.

"Wait."

"Get out of my way, Sandi. You have something to say, say it through your parents' lawyers. God knows, they have enough of 'em." He kept moving.

She shifted, walking backward, still trying to block his way. "Cage, wait—"

"No." He had to remind himself that—whatever his personal feelings were for her—she was equally responsible for the existence of Lucy. Wishing her back to the far corners of the earth had to suffice.

He brushed past her. She smelled as expensive as she'd ever smelled. Only he wasn't a seventeen-year-old kid still reeling from his parents' accident, and that expensive scent that once had him salivating only made his head ache now.

Give him rainwater fresh.

"Cage." Her voice followed him. "I'm sorry. I didn't want it to be like this."

He frowned. Turned on her, incredulous. "Just how the hell did you think it *could* be?"

She approached, her skinny boots clicking like gunshots on the cracked sidewalk. "You surprised me, coming out of the restaurant like that. I just want to see her, Cage. She's my daughter, too."

"And she wouldn't even exist if I hadn't dragged you, kicking and screaming out of that doctor's office before he performed the abortion." He remembered the day clearly. More missed school, in too many days of them after the accident, when he'd had to fight everyone to keep hold of what was left of his life—the ranch. Finishing high school had seemed the least of his worries when there'd been people intent on putting him in foster care somewhere. As if he hadn't already had a man's responsibilities on the Lazy-B. He'd hated people getting in his business ever since.

So he mostly avoided people when he could.

"I was young. Scared," Sandi said. She moistened her lips, looking vulnerable.

He wasn't fooled. There'd been nothing vulnerable about Sandi. Not from the get-go. And, in physical years at least, he'd been younger than she.

He knew in his bones that she hadn't changed her spots in the years since. He'd be damned if he'd lose his daughter to her after all this time, but even more, he'd damn Sandi to hell for all eternity if she hurt Lucy.

He'd already cursed her parents there and back again for that horse.

"I don't give a f—," he reined in his anger. "You signed away your parental rights a long time ago," he reminded her flatly. Right along with signing the divorce decree. He may have been still a kid, and he may have done some stupid damn things along the way, but he hadn't been a complete fool.

She didn't try to deny it, at least. "I know she's inside with that woman you hired." Sandi looked toward the restaurant door. "Belle Day. Nice work, that, Cage. I must admit, I was surprised to hear that name in connection with you."

His fingers curled into fists since he couldn't very well wrap them around her neck where they ached to go. He was glad the windows near the corner didn't afford a view of the table where Belle and Lucy still sat. "Don't go there, Sandi," he warned softly. If she thought she'd already won, she was sadly mistaken.

She angled a look his way. A look that may have acquired some subtlety over the years, but was still purely calculating. "You should have taken me seriously months ago, Cage. All I wanted was to have a relationship with my daughter. But no. You had to have her all to yourself. And now," she shook her head, looking regretful. "You're paying the price. Because now, you have to deal with my parents."

There was nothing but truth in her words and they still sounded vile. Then she reached out and touched the collar of his shirt, her fingertips slowly moving down the buttons. Her head tilted back and she looked up at him. "We can still work something out, Cage. You have to know that I've been desperate. Otherwise I'd never have brought my parents into this. I told you long ago what they were like. Always controlling everything with their money. I don't want Lucy subjected to them, either, but if it's the only way I can see her, then—"

He wrapped his hand around her wrist, trapping her fingers. "What, exactly, are you suggesting?"

She leaned in another inch. "You're the only one I ever married, Cage."

He watched her about as closely as he'd watch a coiled snake. A snake could be taken care of with a well-aimed, sharp shovel blade, though.

"We were still kids and marriage was your price," he reminded. No matter the struggles his parents had faced before his family was destroyed, he believed in family. To the end of his days. Sandi had given him a family, but she'd never been part of it, herself.

"Maybe marrying you was one thing I did do right," she whispered. "You're looking good, Cage." With her free hand, she reached up and brushed her fingers through his hair. "As good as I always expected. And things weren't always bad between us. We had some good times."

He wondered how far she was willing to go in her little pretense. How he could use it to his advantage, turn it against her and get her the hell out of his—Lucy's—life.

"We were wondering what was keeping you."

Cold slithered down his spine at the cool tone and he looked over Sandi's head to see Belle standing on the sidewalk watching them.

Her expression was calm, but he could see the tempest brewing in her dark eyes. "I'll be inside in a minute," he told her. Willed her to turn and go back. To be with Lucy, because there was no contest in his mind with whom his daughter would be safer.

Protected.

It sure wasn't the blonde who'd given Lucy her genes.

And wasn't this a helluva time to realize just how much he *did* trust Belle?

For a tense moment, Belle eyed him. Looked from

him to Sandi. Then she turned, her pretty dress flaring around her delicate ankles, and headed back inside the restaurant.

Relief eased the vise inside him, though he was smart enough to know it was only temporary. He was also smart enough to know his relief was only partially for Lucy.

Belle consumed the rest of it.

As she'd been consuming him all along.

He released Sandi's hand and stepped back so she'd get her fingers out of his hair. "Go back to Europe. Or wherever you've been hanging your broom these last years. There's no way you're going to see Lucy." He'd put Sandi over his shoulder and lock her away somewhere and take his chances with the law over it, if it came to that.

"You're going to regret this, Cage. It'd be easier to deal with me than my parents."

He eyed her. Even though he'd known it in his head, it was still a relief to realize that—face-to-face with her—she left him cold.

"I'll take my chances," he said.

She stared at him for a long moment, lips tight with displeasure. Then she muttered an oath and turned toward the parking lot. He watched her climb in an expensive sports car and didn't go back in the restaurant until she'd driven away with a squeal of tires and a grinding clutch that was criminal in such a vehicle.

Inside, he paused among the throng still awaiting tables and consciously tamped down the anger burning inside him. He caught their waiter and paid the check, then headed over to the table where Lucy and Belle waited.

"Ready?"

Lucy nodded sleepily and reached for her crutches. Belle didn't look at him as she stood also and gathered up the foil-wrapped leftover slices. "I need to get the check from the waiter." Her voice was still cool.

"It's taken care of."

Her jaw tightened. "It was supposed to be my treat."

He tucked his hand around her elbow—absorbing the fine shimmer that went through them both at the contact—and nudged her after Lucy, who was carefully making her way through the crush of tables, chairs and bodies. "Next time."

She shot him a look. Startled. Maybe tempted despite what she thought she'd seen?

"There's going to be a next time?" Her voice wasn't cool now. It was soft. Wistful.

Just that easily, the frozen wasteland left behind by his ex-wife went molten. His thumb stroked over her inner arm. "What do you think?"

"I thought you didn't have *time* for this," she said, barely loud enough for him to hear over the conversations swirling around them.

But the masses had parted for Lucy to make her way more easily to the door, and he didn't want his daughter going out there without him first.

Just in case.

He reluctantly slid his hand away from Belle's arm and slid in front of Lucy to push open the door. Fortunately, he was parked very near the door, and he had the women stowed inside within minutes. And there was no sign of the Porsche having returned.

"Dad?" Lucy was sprawling in the rear seat. "Can you take me to the hotel first before you drop off Belle?"

He looked back at her. "What's wrong?"

She lifted her shoulder. "Nothing. I'm just tired. And my leg is kinda hurting."

And he wouldn't be leaving her unattended in a hotel room for any length of time. Not tonight.

"It's fine," Belle said softly, brushing his leg with her fingertips. "Go to the hotel."

She pulled her hand back quickly, but the whispering contact had more than done its job. His skin was singing. He grabbed her hand again. Ignoring the way she started when he flattened her palm beneath his and pressed it back against his leg.

The warmth seared through his jeans, spearing upward. He was prepared for that. He just wasn't necessarily prepared to feel that warmth head further north than his crotch. But it did, and it was heading up his chest where his heart beat an oddly heavy beat.

"If Nikki's not at her place yet, I'll just grab a cab ride back from the hotel," Belle added. Her voice had gone husky again.

Lucy looked pale in the dim light penetrating the windows from the parking lot. He gave up the brief idea of simply driving back to Weaver that very night. He turned forward and started the truck.

Belle didn't move her hand away, not even when he needed both of his to reverse out of the parking spot.

He drove back to the hotel, watching every set of headlights that seemed to follow them.

*Just because you're paranoid doesn't mean they're not out to get you.*

But there didn't seem to be any car paying them particular attention. And there was no sign of Sandi's car, either. She'd obviously had them followed—a task that had to have begun in Weaver—so there was no point in pretending that the woman didn't already know where they were staying.

He gave up watching the other cars and concentrated instead on getting to the hotel.

It was so obvious that Lucy was in more pain than she let on when they got there, that Cage just handed Belle the crutches and lifted his daughter in his arms, carrying her up to their room.

Belle trailed behind them, hurrying ahead when he jerked his chin at the room to use the key and open the door. She didn't know what was going on—who the woman had been with her hands in Cage's hair outside of the restaurant—but she knew that whatever "it" was, it was important. It was as if the lines of a familiar painting had changed. Ever so slightly.

And now she didn't know what she was looking at exactly.

The hotel offered complete suites. Belle followed him through the living-room area into the bedroom where he deposited Lucy on the wide bed. She set the crutches within easy reach, then turned to give them some privacy.

But Lucy caught her hand, staying her. "I've got a charley horse," she whispered.

Judging by the suddenly tense look in the girl's eyes, this time it was no pretense. Belle sat on the bed and tugged off Lucy's tennis shoe, carefully letting her fingers work up the girl's calf until she could feel what was going on.

Cage sat down on the other side of the bed, his eyes on Belle as she gently kneaded the painful knot loose. It took a while. Every time it seemed to ease up, Lucy would move, and another muscle went into spasm.

Belle's hands ached a little by the time they'd licked the thing for good.

She sat back, realizing the position she'd ended up in on the bed chasing Lucy's muscle spasms—on her knees, her sister's pretty white dress shoved inelegantly between her thighs—was hardly attractive. She slid off the bed, tugging self-consciously at the dress.

"Here. Can you manage?" Cage handed over Lucy's pajamas from the small case they'd brought along.

Lucy nodded. She was already half asleep, barely murmuring a good-night when Cage leaned down and kissed her forehead.

Belle was in the living area when Cage left the bedroom. He pulled the door closed, his gaze angled toward her.

She swallowed and moved across the room, looking blindly out the large window at the end of the room. It looked out over an oval swimming pool. The pool was lit and it glowed, pale, bluish-white.

Like Cage's eyes, almost.

"So." She turned, hugging her elbows. "Who was the woman at the restaurant?"

# Chapter 13

Belle waited, tensely, as her question hovered in the air. She hadn't even attempted to make the question casual. Had she tried, she'd have failed miserably, making this even more humiliating.

"Nobody who matters," Cage said after a moment.

She wanted to believe him. Wanted to hear that *she* mattered, which was so far out of the realm of their nonrelationship that it scared her. "She looked like she knew you well." The sophisticated-looking blonde had had her fingers in Cage's hair, for pity's sake. Looking as though she was staking her claim right there on the sidewalk outside a bustling, family pizzeria.

He shook his head. As slowly and surely as he stepped closer to her. "She doesn't know me at all. Not anymore."

Belle's heart hovered in her throat, making breathing rather a challenge. She stiffened her spine a little.

Brushed her hands down the dress that she'd managed to wrinkle, crushing it the way she had on Lucy's bed. What on earth had possessed her to borrow the outfit from Nikki, anyway? If that smooth blonde was the type of woman Cage preferred... "Well. It's none of my business, anyway."

"You look pretty in the dress," he said.

Was she so easy to read? "I don't need meaningless compliments," she said stiffly.

"You think I don't mean it?" He stepped closer. "Fact is, you look pretty no matter what you're wearing. Red. Gray. White robe. It's all good. Believe me."

Panic streaked through her. She couldn't afford to forget who they were. *Where* they were. "Dagwood," she blurted.

His eyebrow peaked. "Pardon?"

"Oh. That's seven letters." Her feet backed up a step, which only made her bump the large air-conditioning unit attached to the wall beneath the window. Silly of her to have forgotten her shoes in Lucy's bedroom. She'd kicked them off before climbing completely onto the mattress. Another few inches of height on her part would have helped counter the overwhelming, intoxicating size of him.

As if.

"I told you." He stepped closer. "It's unique."

"Please," she sniffed. "Dagwood isn't unique?"

He shook his head, a faint smile hovering around the corners of his lips.

Belle couldn't sidestep him, or move backward any farther. She put out her hand, flattening it against his chest. "What's going on here, Cage?"

"You need me to draw you a map?" He didn't push her hand away. Merely pressed his fingers to her wrist, then slid them along the length of her arm. Curved around her bicep and traveled back again, seriously causing her elbow fits as he seemed to find every ridge and bump, before traveling onward, returning to her wrist.

Shivers danced under her skin.

She needed no map to follow the direction he was headed. "But…why?"

That hint of a smile left his face. His jaw cocked to one side for a moment, then centered again. "Because what I said last night 'bout not having time for this was bull. And I'm tired of pretending."

She decided discretion was the better part of valor, and lowered her hand from his chest, only to tuck both hands behind her back. Out of his temptation. Out of her own. "Your daughter is in the next room."

He made a nearly soundless, wry grunt. "You think I don't know that?"

No. She shook her head. She didn't think Cage would ever forget his daughter. He was too devoted. It was a significant portion of his appeal.

"She's asleep," he assured her after a moment. "She'll stay asleep unless she has a nightmare." He lifted his hand and she watched it, helpless to move, as it neared her face. When his fingers threaded, oh so easily, so gently, through the waves at her temple and glided through it, her muscles turned to warm, running wax. She felt her head falling back a little, like a too heavy bloom on its stalk, still seeking the sunlight.

He'd stepped closer. She could see the little scar below his lip so clearly. Had he gotten it as a rambunctious little boy? A headstrong teenager? "Cage—"

"I love your hair," he murmured, lifting his other

hand to her head, also, and effectively cutting off her ability to think even ridiculous thoughts.

He lifted handfuls of her hair, and let it sift down, watching her from beneath heavy lids. His head drooped an inch closer to hers. "I love that you don't wear it loose very often. Then it's like this—" his jaw canted, then centered again and his hands repeated the motion, lifting her hair, letting the strands rain down "—this private...pleasure only for me."

His voice was too low for anyone to hear except her. And he was maddening her. Seducing her with only his voice. His fingers running through her hair.

She struggled for composure, but the battle was spiraling out of her control. Her fingers tangled in the fabric of the drapes behind her. She was probably mangling the poor things. Better that than letting her hands go where they wanted to go.

Around Cage. Over him. Everywhere.

She lowered her head, her chin dipping. His fingers found her nape. Stroked. Petted.

He might as well have set a live wire to her spine for the sensations he caused. Was causing.

Oh, dear Lord.

"Cage. We...can't. Lucy—"

"Shh." His voice whispered over her ear, followed immediately by his lips as he nuzzled her earlobe. "Just let me do this. For a minute. Or two. Or twenty." He pulled her hair to the other side, smoothing it down her shoulder. Her arm. Over her breast.

Her heart surged against him and her knees nearly collapsed for the pleasure of it. She was drowning in liquid heat.

Then she felt his mouth on her neck. Heard the timbre of his breathing deepen. She started to lift her hands, to touch him.

"Don't touch me." His lips moved against her throat. "It's safer."

She exhaled shakily. He was drifting his fingers through her hair again. Rearranging it around both shoulders. "Nothing about you is safe," she whispered shakily.

"I'm hardly touching you."

Craning her head around until her lips could find his was proving futile. "What you're touching is making me—"

He stilled, one palm cupping her breast through skeins of hair, the other sliding through loose strands, fingers grazing her nape. "Making you…what?"

She tilted her head back as far as his holds on her hair allowed and looked at him. Full on. Gathered enough strength to speak. Heaven help her, to challenge. "Can't you tell?"

She knew what he'd see. Her cheeks were flushed. Her nipples were so tight they ached. She was trembling from head to foot and all points in-between. Particularly in-between. They were both fully dressed and she'd never been more aroused in her entire life.

She'd never had anyone move her—physically, mentally, emotionally—the way he did. Not even Scott. How would she ever survive if Cage touched more than her *hair?* Just then she didn't think he'd even need to, and wasn't that quite a statement on how much the man affected her?

His lips were parted a little, as if even he was having trouble getting enough air.

It was, she supposed hazily, some small comfort.

"Yeah," he finally said, his voice even lower. "I can

see. And I've wanted you looking this way for a while
now." He lifted one hand, flattening the drapes as he
braced his arm against the window above them. He
stepped in another few inches. Until there was no pretending that she wasn't painfully aware of the exquisitely tight fit of his jeans. And the reason why.

"I get only a few hours of sleep at night," he said,
"and what I do get is full of this." He pressed gently
against her. "Thoughts of you. Me. I'll lie there, hard
as a rock, wondering if you're tossing and turning in
that squeaky bed because you're thinking—or dreaming—about tossing and turning with me."

She shuddered. His words were too accurate.

He pressed his forehead against hers. She could feel
the heat of him, the beat of his heart like some freight
train bearing down on them.

Or maybe that was just her blood pulsing through
her veins.

"I went into your room last week," he whispered.
"You were in the living room with Luce. Working on
some math thing you're supposed to be teaching her,
but she was practicing piano and I could hear you complaining about the directions in the math book." His
fingers strayed to her chin only to slide back toward
her ear. Glide through her hair again.

She dissolved a little more. "M-math's not my best
subject."

"I was going to oil those springs but good. Not just
spray them like I did when you first got to the Lazy-B.
But really fix the problem."

She opened her mouth, desperate for some air.

"I didn't oil them," he said. His voice was rougher.
"I sat there and stared at that old bed, imagining you
lying in it, turning from side to side, the sheets tangling

around—between—your legs. Your hair—" he broke off, taking a hissing breath "—your hair spread out all over the pillowcase."

It was as if he'd watched her trying to sleep. Had seen her for himself. Night after night. Week after week. She heard a soft sound, a moan, coming from her throat, and couldn't stop it anymore than she could stop the images he was creating.

Then he twined his fingers in her hair more tightly, tugging back her head until she had to look at him. "Tell me what you dream about at night, Belle. Just tell me. And put me out of my misery. One way or another."

She stared at him, mute. Words dammed up behind her lips, too many words, too little strength to get them out.

He pressed his mouth to her forehead. Tipped her head back. Sifted her hair again through his fingers, spreading his arms wide, luxuriating in the length and weight of it. It slowly drifted, strand by strand, from his long, calloused fingers. His mouth touched her eyes. Her cheeks. Closed with the same exquisite slowness that his hands exercised, over her mouth. Not taking. Not plundering.

Just…tasting. Reveling.

And he trembled. Because of her.

"I dream about you touching me," she mumbled against his lips. Her entire body felt flushed with prickles of heat.

He exhaled and she breathed him in. He tucked her head against his chest, his shoulders curving around her, a world of their own creation right there in that moment of space. Of time. "I dream about that, too," he murmured. "Me touching you. You touching me. Every little touch causing a soft creak in that bed. Every catching breath causing it to moan a little louder."

She gasped, pressing her head harder against him, grabbing his biceps no matter what he'd warned. She was trembling so violently, her legs were barely holding her. "Stop."

But he didn't. "And always, always this hair of yours, a dark river against the sheets."

His hands returned to her head, sliding around, through, shaping her skull, something that shouldn't have been so exquisitely intimate, yet was. And it was sending her right over the edge. "Cage, you're going to make me…ah—" He covered her mouth with his, swallowing her gasping moan.

Then his lips burned to her ear again. "Let it happen, Belle. Let me have this at least. Let me have a little of what you dream. Of what I dream." He stroked through her hair, again. "Maybe you haven't come in that bed, Belle, but I've imagined it."

She whimpered a little at that. At the appalling bluntness of it. At the seduction of it.

"That's why I didn't oil the springs. I've *wanted* it. I've wanted to hear those soft, barely noticeable sounds of you in that bed, and I swear on my father's grave that it's only been you that has caused me to think it. Even if it was only in my imagination."

She shook her head, denial, admission, she didn't know what. All she knew was that he was making love to her, and he was doing nothing but touch her head. Getting inside her head. And it was working.

"I want it now," he repeated.

"Kiss me," she begged, nearly broken with need.

He did. His hands fisted in her hair and his mouth covered hers.

Swallowed the keening cry she couldn't manage to contain as she convulsed.

He caught her around the waist, hauling her against him, absorbing the shudders that quaked mindlessly, endlessly, through her there in that private world. And when she finally came to herself again, when they weren't just a mass of sensation, of emotion, when she could form thoughts, he kissed her again, stifling her embarrassment at her own lack of control back into submission.

And after he'd kissed her long and well, he carried her to the burgundy-and-navy plaid couch and sat down, holding her on his lap. Pressed her tight against him for an aching moment, before she felt the effort work through him to relax his hold.

Then he gave a shuddering sigh and threw his head back against the couch. "Thank you."

She could still feel the shape, the length of him pressing hard and insistent against her hip. Her cheeks felt on fire. And embarrassed or not, she couldn't pretend that she didn't want more. "But you haven't—"

He covered her mouth with his hand. "Don't even say it. Trust me." He blew out a measured breath. "Just sit here with me. It'll go away."

She flushed even harder. Tugged his hand away from her mouth, only to tangle her fingers with his and collapse weakly against him.

"Might take a month of Sundays, though," he warned blackly. "Couple of Weaver winters."

She couldn't help it.

She giggled.

His hooded eyes met hers.

And he smiled. Then he laughed. Out loud. From the belly. A laugh that jiggled its way right through her.

And she knew, in all of her life, she might never hear a more beautiful sound.

# Chapter 14

Eventually—when Belle had regained enough muscle and mind control to attempt simple functions—she used Cage's SUV to drive back to Nikki's place. But it had been wrenching to leave him.

Smart, definitely. But nevertheless wrenching.

She still felt the ache of it when she let herself in with her key, only to choke back a scream.

But it was only her sister sitting there in the living room, hunched over a book in the corner of her enormous couch.

Nikki eyed her for a moment, her blue eyes speculative. "I hope you've come back to clean up the mess you left in my closet."

After everything, Belle had completely forgotten about that. "I will. Thanks for the dress, by the way."

"I hope you at least cut off the tags before you wore it. It looks better on you than me, actually. Keep it. Your closet will rejoice, I'm sure."

Belle dropped her purse on the coffee table and sat down in front of her sister. Grabbed the book out of Nikki's hands and folded them between her own. "Are you all right?"

Nikki sighed a little. Tilted her auburn head to the side and studied Belle right back. "Are you?"

She swallowed a little, but kept her composure intact. "I will be once you tell me what's going on."

"By the looks of it, I'd say you've been playing truth or dare with someone. Since I know you are beyond being over Scott, it must be Cage Buchanan. Truth?"

Maybe her cheeks were a little rosy from Cage's five o'clock shadow, but she knew she didn't look as if she'd just climbed from bed.

They'd never made it to the bed.

Her face went a little hotter at that. It would be a long while before she could think about it without being shocked at her own behavior. At the outrageous and unrelenting way Cage had played her. And she'd sung.

And she wasn't sure she'd be able to sleep in that squeaky bed back at the Lazy-B again. She just might have to sleep on the floor.

"I was with Cage," she admitted. "*And* Lucy."

Nikki eyed her.

"Well. Lucy was asleep in the other room," she admitted grudgingly. Then gave herself a hard, mental shake. "They gave me a ride down here to see *you*. My Jeep is currently kaput."

"Because it's only a hundred years old."

"Not everyone drives around the latest models," Belle countered lightly, "the way you do. So. Talk."

Her sister swallowed. "I'm pregnant."

Belle waited.

Nikki pushed to her feet, shoving a shaking hand through her thick, auburn hair. "You'd think I'd get used to hearing those words come out of my mouth, wouldn't you? I'm pregnant. I'm pregnant." She shook her head. "Nope. Still freaks me out." Her smile wavered.

Belle hopped up and wrapped her arms around her sister.

"Do you love him? This guy? The one you're not ready to talk about?"

"Do you love *him?* Cage?" Nikki's whisper was ragged.

Belle swallowed hard. But this was her sister. The one with whom she'd shared their mother's womb. They were twins. Different. Alike. But always honest.

"I'm afraid I'm starting to," she admitted. "I can't even imagine going back to Huffington, and that's—" She shook her head, unable to explain. "But I want to know about *you.*"

Nikki sighed heavily. She pushed Belle back and studied her face for a moment. "Later. For now sleep or chocolate?"

Nikki had always been an independent soul. "Chocolate," Belle declared. Sooner or later her sister would talk. "Most definitely."

Nikki turned toward the kitchen, padding along in her bare feet. "Fortunately, in the chocolate area, I'm well prepared."

They ended up falling asleep on the couch facing each other, the carton of Double Chocolate Fudge Madness empty on the bare inch of cushion not covered by their sprawling legs.

Belle woke first and watched her sister sleeping.

Nikki was going to be a mother.

She pressed her palms flat against her own abdomen, as she wondered what it felt like. Not the worry over being a single mom, but what it felt like to have something—a new creation—growing inside.

But thinking about that naturally led to thinking

about how one became pregnant, which naturally led to thinking about Cage, which naturally led to Belle not having any hope of going back to sleep.

So she carefully slid off the enormous couch. Nikki sank down a little more, unconsciously taking advantage of the extra space just the way she'd always done whenever she and Belle had had to share the back seat of their family car.

Belle draped an ivory afghan over her sister and plucked the empty ice-cream carton off the couch. Silently gathered up the spoons and napkins and carried it all into the kitchen, tidying up. She flicked on the coffeemaker, then went upstairs, took a quick shower, and changed into the spare outfit she'd brought.

Then she cleaned up the mess—which admittedly was more mammoth than she'd thought—of clothes she'd left when she'd raided Nik's closet the night before.

She left a thermal mug of decaffeinated coffee on the table beside Nikki, and with a matching one in her own hand, let herself out of the house, locked it behind her and drove back to the hotel. She buzzed Cage's room from the lobby as he'd suggested she do before she'd left him the night before.

He and Lucy arrived within twenty minutes.

It wasn't taxing to wait. The hotel had that pretty pool, after all. And plenty of chairs around it that weren't yet occupied at the early hour.

She had her coffee. She had the beautiful promise of an early Sunday morning, with a sky that couldn't be more perfectly blue, and clouds that couldn't be more perfectly like big, squishy cotton balls. She had a year's supply of chocolate circulating in her bloodstream and the certainty that her sister—while still reeling—was, bottom line, as strong as she'd ever been.

And she had the sound of Cage's laughter in her heart.

Lucy swung into view first, her freshly washed hair lying over her shoulders in twin braids. She waved and aimed toward Belle, plopping down onto a chair with no sign of the stiffness she'd exhibited the night before.

Cage followed more slowly, a foam cup eclipsed by his long fingers.

She gulped her coffee, dragging her eyes away from his fingers. And nearly choked on the liquid.

Served her right for thinking *those* thoughts about his wonderfully shaped, perfectly masculine hands.

He gave a crooked smile and sat down in the third chair, setting his coffee cup on the table where his fingers hovered around the rim. He lifted his other hand, and she realized he'd been carrying a blueberry muffin. "Want one?" She shook her head and he handed the muffin to Lucy. "Ever catch up to your sister?"

"She was there when I got back last night."

"And?"

"And…I feel better. Thanks a lot for driving me. Really."

He lifted his coffee, the faintest sketch of a toast in his movement. "My pleasure."

Well. She nervously tugged her ponytail over her shoulder. When his gaze shifted a little, she hurriedly pushed it back behind her shoulder and tucked her hands beneath her legs on the chair. "So. Any preferences for breakfast?"

Cage just looked at her.

Fresh heat streaked through her.

She focused on Lucy and it took no small effort to do so. "Well? What are your druthers, miss? Waffles? Eggs?"

"If we go to Grandma's care center, we could have

breakfast there. They always have a huge Sunday buffet. That's what we usually do. Right, Dad? Then we can introduce Belle to her."

Belle absorbed that. She looked at Cage, who had begun studying the contents of his coffee cup. "Yes," he said after a moment. Then his gaze lifted and focused once more on Belle. "Let Belle decide."

Lucy looked hopefully at her.

Belle would have preferred to go anyplace else. She'd have preferred to drive straight to the moon and back rather than go to the care center.

All of which only proved that a coward still lurked beneath her skin. "A *huge* buffet?" she questioned Lucy. "Huge in relation to what? To the number of history papers you've written in the past eight weeks? To the number of birds congregating in that tree over there, hoping you leave some crumbs of your muffin behind?"

Lucy laughed, delightedly. "They have, like, five kinds of eggs. And I *know* you like eggs."

Belle smiled and tugged on Lucy's braid. "So I do," she admitted.

So, after Cage took care of the checkout, they drove across town to the pretty tree-shrouded facility where Cage's mother lived.

Belle's eyes took in every corner. Every sight and sound and smell. She'd feared the place would be unbearably institutional. But it wasn't. It was more like a sprawling, gracious home. The front door was double width and could accommodate wheelchairs, but it was a far cry from some sliding metal-and-glass monstrosity that so many places possessed. Inside, there were plants everywhere. The staff members weren't wearing starched whites.

Cage and Lucy headed down a hall, obviously familiar faces from the greetings they received. The exclamations of how well Lucy was maneuvering with her crutches since the last time they'd been there.

Belle would have followed behind them, but Cage slowed up a little until she walked *with* him.

At least he didn't pretend that this was something either one of them could have predicted when she'd become Lucy's PT.

After a couple turns of corridors lined with lovely artwork and occasional chairs, Lucy stopped in front of an open door. She barely knocked before unceremoniously entering. "Hi, Grandma."

Belle swallowed and hung back. She was used to working with people in all manner of physical conditions. She didn't know exactly what Mrs. Buchanan's condition was, but she knew with certainty that no amount of training could have prepared her for this moment.

And Cage, no matter what, couldn't possibly want her here.

The man she'd thought she'd known these past months surely would be affronted by her very presence here.

But he gave no indication of anything. Unlike the previous night in his hotel room when he'd been excruciatingly verbal, his thoughts now were far too well contained.

Lucy had no similar affliction. She pointed the tip of her crutch at Belle, startling the life out of her.

Belle grabbed Cage's arm. "Look."

"What?"

"Lucy took a step without her crutches," she hissed under her breath. "She's standing on her own."

And the girl had. She was. She continued gesturing with her crutch, an extension of her hand, for Belle to come closer. "Come in and meet my grandma," she urged.

Belle blindly walked into the room. She was still

amazed at what Lucy was doing so unconsciously. Fortunately, too amazed to say something that might send Lucy backtracking. And she found herself facing Cage Buchanan's mother.

She was sitting in a side chair, next to a small round table, a book on her lap. A mystery. Belle instinctively knew without having to look closely that the stack of books on the bookshelf beneath the window held books by the same authors that filled the shelves at the Lazy-B. The books Cage read.

The window was open and a slight breeze billowed gently through the delicate white curtains, lightly stirring the bronzy curls of the woman.

She was beautiful. More than the aging black-and-white photos hanging in the house at the Lazy-B could ever have predicted.

A female version of the beautiful son she'd borne. The same color hair, the same breathtakingly clear blue eyes. Her skin was soft, nearly unlined. She wore a simple, pink sheath-style dress. Her feet were tucked into delicate pink pumps. She could have been a perfectly healthy woman dressed for church.

"This is my friend, Belle Day." Lucy introduced her cheerfully.

Belle held her breath. But Cage's mother merely slid her softly smiling gaze from Lucy to Belle's face. Obviously, to her Belle's last name was just a name. Her breath leaked out. She stepped forward, holding out her hand. "Hello, Mrs. Buchanan."

"How nice of you to bring Lucy," she said, squeezing Belle's hand with both of hers. They were soft. Cool. Utterly gentle. Only a close ear would have noticed the halting tempo of her speech. And Belle felt a faint smile on her own lips in return of the one directed so sweetly at her.

Then Mrs. Buchanan looked beyond Belle at Cage. She reached out her hands to him, perfectly friendly. "And who would you be?"

Knowing that his own mother didn't recognize him was one thing. Witnessing it another.

The sadness of it was encompassing. Wide and deep. Belle kept her smile in place only through sheer effort as she watched Cage step forward.

He leaned down, holding her hands, and kissed his mother's cheek.

His knuckles were white.

Belle wanted to look away, but couldn't.

"Hi, Mom." His voice held only gentleness. "We came to have breakfast with you, so I hope you haven't already been down to the dining room."

The woman nodded easily. Cage's greeting had no more effect on her than Belle's had. "I was reading. And nearly forgot to eat." She laughed a little, realizing the book had fallen to the floor and took it when Cage handed it to her. She set it on the table, then rose. She smoothed her hand over Lucy's head, pure delight in the gesture. "You look very nice today, Lucy. Are you getting taller?"

"I'm a teenager now, Grandma. My birthday was two days ago." Lucy swung through the doorway. "Maybe I'm taller 'cause of these tennis shoes I'm wearing. They look cool, don't they? Belle gave 'em to me. For some reason, she thinks I like pink. Do you think they'll have blueberry waffles this week? I really missed them when we were here last time."

Belle watched them go, Lucy's cheerful chatter so natural and unaffected, floating down the hall as they went.

Cage stood beside her. He touched her arm through the filmy sleeve of her blouse. "Are you okay?"

She looked up at him. That he could ask *her* that,

when it should be she posing the question to him…she shook her head a little. "I'm so sorry, Cage."

"So am I."

She pressed her fingers to her lips for a moment. Felt the drift of the air through the window. "You know, after the accident, my dad was never the same. He wasn't hurt. Not physically. But…he just wasn't the same."

Cage's lips twisted, but he said nothing.

"He had a massive heart attack three years later. I was sixteen. But sometimes I think he left his heart on the highway that night."

"You still had your mother. Your sister," he said after a moment.

"And you had no one." Her eyes blurred. No family at all. And there was no question that family meant everything to this man. It had just taken her a while to see it. "Your mother—"

"Traumatic brain injury," he said evenly. "The only person since the accident that she remembers from one day to the next is Lucy. We don't know why. Maybe because I've been bringing Lucy here since she was born. My mother functions well. Her speech is good. Her motor functions are good. But she wouldn't remember to look before crossing a street. She wouldn't remember to take off her shoes before getting into bed. She wouldn't remember that a sharp knife would cut her hand."

The tears flowed down Belle's cheeks.

"I took her back to the Lazy-B once. Lucy was five." His gaze turned inward. "The insurance settlement had run out and I wanted her home. Thought it might help. But she never connected. And whether or not I wanted to admit it, I couldn't help her. She needed to be in a safe environment. The ranch wasn't it." He glanced around the room. The walls were a pale pink, so similar to

Lucy's at the Lazy-B. Everything about the room was pretty and soft and feminine. "So I sold nearly everything I owned except the ranch and brought her back."

And Belle knew that it had broken his heart.

"It's my fault."

"Right." His expression was plain. He blamed her father. He always had. Even though no fault had ever been officially declared. Gus Day had walked away from the accident, and Cage's family had not.

"I wanted to go on a winter break with a friend of mine from school. They were going to Mexico for a week. And I wanted to go along in the worst imaginable way. I was thirteen and I thought Cheyenne was about the most boring place on the planet, and Mexico—" she shook her head "—well I knew it wouldn't be boring. But my father said I couldn't go, and my mother—as usual—agreed with him. He didn't like my friend's parents, you see. He thought they were... irresponsible. I thought they were a hoot. More like friends than parents."

"Belle—"

"Let me finish this, Cage." She had to finish. If she didn't now, she wasn't sure she ever could. And face-to-face with the reality of what he'd been left with that night grieved her so deeply, she knew she couldn't live with herself if she *didn't*.

No matter if it meant he'd never look at her the same again. He deserved the truth. All of it.

"My father was right, of course, but I learned that only after a while. They were busted for some stuff. Anyway." She knew she was babbling. Tried to focus.

"You don't have to cry about this, Belle. I don't blame you for what happened that night. Maybe I started out that way—hell, I know I did. I resented the fact that you and your sister grew up having what had been ripped away from me."

"But I am to blame," she burst out. "The trip to Mexico. I was determined to go, you see. And Daddy just kept telling me I couldn't go. And I told him that I hated him and would *never* forgive him, and stormed out of the house. I went to my friend's and, even though her parents had to have known I didn't have permission to go, we all headed out of town."

Despite her tears she could see his expression had gone still. Stoic. And her heart broke. For him. For the past. For the future.

"Dad caught up to us after twenty miles," she went on. Pushing the words past the vise of her throat. "If it was even that far. I wanted to crawl in a hole and die of embarrassment when he made the van pull over. Now, I think it was surprising he hadn't just sent the police after us. We were driving back to Cheyenne when the accident happened. I was so angry. I wouldn't even sit in the front with him. I was ignoring him. Lying in the back seat like some…some spoiled child."

She pressed her eyes shut. "If my dad was distracted, if he wasn't paying enough attention, if it *was* his fault, then it was because of me. And even if it wasn't his fault, if it was just the ice, or the snow, or whatever the way I was always told, it was still because of me. Don't you see?" She opened her eyes again and faced Cage. "We were only out that night, because of me."

## Chapter 15

Belle stood there, feeling as brittle as the last autumn leaf. Waiting for him to look at her again, for his eyes to go cold and flat. For him to tell her that she'd interfered in his life enough, to get the hell away from his family and stay away. Far, far away.

"Why are you telling me this?"

She stared down at her hands. She *had* helped Lucy. She knew she had. Knowingly or not, the girl had stood squarely on both feet and taken a step without the aid of her crutches. It didn't mean the job was done. But it meant that Belle had helped. Finally.

"Belle."

She lifted her chin and looked up at him, wanting to memorize his face. *Him.* From the top of his bronzed head, over the cobalt-blue shirt that made his eyes even more startling, to the bottom of his black boots. A different pair than what he wore around the ranch. These were newer. Shined.

Because he'd known he was visiting his mother, even though she wouldn't remember him from one week to the next.

"Because I…I'm falling in love with you," she said. And she'd told him the one thing sure to put an end to whatever possibilities might exist for them. "Because you have a right to at least blame the right person." She wiped her cheeks and turned to leave.

He caught her wrist.

The pain sweeping through her was physical. Nearly sending her to her knees. But she stood there, knowing the pain he'd endured—was still enduring every time he came to this comfortable room where his mother's life was contained—eclipsed hers by legions.

"Do you mean that?"

Confusion made her hesitate.

"That you love me," he said impatiently.

Did he want his pound of flesh, then? If it made him feel better, he could have it. And more. "Yes." What was the point of recanting?

A muscle worked in his jaw, more noticeable because his face was pale beneath the tan he'd earned putting in alone the work of ten men on the Lazy-B.

Her wrist was beginning to ache beneath his shackling grip. But she'd have done anything just then to take every ounce of pain he felt inside herself, if only to ease him, somehow.

Then his fingers—as deliberate now as they'd been the night before when he'd sat them on the couch, both of them wanting *more* than they could have in that hotel room—carefully eased their tight hold. He lifted her hand, his eyes downcast.

"Maybe it's time to leave the past in the past," he said, his voice sliding over her, deep and gruff.

"The past isn't bringing Lucy here week after week to visit your mother." It was his present, and his future.

He let out a long, deep breath. "No," he agreed. "But Lucy's happy. My mother is happy. She doesn't know anything else now. She's content. This is what *is*."

He slid his hand behind Belle's neck, tipping her face up. Everything inside her gathered into a hard knot centered somewhere under her heart. He lowered his head, pressed his forehead to hers, eyes shut.

Hot tears burned down Belle's cheeks. She cautiously touched his shoulders. Her fingertips trembling along his neck. Feeling the tension inside him. Not daring to believe that he wasn't pushing her away.

"Maybe it's time I let myself be happy with what is, too."

A shudder of grief was working through her shoulders, no matter how hard she tried to suppress it.

Then his fingers slid under her chin, lifting it and his mouth covered hers, swallowing her hiccuping sob. "Don't cry," he muttered. "I can't take it."

A statement that only had the opposite effect. Belle buried her face against the front of his shirt. He swore under his breath, tugged her over to the chair where his mother had been sitting and sat down, arranging Belle in his lap as easily as if she were smaller than Lucy. His shoulder moved, then he was handing her a tissue he'd plucked from the box on the bookcase.

But the tears just kept coming and he moved again, and she felt the cardboard cube being pushed into her hands.

"Go to it, then," he said gruffly.

She leaned against him, sliding her arm over his shoulder, holding him. The box crumpled between them. His hand moved down her back. Back up again.

And after a long while, Belle felt an odd sort of peace

creep through her. She sat back a little. Mopped her face with tissues. Finally looked up into that gaze of his. "What do we do now?"

He was silent for a moment. His fingers toyed with the length of her ponytail, pulling it over her shoulder. And even though her emotions were fully spent, the action felt as if he was spreading a layer of soft warmth over her. "We go have breakfast," he finally said. "And then we go home to the ranch."

She absorbed that. Nodded a little. Step-by-step. "And then?"

"Then we'll see what happens."

"You, um, you still want me to work with Lucy?" Her voice was shaking again.

"Yes."

"Okay." It was more than she could have expected.

"I want you to work with me."

"On…what?"

He leaned over her, catching her softly parted lips between his. First the lower. Then the upper. "Learning how not to be an ogre."

"You're not an ogre," she assured thickly. And hoping that she wasn't making the biggest misstep of all, she pressed her mouth against his.

His arms tightened around her.

"Whoa. Wowzer. No *wonder* you guys are taking so long!"

Belle yanked back at the exclamation. Her lips felt as puffy as her eyes. Her ponytail was askew.

"Caught in the act," Cage muttered against the shell of Belle's ear. She was blushing like a spring rose and he looked past her to his daughter, gaping at them as if she'd just discovered fire or something. "We'll be along in a minute, Luce."

Her eyes were bright. No surprise there. She adored

Belle. But he was a little surprised that she didn't seem more shocked. Her head bobbed and she planted her crutches, turning smartly only to take another quick look back at them, a grin already on her face. "Wow," she said again. Then swung right out of sight again.

Belle was scrambling off his lap. "Maybe you should go talk to her, or, or something."

"About what? You think she doesn't know what a kiss is all about? She already told me you made sure she knew the facts of life after she got her period."

Belle gulped a little and looked away. "Well, I wasn't sure you were up to—"

"I told you. Luce has always been able to talk to me." But damned if he hadn't been more than a little relieved when he *had* cornered his girl after that particular episode. Not that they hadn't discussed the facts of life long before then. Lucy was a rancher's daughter, for cripes sake. She knew how babies came to be.

But it was one thing when it was talking about puppies or calving. It was another thing entirely when it was his *daughter*.

"I'm always underestimating you," Belle said quietly. "Aren't I? I'm sorry."

"For caring about my daughter?"

"I love her, too."

He let the fact of it settle inside him, only to have to acknowledge that it wasn't all that much of a surprise, after all.

"Come on," he said, taking up her hand in his. "Breakfast."

Her fingers slid through his, holding tightly.

And they went to breakfast.

Later that afternoon, Cage dropped Belle off at her house in town since there still was the matter of her

Jeep to be seen to. The dropping off took longer than it might have, since Lucy was curious to see where Belle lived, necessitating a brief tour.

By the time Cage and Lucy drove off again, Belle knew that Brenda Wyatt had gotten quite an eyeful, hovering obviously out in her front yard. No way could she have failed to miss the kiss Cage planted on her before climbing into his truck and driving on down the road.

By the time Belle had thrown a hasty load of laundry into the wash and tracked down the whereabouts of her Jeep, her mother was standing on her front step, knocking on the door before unceremoniously letting herself in.

Gloria Clay propped her hands on her slender hips and tilted her auburn head that was only showing a few strands of silver. Her blue eyes were expectant. "Well? Has your phone stopped working? Where have you been all weekend? And *what* is going on with your sister? She's harder to get hold of than you are."

Belle warily dumped the towels she'd taken from the dryer on the couch and sat down beside them. "I went down to Cheyenne." She reached for a towel and spread it out, taking inordinate care over the folds.

Her mother lifted an eyebrow. "And?"

"And nothing. Well. I met Cage Buchanan's mother." The admission came out fast. She felt as if she was ten years old again and she and Nik had been caught sneaking Christmas cookie dough out of the fridge.

"Oh. My." The news was enough to distract Gloria for a moment, but Belle didn't hold out much hope it would last. Gloria sat on the other side of the towels and grabbed one, smartly flipping it into a perfect fold in a fraction of the time it took Belle. Then she rested her folded hands on top of the fluffy terry cloth. "Is she doing well?"

Belle wasn't sure how she'd expected her mother to react. "She looked lovely."

Gloria made a soft *mmm*. "What's going on, Annabelle?"

"Brenda Wyatt didn't give you the skinny?" She finished folding and stacked the towels together. Then wished she hadn't finished so quickly.

Her mother waved a hand. "As if I care what nonsense that woman spouts. She's been gossiping since long before either one of us came to Weaver. Managed to cause all that fuss Tristan and Hope had to deal with when that reporter came snooping for a story about him." She tilted her head a little. "Of course, that all had a rather nice result in the end since they got married because of it and fell in love. Hope's expecting again, you know. Erik's over four now. We were all beginning to wonder if he was going to get a little brother or sister "

A quick rush of pleasure jolted through Belle, right along with a sturdy helping of guilt for keeping silent about Nikki's news. "I didn't know. That's great."

Her mother's blue gaze rested on Belle's head for a moment. "Well. Sawyer told me about your Jeep."

"It's been hauled to the garage."

Gloria held out her hand and dropped a key into Belle's. "You can borrow this until yours is running again."

"Mom—"

"Don't argue, now. Squire insisted and you know what *he's* like. There're plenty of vehicles to spare around the Double-C. You can leave it off again next week at Angel's party if yours is done by then. And none of us has to worry about you driving that old thing on those roads out to the Lazy-B. I know it was your father's, sweetheart, but even he wouldn't expect you to drive it forever."

Belle shrugged. "I like the Jeep, Mom."

Gloria nodded. "So, does this man mean something to you, or are you just using him to get over that fool, Scott? That boy had no integrity at all, proposing the way he did when he already had a wife. And *then* blaming you because he didn't recover as fast as he wanted to."

"My feelings for Cage have nothing to do with Scott," she assured. "I can't believe I ever thought what I felt for him was love." Or let him convince her she wasn't a good enough therapist to help *anyone*.

"Because you know what real love feels like now?"

Belle pulled the stack of towels onto her lap. Put them back on the table. Rose and paced. "What really happened that night, Mom? The accident. Whose fault was it?"

Gloria watched her, a hint of sympathy in her eyes. "Accidents can happen with no one being at fault, darling. And that night was icy. Your father did feel responsible, though. Which is why—"

"Why what?"

But Gloria just shook her head. "Nothing. It's in the past."

The past. "I told Cage why we were out there that night at all."

"I see."

Belle suddenly sank down on the coffee table. "I'm falling for him, Mom. And Lucy. And that brick house with its antiquated furniture and everything."

"And how does Cage feel about you?"

"He doesn't seem to hate me." A miracle she still had trouble believing.

Gloria lifted her eyebrow again. "Is that all?"

She was too old to be blushing, yet she did. "Maybe not. I don't know."

"I imagine you do, but you don't have to tell me all the details," Gloria assured her wryly. "My heart won't be able to take it. Now. It's getting to be supper time. Squire wants ribs from Colby's. Everyone's meeting over there. The entire family. Newt is saving the back room because we'll need all the space to fit. You'll join us."

There was no question in it.

"Where is Squire?"

"Right here, girl," the tall man said, stepping through the door. He wasn't quite as tall as his five sons, but his iron-gray head ducked a little anyway as he entered. A habit she'd noticed more than once in her stepbrothers, who'd undoubtedly conked their heads on low doorways often enough to be conditioned. "Was just checking the rain gutters on the side of your house. One of 'em is coming loose. If that man of yours doesn't come back to town this week to get it fixed up, I'll have one of the boys come over and take care of it."

Belle just shook her head a little and reached up to hug him. There was no more stopping Squire than there was any of the Clays. The "boys" he'd referred to were all grown men, and gossip in town must have been plentiful indeed if people were already calling Cage "her man."

Once she'd spent a few hours in their company over a half-dozen tables pushed together in Colby's back room to accommodate the mass of Clays who seemed to keep filtering in—she stopped counting after twenty—she felt as if she'd filled up some wellspring inside of her.

That was what family could do.

After supper, while everyone was still passing out hugs and chattering a mile a minute, Belle decided she was not going to wait until morning to go back to the Lazy-B. She had a car—maybe not her beloved Jeep—

and no desire whatsoever to sleep in the house of Hope's that she'd been using and every desire to be at the Lazy-B. No matter which bedroom she used.

But her plans were preempted by the sight of Cage, sitting on her front porch.

Her heart kicked hard against her ribs as she climbed out from the back seat of Sawyer's SUV. She was hardly aware of what she said to him, just that she was relieved when he wheeled around and drove back up the street to collect his own family before going home.

She watched Cage stand. He doffed his brown cowboy hat and his hair gleamed a little under the glow from the porch light. He was twenty yards away yet she could feel the intensity of his gaze.

Tension slipped up her spine, fiery pinpricks careened through her nerves. She couldn't seem to draw enough oxygen into her lungs and her mouth ran dry. She moistened her lips, torn between fleeing or standing her ground. But her rooted feet took the decision from her because she couldn't seem to move to save her soul.

And then he took a step toward her. And another. And there was nothing but purpose in his movements, purpose that no amount of pretense could hide.

Her heart climbed up into her throat.

Closer now. She could see the flame in his eyes, otherworldly pale, blue fire. "Luce is over at Emmy's," he said bluntly. "All night."

"Oh."

"You gonna stand there all night?"

"Maybe." She swallowed. "I can't seem to make my feet move."

"Where were you?"

As if he had every right to know. It didn't occur to her to prevaricate. Or even to challenge. "Colby's. The whole family was there. I was going to drive out to the ranch tonight," she admitted in a rush.

"The Double-C?"

She shook her head.

"The Lazy-B."

She nodded.

"Whose car?" He jerked his chin toward the sexy little convertible sitting in front of the house.

"A spare from Mom and Squire."

"I'm glad." He stepped closer. "Was wondering about it." His voice was low. Quiet. "Like I wondered about that white shirt."

"There's no man but you." The admission felt as momentous as dropping a boulder into a still, still pond. And she wasn't at all certain how high the ripples might roll. Or, even if she were brave enough to find out. "You've had a lot of driving today. Cheyenne. Back and forth to Weaver. You must be tired."

"Inside?"

She pressed her hands down the sides of her jeans. Then nodded and willed her feet to move, heading up the small porch ahead of him. Fumbled with the lock and then the door. He finally reached around her and shoved it open, then nudged her through, and closed the door with a slam, turning and pressing her back against it, his body imprinting itself against hers.

She went straight past wary to aching. No line, no waiting. "I always wondered what swooning was like," she mumbled, staring blindly up as his weight pinned her. "I, um, I guess you're not that tired after all."

"Evidently." His fingers were busy on the tiny black buttons of her blouse then his hands swept inside, finding nothing but bare skin and the world seemed to stop spinning.

Her eyes nearly rolled back in her head. "Good," she

gasped. She tore at his shirt. Made a mess of it since she got it off his shoulders but not his arms. The crispy swirl of black hair sprinkling his chest abraded her breasts. The contrasts between them were inciting. Delicious.

And then she felt the tease of his tongue along her lower lip, and the world wasn't still at all. It was racing, spinning, and the only steady port was Cage.

She shuddered, her fingers clenching his corded forearms. Her clothing provided no protection whatsoever against his searing heat. And, oh, she didn't want to be protected. She ran her hands up his arms, fumbling over folds of cobalt shirt, pressed her fingers into the unyielding biceps, her head falling back at his drugging onslaught. His breath was harsh when he finally lifted his head a few inches, hauling in a ragged gulp of air.

"I didn't expect you to happen." His mouth found her temple. Slid down her jaw.

"I know," her voice was woefully faint. Her fingers walked up his shoulders. Felt the cords of his neck. She felt the brush of silky bronze hair against her chin as his kiss burned along her shoulder blade. Pressed against the pulse beating frantically in her throat. "I didn't, either."

"Don't talk," he murmured, straightening. He tilted her head to suit him. "Just kiss me again."

So she did.

She kissed him until her head spun, until her skin felt molten, and her blood sang. She kissed him until she couldn't think, until the only thing she knew was the shape of him, the taste of him. Until she went beyond fear that kissing him would never be enough to certainty that the fear was irrelevant.

His hands raced over her only to stop and tarry, maddening her with the graze of his calloused fingertips along the bare skin of her back, her abdomen. He lifted his head, and she was conscious enough to flush at the moans rising in her throat when his gaze ran over her, only to stall at the thrust of her rigid nipples through the loosened blouse. His hand slowly drifted from her shoulder, over the push of her breasts against the fabric. His fingertip slid in tightening circles around her nipple, and if it wasn't for his other arm around her waist, her knees would have failed her completely. Then he dragged his finger over the peak, and the sensation was so exquisitely intense, she cried out.

His gaze slashed back to hers as he repeated the motion. She shuddered, mouthing his name.

He exhaled roughly, and covered her mouth again, kissing her deeply. She felt his fingers slide beneath the blouse again, drawing it down, past her shoulders. Off her arms where it floated to their feet. Then his palms covered her flesh.

Belle gasped at the sensations battering her from all sides. His drugging mouth on hers. His clever hands touching her. The unyielding wall of his chest against her. "Hold on," he muttered. Then he simply lifted her off her feet. Her pulse stuttered and she twined her arms around him, burying her face in the curve of his neck. He tasted hot, slightly salty, totally male, and at the flicker of her tongue against him, his grip tightened and his stride faltered. He muttered something under his breath, then moved again. He carried her down the hall. "Where?"

"End of the hall."

His mouth covered hers. Her legs bumped the wall. He swore. She laughed softly. Then he was moving again, turning sideways through the doorway to her bedroom. And even though they were the only ones in the house, he kicked the door shut behind him.

The abrupt slam of wood rocked through her as he

let her legs swing down. Closed in her bedroom. Why did it feel more intimate just because he'd closed the door? She shivered.

His hands cupped her face. Calloused thumb slowly brushing the corner of her lips. "Say no now, Belle."

She wanted to feel the hard press of his chest again against her breasts, but he held himself away, touching only her face. "Is that what you want me to do? Say no?" Moonlight shafted through her windows, painting the corner of her bed in its tender light. She reached up, unable to resist, and pressed her palm against the muscle flexing in his jaw. "Are you already regretting this, then?"

"No." He lowered his forehead, pressing it against hers. "But you can still change your mind. Now. If you do later…" His voice was low. Rough.

Her palm slid to his nape, fingers slipping through his silky hair. "I'm not changing my mind." Stretching up, she brushed her cheek along his. Whispered in his ear. "Not now. Not later." Not ever, she feared.

He exhaled sharply, and in less than a breath, there was no space for even a whisper between them as he turned to her bed. Settled her in the center of it. She felt the kiss of air on her abdomen in the moment before his lips displaced it as he drew down her jeans. It was like being dipped in fire. She scrabbled at his shoulders, but he caught her hands in his, fingers sliding between fingers, palms meeting palms.

"Let me." His lips brushed her thigh.

And then she wasn't being dipped in fire, the conflagration came from the inside out. Only when she was gasping, then crying out his name, did he slowly work his way upward. She knew she was shaking, but couldn't seem to bring order to her senses, couldn't seem to grasp anything solid or real, except him.

He caught her nipple between his lips, teeth scraping oh-so-gently. His thigh, hair-roughened and hard, notched between her legs. When had he gotten rid of the rest of his clothes?

Then his mouth slid along the column of her neck. His breath was rough. His heartbeat pulsing hard against hers. He slid one hand behind her knee, urging it higher against his hip and groaned softly as his flesh tantalized hers.

She arched, greedy for so much more, and he laughed softly, turning until she lay over him. She arched against him, so much emotion inside her that she feared she might never recover. "I need you," she whispered.

He went curiously still. "Do you?"

If there were any places inside her that hadn't been softened beyond hope where he was concerned, his tense, urgent expression found them. Her throat went tight. Her fingertips grazed the sharp lines of his jaw, her palm cradled his cheek. "Yes."

She could feel the muscle flexing in his jaw. Feel every muscle he possessed seeming to gather itself. Her heart sped, the world spun as he pulled her beneath him.

"Remember that," he said. His fingers fumbled with her ponytail, and then he was spreading her hair out around her. And when he was done, he found her mouth as he took her. Unerring. True.

She pressed her head back against the bed, hauling in a keening breath, feeling her emotions stripped bare. Wanting the moment never to end, wanting to hide from it forever.

He breathed a soft oath that sounded more like a plea. Her fingers curled, but he pressed his hands against her arms, smoothing upward until his palms met hers. Fingers linked. "Open your eyes," he whispered.

Such a simple act. It took all her strength. She looked

at him. At the naked desire burning in his eyes, in the tendons standing out of his neck, his shoulders. Pleasure flooded through her and she shuddered wildly, on the precipice of something deeper, stronger than she could have ever suspected. Her fingertips dug into his hands. And he moved again.

"Next time," he promised roughly, "I'm going to make this last all day."

She laughed, but the sound was thick, and helpless tears leaked from the corners of her eyes.

He made a soft sound, almost *tsking,* and drew their linked hands closer to her head, where he caught the moisture with his thumbs. His movements were suddenly, indescribably gentle. "What? Did I hurt you?"

She shook her head. "I feel you…in…my heart." Her voice shook. She pressed mindlessly against him. "Don't stop," she begged.

"Not possible." He kissed her again, conquering her mouth as surely as he conquered her body. Then he tore his mouth from hers, his breath harsh, and the sight of him, muscles cording, eyes hot with need, sent her that last, infinitesimal distance and she went screaming into the abyss.

He went with her.

# Chapter 16

Belle tucked her hand beneath her cheek and lay quietly in her bed.

Early-dawn light was sneaking through the window, slowly creeping over the foot of the bed and the tangle of sheets and blanket. Any minute, she expected Cage to wake.

But for now, for now she watched him sleep. As he'd been sleeping for hours.

His hair was tousled. His lashes thick and dark and still. There was no tension coiled in his long, strong body. There was only sleep.

It was a sight to behold, Belle thought. And difficult not to touch him. Not to let her hands drift over his wide shoulder. Sift through the hair on his chest and feel the slow, easy rise and fall of his breathing.

She didn't touch him, though. Didn't want to break his slumber.

So her eyes traveled where her hands dared not. Her body, aching in unaccustomed places, her senses, still alive from the feelings he'd wrought absorbed the close warmth of him.

What the future held for them was a mystery. We'll see what happens, he'd said.

She wanted to believe that left an open vista of hope. Needed to believe it. Her gaze drifted over his hand, thrown above his head, fingers lax. Palm exposed. His bicep, a perfect relief.

She closed her eyes, exhaling slowly. There was no objectivity in her appreciation of his male beauty. She couldn't admire him without wanting to touch him.

But he was sleeping. Soundly and undisturbed for the first time in Lord only knew how long. She carefully turned on her back. Then her other side. Gave the small clock sitting on her nightstand a baleful look and turned her face into her pillow. Another few hours and Cage would be wanting to collect Lucy. Champing at the bit to get back to the Lazy-B and the chores that waited for no man's weekend away.

Cage shifted. "Too far away." His voice was husky, full of sleep. A long arm slid around her from behind, easily removing the six inches of space separating them. She sucked in an absurdly needful breath as his hand flattened across her abdomen, pressing her back against him before sliding up and covering her breast. His chest felt hot against her spine and everywhere that she was soft, he was…not.

She snuck a glance up at him, but his eyes were still closed.

She attempted to do the same.

"Quit wiggling," he said after a moment.

Forget another hour of *z's*. "I can't help it," she whispered. "I'm not used to this."

His thumb roved lazily over her nipple. "This?"

Her blood was heating. Collecting. "Waking up with a man," she admitted.

His hand left her breast. Slid along her side, her waist. Cupped her hip. He hadn't seemed to notice the scars there the night before.

"Are you sore?" He wasn't referring to the long-healed ridges his fingers slowly traced.

"Are you?" she challenged, if only to pretend she wasn't mortified.

His chest moved against her back and she realized he was chuckling, soundlessly. "Cage—"

"Shh. Relax." He pulled her hair aside and kissed her shoulder. Slid his hand along her thigh. Lulling. Drugging. Then his hand was between her thighs. And he sighed, a sound of such deeply basic appreciation that she melted even more. He kissed her shoulder again. "I want you. Every night. Every morning."

She was swimming in pleasure.

"Marry me, Belle."

She couldn't have heard right. "What?"

Then he moved again, pushing her leg forward just enough to find, to take. Sinking himself into her so smoothly, so sweetly and gently that he stole her heart all over again.

"Oh, yeah," he murmured. "This way. Every way. Marry me."

She arched against him, taking him even deeper. Twisted her head, looking up at him. "You can't mean it." It was supposed to be women who got their emotions all tangled up with sex. Love. It was happening to her, for pity's sake. It wasn't supposed to happen to him.

But it was.

And his eyes were dead serious. Passion pulled at him, she could see it. Feel it. But he was…serious.

"I want all your mornings," he said evenly. "All your nights. Say yes." He covered her mouth with his and her heart simply cracked wide.

"Yes," she breathed into him.

His arms surrounded her, holding her tight as he rocked into her.

It felt as if he'd rocked right into her soul.

They showered separately. Not because either necessarily wanted to, but because he did need to collect Lucy and get back to the Lazy-B, not spend another endless session drowning in Belle.

There would be plenty of time for that, later.

Much as Belle would have preferred to sit beside him on the long drive, her hand pressing against his leg as if to remind herself of all that had occurred suddenly and not so suddenly, practicality managed to assert itself and having her own vehicle at her disposal was only sensible.

And it gave her more time to pack a real suitcase. To let…everything…sink in a little more.

Cage Buchanan wanted to marry her. And she'd agreed.

When she arrived at the house, Cage wasn't in sight. But Strudel greeted her, barking and dancing around, and Belle hugged the dog, feeling as thoroughly and utterly content with the world as the dog. She lugged her suitcase in through the front door. Cage wanted to tell Lucy their plans together, so she knew he wouldn't have shared the news yet.

But there was no sign of Lucy in the house, either.

She lugged the suitcase up the stairs. Debated briefly where to unpack it. Settled on the guest room since she didn't really have the nerve yet to make herself at home in Cage's room.

She'd never even been *in* Cage's room. So after she'd quickly unpacked, she went in. Smiled a little at the hasty way he'd made his bed. Couldn't very well lecture his daughter about the habit if he didn't try to make his own, could he?

She walked over and picked up the photo beside the bed.

Lucy. Wearing a fancy little ballet tutu, in mid-pirouette. Her limbs strong and true, her face beaming.

Belle set the photo back in its place and went downstairs. Maybe the barn. She'd barely stepped out of the back door before realizing there was a car parked behind the house. A Porsche covered with a fine mist of dust. She eyed it and headed toward the barn.

She hadn't made it halfway when she heard Cage's raised voice, so angry it made the hair on the back of her neck stand up. "She'll have a mother!"

Belle quickened her steps only to stop outside the barn at the sound of her own name.

"Who? Belle Day? Come on, Cage. You really think you can pull that off?"

"She'll marry me."

A ring of amused, female laughter shattered over Belle. "So you'll finally have some revenge. Gus Day drives your parents off a road and finagles out of any sort of financial settlement, but now you're going to marry his daughter and have your hands on his money through her. And those rancher people, too. The Double-whatever. I'm told they are *very* well off. Not like my parents, of course, but—"

"Is it true?" Belle stepped around the corner of the barn to see Cage squared off with the woman from the pizzeria. He looked as if he'd been pulled backward through a knothole. In contrast, the woman looked perfect. From the top of her gilded head to the toes of her white leather boots.

And they both turned and looked at her when her tennis shoes skidded a little on the hard-packed ground.

Her eyes were green, Belle thought dully. And her face was Lucy's. Why hadn't she noticed that before? "Is that why you proposed?"

Cage's filthy mood at finding Sandi in the barn with Luce when he'd ridden back in after battling with a bawling cow and barbed wire went even farther south. He'd rather battle a mile of barbed wire than have to deal with this moment.

Belle eyeing him, clearly waiting for some explanation. Some *something*. "No," he assured flatly.

"Of course it is," Sandi said clucking, her voice dripping kindness. "You swore on your father's grave, remember? Told me all about it," she said to Belle. "How one day he would make the Days hurt as badly as the Buchanans had been." She looked back again at Cage. "Too bad your success doesn't really matter since Lucy's going to be living in Chicago with my parents. Talk about the original rock and a hard place, right, Cage? Which one to let go of. The ranch or the kid."

He was grateful that Lucy was still out of earshot in the stable where he'd sent her to feed the horses as he rounded on Sandi. "Get…off…my…land." His voice was deadly.

Finally, Sandi had the sense to back off. Her sense of self-preservation kicking in, no doubt because he was two inches shy of dragging her off his property by the roots of her hair and he didn't much care if he broke her neck along the way or not.

She strode toward the barn door. "Good luck with him, honey," she advised Belle. "You're going to need it. If you're smart, you'll rethink the whole marital-bliss thing. My parents will drive him up to his ears in hock if he's not there already, then walk away with Lucy as the prize when they're finished with him." She slid a key chain out of her white purse and jangled the keys. "Of course. He'll have a Day around to finally give him his due." Dust puffed a little around her high heels as she strode out of the barn.

Moments later, her car shot past, gravel and dust spewing from beneath the tires.

Belle was staring at him, her eyes wide. Wounded.

He raked his hands through his hair. He smelled like just what he was. A guy who'd been rolling in mud and manure. Dammit all to hell and back again. Their first day under his roof—together—wasn't supposed to be like this.

Sandi was supposed to be rotting somewhere and he was supposed to be able to pick his time to tell Belle about his legal hassle with the Oldhams and not send her running.

"You could have told me who she was."

"She doesn't matter."

"Of *course* she matters! She's Lucy's mother."

"I didn't think she'd have the nerve to come out here."

Belle's eyes narrowed. "Well she did. This is what all that correspondence with the attorney is about?"

"Yes."

Her chin trembled but she collected herself. "How bad is it? Really?"

"Bad."

"And you need money."

"Yes." The word nearly choked him.

"So." Her knuckles were white. "Everything...
Sandi—Lucy's mother—"

"Stop calling her that."

"It's true, though. Along with everything she said.
It's all true."

His hands curled, impotence raging through him.
"No."

"And I really played right into your hands, didn't I?"

He reached her in two steps, grabbed her arms. "It
*wasn't* like that."

"Oh?" She was pale. "Then you're going to tell me
that you proposed to me because you *love* me? I should
have known better. Realized that there was no way you
could have changed so much in these weeks, these last
few days. Stupid me." She shrugged out of his hold and
ran out of the barn, heading toward the house.

He practically tore the screen off its hinges going
after her. Followed her up the stairs and into the guest
room. She was shoveling stuff into her suitcase.

He grabbed a handful of sports bras and threw them
back out onto the bed. "What I feel for you has been
coming on for longer than these past few days and you
damn well know it. You're not going to leave like this."

"Really? Do you think you can stop me?"

"I love you, dammit!"

Her hands paused. Shook. Then she scooped the contents out of a drawer and tossed them in the suitcase, her
motions stiff. Jerky. "And you never once thought, well,
hey, I can make use of this woman? Never, not once?"
She waited a long beat. "I didn't think so."

Was he damned forever? He grabbed her shoulders. "It was before I knew you. Really knew you."

"And what about my family? What about if we did—" She broke off, her face a struggle. "If I married you. Then what? You're going to accept my mother? My sister? We're all *Days*. They're my family and they're as important to me as yours is to you."

"Jesus Christ, Belle. The past is the past. I know that. And you're in need of leaving it behind as bad as I am."

"Maybe, I am," she agreed.

"Then we can make a new family. Together. Nothing's changed!"

She stepped away from him, her expression closing. "Everything's changed." She flipped the suitcase closed, despite the edges of shorts, shirts hanging out, and dragged it off the bed. "And just to clear things up. I have *no* money to speak of. When my dad died, my mom had to work just like a million other people to keep a roof over our heads. I went to college on scholarships, not on trust funds. *I* work because I need a paycheck. So, I guess I wouldn't be all that useful to you, after all." She walked out of the room. Thumped her way down the stairs.

His hands fisted. He glared at his old iron-framed bed. Kicked it.

It groaned.

He caught up to Belle before she reached her car. "You love me. Need me. You meant those words, Belle. I know you did."

She threw the suitcase into the passenger seat. It bounced open, spewing its contents. "I'll get over it," she promised thickly, and yanked open the car door, sinking down behind the wheel only to stare at it, mute frustration screaming from her. Her palms slapped the steering wheel and he realized she didn't have the keys.

He blocked her from opening the car door simply by planting himself there. She'd have to climb over the mess of clothes or him to get away. "Don't leave me."

Her head tossed, hair rippling. "Why? Because of Lucy?"

"Because of me."

Her mouth parted. She shook her head. "I don't believe you."

"Goddammit, Belle—"

"Ohmigod." She grabbed the top of the windshield and hoisted herself up in the seat. "Cage. Lucy—"

He caught a blur of motion, the moment seeming to turn to stone in his head. Turning to see what put the horrified expression on Belle's face. Lucy on Satin's back. Struggling to keep him reined in.

He swore and raced out ahead of the horse, aiming straight at him. In some distant part of his mind he heard Belle scream. Maybe it was the horse.

Maybe it was Lucy who was falling, falling. All over again, even before he could get close enough to snag the beast's reins and drag him under control.

Belle scrambled past him, reaching Lucy first. She huddled on the ground, her hands carefully, gently running over his baby. He fell to his knees beside them.

Satin raced off, hell-bent for leather.

Lucy's eyes were open, tears streaking her face. She tried to move and cried out, clutching her leg and Belle hoarsely ordered her to be still.

His daughter glared at him, her face set in rigid lines. "I heard you guys yelling in the barn. You're sending me away to live with them, aren't you? Just like my mother said."

"No. I won't let it happen."

"She told me she was here for my birthday. That she tried to get here the other day, but she was stuck in an airport in France. But that wasn't it at all, was it?"

He shook his head, wishing he'd been smarter, wishing a million things, all of them too late. "I'm sorry, Lucy."

She angled her eyes over at Belle. "Were you really gonna marry my dad?"

Belle didn't answer that. She looked at Cage, but didn't look at him, and it was worse now than it had ever been in the beginning. "I'm calling Sawyer. We need to get her to the hospital but I don't think we should move her." She touched Lucy's hair gently, then pushed to her feet, running like the wind toward the house.

Lucy closed her eyes. A sprinkle of freckles on her nose stood out, stark against her white face. "I don't wanna be a dancer, Dad. I don't wanna be anything like my mother."

He folded her hand in his. "You will dance," he said roughly, "and you will ride and do all the things you love, and you have *never* been like her. And I'm not letting you go anywhere you don't want to go. Clear?"

She started to nod, groaned.

Belle returned, blankets in her arms. "The medivac's on its way. Twenty minutes, max." She knelt next to Lucy, spreading the blankets over her. Held up her fingers for Lucy to count, making comforting noises.

Then the chopper arrived, settling out in the field. Same place as it had done seven months earlier. Only then, it had landed on a skiff of snow.

Cage and Belle ran alongside the stretcher they quickly loaded Lucy on. He ducked low, avoiding the blades that had barely stopped rotating. Belle hung back, already moving away from the clearing. She didn't need to be told there was a premium of space inside the helicopter.

One of the techs was telling Cage to finish fastening his safety harness. He did so, watching out the side as the helicopter lifted. The wind whipped Belle's hair in a frenzy around her shoulders as they left her behind.

As far as hospitals went, Weaver's was pretty small. Cage had paced from one end of the building to the other about a million times over before Dr. Rebecca Clay finally reappeared after closing herself with his daughter behind a series of doors some bull of a woman in starched whites had dared him to cross.

The slender brunette held an oversize folder in her hands and he knew from experience they contained the X-rays Lucy had just received.

The doctor smiled at him and gestured at the row of hard plastic chairs lining a sun-filled waiting room. "Let's sit," she encouraged. "Lucy's doing pretty well. No signs of concussion. I want to keep her awhile just to be cautious. A few days."

He stared, waiting for the big *but*. "What about her leg?"

Rebecca sighed a little. "There are no fractures, which is a good thing. We've immobilized it for now. But she has done some damage. How extensive, I couldn't tell you. She'll need to see her orthopedist. I know you have a perfectly fine one, but George Valenzuela from the Huffington Clinic has agreed to come up and consult, if you'd like. Belle called him while you and Lucy were on your way in. He specializes in pediatric cases. But you don't have to decide anything right now. We've given Lucy something for the pain."

She patted his hand. "They're getting her settled in a room. I'll have someone take you to her."

He nodded. An hour later, he was sitting beside his daughter's hospital bed. She was sound asleep, her leg back in a brace similar to the one she'd worn for so many weeks after her first round of surgery.

He called his house but there was no answer. Called a dozen times throughout the night. His house. Belle's house. The cell phone she avoided as often as not.

By morning he faced it.

Belle was gone.

But if she thought things were over between them, she didn't know him as well as he'd thought.

*Chapter 17*

Cage eyed the row of men. And women. When he'd driven up the circular driveway of the Double-C Ranch, they'd all turned to watch, seeming to form a line. A significant line looking incongruous against the backdrop of colorful balloons tied by ribbons to nearly every stationary object.

"They don't look real happy to see us." Lucy's voice was subdued.

He hadn't figured showing up this way would be easy. "They invited you weeks ago to Angel's birthday party. It's not you they're not happy to see," he assured her. And, he reminded himself, Belle had visited Lucy each of the three days she'd been in the hospital. Avoided him like the plague, true, but she'd come all the same.

The driveway was congested with dozens of vehicles, not all belonging to the various members of the

Clay family, he figured. Their reputation for throwing a celebration was well known, and it wouldn't have surprised Cage to count nearly half the population of Weaver as present.

It was the first time Cage had ever been to the Double-C Ranch, though. For any reason.

He didn't bother with trying to find an open place to park. There were none, so he just stopped his truck close enough where Lucy wouldn't have to drag her brace around any farther than necessary.

Even though there was music riding the air, right alongside the distinct smell of grilling meat that would've made his mouth water if it hadn't already been filled with crow, it still seemed as if a silence settled over the throng as he and Lucy slowly crossed an oval stretch of green grass toward that line of people.

"I don't see Belle." Lucy muttered an aside, looking worried.

Neither did Cage.

"Hey, Lucy." Ryan Clay grinned, seemingly unaware of the collective stares of his parents—Sawyer and Rebecca—aunts, uncles and grandparents as he walked into view, a plate in his hand on which a tower of food wavered dangerously. At sixteen, he was the oldest of Belle's nieces and nephews and the brown-haired kid with his father's blue eyes seemed to take the role with due seriousness. "Nice hardware you got on your leg there. Does it come off? 'Cause some of us're heading out to the swimming hole in a while and we wouldn't want you to sink." He jerked his head, assuming that she'd follow.

Lucy cast a look up at Cage. "Go ahead."

She needed no second urging and slowly worked her way toward Ryan.

Which left Cage facing that line of people alone.

He focused on the slender, auburn-haired woman who stood at the center. Gloria Day. Gloria *Clay*. And of all the men there, eyeing him with various degrees of warning, it was facing her that struck him the hardest. He walked closer. Until he could see the strands of silver in her auburn hair and the gentle lines beside her eyes that were the same shape and size as her daughter's, if a different color. They were the lines of a woman who'd done a lot of smiling in her life.

Definitely not in evidence now.

"If you've come to bring your daughter to celebrate with us, you're welcome," she said after a moment. "But if you've come to cause my girl more heartache, you can turn right on your heel and go."

"Give the boy a chance to talk, Gloria." Squire stood beside his wife and Cage could see the speculation in the man's squinty gaze before he turned his focus back to the fat wedge of cake on the plate he held.

Cage pulled off his hat and got to it. "I've nursed a grudge for a long time, Mrs.—" get it right "—Clay. Way back, it was sometimes the only thing that got me through another day." He figured he imagined the speck of sympathy in her eyes before her lashes swept down. "And I'm willing to admit that I managed to make a comfortable habit out of blaming your late husband for things. When you married Squire and moved up to Weaver—well, I let it bug me more than I should have. And I'm sorry for that. For a lot of things."

"I don't need your apology, Cage." Gloria looked up at him. "Nor do you need mine. What happened all those years ago was a tragedy. So, if that's all you came to say, then—"

"It isn't." A lifetime of fending for himself, on his

own, struggling to keep what was his clawed at him. "I'm in love with your daughter, Mrs. Clay. And it's the first time I've ever *been* in love. The kind of love that matters. The kind that'll last a person their whole life if they're smart. And up to now, I've pretty much made a mess of it. I know I'm a stubborn man."

"He's right," Squire put in conversationally. "Cussed stubborn. I've offered plenty for that pretty piece of property he's got many a time and it took him until—"

"Squire," Gloria chided. "Hush up."

"What?" He looked around, innocence personified, which nobody bought because Squire Clay's craftiness was too well known. "I'm only agreeing with the boy. He's stubborn." He lifted his fork and pointed before stabbing it into his cake. "But he's got gumption, too. I'll give him that."

Damned if Cage didn't feel his neck getting hot. He'd had a meeting or two with the man over the past few days. But he hadn't bared any more thoughts than necessary and he hadn't said squat about Belle. It wasn't Squire he needed to get square with.

It was Gloria. "And I'm proud," Cage went on, determined to get through this even if it killed him.

"Too proud, I'd say."

He jerked, the sound of Belle's voice ripping a layer of skin off his soul. He turned and there she stood in a skinny red top and narrow black jeans. Want slammed hard in his chest and it had nothing to do with the physical.

"You cut your hair."

Her hands flew to the shoulder-length strands as if she wanted to hide that glaring fact. Then she straightened and lifted her chin. "So?"

She'd done it because of him. There was no doubt

inside him. And it hurt. Not because he cared if she had long hair or short hair or no hair. But because he knew what she'd been trying to do. Amputate the memory of them by lopping off her hair.

He set his shoulders, his fingers digging into his hat. "I'm *too* proud," he continued evenly. If Belle wanted him to crawl, he'd crawl, but damned if he was gonna enjoy the process.

"And stubborn," she said, crossing her arms, staring down her nose.

He gave her a sideways look. "I believe that's ground I've covered already."

She sniffed and looked away. But her high-and-mighty act was just that. Because he'd seen her eyes. Looking wet and bruised as pansies after a hard rain. Knowing he'd put that look there made him ache inside.

Gloria lifted her hand, sighing a little. "Stop." She stepped forward, breaking the ranks, and continued until she looked right up in Cage's face. "How is your mother?"

It ought to have ripped, that question. And maybe it would have just a few weeks earlier. "She's doing well. Thank you," he tacked on.

"I'm glad. My husband would have been glad. He worried about you and her a lot. He tried to speak with you, more than once, to tell you how sorry he was. But he was also deeply concerned about intruding on your grief."

He hadn't imagined the sympathy in Gloria's eyes, he realized. But along with that was also a vein of steel. He was a parent, too, and he could respect that. He'd messed with her daughter. "I appreciate knowing that."

"He tried to help, financially. The money you thought came from your parents' insurance came from him."

Belle's *"What?"* was an echo of his own.

"I know it wasn't much," Gloria went on. "Not enough to have lasted out all these years for your mother's care. You've done that. On your own, I'm sure. Doing a fine job of it."

"Why are you telling us this now?" Belle stopped beside him, facing her mother. "Why, after all these years?"

"Because I think—" Gloria's eyes were thoughtful "—Cage is ready to accept the truth of it, now. Aren't you?"

He remembered the day the check had come from the insurance. "I fought the insurance company for months," he said. "Trying to get them to settle. They claimed my father'd let the policy lapse. Then I later got a letter. And a check. Saying they'd been in error." The lawyer he'd hired had finally come through. Cage had always figured the guy had kept on the case only so he could collect his contingency fee.

That money had done a lot of things, not least of which was getting Sandi Oldham on that plane to Brazil and out of his life. "The insurance company wasn't making up for an error, like I was told," he concluded swallowing down hard on that. It wasn't an easy pill.

Gloria shook her head. "Given your situation, and what he learned about you, Gus believed that you'd never have accepted the money outright from him. He knew that the only thing you wanted was for your parents to still be with you. And that was something he couldn't accomplish. No matter how much he wished otherwise. I never was sure it was the right way to handle it, but it was Gus's decision and there was no moving that man when he'd set his mind on something." Her lips curved a little. "I know a little bit about dealing with stubborn men," she added.

And the man's actions hadn't left much over for his own family when he'd died not three years later, Cage figured.

"I'm sorry." He was.

Her hand brushed down his arm in a soothing motion. "There's no need to be," she said quietly. Then she stepped back, folding her arms across her chest. Squire was there and she leaned against him. "Not about that, anyway," she said. Her gaze encompassed him and Belle. And he knew that Gloria already knew some of what he'd come to say. He doubted there were many secrets, if any, that were kept between herself and Squire.

He looked down at Belle. "I'm selling the Lazy-B."

Belle sucked in a breath as Cage's words penetrated the glaze she'd been dwelling in for days. "What? Why? To who?"

"Because it's time," he said.

Her eyes burned way deep down in their sockets. "You shouldn't have to sell the Lazy-B, Cage. It's your home. There must be another way to fight against the Oldham's suit."

"I'm not selling 'cause of them. I'm moving Lucy to Cheyenne."

She wrapped her arms around her middle, glancing over at the girl who was sitting in a lawn chair someone had given up for her, a hot dog in her hand that held nowhere near the interest that watching *them* did. "Have you *told* her that?"

His lips tightened a little. "Don't you want to know why?"

"No," she lied. "Have some food. There's plenty. If you can stand to eat anything touched by a *Day's* hands."

"Annabelle!" Gloria stared at her.

Belle's eyes flooded. Seemed they weren't eternally dry after all even though they ought to have been given the number of times she'd bawled over the past week. And she was making a scene, just exactly what Cage had to hate most of all, airing his personal matters in public.

Particularly *this* public.

"Don't worry, Mrs. Clay," Cage said evenly. "She's not saying anything I haven't thought at one time or another." His jaw slanted. Centered. "And I'm sorry for that, too."

Belle pressed her hands to her temples. "Maybe we should talk about this somewhere else."

"No," Cage said, shocking her silent. "Right here will do. I'm in love with you, Belle Day. I proposed to you once, but I'll keep doing it until you realize I'm not giving up on you. On us. You think I can't handle being a part of your family. Well, I'm here. And I'm not going anywhere until you can start believing otherwise."

She dropped her hands. Stared at him. All conversation had ceased. They could have heard the grass growing if they listened.

"I'm a simple man, Belle. And I don't have a lot." He made a wry sound, nearly soundless. "I've got…baggage." He looked over at his daughter and smiled a little. "And I'm not talking about that one, there, 'cause she's definitely the best thing I have going for me. Which I guess you know better than most. I've spent nearly my whole life fending for myself and opening up about it isn't my forte."

Belle gnawed the inside of her cheek as Cage stepped closer to her. His black shirt rippled in a sudden flutter of wind that tugged the tablecloths and dragged at the balloons.

"We can't change the past," he said. "It shapes us, but it doesn't have to define us. Luce and I are going to Cheyenne because that's where *you're* going."

"Says who?" she challenged thickly.

"That doctor you arranged to come up and consult on Lucy's case. Dr. Valenzuela. He said you're the best physical therapist Huffington's got and was mighty glad you were finally going to be back on staff."

"Well, gee." Her tone was stiff enough to hold up barbed wire. "Thanks for the validation."

"Is this a battle over *your* pride, then?" he asked. "Yes, Lucy can be treated at Huffington. But we're going to Cheyenne because of *you* and it doesn't have jack to do with your job, so get off your bloody high horse!"

She glared at him. "I'm interfering. I'm nosy. I'm riding high horses. What on earth could you possibly want with me, then?"

"God only knows," he said tightly, "because you're a pain in my heart like you would not believe. I married a woman when I was seventeen years old, but she was *never* part of my family. She was never my wife in any sense of the word. You're the only one I've ever asked to be, and you throw it in my face."

"You only proposed because you—" She barely managed to bite back the words. He'd proposed while they'd been making love.

"Because I wanted to spend my next fifty years loving you? Making a home with you?" His voice was rising furiously. "Giving Lucy a brother or a sister maybe? Watching them grow up with your brown eyes and your laughter? Yes, I should have told you about the custody suit. But it didn't have squat to do with my loving you and it still doesn't! Now are you going to marry me, or not? And don't be looking around for everyone's opinion, here. Because this is not between us and them, it's you and me, Belle."

She was shaking. "Could have fooled me," she whispered, "considering the way you're announcing it to all the world, here."

His eyebrows drew together. His tone gentled. He took another step nearer. "You want me on bended knee with all these witnesses to beg? Will that convince you?" He started to go down.

She shook her head and grabbed his arms, staying him. "I've never wanted you to beg," she whispered. "I just wanted you to love me."

"You have that, Belle." He slid his fingers through her hair, drawing it away from her face. "I've worked out this stuff with the Oldhams," he said quietly. "They took Satin back where he belongs."

"But…how? When? Isn't Lucy upset?"

"When you were hiding from me around hospital walls, and not answering your phone no matter what time I called," he murmured. "When it seemed I had to prove my feelings for you didn't have anything to do with anyone other than you. I did exactly what my attorney advised me not to do, and called them myself. And no. Lucy isn't upset. Now that the horse is gone she's stopped pretending she wasn't scared spitless of it. She thought she needed to be ready to ride, but she wasn't. When she is, when her leg is better, it might take a while to get her back in the saddle, but she'll get there with a horse she's not already afraid of."

She could hardly draw breath. "And what about the Oldhams?"

"I should have done it a long time ago. But there's that stubbornness of mine at work again, trying to prove

I can do anything and everything better than everyone else. They never wanted complete custody of Lucy. They just wanted to have the grandchild Sandi'd been denying them."

"And you believed them?"

"I did once they faxed me confirmation they'd dropped the suit. Came this morning." He patted his pocket. Pulled out a piece of paper and showed it to her. "If I hadn't been so stuck on pride and just let them visit when they asked, none of this would have happened. The gifts they sent. The horse." He shook his head. "But then we wouldn't have had a reason for *you*." His voice went a little hoarse at that and he cleared his throat. "In exchange, they can come and visit Lucy *at* the Lazy-B and she doesn't have to sneak phone calls to them, anymore."

"Oh, Cage." She could see the relief in his eyes as he slid the notice back in his pocket. Knew how deep the relief ran. "It was that simple?"

"Well." His lips twisted a little, and she knew then that it hadn't been quite so simple. "In this case it's the end result that matters," he said. "So you see. I'm here strictly on my own. No agendas. Nothing. Maybe nothing is the word you need to focus on, though. I've got some prospects once I finish the sale of my place and get my neck out of debt. It won't be like running my own spread, but I—"

*"We,"* she corrected huskily, catching his hand in hers, pressing it against her face. "We, not I, Cage. That's what families are about, aren't they?"

"We," he repeated slowly, as if he were testing the taste of it. The weight of it. "I guess they are. So is this a yes, Miss Belle Day? No changing your mind, no turning back. Will you marry me?"

She nodded. A tear slid past her lashes and his thumb caught it.

"Mrs. Clay?" He raised his voice, never taking his vivid gaze off Belle's face. "Do I have permission to marry your daughter, or not?"

"I guess you'd better," Gloria said faintly. "Or we might have a revolt on our hands."

Belle slowly looked past Cage's wide shoulders to see a horde of expectant faces. Her mother. Her sister. And then there was Lucy, who looked ready to vibrate right out of her shoes.

"Welcome to the family, son," Squire said blandly.

Cage's lips tilted and his eyes met hers. "I love you, Belle."

"I love you, too, Cage."

"So hurry up and kiss her already, 'cause I want to go to the swimming hole with Ryan and his friends," Lucy said loudly.

"She has kind of a smart mouth sometimes," Cage murmured. "Don't let it scare you off."

"Not in this lifetime," Belle promised.

"Now," Squire said. "About the ranch. Some details we gotta—"

"Hush up, Squire," Gloria chided.

He grunted.

"Don't let them scare you off," Belle whispered back.

His hands held a fine tremble as he cupped her face in them. His eyes gleamed. "Not in this lifetime," he promised.

And at last, Belle believed him.

Then he wrapped his arms around her and kissed her.

And neither one heard anything further.

# *Epilogue*

"Howard. Gorgon. Beowulf." Belle kept her voice low and watched Cage's lips turn up at the corners. Three months had passed since the day he'd shown up at the Double-C. Three months during which she found every opportunity to make him smile. She loved that smile.

She loved him. And each day that passed, she loved him more.

"Unique," he whispered easily, shifting in the folding chair. He looked over his shoulder, but there was still no sign of the bride and groom. "I hope our wedding doesn't last this long," he murmured. "I should have brought a book to read or something."

She contained a laugh. "You've been friends with Emmy Johannson for a long time. You *should* be here for her wedding. She and Larry are probably getting some pictures taken. They'll be here soon enough. Here. You can finish my punch." She nudged her cup toward him.

He took it. Drank it down. Even though he seemed calm, she knew he wasn't entirely comfortable. Emmy and Larry's wedding wasn't as large as theirs was shaping up to be, but it *was* well-attended. Since he'd proposed, he'd been a more frequent sight in Weaver, but this was the first time they'd attended such a thoroughly social event.

"Come on," she wheedled, tilting her head a little. Sliding her fingers inside the cuff of his handsome gray suit. "We'll be married soon ourselves and you *still* won't tell me your real first name. Don't you think you're taking things a little far? When we pick up the wedding license I'm going to find out, you know."

He caught her exploring hand, lifted it and kissed her knuckles. "I never kept it secret from you, Belle."

She sniffed, but they both knew it was more for effect than anything else. Then Hope—who was a teacher like Larry was—and Tristan rejoined the table. They'd been dancing.

Hope let out a breathy laugh. Her pregnancy barely showed yet, but she was the picture of health from her toffee-colored long hair to her gleaming violet eyes. "Lucy must have worked really hard to be ready for today without needing her crutches. She and Anya look so pretty in their bridesmaid dresses."

"Too grown-up if you ask me," Cage murmured, looking over to where his daughter stood. Lucy and Anya— dressed in matching long red velvet gowns—were surrounded by friends. Many of them male. He looked over to Tristan. He and Hope already had a five-year-old son. "If you two have a girl, you'll know what I mean."

Tristan grinned. His fingers looped through his wife's. "I've got nieces," he said. "So I already have an idea." He looked at Cage. "How's it feel to be partners with Squire?"

"He takes some watching." Cage looked amused. "He's got Double-C hooves grazing on Lazy-B land now."

"You'll buy him back out again," Belle assured. Knowing that Cage one day would. He was simply too proud not to. She understood that now. Understood so much about the boy he'd never really been allowed to be. And she was eternally grateful that he hadn't sold the Lazy-B outright. Not even to her stepfather who was currently circling the dance floor with her mother.

A commotion near the door of the church hall brought their attention around. Emmy and Larry had arrived. They didn't form a traditional receiving line, but went around to greet their guests in their seats. When the couple reached their table, Cage stood and gruffly bussed Emmy on the cheek and shook Larry's hand. "Congratulations."

Emmy beamed at Belle. "I know *you're* the one to get Cage here. Thanks."

"He wouldn't have missed Lucy being a bridesmaid," Belle assured. And Emmy had been one of the few people in Weaver he'd peripherally let into his life in the first place. It may have been more of necessity than anything else since she'd helped so much with Lucy over the years, but she knew he was happy for Emmy and Larry.

"Anya's so excited about going to New York with Lucy and the Oldhams next summer. I don't know which thrills her more. Seeing a Broadway show, or riding on the plane there." Emmy squeezed Cage's hand briefly. "Thanks for including her."

"Thanks for letting her go."

She smiled happily and with Larry's arm around her, they moved on to the next table.

Belle leaned toward Cage. "You've known Emmy since you were kids. Does *she* know your real name?"

The DJ had switched tempos and a slow sexy tune wailed from the speakers, heavy on sax and bass. Cage held out his hand for her. "You know my real name. Come on. I know you want to dance."

She did. But she'd been content to stay by Cage, believing he'd have no interest in it. She put her hand in his and he took her into the center of the swaying couples, ignoring the surprised looks they received. Then he pulled her into his arms. Two seconds later, she knew he wasn't just a shuffle-your-feet dancer. He knew how to dance. Properly.

"Don't look so surprised," he said after a moment, his eyes smiling. "My mom made sure I learned a long time ago. Did you think Luce gets her coordination all from Sandi?"

Belle shook her head. "She gets her heart from you," she whispered. And right now, *her* heart felt so full she was afraid it would start leaking out her eyes. "And how would I know your real name? You've only told me it's unique. What am I supposed to—" She broke off, suspicious at the glint of humor in his eyes, and realization finally dawned. "Oh. No. No way."

"It's an old family name," he said gruffly. "And I know it's—"

"Unique," she inserted. "All along, you've told me. Your name is actually *Unique*." She laughed. Pressed her lips together and giggled some more. "Please tell me we don't have to stick with the family name when you and I start having children," she finally managed.

"You don't have to do anything," he assured. "Except let me love you for the rest of my days. You're my life, you know," he whispered softly, for her ears alone.

She twined her arms around his neck and it didn't matter that they were in the middle of someone else's wedding reception. Her heart *did* overflow.

That's just what happened sometimes when a woman found everything she'd ever wanted with one very unique man.

"And you're mine, Cage Buchanan. You're mine."

\* \* \* \* \*

# JUST FRIENDS?

For my family.

# *Prologue*

It didn't turn out at all the way Evan had intended.

When it started out, it was just supposed to be a quick trip home during a break between classes. He'd known she'd be home, too, because he'd made a point of finding out. Subtly, of course. It had never paid to show one's cards too easily where Leandra Clay was concerned. She was too quick. Too smart.

Too…everything.

Fool that he was, though, in his determination to appear *any*thing but obvious, he'd invited his dorm-mate.

Jake sure in hell hadn't worried about being subtle.

One look at Leandra and he'd been a goner.

Evan's fault. If he'd told Jake he'd already staked out that territory, his buddy wouldn't have trespassed.

Problem was, Leandra hadn't been Evan's territory. *Never* had been.

So what had Evan done?

Nothing.

And now what was Evan doing?

Nothing.

Nothing except stand there in his suit and a tie that felt like it was strangling him, and lift his champagne glass the way all the other wedding guests were lifting theirs.

"To the bride and groom," he managed to say. "We wish them a lifetime of happiness."

Jake wore a tux, too, and Leandra looked like some princess out of a storybook in filmy white stuff from head to toe. Their arms were slung around each other, giddy grins on their faces.

They'd hardly let go of each other in the year since Evan had introduced them.

The couple drank to the toast, and to the others that followed, kissed softly, sweetly, and Evan turned away, downing the rest of his champagne. But no amount of alcohol was going to deaden the pain inside him.

He hadn't spoken his piece when he should have.

"Hey, you." Leandra had untangled herself from Jake and touched Evan's arm. "Don't go running off now. You've got to promise me a dance after Jake and I do our thing."

He had to steel himself against flinching. "I was just going to find more of your dad's fine bubbly."

Her gaze, as rich as the fudge pudding Evan's mom had made since his childhood, was sparkling and that sparkle was all for her brand-spanking-new husband. "I'm not sure I ever said thank you. You know. For introducing Jake and me. If it hadn't been for you, we'd have never met."

"What are friends for?"

She missed the dark note in his voice. Nothing in her world right now was dark.

She was Leandra Clay and she'd just married the man of her dreams.

She suddenly reached out and hugged him. A quick dip into sweet perfume and soft, rustling white gown. "Thanks." Then she was moving away again, heading back to Jake, never knowing that she was taking Evan's heart along with her.

No, things definitely hadn't turned out at all the way he'd planned.

# Chapter 1

He woke to the sight of a strange man standing in his bedroom.

"Son of a—" Evan Taggart sat bolt upright, grabbing the bedding around his waist even as realization hit that the young guy with the lumberjack's build wasn't *entirely* a stranger. Nor was the red eye of the television camera the guy held entirely a surprise, either.

He stifled the ripe curse on his lips just in time to keep it from being captured for all eternity—or at least the viewing life of a certain cable television reality show. "I've never been videotaped in bed, with a woman or without, Ted," he said grimly, "and I'll be damned if we're going to start here and now."

Ted Richard's grin was visible thanks to the annoying light he'd erected on a metal stand next to the bed, but he still didn't lower the camera. "The producer would be a lot happier if you *did* have a woman under those sheets. Marian would figure it'd be good for ratings."

Evan wasn't amused. "How did you get in here?"

"Leandra always says Weaver is so safe that nobody ever locks anything. Guess she was right."

*Leandra.*

Evan should have known. He squelched another oath, this time directed at Leandra Clay and her part in the farce his life seemed to have become over the past week. "Shut that thing off," he warned. If he hadn't been out nearly all night tending a sick bull, he would never have slept through an intrusion like Ted's.

Not that this particular situation had ever arisen before.

Ted still didn't lower the heavy camera from his shoulder. The distinctive red light on top of the thing stayed vividly bright. "Don't shoot the messenger, dude," he said easily. "I'm just doing my job."

Ted's *job* was to follow Evan Taggart around for six weeks for *Walk in the Shoes,* or *WITS,* the cable television show of which Leandra was an associate producer. "Nobody told me your job was to invade *all* of my privacy."

Ted still didn't seem fazed. Nor did the young guy seem inclined to turn off the camera. But he did turn his shaggy blond head when they heard the sound of footsteps on the stairs outside Evan's bedroom.

A moment later, the woman responsible for Evan's headaches of late practically skidded into the room. He got a glimpse of chocolate-brown eyes before Leandra turned her attention to her cameraman.

"Ted, turn off the camera. You shouldn't even be here." She hefted the enormous satchel that hung from her shoulder a little higher and raced a slender hand over her short, messy hair.

Evan grimaced when the cameraman obediently lowered the camera.

"I'll just go back to the motel and catch a few more *z's*," Ted said cheerfully. "Any changes to today's schedule?"

Evan caught Leandra's gaze skittering over him before she shook her head and stepped out of Ted's way. "Not yet. I'll see you later."

Ted nodded and took the heavy camera, his steps pounding far more loudly on the stairs than had Leandra's. A moment later, they heard the sound of a door slamming.

Evan raked his hands through his hair, wishing he'd gotten more than the two measly hours of sleep he'd snagged. He needed all of his wits about him when it came to dealing with Leandra.

Leandra, who was still standing there in his bedroom, twisted her hands together at her waist. "Sorry about that," she murmured.

For what? Bringing chaos to what was ordinarily a pretty peaceful life? Peaceful, just the way he liked it.

"I didn't send him." Apology turned down the corners of her soft lips. "And I came as soon as I knew he was here," she added. As if that made up for everything.

Peaceful, he thought. Whatever had happened to it?

He'd grown up around Leandra. *And* her siblings. *And* her cousins, and there were plenty of 'em. But what on God's green earth had he done wrong that every time he laid eyes on this particular Clay he felt a jolt?

Bad enough she'd once been married to one of his best friends.

Bad enough she'd chosen Jake over Evan in the first place.

"Well?" Her chin had come up. "Aren't you going to say something?"

She wore loose flannel pants covered in cartoon chickens and a pink long-sleeved T-shirt with *WITS* printed over her breasts. The shirt did nothing to hide the fact that the woman was graced with all the appropriate curves. A woman who looked as if she'd bolted from her bed almost as precipitously as Evan. If she hadn't, she'd have grabbed a jacket, at the very least.

He didn't need the evidence staring him in the face to know it was pretty damn chilly outside.

It was September. It was Wyoming. It was four bloody o'clock in the morning, and he had Leandra Clay's sexy body smiling at him through her shirt.

"I've never seen chickens wearing bunny slippers," he finally drawled. "That the style out in California these days?"

Her lips pressed together. "That's not what I meant."

He was sure it hadn't been.

And he was pleased with the tinge of red he could see in her cheeks as she turned off the blazing lamp that Ted had left behind.

Made him feel a little better at least.

Now he just needed to get her out of his bedroom.

Because it *was* 4:00 a.m. and she *was* Leandra Clay.

He grabbed the sheet and started to slide off the bed.

At the first sight of his bare legs, Leandra frowned and abruptly headed for the doorway. "I'll, um, I'll put on some coffee."

He grunted. At least that would be something useful.

She glanced back at him and he dragged the sheet around himself, managing not to bare his butt to her eyes.

She fled, her footsteps racing down the staircase.

If he'd needed any hint that Leandra wasn't the least bit interested in seeing his butt, he supposed he had it now.

He dropped the sheet back on the messy bed and went into the bathroom, slamming the door shut.

How in the hell had his life come to this?

The question required no searching thought when the simple answer was right downstairs putting on the brew.

He rummaged in the small pile of laundry he'd kicked into the bathroom the other day to keep the mess from being caught on tape. His clothes smelled of God-knew-what, but he pulled them on anyway, then went downstairs to face Leandra and her coffee.

But when he got there, the coffeepot still sat piteously empty.

"Thought you were putting on the java."

"I was. Am." She closed the refrigerator door with a soft rattle of bottles. "I can't find the coffee."

He opened the cupboard above the maker and pulled out the can. "Suppose you're used to some fancy brand you grind yourself."

She made a face but didn't answer. Which probably was her answer.

Evan knew good and well that Jake—his good buddy Jake—liked his coffee expensive and ground only moments before it was brewed.

Why would Jake's wife be any different?

*Ex*-wife, an internal voice reminded him. For all the good it did.

Evan was a fool. That's what he was. Pure and simple.

And God didn't protect fools by the name of Evan Taggart.

Punishment was the course, there. Punishment in

the form of a golden-haired wisp whom he still didn't have the good sense to say no to.

Now that sprite in question was eyeing him through the brown eyes that had always seemed too large for her heart-shaped face.

He dumped his simple, grocery-bought coffee into a fresh filter and shoved it into the coffeemaker. "You going to drink some of this?"

"If you're offering."

He pulled out the filter, added another scoop of ground coffee, and pushed it back in place. Before he could reach for the empty coffee carafe, she'd plucked it out of the sink and was rinsing and refilling it with water.

Their fingers brushed when she handed it to him.

He sloshed the water into the machine and hit the power button, not looking at her. A reassuring gurgle answered him. "I'm grabbing a shower before that peeping Tom comes back."

"Ted's not a pervert," she called after him as he practically bolted from the room. "He's doing what Marian told him to do."

"Then maybe Marian's the one who's twisted," Evan called back, heading up the stairs.

*What* had he been thinking when he'd agreed to be part of that stupid show?

What had she been thinking to approach Evan Taggart about *WITS*?

Leandra pushed her fingers through her hair, pressing the tips against her skull as if the pressure could relieve the throbbing ache inside. She'd figured that following the life of a good-looking veterinarian would be just the ticket for the show that had been her home

for the past eighteen months. She'd *figured* that veterinarian would be her ex-husband, Jake Stallings, who,
despite their divorced status, was usually willing to do
most anything that Leandra asked of him.

Jake was everything that her boss, Marian Hughes,
loved. Charismatic. Handsome. A veterinarian to a
whole host of pampered celebrity pets.

But for reasons known only to Jake, he'd refused
her request and reminded her instead about his friend
from college.

Evan Taggart.

Evan, who wasn't *only* Jake's old friend, considering Leandra had known him since they were tots. He'd
been as much a thorn in Leandra's youth as he had been
a friend, and he was the one who'd introduced Leandra to Jake when he'd brought his college mate home
one weekend.

Huffing out a breath, remembering that she hadn't
even brushed her teeth when she'd made her mad dash
over to Evan's, she went to her purse and rummaged
inside for her cosmetic case.

She could hear water rumbling in the old horse's
pipes and tried not to think too much about Evan upstairs in his shower.

It was bad enough to have seen him upstairs covered
to the waist in a rumpled sheet.

She'd found herself wondering just what he'd had
*under* that sheet. That, in itself was pretty darned disturbing.

She shook her head, trying to eradicate the image
and yanked open the little case. She found her travel
toothbrush and squirted toothpaste on it, then brushed
her teeth at the kitchen sink, washed her face and
streaked some water through her hair.

She had a pair of jeans and a shirt inside her bag, too, but she wasn't going to change into them until she'd had her *own* shower.

Which she would have back at her cousin Sarah's place, where she was staying for the duration of the *WITS* shoot.

She certainly wasn't going to ask Evan if she could cop a soak in his bathroom. The man had made it more than plain that he considered every moment they spent together an intrusion in his life.

She still wasn't certain what had made him agree to participate in the first place. Sure, they were friends from way back, and he and Jake were still buddies, but Evan's consent had been a surprise to her. A pleasant surprise, even. That is, until she'd arrived with her crew the week before and came face-to-face with how disagreeable Evan could be—disagreeable and disturbing.

But she was pretty desperate to have this shoot go well. If it did—no, *once* it did—she'd finally get out from under Marian's thumb and produce her *own* projects. And they wouldn't involve any shirtless hometown veterinarians, either.

The pipes overhead gave an ominous groan. Leandra looked up at the ceiling, half expecting the pipes to burst right then and there. But the ceiling—plain white with not a speck of dirt or a cobweb in sight—remained intact until the demand ceased and the pipes went silent. Rather than be caught gawking at Evan's spotlessly clean white walls, she hurriedly rummaged around in his refrigerator and cupboards and had the makings of breakfast well underway when he came back downstairs a while later.

"Smells good." He walked across to the waiting coffee. She wasn't sure if he meant his coffee or the bacon and eggs. "Mmm." She flipped the omelet with a toss of the pan and picked up her own mug of coffee, watching him over the rim.

At least he'd put on a shirt, even if it was just a white T-shirt that hugged every muscle from which good genes and an active lifestyle had graced him.

His jeans looked the same as the other pair he'd just had on. Except this pair was clean.

When it came down to it, all of Evan Taggart's jeans looked pretty much the same.

Well-worn and sexy as hell on him.

Drat it all.

She buried her nose a little deeper in her coffee mug and reached for the spatula again.

*Now* was not the time for her libido to kick back to life after years of lying unconscious.

As far as Leandra was concerned, she preferred the unconscious state. Life was a lot less complicated that way.

She tipped the omelet onto a plate, drizzled hollandaise over it, then added toast and several slices of bacon and held it out to him.

He stared at the plate as if he'd never before focused those brilliant blue eyes of his on such a thing. "Jake always said you weren't much one for cooking."

"Is that going to keep you from eating it?" She gently waggled the plate. "It's only bacon and eggs."

"Fancy eggs." He lifted the plate out of her hand and set it on the square oak table that he'd shoved against one wall of the kitchen. Presumably to make room for the modern playpen that took up a good portion of the center of the kitchen. The playpen was currently empty, but Leandra knew it was for babies that weren't of the human variety. A few days earlier, it had contained a lamb. "You made enough for yourself, I hope," he added when she just stood there like a bump.

Spurred, she began dishing up her own plate. "Girl's gotta eat." She settled herself across the table from him. "Hope you don't mind that I made myself at home."

The corner of his lips twitched. He angled a look at her from beneath long eyelashes that were practically pornographic. "I'm eating, aren't I?"

He certainly was.

She watched him bite off a corner of toast and looked down at her own plate. Who needed a jacket in September when she was steaming from the inside out? She gulped down a mouthful of coffee and coughed at the intense heat.

"You okay?"

"Fine," she lied a little hoarsely. "And I *am* sorry about Ted busting in on you this morning. If that had been on Marian's schedule, I'd have talked her out of it."

"Marian's *your* boss. How would you plan to do that?"

"The same way I've talked her out of a few other ideas. How long was Ted here filming you?"

"Long enough to be satisfied when he left."

Leandra couldn't deny the truth of that. The guy had been perfectly agreeable about leaving. Which could mean that he'd gotten whatever shots Marian had been after. "At least you were alone."

He gave her a measuring look. "Oh?"

She was appalled at the way her stomach dropped. She hadn't stopped to consider the fact that Ted had clearly been filming for more than a few seconds. Had Evan had company who'd absented herself before Leandra came riding to her supposed rescue? "*Weren't* you?"

His expression didn't change and her nerves tightened even more. "Yes," he finally said. "The only ones upstairs who didn't belong there were you and your cameraman. And a helluva sight he was to wake up to. So how *did* you know he was here?"

Relief loosened her tongue. "Marian told me when we were speaking this morning."

"You talk to your boss before four every morning?" He made it sound like an accusation.

"I do when she's calling from the East Coast, where she's filming another project, and is a few hours ahead of me."

"That why you're still in your pajamas? You jump out of bed to come rescue me, Leandra?"

Her cheeks went hot again. The truth of it was, once she'd heard that Marian had set Ted, unscheduled, upon Evan, she had pictured just that. Which was ridiculous. "You're the least rescue-needing man I know," she said truthfully. "And this outfit doesn't have to be pajamas. It's pants and a shirt."

"Right."

She decided not to argue the point. After all, she *was* sitting there in her pj's.

"So, where *did* you learn to cook? I know it wasn't at your mother's knee. I remember Emily moaning about the fact that you were always too antsy to stand still long enough to listen to anything that concerned the kitchen."

"There's the problem working with someone you knew while growing up." She wasn't exactly thrilled with the notion that Evan knew so much about her.

"Well, if I hadn't known you growing up, do you think I'd have agreed to this damn situation?" He raked his hair back with long fingers. The short strands were still damp from his shower, and they stood out in gleaming blue-black spikes. "Tell me again why this show is so important to you?"

"All of the stories we've done for *WITS* are important to me."

His sharp focus didn't budge from her face.

"Well, okay, the series focusing on you is a little more important. Do you have to debate every single thing I say?"

"Not *every* thing. The breakfast was good."

"Small mercies," she murmured.

"Which you didn't explain, by the way."

"Nuking bacon and tossing together an omelet doesn't require an advanced degree."

He dragged his toast through the hollandaise sauce. "This sauce stuff didn't come out of a mix."

She shrugged. "Just more butter and eggs and a little lemon juice. No big deal. What's with all the lemons you have in your fridge, anyway?"

"My folks shipped them back while on vacation in Florida. And no changing the subject."

"I learned a few tricks when I was in France."

He went still for a moment.

France. Where she and Jake had gone on their honeymoon. And where Leandra had returned four years ago after their divorce. After they'd lost Emi.

Fortunately, Evan broke the tight silence when Leandra found herself unable to do so.

"Guess if you're going to finally learn to cook, France is one place to do it."

"I didn't take a class. I just picked up a few things from Eduard."

Evan's eyebrows rose. "Ed-wa-ahrd?"

"Don't give me that look."

"What look? You're a grown woman, Leandra. Free to take up with some French guy if you so please."

She rose, gathering their plates to take to the sink. She wished she'd never brought up the topic of France.

"Does Jake know you met some guy over there?"

The plates clattered against the sink as she set them down. She flipped on the water and it splashed hard against the dishes, spattering the front of her T-shirt. "There's nothing for Jake to know. We're divorced, remember? We have been for several years now."

"Yet you still went to him about doing this show before you came to me."

Her nerves felt like a match had been lit against them. It'd never been a secret that Evan hadn't been her first choice where *WITS* was concerned. "What's the matter, Evan? Feeling second-best?"

It didn't matter that Evan's one-time crush on her felt about a million years ago; not when it had been inspired just because he'd been fighting with his girlfriend—who'd happened to be her cousin, Lucy. Leandra still felt catty the moment the words left her lips.

He didn't look fazed, though, when he leaned his hip against the wood cabinet about a foot closer to her than was comfortable. "I guess if either one of us were worried about that, we wouldn't be here, now would we." His deep voice was smooth. Friendly. Easy.

Yet…not.

She frowned, feeling off-kilter. And she didn't know why. Evan had never been serious about her despite that one time when he'd claimed otherwise. He'd been too busy being in love with her cousin. Only Lucy had gone on to New York after high school for a career in dance, and Evan had never been serious about anyone since.

Particularly in college when, according to Jake, Evan

had become a complete love-'em-and-leave-'em kind of man.

"I'll take your silence as agreement with me," he said after a moment. He reached past her and shut off the water, his arm brushing her shoulder as he did so.

She barely managed to keep from jumping out of her skin. "I'm not worried about a single thing," she assured him.

His lashes drooped for a moment, as if he were studying something. "Good. Thanks for breakfast."

Then he handed her the dishtowel that was folded over a knob, and walked out of the kitchen.

Leandra squeezed the towel between her hands and tried to ignore the unfathomable shivers that were sliding down her spine.

What *had* she been thinking?

## Chapter 2

The sun had still not quite risen when Leandra returned to Sarah's place. The little house was located in the center of Weaver, across from a park and the high school. The bungalow had been home to Leandra's various aunts, and now Leandra's cousin called it hers.

Not until now, though, had Leandra ever appreciated the charm in the little place.

No, she'd been too busy wanting to get *out* of Weaver to understand some of the nicer aspects of her hometown.

She parked behind the house near the garage and let herself in the back door. Like Evan's place, it opened right into the kitchen and again, like Evan's, it was as unlocked as it had been when Leandra had bolted out of it earlier.

She tried to be quiet as she dumped her purse in the second bedroom and padded into the single bathroom, where she flipped on the shower and waited for the hot water to steam up the small room. She felt cold to the bone.

She hadn't exactly dressed for a cold morning trek over to Evan's, after all. *That* was why she still felt haphazard shivers attacking her.

No way were they caused by Evan Taggart himself.

She stepped under the streaming water, nearly groaning with relief as the hot needles stung her skin.

"I thought I heard you leave already." Sarah's voice rose above the rush of water, breaking through Leandra's dazed heat-giddiness.

Leandra looked around the tastefully striped shower curtain to see her cousin peeking around the corner of the door. "I did. I'll just be a sec. I know you need to get ready for school."

Sarah pushed the door open farther and entered. "Sorry," she said as she flipped on the faucet and reached for her toothbrush. "Have a parent meeting before school this morning. Time's tighter than usual."

Leandra ducked back under the shower, which ran even hotter now that Sarah was using some cold water, and rinsed the shampoo out of her hair. "I'm the one who should be sorry. I could have stayed at the motel with the rest of the crew and not put you out."

"You are *not* putting me out." Sarah's voice was muffled by the toothbrush. "Idiot."

Leandra made a face and hurried through the motions. When she turned off the shower, Sarah tossed her a thick towel over the shower curtain. Leandra quickly toweled off and wrapped it around herself, then stepped out so her cousin could take over occupancy. "All yours."

"Where *were* you earlier, anyway?" Sarah reached beyond the curtain and turned the water back on.

"Evan's." She dragged her fingers through her hair.

"In the middle of the night?" Sarah looked amused. "Anything you need to confess to Auntie Sarah?"

Leandra just shook her head as she left the bathroom. "I'll put coffee on if you've got the time to drink it."

"I always have time for coffee." Sarah's voice followed her down the short hall.

Sarah was a Clay, too. For the most part, the Clays were all inveterate coffee drinkers.

Leandra quickly dressed and started the coffee. The grind-your-own-beans kind that she'd sent Sarah the Christmas before. There was a half pot brewed by the time Sarah entered the kitchen. Her long, strawberry-blond hair was twisted into a thick wet braid that roped down to the middle of her back. She wore a loose-fitting knitted beige sweater over an ankle-length red skirt and looked exactly like what she was—a somewhat prim elementary school teacher.

Only Leandra knew her cousin wasn't *all* prim and proper. They'd been thick as thieves while growing up, after all. "Here." She handed Sarah a tall travel mug filled with black coffee.

"Thanks." She took a sip, winced a little, and set the mug on the small kitchen table. "So, what was the deal with Evan? He trying to back out of the show?"

"He might hate every minute, but I'm not worried about him doing that. It's been a long time since I moved away from Weaver, but I doubt Evan has changed in *that* regard. Particularly when the first episode airs in a few days."

"True. He's generally a reliable guy. But in what other regard is he supposed to have changed?"

Leandra shrugged. "None."

Sarah looked skeptical, but she didn't pursue the point. "So, you're still going to be free tonight for supper, right? Family is all meeting at Colby's to talk about Squire's surprise party."

Squire Clay was their grandfather. "Friday night at Colby's. Wouldn't miss it for the world."

"Good. You've been so busy with the shoot since you arrived that hardly any of us have had a chance to sit down for long and visit with you." She grinned as she tossed a jacket around her shoulders and grabbed up her satchel. "Everyone's been bugging me to fill them in on all your latest, and I had to break their hearts by telling them there *has* been no latest, even for me."

Leandra felt a quick knot in her stomach. Not even with Sarah had Leandra been able to share everything over the past several years.

Not since Emi had died.

How could she? Sarah—nobody—could ever understand just what Leandra had endured.

Endured because of her own failings.

"I'll be there," she promised. "After spending a day shooting with Evan and my crew, I'll be *more* than ready to sit back and chill for a while."

"Well, I promise we won't make it too late of a night."

Leandra smiled faintly. "There was a time when late nights didn't stop us."

Sarah's light blue eyes twinkled. "True. But right now, you look like you need about twenty hours of sleep, my friend. And those days when we could play all night have passed me by. Too old, I'm afraid."

"Old? Please. We're only twenty-eight. I can still hold my own, even against Axel and Derek."

"I seriously doubt it. Particularly where Axel is concerned. I know he's your little brother and Derek is mine, but even *he* has said that Axel can wear him out. And they're the same age." She glanced at the round clock on the wall. "Gotta run. Hope things go well today."

Leandra hadn't even gotten her "thanks" out, before Sarah had hurried out the door.

She exhaled, her gaze slipping around the confines of the kitchen. Currently, it was painted in muted green tones. There were pretty pale yellow canisters lined neatly on the counter, matched in color by the place-mats on the table and the woven towel draped over the oven door latch. The only mishmash of anything was the collection of photographs sticking to the front of the off-white refrigerator door.

She hadn't looked closely at Sarah's collection before. Hadn't dared.

She still didn't really want to look but, for some reason, her feet inexorably closed the distance until she was standing only inches away. Her heart was in her throat. Nausea twisted at her insides. She felt hot and cold all at once as she looked.

Her mind automatically dismissed the tiny snapshots that were distinctly school photographs. Sarah's students, undoubtedly. And she really didn't pay much attention to the assortment of milestones marked by someone's trusty camera.

But the more she looked, the more she'd convinced herself that she did *not* want to see that beautiful, perfect face, the more she realized that the one face that was *not* captured here was the one face Leandra most wanted to see.

Her daughter's. Emi.

Eyes burning deep inside her head, Leandra turned away. She felt shaky and her stomach pitched even more turbulently.

Sarah had removed Emi's photographs.

There was no doubt in Leandra's mind that her cousin's refrigerator door had once been graced with many pictures of Emi.

Emi's birth had marked the beginning of the family's next generation. There had been dozens of pictures. Leandra had sent them herself. Taken them herself.

Her heart ached and she bolted for the bathroom, overwhelmed by nausea. But even after, huddling on the cool tile floor with a washcloth pressed to her face, there was no peace for her.

Coming home to Weaver, no matter how temporarily, was only making the pain inside her worse.

When she heard the distinctive ring of her cell phone from the kitchen, she dragged herself off the floor. There was only one caller programmed into her cell phone with that particular ring tone.

Beethoven's Fifth.

It had been Ted's idea of a joke when he'd been messing around with Leandra's latest cell phone to link the dramatic tune to their boss's phone number. Leandra hadn't had a chance to figure out how to change it. Given her propensity for losing cell phones at the rate of two or three per year, was it any wonder that she didn't sit down with the programming guide every time?

She made it to the kitchen and wearily pulled out one of the chairs as she flipped open her latest phone. "What's up, Marian?"

"Have you talked to that vet of yours yet about our problem?"

A fresh pain crept between Leandra's eyes. Only this pain, at least, was not one that tore her soul to shreds. "I don't consider Evan's love life our problem, Marian. That's not the focus of *WITS*. Remember?" Her tone went a little dry. "We're presenting his life as a veterinarian."

"Hon, if that were all we were doing, we'd call *WITS* a documentary. Not reality TV."

The only reason Marian wanted to call her show *reality TV* was because it sounded more contemporary. More appealing than a documentary series to her all-important demographic—women aged 24-35. The fact that *Walk in the Shoes* had been just that—a small, but relatively well-respected documentary series about people and the careers they chose—before Marian came on board over a year earlier was obviously unimportant to all but a few.

And arguing the point had been getting Leandra absolutely nowhere. "I'll see what I can find out." She crossed her fingers beneath the table. Childish, perhaps, but the best she could do for her conscience.

"Don't just *see,* Leandra. *Do.* This guy you found may be eye candy, but sweets only go so far. I want spice!" Marian's voice rose. "Either you find it for me, or I'll find someone who will." Marian let out a huge breath. "Now," she said more reasonably and Leandra could picture her sitting there, smiling through her big white teeth. "Are we on the same page here?"

Leandra grimaced. "I understand your page perfectly, Marian. Unless there's something else, I need to get on with it. We'll be taping again in a few hours."

"Fine. But don't forget. Spice, Leandra, *spice.*"

Leandra hung up her phone and shoved it in her purse. "Spice," she muttered. No doubt the reason why Marian had sent Ted unannounced into Evan's house that morning. A quest for *spice.*

"Artificial insemination. Ought to look sexier than it is."

Leandra frowned at Ted. It was late afternoon and

they'd been taping since midmorning. It was a toss-up who was more tired. Leandra and her crew set up on the outside of a small arena, or Evan and his, working with a showy black horse on the inside.

"Breeding horses is not just a business. There's an art to it." She kept her voice low, not wanting to add any more disruption to the day's already frustrating attempts. "And the insemination isn't happening right now, anyway."

"No, they have to get that black horse to shoot his—"

"Yes," Leandra cut him off. She'd been listening to jokes about the semen collection process long enough.

"Well, I guess you'd know all about it, growing up here."

*Here* was Clay Farm, the horse ranch that her father had founded when he and her mother had been newly married. "Mmm-hmm." She kept finding herself more distracted by the action they were trying to film than by her duties behind the scene. More specifically, she was more distracted watching *Evan*.

It was ridiculous, really. The man stood the same height as her own father, Jefferson, who was working alongside Evan. He wore similar clothing—dusty blue jeans and a T-shirt. His short black hair was slightly disheveled and there was definitely a hint of a five-o'clock shadow darkening his jaw—and it was only around two in the afternoon.

*What* was it about the guy that was so intriguing?

"Earth to Leandra."

She moistened her lips, dragging her gaze from Evan to focus on Ted. "What?"

"I asked if you'd ever done that to a horse?"

"Only a stallion," Leandra reminded wryly, ignoring her cameraman's suggestive tone, "and, yes, I've helped collect semen before. And before you start making comments, it's *business*. Big business. Do you know how high stud fees can run for a really impeccable pedigree?"

It was a moot question, since they'd been talking about such matters most of the day. Northern Light had yet to prove himself at stud, but his sire had commanded stud fees in the six figures. "They're having some problems with Northern Light there because he's never been ground collected before. He's inexperienced."

"Inexperienced?" Ted grinned slightly. "I'll bet it's more like he wants a warm body to snuggle up to instead of that cold tube thing Evan's holding."

"It's called an A.V.—an artificial vagina. Oh, heads-up," Leandra warned. "Howard is bringing out the mare again to tease Northern Light."

Ted trained the camera again on the group of men surrounding the stallion and started filming. Leandra stepped slightly away, watching Northern Light's reaction to the mare. His ears perked. The horse's gleaming black coat twitched. His tail swished.

Bingo, Leandra thought, smiling to herself as the horse tried to lunge forward against the teasing rail, wanting to get at the mare.

Her father, at Northern Light's head, kept the stallion from getting light in the front, making the horse resist his natural urge to rear up and mount something. Preferably the mare that had clearly, finally, spurred the young stud's libido.

Even Ted jumped a little at Northern Light's sudden interest, and in Leandra's memory, there were few occasions that managed to startle the cameraman. But, she was pleased to note, the camera didn't waver.

A nervous hand tugged at Leandra's elbow from behind. Janet Stewart, another crew member, was frowning mightily, looking worried about the sight of the half ton of horse flesh seeming to struggle against his handlers. The girl put her mouth close to Leandra's ear. This was only her second shoot, but so far Leandra had been pleased with the quiet girl's work. "The horse can't hurt the men, can he?" she whispered.

Leandra shrugged. The truth was, a stallion could crush a man if he chose. But she'd grown up around horses. She knew her father's capacity to handle the animals. He might be in his 60s now, but he was fitter than many men half his age. And she knew Evan's capacity equaled her dad's.

Evan, who happened to glance their way as Northern Light gave another thwarted lunge. The gleaming black tail spiked and they could all hear the horse's breath streaming from his nostrils.

Janet drew in a hissing breath. "Ee-uu-ww. Is he going to, uh—?"

Leandra frowned, putting her finger to her lips, silently hushing her. The answer to her production assistant's half-formed question was clear in the satisfied actions of the men as Northern Light's interest subsided in the mare still standing safely some distance away.

Howard, her father's oldest ranch hand, took away the collection tube carrying Northern Light's soon-to-be-pricey contribution to the breeding process. Leandra knew this particular specimen would only be used for analyzing. Leandra's father led Northern Light back into the shadowy interior of the barn, where he'd be closed in his stall with fresh feed and water until his next encounter with the A.V.

Evan's presence wasn't ordinarily required at such proceedings, but since he and Axel were co-owners of the stallion, he had a vested interest. As he headed toward them, his gait was loose-hipped and easy and in Leandra's mind, she envisioned the slo-mo and music that could accompany the movement once they put the piece together.

Eye candy, exactly as Marian had said. Oh, yes. Definitely eye candy.

"You realize that Northern Light was distracted by all of you over here." Evan directed his irritation straight at Leandra. "What took most of the day should have been accomplished in a third of the time. It's a wonder that Jefferson allowed you to even tape here today."

"I guess that's one of the perks about being the boss's only daughter." Her voice was as cool as his. She didn't appreciate the lecture, particularly when she was very much aware of the delay they'd caused.

Evan's lips thinned. He glanced at the camera. "I suppose you're still filming."

"That was the agreement, remember?" Despite that very fact, Leandra stepped closer to Evan. "Our crew follows your daily activities for a month and a half. How else can our viewers expect to *walk in your shoes?*"

"With boots," he drawled. "And I remember the agreement. Doesn't mean I have to love it. Definitely doesn't mean I appreciate extending that inconvenience to my *clients*. And daddy of yours or not, Jefferson Clay is one of my best clients. We're planning to breed one of his mares to Northern Light, and I'd still like him to stay one of my best clients even after you've taken your sweet tush off onto your next escapade."

"Cut," Leandra told Ted, barely managing to get the word through her clenched teeth. "Janet, you and Ted go over to the lab where Howard's working and catch what you can. There's quite a bit of science involved in this. You never know what might come in useful." She could feel her phone vibrating silently at her hip, where it was clipped to her pocket, but ignored it. She didn't have to guess hard to figure it was Marian. "Then we'll take a stroll through the horse barn and call it a day."

The idea of ending shooting even an hour early clearly appealed to Janet. Leandra knew she and Paul Haas, the other crew member, were planning to drive down to Cheyenne for the weekend. Both in their mid-twenties, they figured their free time would be a little more lively there than it would be if they remained in town. Ted, however, was staying put. He had a wife and a toddler back home in L.A. and, though he hadn't said anything specific, Leandra had the impression that things weren't entirely smooth between the couple. They'd all be back in Weaver on Sunday, though, in time to watch the show on television.

When Ted and the camera were no longer there as silent witnesses, Evan leaned his elbows on the metal rail between them. "You showing off that you're the boss, Leandra?"

"When it comes to this, that's exactly what I am."

"As long as Marian lets you be."

She stiffened, ignoring the jab. "Regardless, I don't need you taking me to task in front of my people just because you occasionally find this situation a little less than comfortable."

"Occasionally?" His eyebrows lifted. "Have *you* ever had a camera following you around all damn day? You don't know what it's like. You only know what it's like from behind the lens."

The fact that he was right didn't help her beleaguered conscience any. Nor did the phone cease vibrating. She snatched it off her belt, flipping it open. "Yes?"

There was a brief pause, then a short, masculine laugh. "Judging by your voice, I can tell you're happy to hear from me."

It wasn't Marian at all. "Jake." Leandra greeted her ex-husband. Evan's shadowy jaw cocked and he turned, stepping away from the rail. "I thought you were Marian calling. What's wrong?"

"Who said anything had to be wrong?"

"You don't usually call me when I'm on location." Her ex-husband called about once a month, insisting on checking up on her. He'd been doing it for as long as they'd been apart. At first, it had been simply painful. Then, it had been…simply simple. That was Jake.

They might not have made it as a couple—particularly after Emi—but that didn't mean that they didn't care about each other.

"As it happens, I was calling to see how Ev was doing."

*Ev* was twenty feet away from her now, joined by her father, who'd ambled out of the barn a few moments earlier. "Why? He's a big boy."

"Yeah, but he hates attention. You know that."

"Then he shouldn't have agreed to the shoot. I still don't know why he did. I know he regrets it. It would have been a heck of a lot easier if you'd agreed to do this, Jake. I would never have had to come to Weaver. You didn't even tell me your good excuse," she reminded him. "Just that you had a reason."

"I did. Do. So, put the man on the phone, would you? I need to talk to him."

"Oh, so that's why you called my phone," she teased wryly as she crouched down and slipped through the horizontal space between the wide-set metal rails. "Not to talk to me after all, but to your good buddy."

"At least from him I might get the straight scoop on how you're really doing." There was no joking in Jake's voice.

Leandra stopped next to Evan and extended the tiny phone. "Here, spy man. Your accomplice wants to talk to you." She jiggled the phone. "Jake."

Evan took the phone. "Yo."

Leandra grimaced and turned away.

Her father caught her gaze, his dark blue eyes unreadable. "You still talk to Jake?"

She shrugged and he fell into step with her as she walked away from Evan, heading toward the big, state-of-the-art barn. She didn't really want to hear whatever report he might be giving Jake.

The fact that there might be any *reporting* at all annoyed her right down to her bones. She was having lustful thoughts about Evan and *he* was merely keeping tabs on her for Jake.

"Don't worry, Dad. We're not getting back together or anything." There was too much water under that bridge. And Leandra wasn't up to emotional entanglements, anyway.

"Jake was—is a good enough guy." Jefferson's low voice was wry. "Maybe not good enough for my girl, but—"

She tucked her hand under her father's arm. At six-plus feet, he still towered over her. And though his blond hair had a good portion of silver now, it was still thick and often longer than his wife's shoulder-length hair.

"Nobody would be good enough to suit you, Dad."

"Me?" His lips quirked. "It's your mother who's the hard one to please." He nodded his head toward the slender, dark-haired woman who was striding toward them. "Tell her, Em," he said when she reached them.

"Tell her what?"

Leandra suffered a head-to-toe examination from her mother's all-seeing brown eyes. She was ten years younger than Jefferson, and more than once had been mistaken for Leandra's sister, rather than her mother. "He's claiming that instead of him, it's you who thinks no man is good enough for me."

Emily smiled. "Well, we both know what a tale your father can spin. So, how much longer are you going to be following poor Evan around? You know we're all going into town tonight to meet at Colby's, right?"

"Sarah told me."

"I really wish you could stay out here with us." Emily closed her arm around Leandra's shoulder. "I know it's not too practical during the week because of the drive, but what about the weekends?"

A part of Leandra wanted nothing more than to escape to the sanctuary of her childhood home. To sink into the comfort and care of parents whose love was a constant in her life. A bigger part of her resisted those very same things for fear that she'd never make her own way. "I'll still be working on the weekends," she told them truthfully. "We just won't be actively following Evan."

"Working on the weekends." Emily sniffed wryly. "Why does that sound familiar?"

"Because you grew up on Squire's ranch," Jefferson drawled. "And there ain't *no* time off on a ranch."

Emily tilted her head up, looking at her husband. "Oh, and you're so different from your father, are you?"

Jefferson closed his hand around his wife's hand. "Hell, yes. I'm nothing like Squire Clay."

Leandra snorted softly. Her mother laughed and her

father smiled before dropping a kiss onto his wife's forehead.

There was no way that Leandra could ignore the contentment radiating from her parents. It blossomed around her as surely as the sun rose and set. "I've got to round up my crew and get them back to town," she told them. "So I'll see you later at Colby's."

"Even if you're not staying with us, I'm glad you're here." Emily kissed Leandra's cheek. "It's been so long since you were home."

*Not since Emi.*

Leandra kept her smile in place, but it suddenly took an effort. And she knew that her parents were aware of that fact, which made the effort even harder. "I know. So…later." She hurried away from them, retracing her steps back to the small arena.

Evan, though, was nowhere to be seen.

Paul and Janet were busy loading up the rental van with equipment. "Looking for this?" Janet handed over Leandra's clipboard.

She hadn't been, but that didn't mean she didn't need the jumble of schedules and notes and other assorted items that were clipped together on the large brown clipboard. "Where's Evan?"

"He left a few minutes ago."

For some reason, the news startled Leandra. "When?" She hadn't noticed his pickup truck driving away from the ranch, but then she'd been on the opposite side of the barn, facing away from the road.

"A few minutes ago. We're still finished, right?"

"Right." Leandra realized she was looking in the direction of the road, as if she would be able to see Evan's departure. They probably wouldn't see each other until Sunday, when the show aired and the crew threw a promotional event in town to play up Evan's debut. The thought nagged at her, and she deliberately looked down at her clipboard. She was there to work and that was all. Work was good. Work was safe.

And amid her work was a big pink note, taped on top of her collection of pages. *Call Marian.*

She automatically reached for her cell phone.

Which she'd given to Evan.

"Don't suppose he gave you my cell phone before he left?"

Janet shook her head. "Nope. Sorry."

Well, if for no other reason than to retrieve her cell phone, Leandra would be seeing Evan before Sunday, after all.

"Guess you'd better lend me yours, then," she told her assistant.

The young woman handed it over and Leandra dialed Marian's phone number.

Even the prospect of talking to her half-sane boss *again* wasn't enough to dull Leandra's sudden burst of cheerfulness.

She wouldn't be waiting until Sunday, after all.

# Chapter 3

"Does your daddy know you still play pool?"

Bent over her borrowed pool cue and the side of one of the pool tables situated inside Colby's Bar & Grill, Leandra's stroke hesitated. When had Evan arrived at the bar? She angled her chin, looking beside her. "Does *your* daddy know you've taken up drinking beer?"

The corner of Evan's lips twitched. "I'd have to say he did since he's the one who bought it." His fingers were looped around the slender neck of the bottle and he tilted the bottom of it, gesturing. "He's at the bar over there."

Leandra followed the gesturing beer bottle. Sure enough, Drew Taggart was standing at the bar.

From Leandra's vantage point, it looked as if the only thing that had changed about Evan's father were the strands of silver threading through his black hair. He was talking with one of her uncles. Tristan Clay was as golden blond as he'd ever been, and standing there, the two men—one dark haired and one light—made a striking image.

"I thought you were going to Braden this evening." She distinctly remembered him saying as much that afternoon.

"Plans change." He shifted beside her.

"You said your parents have been to Florida?" She focused again on lining up her shot, instead of on his well-worn jeans.

"Got back yesterday."

The cue ball struck the racked balls with a satisfying *thwack*, scattering them nicely. "Were they gone long?"

"Two weeks." Evan set his bottle on the wide ledge of the pool table and pulled a stick from the selection hanging on the wall rack. Colby's might serve the best steak in town, but it was still a bar, complete with jukebox, wood floors, a very long, gleaming wood bar and a half-dozen pool tables. "They came back early. Because of the show being on television." His voice sounded disgruntled.

"I'll have to catch up with them and say hello," Leandra murmured, stepping around the table and lining up her next shot. She hoped Evan didn't get any grumpier about the shoot. She truly didn't like the idea of making someone miserable just so she could achieve her own goals. "Where's your sister been staying while they were gone?"

"Tris and Hope's. Though she's eighteen now. She could have stayed by herself at the house. Jake doesn't know anything about Ed-wa-ahrd."

Her shot went wide, the ball banking uselessly off the side cushion. She straightened, propping the end of the stick on the toe of her tennis shoe. "What did you do? Ask him about it when he called?"

"Yes."

An invisible band seemed to tighten around her skull. "I told you it didn't concern Jake. It doesn't concern *you,* for that matter."

"Sounding a little defensive there, Leandra." Evan leaned over and sank two balls in the corner pocket.

So much for her sympathy. She had an intense urge to smack him over the shoulders with her own pool cue. "And you are sounding pretty interfering there, Evan. What does it matter, anyway? Why do you care?"

He was studying the table, his head slowly tilting to one side, then the other. "Jake's one of my best friends."

"So out of loyalty to him you figure he needs to know about Eduard?"

He leaned over again, his movements with the pool cue infuriatingly confident. "Does he?"

Despite her intense concentration on them, the infernal balls didn't have the sense to thwart his rapid shots. They went sailing exactly where he wanted. At the rate he was going, he'd have the table cleared in minutes. "I've already said there's nothing for him to know. Why are you making a deal about this?"

"You're the one being closemouthed." Only the eight ball remained. He lined it up. A second later, it rolled neatly into the pocket. Looking smugly superior, he straightened.

"Bet you can't do that a second time."

His lips quirked, amused. "Bet I can. Don't forget, sport, I've been hanging out here at Colby's since before you moved away."

"Maybe I hit the billiard circuit in California."

"You're a rotten liar. Have been ever since you tried to convince Mr. Pope that you didn't cheat on that junior high math test."

"I *didn't* cheat!"

"Have you convinced yourself of that in the years since?"

"I don't have to convince myself of anything. I know what happened with that test whether Pope—or you—believed me or not." She walked around the table to the other side, facing him. "If you must know, it was Tammy Browning who was cheating off *my* test. I've never cheated on anything. And you're trying to side-step the bet. What's the matter, Evan?" She leaned over, propping her forearms on the side of the table. "You afraid of losing to a girl?"

"Wouldn't matter if you *weren't* a girl. How much?"

She rolled her eyes in thought. "Twenty."

"Sissy bet."

"Forty."

He waited.

"Fine." She pulled some of the cash from the front pocket of her blue jeans, counted through it. Slapped several bills down on the rail. "Fifty."

Of course, *now* the man smiled. Slow and easy. As if he'd been the one baiting her all along.

It annoyed her to no end.

"Rack 'em up, sport."

She made quite a production out of it. "What's with the 'sport' thing?"

He leisurely chalked the tip of his cue, watching her. "You're the one dressing like a Little Leaguer."

She looked down at herself. Blue jeans and a zip-front sweatshirt. Well, okay, she *was* wearing a ball cap with the show's *WITS* acronym sewn on it, but that was hardly a damning fashion statement. Most of the crew wore the caps. Even people around town were sporting them.

She captured all of the balls within the triangular

rack and rolled it back and forth, finally positioning it at the footspot. "Knock yourself out, Doc."

He hit a sound break, solids and stripes bursting outward in a rolling explosion. He waited until they all came to a rest, his blue gaze studying the positions.

"Getting cold feet?" Her voice was dulcet.

He snorted softly and leaned over to begin smoothly picking them off, one by one—and sometimes two—into the pockets. He didn't miss a single shot.

"Who taught you to play, anyway?" She silently bid her money a farewell.

"My dad."

"Figures. And I know he must have played plenty with my uncles during their misspent youth." The Clay brothers, and Tag, had all been notoriously wild teenagers.

"And your dad. He's one of the worst ones when it came to playing hard."

"Worst as in best," she muttered. Not once in her life had she been able to best her father at the pool table, whether it was the one housed in their basement or elsewhere.

"It's all Squire's fault." Sarah had come up to stand beside Leandra. "He's the one who taught his sons how to play in the first place."

Leandra nodded. "True." Their grandfather had raised his sons alone after the death of his first wife, Sarah, after whom Leandra's cousin had been named. According to the stories, he'd been a hard-nosed man with little softness afforded to his boys after his wife's death from giving birth to Tristan, their youngest. And then Leandra's mother, orphaned before she was even ten, had gone to live with Squire and all of those boys. And all of their lives had been forever changed.

Evan sank two more balls. The table was nearly clear

again, and Leandra's hopes that Evan would make even one small misstep were dwindling.

"He's going to keep running the table if you don't do something," Sarah murmured as she lifted her soda to her lips. She'd changed out of her schoolteacher clothes into jeans that were nearly identical to Leandra's. But instead of a shapeless gray sweatshirt, Sarah wore a pretty pink crocheted top over a matching camisole, and instead of scuffed tennis shoes on her feet, she had pointy-toed black boots with killer heels that made her look even more leggy than she really was.

And Leandra was beginning to feel decidedly frumpy. She turned on her heel, looking at her cousin. "What am I supposed to do about it? I already feel stupid for putting the money down."

Sarah shook her head slightly and her long hair rippled over her shoulders. "Distract him."

Leandra wanted to snort. Her cousin was a distracting-type woman. Leandra was not. She was not especially tall, nor especially curvy and her last haircut had been at the courtesy of her own hands because she'd been too darned busy to keep a hair appointment. "Just what am I supposed to distract him *with?*"

Sarah rolled her eyes. "Have you forgotten everything we used to know? You're wearing something under that sweatshirt, aren't you?"

"An undershirt."

"Is it completely disgraceful?"

It was thin, white and sleeveless. "It's clean."

Sarah laughed softly. "What would you advise someone on your show? And you'd better hurry up. At the most, he only has three shots left."

Frowning at the lengths she'd go to in order to save her fifty dollars, Leandra unzipped the sweatshirt and tossed it onto the nearby high-top table. Picking up her cue stick again, she sauntered around the table until she was opposite Evan once again.

She leaned the stick against the side of the table and braced her hands on the rails. "Want to go for double or nothing?"

He didn't even glance her way. "We could just save the time and have you hand over the money, instead."

Leandra rolled her eyes. Caught Sarah's gaze. Her cousin nodded encouragingly.

Swallowing an oath, she slowly moved around the table, taking advantage of the time Evan was spending as he studied the table and the not-so-easy position of the remaining balls. She stopped beside him as he began to line up his next shot and murmured close to his ear. "Maybe I think three times is not going to be the charm for you."

He jerked as if he'd been bitten. She almost chuckled at the comedy of the moment. But she managed to contain herself when he straightened again, not taking the shot after all, and she found her nose about five inches away from the soft brown shirt covering his chest.

Or, rather, the chuckle nearly turned into choking because the man was just too *male* for her stunted senses.

"What are you doing?" His voice was mildly curious.

She would not blush. She was a career woman, for heaven's sake. Blushing was not supposed to be part of her repertoire.

She still felt her cheeks warming and thanked the heavens that the bar was crowded and slightly warm as a result. She'd blame it on that. Much more palatable than thinking he could reduce her to a blush so easily.

Searching desperately for an answer, she spotted Sarah, who lifted her eyebrows slightly, meaningfully.

"Just cooling off," she assured. "Don't you think it's getting warm in here?"

His lashes drooped, his gaze moving over her from her face to her toes.

And dammit, she actually shivered. Shivered!

Maybe she was coming down with the flu. Maybe she was simply off her rocker. *That* was far more likely.

"Yeah, it's warm all right." His voice dropped a notch. "A hundred bucks? *You* sink every striped ball and I'll pay you a hundred bucks."

"Interesting idea. But this wasn't about my ability. It was about yours."

He set the bottom of the cue stick on the floor. The tip of it stood higher than Leandra's head. "I don't think either one of us question my ability." He took Leandra's hand and wrapped it around the shaft of the stick, keeping it in place with his own hand around hers. "Do we?"

There was a knot in her throat, making it difficult to breathe. His hand felt hot against hers.

"Well?" He prompted when she failed to answer.

She shook herself, snatching the stick and her hand away from him. Ignoring the faint smile that touched his wicked, wicked mouth, she turned to the pool table only to find that at least a dozen people had joined Sarah in watching them.

She felt her face flush even hotter.

Her parents. Her cousins. Ted. They were all there. Even the players at the other pool tables had gone silent.

Great.

"One hundred dollars," she said brusquely. "You sure you're good for it, Taggart?"

He cocked an eyebrow.

Making a face, she pointed the cue at the table. "Rack them up, then. Striped balls, any pocket."

While Evan gathered all of the balls in the rack, Sarah scooted next to Leandra. "You were supposed to be distracting *him,* remember?"

"Yeah, a fine idea you had," she muttered. "I'm going to make an ass out of myself, right here in front of everyone. Even Ted and his little camcorder, there."

Sarah glanced over at the cameraman. "I didn't even realize that thing he's been playing with all evening was a camera."

After more than a year of working together, Leandra wasn't the least interested in Ted and his penchant for electronics. Instead, she kept her focus on Evan's work at the table. He removed the rack with a goading smile, and waved his hand over the table, as if inviting her to humiliate herself.

"Just take your time," Sarah advised under her breath. "Remember everything we've ever been taught about pool."

The first thing Leandra had been taught was not to place a bet that she wasn't absolutely certain of winning.

She centered the cue ball over the headspot, settled her left hand on the felt, making a bridge for the stick and sliding it slowly back and forth, experimentally, as she focused on the leading ball of the rack.

"Gonna take all night there, sport?"

She drew back and let fly.

The racked balls exploded. Two balls, one solid, one striped, plowed into the corner pockets.

A couple of hoots followed from the peanut gallery. Leandra closed them out.

It was not so easy to close out Evan, though, as she moved around the table, studying the position of the remaining striped balls. He leisurely moved out of her way when she pointedly stopped next to him.

"Sure you want to try that shot?" His voice was solicitous. "You're gonna have to cut the eleven ball to get the right angle."

Shut up, she thought. She leaned over, lining up the

shot. He was right, though. She'd have to hit the cue ball into the striped ball exactly to one side of center in order to gain the forty-five-degree angle she needed for the ball to head toward the corner pocket. Narrowing her eyes, she drew in a breath, and made her stroke.

The balls clacked together and old eleven rolled right into the pocket. More slowly than she'd intended, but at least it dropped.

"That's my girl," she heard her father say.

"Five more to go," Evan murmured as she slipped by him yet again.

As a distracter, he was much more effective than she'd been. "I should have let Ted tape you snoring all night long."

"Who says I snore?"

She leaned over and sank two balls, slam bam. "Jake. You *were* college roommates." She straightened for only a moment before leaning over again. "Hope you don't need that hundred too badly, *sport.*"

He'd moved around the table, opposite her. "Did you know that I can see right down your shirt?"

She barely kept the tip of her stick from hitting the felt. Her skin prickled and she fought the urge to straighten. To press her hand against the scooped neckline of her T-shirt and hold it flat against her meager chest, just in case he was not merely spouting tripe.

Whether or not he could see down her shirt, she still felt her nipples tighten, and prayed that he wouldn't notice.

Three striped balls to go, she reminded herself, and she would get out of the bar, go home and not have to see Evan again until Sunday evening.

She set her jaw, kept her grip on the stick loose and stroked.

Only when the green-striped ball toppled into the pocket did she let out her breath.

"Looking a little stressed there," Evan murmured. "Sure you don't need a break?"

She rounded the table, knocked into his shin with the butt of her stick and smiled sweetly. "So sorry."

He merely lifted his beer bottle and sipped.

She envied him a bit. Her mouth felt parched. And when she leaned over for the next shot, she couldn't help but glance down to see how, exactly, her T-shirt behaved.

It was as snug against her torso as ever and when she looked up, the glint of laughter in Evan's expression was unmistakable.

He'd caught her looking.

She slammed the sixth ball into a corner pocket. Only one striped ball remained. But it had a nightmare position, nearly blocked by two solids and frozen against the side cushion.

She could hear the murmur from the peanut gallery and didn't dare look their way. Knowing the family as she did, she was afraid they might well be placing side bets.

"Feeling the pressure?" Evan leaned down on his forearms beside her, acting for all the world as if they were bosom buddies. "Not even sure I could make that shot, truth be told."

For as long as Leandra could remember, there had always been a haze of smoke clinging to the interior of Colby's. Now was no different.

Yet despite the smoke, she could still smell the fresh, clean scent that she was beginning to identify with Evan and *only* Evan.

"I can make the shot," she assured, lying right through her teeth.

He shrugged. "Maybe. Or you could just fess up about Ed-wa-ahrd, and we'll call it even."

She narrowed her eyes, ostensibly studying the table. "A person might think that your curiosity where Eduard is concerned has nothing to do with Jake, and everything to do with you."

"Maybe it does."

She bit down on her tongue, not at all expecting that admission. She'd just been tossing out the accusation to goad him.

"You going to give up, Leandra?" Ted's voice drew her attention. He had moved closer to the pool table from the high-top where she'd last seen him, and was holding up his palm-size video recorder.

Evan was still watching her.

And she had an unbidden vision of him lowering his head toward hers, brushing his lips across hers.

Feeling thoroughly unsettled, she shook her head in answer to Ted, but just as much to shake the image of Evan kissing her from her head, and lined up the shot.

The stripe missed the pocket by a good six inches. Smiling wryly, she turned to face the gallery, shrugging. "Them's the breaks," she said lightly as she extended the cue stick toward Evan.

What was she doing, thinking about Evan kissing her? The only time he'd ever kissed her had been on the cheek at their high school graduation.

She pulled her cash out of her pocket again and counted out another fifty, picked up the cash that was still sitting on the rail, and folded it all together. "There you go, Doc. Add that to your lunch fund."

Evan eyed the woman and the cash she was holding out. He didn't want Leandra's damn money. He *wanted* to know who the hell the French guy was and what he'd meant—or still meant—to Leandra. Loyalty to Jake was only an excuse.

A poor excuse, since Evan's feelings where Leandra Clay were concerned *weren't* exactly loyal.

But Evan knew what Leandra didn't—that Jake was engaged to be married again and he didn't have the *huevos* to tell his ex-wife about it for fear of hurting her even more than she'd been hurt. But if Leandra had been involved with some other guy, then maybe Jake could take off that particular hair shirt of thinking that Leandra was so damn fragile, and get on with his life.

And Evan could maybe get on with his.

When he didn't take the cash, though, Leandra finally stepped toward him. The top of her tousled blond head didn't even reach his shoulder, but he still swore he could smell the enticing scent of her shampoo.

Then she reached out and tucked the money into the front of his leather belt. "Enjoy the dough," she said smoothly, and turned away.

It was all he could do not to grab her by the shoulders and haul her up against him.

The fact that half the patrons of Colby's—including Ted and that toy-size camera of his—were watching, kept his hands firmly at his sides.

Then Leandra lifted her hands and addressed the crowd. "Don't anyone forget. Sunday evening at seven right here at Colby's to watch Evan's television debut!"

Evan endured the hoots and hollers and reminded himself that six weeks wasn't *really* all that long of a time.

He could survive it.

Maybe.

## Chapter 4

"You know what I like about Saturdays?" Leandra was stretched out on the couch in Sarah's living room. Her cousin was sitting on the floor, surrounded by school materials as she made lesson plans.

"Hmm?"

"The possibility of endless sleeping."

"Having Snow White fantasies again? Like the idea of those seven short guys?"

"As long as they're catering to my every whim?" Leandra smiled lazily. "Sounds okay to me."

"Sort of boring, though, laying there in the glass case, waiting for your prince to come and lay some lip on you."

What would Evan's kiss *be* like?

Leandra threw her arm over her closed eyes, mentally brushing at the thought, but it kept circling like some pesky mosquito buzzing around her head. "Well, note that I said the *possibility* of sleeping. It's nice to just ponder the whole idea of it. Not that I'll be doing it or anything. Too much work to do." Which reminded her that she'd forgotten all about her cell phone again.

Leandra would go to Evan's later and retrieve the phone.

She pressed her lips together, trying to stop the tingling.

Maybe she'd have developed some self-control over her wayward notions by them.

She turned on her side, propping her head on her hand. "Sounds like we'll have quite the crew around next month for Squire's birthday party." Before the ill-fated pool table episode, the family had gone over the developing plans while crowded around several pushed-together tables in the restaurant portion of Colby's.

"We still don't know if J.D. and Angeline will make it back from Atlanta. J.D.'s schedule is probably easier than Angel's, though, given the way she's on call so much."

Angel was an emergency medical technician in Atlanta. J.D. lived in that vicinity, too, working at some blue-blooded horse farm. "And nobody's been able to get hold of Ryan?" Ryan was the oldest of the cousins, serving in the Navy, like his father, Sawyer, had once done.

Sarah continued flipping through a project idea book. "Between you and Ryan, it's a toss-up who has been home to Weaver less."

"Well, I'd guess he'd win, since I'm here now."

"You're here because of the show. But we'll take what we can get. And it's ideal that Squire's birthday falls during your visit." Sarah set aside her book and propped her elbows on the coffee table in front of her. "So…you really like working in show business?"

"Documentary filmmaking. And, yes, I do."

Sarah watched her for a moment, as if she wanted to say something. But she just lowered her arms again and picked up her oversized book once more.

"What?"

Sarah shook her head. "Nothing."

*"What?"*

"Nothing. Really. I was just going to say that it is amazing the places that life takes us."

Leandra really didn't want to get into that particular discussion. Only pain colored that philosophy.

"Do you think if you hadn't gone to France you and Jake might have gotten back together?"

It wasn't quite the comment she was expecting, but it was easier than discussing Emi. "No."

"You two were crazy about each other."

"Yeah, but we never really managed to know each other very well before we got married. And when… when…things got bad, instead of helping each other through it, we blamed each other."

"I'm sure Jake didn't blame you."

Arguing the point now served no purpose. "I did." *I still do.* Leandra swung her legs down from the couch and pushed to her feet. "So is there anything I can help with around here?" The house was as tidy as a pin. The yard outside was even more so, seeming to lay in wait with its lingering summer colors before autumn truly hit with all of its glory.

"Not unless you want to come up with arts and crafts ideas for two elementary school classes."

Even that humorously meant offer made her hurt inside. "Thanks, but I think I'll pass." She brushed her hands down the front of her jeans. "I'm going to head over to Ruby's Café for something to eat. Do you want to go with me?"

"Not this time. I need to get this done. There's a meeting with the parent association this afternoon."

"They meet on Saturdays?"

"They do when half of them have to drive over from Braden."

Even though Weaver had grown considerably since she was a little girl—mostly because of the computer gaming business her uncle Tristan had started here—it was still at heart a ranching community. "Some things never change."

"If Justine has any cinnamon rolls, bring a few home, okay?"

"Will do." Justine Leoni was the granddaughter of Ruby Leoni, the café's founder. She was also the mother of Tristan's wife, Hope. And fortunately for the town, Justine had inherited not only the café after Ruby died, but she'd inherited her grandmother's ability to make the most delicious cinnamon rolls.

Leandra didn't bother with her purse. She merely tucked some cash into her front pocket—which unfortunately reminded her again of the previous evening—pushed her feet into tennis shoes and headed down the road.

There was no need to drive.

Ruby's was located barely two miles away and the weather was pleasant. Bright blue skies. Morning briskness giving way to the sun's warmth, hanging strong despite the steady breeze in the air. Leandra knew it wouldn't be long before that warmth was only a memory for the residents of Weaver. With the lengthening year would come shorter days, cooling temperatures, and in another month or so, there could easily be snow on the ground.

She looked across at the park as she walked along the street. Homes on one side, green grass on the other.

During the wintertime, there would be an ice-skating rink covering part of what was now the baseball diamond, where a handful of kids were even now tossing around a ball.

A young man was mowing the lawn in front of one of the houses she passed. She didn't recognize him.

Not surprising. There were a lot of people she didn't recognize anymore in Weaver. That's what happened when someone moved away and stayed away for years at a time.

The logic was sound. The feeling in the pit of her stomach didn't seem to care.

Sighing, she quickened her step, rounding the corner onto Main Street. She could see Ruby's from here. The door stood open to the fresh air, and when she angled across the road, waiting for a slowly passing car first, and walked into the café, she couldn't help but smile.

Here, everything was familiar. The only missing element was Ruby herself. But she'd died when Leandra was away at college.

The entire town had attended the diminutive woman's funeral. But Leandra hadn't returned for it, even though Ruby had been part of her extended family—great-grandmother to Leandra's aunt, Hope. No, Leandra had been too busy to come home for that event. Too involved in her studies, too involved in her own life.

She stepped through the doorway.

The first thing she smelled were the famous cinnamon rolls.

The first person she noticed was Evan Taggart.

He sat at a booth, facing the doorway, and, as if he'd been waiting for her arrival, he was watching her with not one wisp of surprise in his expression. She gave him a brief nod as she moved through the somewhat-crowded café toward the counter, but the casualness of the motion was belied by the butterflies that were suddenly batting around inside her stomach.

"Hey there, Leandra." The girl behind the counter smiled widely as she poured coffee for the patrons sitting at the counter in front of her. "You need to tell my brother that I should have some face time on your show."

"Tabby, if we put your pretty face on *WITS*, nobody is going to be interested in watching your brother," Leandra teased as she slipped onto the only vacant red stool at the counter.

Tabby dimpled. She really was as striking as her brother. "Yeah, that's what I was afraid of." She sighed dramatically, managing to deliver a plate of corned beef hash and eggs without spilling a drop of coffee as she continued topping off coffee cups. "You here for breakfast? Daily specials are up on the board."

Leandra glanced at the chalkboard that was propped on a shelf. It, too, was a familiar sight. The looping handwriting, though, was undoubtedly Tabby's. "Just give me the special," she said. "And a half-dozen cinnamon rolls to go for Sarah, if there are any left."

Tabby nodded. "I'd already saved in back a dozen for my brother. But you can have half. He won't mind."

Leandra wasn't so sure. She resisted the urge to look over her shoulder back at the booth where he'd been sitting.

"You want to join him, I'll bring your food on out in a sec."

No, Leandra didn't want to join Evan. But even as she told herself she wasn't going to, she was aware of more people entering the café. She was taking up a seat at the counter out of cowardly orneriness.

She took her coffee cup—flipped over and filled up by Tabby without a word—and headed over to Evan's booth. She was halfway there, and everyone in the café knew it, when Leandra's feet dragged to an abrupt stop.

The coffee sloshed over the cup's rim, stinging hot on Leandra's hand.

Evan wasn't alone.

A pint-size little girl sat opposite him in the booth.

She had striking blue eyes, creamy white skin and shining black hair that was as dark as midnight.

She looked like a miniature, female version of Evan, and the sight of her was a blow to her midsection.

She'd heard of Evan's niece, of course, but she hadn't expected to come face-to-face with her.

And she'd never known that she was so like her uncle she could have been *his* daughter.

Evan breathed a soft curse as he saw the color drain from Leandra's face. He was already moving out of the booth and heading for her when she seemed to sway a little, spilling coffee over her hand.

She looked up at him as he took the coffee cup from her. Her eyes seemed to dwarf the rest of her small face. "I'm sorry. I didn't expect—"

"I watch Hannah for Katy sometimes." Katy was his half-sister by blood and his cousin by marriage. Mostly, though, she was Hannah's mom.

She blinked once. Twice. "Right. Of course."

He could see the reluctance in Leandra's expression as it began edging out the shock that had encompassed her. He could also see that she looked decidedly shaky.

Jake had warned him that Leandra still found it difficult being around small children. But seeing it with his own eyes twisted something painful inside him. She looked like a wounded, trapped animal.

He didn't even think about it. He just slid his arm around her and nudged her down onto the bench, across from where Hannah sat, watching them both with her evasive way of viewing the world around her. "Hannah," he said calmly as he sat down beside the little girl, "this is my friend, Leandra. Can you say hello?"

She kept her gaze half-averted from them. "Say hello," she repeated obediently. Her thumb steadily stroked the wheel of the matchbox car she was holding, turning it again and again.

"Tabby." He caught his little sister's attention as she was bustling around behind the counter. "Can we have some more coffee over here?"

"Coffee here," Hannah repeated softly. She shifted, pressing her shoulder against Evan's side. He smoothed his hand through her shoulder-length hair. Despite the convoluted history entwining their families, she was a light in his life.

"I should be going," Leandra said.

"Wait until Tabby has a chance to top off your coffee. And when's the last time you ate? I heard you order the special. So unless you plan on walking out on the order, you might as well relax."

Her lashes shielded those dark, dark brown eyes. Bambi eyes, he used to think. Round, velvety soft and surrounded by lashes that were long and delicate, all at the same time.

Tabby arrived with the coffee carafe, saving him from his teenage, angst-ridden memories. "Your food will be up next, Leandra. Ev, you or Hannah want anything else?"

Hannah had made a typical mess of her toast and scrambled eggs, eating half of each and decorating the table with the other half. "We're good, Tabby. Thanks."

"No prob." She was moving off in a flash.

"For some reason, I'm always surprised at how good she is at this. Tabby's worked here for more than a year now, but it is still a surprise."

"Your thoughts have her perpetually stuck in pig-tails, playing with dolls?"

"Playing Little League baseball, more like. But, yeah."

Leandra's lips curved ever so faintly. The tiny smile was heartbreakingly sad, though. "I know the feeling."

He hadn't gone to California for Emi's funeral.

He should have.

He was Jake's best friend, wasn't he?

Something, though, had kept him away. And he'd never forgiven himself for that particular display of cowardice. But before he could form any words, Leandra was looking—somewhat stalwartly, he thought—at Hannah.

"How old are you, Hannah?"

She didn't look up from spinning the wheels on her little car. "Leandra is talking to you, Hannah," he prompted calmly.

"Talking to you," she repeated.

"It takes her a while to warm up to new people," he excused.

"I understand."

Did she? He wasn't all that certain. Leandra Clay may have grown up in Weaver, but he knew her life had been fairly charmed—at least until the devastating loss of her daughter. And now she worked on a show that followed veterinarians around, for God's sake. She observed life now, instead of living it.

"Four," Hannah suddenly said.

If Leandra was surprised by the belated response, she didn't show it. "Four is a fun age to be. I like your car, there. Is it your favorite one?"

"Yes. It's red." Hannah didn't look up as she replied.

"I like red, too."

Hannah's thumb spun the wheels. She didn't reply.

Tabby delivered Leandra's meal, as well as two neatly wrapped packages of cinnamon rolls, and disappeared just as quickly. Leandra picked up her fork, but didn't move it near enough her food to suit him. "How is Katy doing these days? Is she still in the service?"

"She's in Afghanistan."

Her eyebrows drew together, and he caught her sliding a glance at Hannah. "Scary," she murmured.

"Yeah. But she's supposed to be home soon."

"You all must be relieved."

He nodded. "Hannah's been staying with her grandparents in Braden while Katy's been serving overseas. She had been living in North Carolina near her base, but when she got sent to Afghanistan about a year ago, she brought Hannah here to Wyoming."

"What about—" she hesitated for a moment "—Keith?"

He was surprised she remembered the name, since he was pretty sure Leandra had never even met his half-sister's husband. "Yeah. Keith. He split a few years ago. Permanently."

"Will Katy stay in Wyoming when she gets back?"

He shook his head. "She plans to go back to North Carolina."

She slipped a glance at Hannah. "Does she visit you often?"

Not as often as he would like. "She spends a day with me now and then. Gives Sharon a break."

She was silent for a moment, studying him, as if she were trying to put together a puzzle she'd never before noticed. "You'll miss Hannah when she goes," she finally observed.

He didn't bother denying it. Just nodded and wondered darkly why the hell Leandra would sound so surprised by the realization.

"And your…Katy's parents. How are they?"

His lips twisted. "You mean Darian, I suppose."

"I mean both of them," she said.

Given the way her brown eyes had flickered, he doubted it. "Sharon is fine." If you didn't count her increasing propensity for pretending Hannah was just like any other kid around Braden and Weaver.

"And Darian?" Her chin had come up again in that way he remembered from days of old.

"My old man is the same as ever," he drawled.

Her lips tightened. "Drew is your dad."

Thank the good Lord. And he felt his usual tangle of guilt for feeling the way he did when Drew *was* his dad in every way that ought to matter. "Yeah, and we all know why that came about." Drew had married his mom after his half brother Darian had gotten her pregnant and left her flat.

Her eyebrows pulled together, making a crease in her pretty face. "Nobody in this town has *ever* thought that way."

He let that slide, since she was probably right.

His feelings about Darian were his own.

Didn't make it any easier to get rid of them, though.

"Is your grandmother well?"

"Other than that she still hates my mom, dotes on Darian, pretty much ignores Hannah and sort of tolerates the rest of us, she's fine."

"She never was the brightest of women," Leandra muttered. Her cheeks turned pink. "Sorry."

He shrugged. "Not everyone has grandparents like yours."

"Well, Squire is a one-of-a-kind man." Her lips curved faintly. "And Gloria's pretty much a saint."

"How're the plans for the party shaping up?"

"Good." She seemed almost as relieved as him at

the change of subject. "The trick of course, is to keep Squire from finding out. Not an easy task when practically the entire town will be turning out for the fete."

"He and Gloria are still out of town?"

She nodded. "I can't believe he's turning eighty-five." She didn't seem to realize that she'd forked up some scrambled eggs, and looked at the results with some surprise.

"But he's a *healthy* eighty-five."

"True." With nothing else to do with the food, she tucked the fork between her lips. Slowly drew it out.

He realized with an inward groan that watching Leandra eat was just one more thing about her that charged his batteries. But he was sitting in a bustling café, with Hannah leaning against his side. It ought to have been as effective as a cold shower.

But then again, this was Leandra Clay he was dealing with.

Or not dealing with.

And that meant that any reasonable thought processes were hard to come by.

She tilted her head slightly. The sunlight streaming through the window beside them caught in the wispy feathers of her funky hairstyle, making each strand gleam like it had been dipped in gold dust.

His fingers itched.

He ignored the desire to feel her hair between his fingers and smiled instead at Hannah. She smiled back.

Leandra took another forkful of food. "My family has been blessed that way," she said. "You know. Good health. Nothing bad happening."

"I wouldn't say nothing bad had ever happened."

"To me," she said. "But not to them."

He brushed a handful of crumbs away from the edge

of the table before they could fall on Hannah's lap. "You think that Emi's death didn't hurt them, too?"

He heard the breath she sucked in when he spoke her daughter's name. "I didn't say that." She stared at her forkful of eggs, only this time she didn't partake. She set the utensil ever so carefully down on the plate and shifted in her seat, pulling money out of her pocket. She dropped several bills on the table.

The interlude was definitely over.

"Hannah—" she looked at the little girl with a determined smile as she picked up one of the packages holding the cinnamon rolls "—it was very nice to meet you. Evan, I'll see you later."

He wanted to say something, to stop her from racing out of Ruby's. But whatever words that might have taken, he didn't seem to possess.

So he just sat there and watched her hurry out of the café. She barely slowed as she crossed the sidewalk and headed out into the quiet street, the package of rolls clutched against her chest like some sort of life preserver.

"She's sad," Hannah said suddenly.

"Yes," he murmured, still watching through the window. "She is." And though he wished he could help her change that, he was pretty sure that he was not the man to do it.

After all, they were just friends.

Weren't they?

# Chapter 5

"Axel, just do me one favor and pick up my phone from Evan's, would you?" She couldn't believe that she hadn't given the cell phone one single thought when she'd run into Evan earlier that morning.

Leandra's brother gave her a lazy look. He was sprawled on a kitchen chair in Sarah's kitchen, a can of soda balanced on his belly. "God, Leandra, are you that lazy? He's five minutes away."

"Exactly. It won't take you long. And as you can see—" she waved her hand over the pile of materials that had been delivered by courier about the same time that her little brother had meandered up Sarah's neat walk "—I'm sort of busy."

"So am I."

She lifted an eyebrow. "Doing what?"

"Enjoying the company of my errant sister."

"Think *errant* describes you more than me. You've

been out of college a year now, right? Still sponging off Mom and Dad?"

His lips twitched. "Damn straight."

She shook her head, amused despite herself. She set down her pen and focused on Ax. They had the same brown eyes, and though he was blond like she was, his hair was a much darker gold than hers. Only, in the irony of the universe, he not only had longer lashes than she did, his hair was thicker, too. He was four years younger than she was; she loved him to death, but she felt like she was a lifetime older than he was.

"You've spent the last year traveling around the world, seems like. So what *do* you plan to do? Seriously?"

"Maybe I'm already doing it," he said.

"Drinking cola?" Not even the diet kind. No, her brother was graced with a metabolism that didn't worry about that sort of thing, either.

"I work for CeeVid," he reminded her, and she was surprised at the hint of defensiveness in his voice. "Just because it's Tristan's company doesn't mean I don't earn my keep."

"I wasn't suggesting that. I just didn't think you got a degree in political science so you could ride a desk right here in Weaver."

"Some people like Weaver, Leandra. Not everyone figures it's a place to escape."

"I wasn't escaping. I was…living." And what would have happened if she *hadn't* left Weaver? Would she have been a better wife? A better mother?

If she hadn't left Weaver, she'd never have married Jake, so the questioning was entirely pointless.

"What's your phone doing over at Evan's, anyway?"

Because, twice now, she hadn't managed to remember the darn thing. "I loaned it to him yesterday out at the farm." It was true in a sense.

"Heard you sat with him this morning over at Ruby's."

She should have known. Her little brother had always had a bodily connection to the Weaver grapevine. "So?"

"Why didn't you get it then?"

"What does it matter to you?"

"You're the one who wants me to play errand boy."

She picked up her pen, determined to remain nonchalant. "Forget about it. I'll get it later."

"What'd you think of Hannah?"

She squelched a sigh. "Axel, I have *work* to do, here. Aren't there any available females around anymore?"

"I save that for later in the day, when the sun goes down and stars come out." His eyes gleamed. "So? What'd you think?"

She shoved her pen behind her ear and fixed her gaze on her brother. "I think she's a very pretty little girl who looks a lot like Evan."

"And Katy."

"Undoubtedly. They are related."

"She's autistic, you know. Hannah, I mean."

"I figured it was something like that."

"Did Evan say so?"

"He didn't need to. Some things I can actually discern for myself. Now, either go get the phone, or go drink soda elsewhere."

He jackknifed his legs and rose. "You haven't changed since you were ten, you know. Still bossy as hell." He rumpled her hair as he passed her on his way to the living room. "Dad would be proud that you're displaying the Clay genetic trait so well."

She shook her head, but she was smiling as she

turned her attention back to the production notes that Marian had sent.

There was a ton of work yet to be done on Evan's shoot, particularly with the first episode airing the next day. There was also a mammoth amount of work going on for the next series, set to feature a young cheerleading coach who was trying to break in to singing. The only problem was the girl—beautiful and wonderfully fit though she was—couldn't carry a tune in a bucket. There would be plenty of ear-splitting, wince-inducing footage of her efforts, no doubt.

Marian, currently filming it, predicted that the viewers would love it, and Leandra supposed there was some truth in that.

Thank goodness Evan's story wouldn't include anything so embarrassing. It wasn't as if she was exploiting any of his dearest dreams the way Marian was with Whitney Sanchez. But the business was weird. For all Leandra knew, Whitney could end up as famous as she'd ever dreamed as a result of *WITS*.

Leandra heard her brother's footsteps behind her. "Twenty bucks," she offered. "Easy money, Ax."

"I'm all for easy money," a voice—not her brother's—answered. "As proven by last night at Colby's. What's the gig this time?"

She looked around to see Evan standing there. Of Axel the rat, there was no sight. "Nothing," she assured him. "I hope you have my phone." Better to get it out quickly, lest she forget yet again. When it came to her thought processes around Evan, she was beginning to wonder about herself.

Fortunately, he pulled the small phone from his pocket. An action that *unfortunately* drew her attention to the shape of the man beneath the soft blue denim.

His fingers grazed her palm as he dropped the phone into her outstretched hand. She set it aside on the table, quickly looking away from him. "Thank you. Where's your niece?"

"Having a nap at my mom's. And I ought to thank *you*. That phone rings every hour on the hour, practically. Made me want to curse Beethoven's composing skills. It's no wonder you weren't in any hurry to get it back."

"I—" she bit off the denial that she *had* been anxious for the phone. How would she explain her reason for continuing to forget it was tied entirely to the way he had of scrambling her brains? "Sorry," she said instead. "It does ring a lot. Comes with the territory." Even as she said the words, the little phone vibrated against the table, and sent out its first tinny note.

He made a humorous grimace and turned out of the kitchen as she picked up the phone. "Hello, Marian," she greeted. "I got the courier pack. I'm nearly finished."

She held the phone a few inches away from her ear as her boss went into her latest litany. Through the doorway from the kitchen, she could see Evan standing in the small living room. He seemed completely out of place among the fine lines of Sarah's furnishings. He was much more suited to rustic woods and knobby fabrics than to Chippendale and English chintz.

"Dig up his old girlfriends," Marian was saying when Leandra belatedly tuned back in. "I'm sending a second crew to New York to get some background."

"Wait a minute. Why? For what?"

"Not for what. Who. Why did I have to learn from Ted that your hunky hometown vet had a thwarted love affair with a citified ballerina? You're holding out on me, Leandra, and I don't like it."

"Lucy Buchanan comes from Weaver, too," Leandra said quietly, not wanting Evan to hear. "And that story goes back way too far to be of interest. They dated in school, for heaven's sake."

"Well it's the only love life that apparently exists for studly Evan Taggart. Or maybe he's more of a dud than a stud. Is that it, Leandra? Is Evan more interested in the gents than in the ladies?"

Leandra pressed her fingers against her temples. "Marian, I can assure you that Evan Taggart is *not* gay. And even if he *were,* it would have no relevance to our shoot! *WITS* isn't about his sex life. It's about his career."

"Honey, if you haven't learned yet that *everything* is about sex, then you're in the wrong business."

"Maybe I am." Leandra's temper sizzled. Which was exactly the reason why she wanted to get out from beneath Marian's thumb. There were interesting stories and people all around the world. Informative, empowering stories. Stories that could change people's lives, even. And they didn't have to be steeped in titillation to be told. "But right now, this is where I am at."

"And don't you forget who put you there."

"Eduard put me here," Leandra reminded just as coolly. She'd been on the *WITS* crew longer than Marian had been.

The reminder was enough to silence Marian, for once. After all, Eduard Montrechet was the money behind *WITS*. Marian worked for him just as much as Leandra did.

"I'll send my production notes before Monday morning," Leandra said more calmly. "Is there anything else we needed to discuss?"

"Get them to me by tomorrow night," Marian

snapped, clearly still feeling a need to establish her authority. "Before the show airs. I'll probably have to work all night just to get things in order for Monday's taping."

"Fine." Leandra let the insult pass. "You'll have them by tomorrow night."

Her answer was a click. Marian had hung up.

Leandra sighed, closing the phone. Escape, she thought faintly. Just let me escape.

"Why are you doing this, Leandra?"

She couldn't look at Evan. Not yet. She lifted her shoulder and set aside the phone, keeping her attention on the schedules and lists and budgets that were spread across the kitchen table. "You have your living, I have mine. Thanks, again, for the phone."

"Why were you talking about Lucy?" He pulled out the chair beside her and sat on it. Sprawled, really, much the same way Axel had done. He picked up the cell phone and toyed with it, balancing it on end between his palm and the table top. "Can I only hope that you're thinking she'd be a subject for *WITS?*"

Following a New York City ballerina around would definitely be interesting—and it had definitely been done before, something that *WITS* tried to avoid. "Marian heard that you and she were high school sweethearts."

"And?"

There was no reading the expression on his face. His voice was calm, also revealing exactly nothing.

There was no point in prevaricating, even if she'd wanted to do so. Evan would know soon enough what was in the wind. "And Marian wants to pursue whether or not there remains any interest or involvement between the two of you." Her voice was flat.

His lips twisted a little at that. "The local yokel and the girl who made good?"

"Lovers thwarted by whatever reason."

"What do you think? That Lucy and I are thwarted lovers?"

She shifted, gathering pages together in a careful pile. "It doesn't matter what I think."

He didn't respond to that. After a moment, he stretched out a long arm and plucked one of Sarah's photos off the refrigerator. "Remember when this was taken?"

She glanced at it. Five girls. Five boys. The girls dressed to the nines and the guys looking like they wanted to rip off their bow ties. "Prom night."

"Weaver and Braden had to combine their high school proms. Only way they could get enough kids together to qualify as a prom."

"I remember."

"They still do it the same way, even now. Trade locations each year. One year in Weaver. The next in Braden."

"The trip down memory lane isn't necessary. I remember how it was."

"Do you?" He set down the photograph. It was facing away from Leandra, but she had no trouble seeing the image. Evan's arm had been looped around Lucy's shoulder. Except for those brief few weeks in high school when Evan had claimed to be crazy for Leandra, his arm had nearly *always* been around Lucy's shoulders. Even at that age, Leandra had known not to take the word of a guy who was in love with someone else.

"Of course I do." She signed her name to the bottom of Janet's latest expense sheet and added it to the pile, then reached for Paul's report.

Evan caught her hand, pen and all, before she could reach it. "You think Lucy and I were lovers? That I've spent all these years—an entire decade—pining for her?"

Her hand tingled. "I've already said that it doesn't matter what I think. Could I have my hand back, please?"

He ignored the request. "That I didn't have the wherewithal to go after a woman I wanted, even if it meant going all the way to the big...bad...city?" He finished with an exaggerated drawl.

"I don't know, Evan. Do you?" All the irritation she felt probably showed in the look she gave him. "You're the one who—with the exception of veterinary school—has pretty much stuck close to home. Unlike nearly every other single man of your age in this town, you're still unattached. Who *wouldn't* think you were pining for Lucy? For a while there in school, you guys talked about getting married, remember?"

"We were kids. That's all. And believe me. I usually do go after what I want." His fingers tightened on hers. "Sometimes the smarter thing is *not* going."

She frowned at him. Heat was seeping—no, it was tingling its way right up her arm. "If that's some sort of comment on *my* leaving Weaver, then—"

"Then what?" He leaned closer to her. "If you don't like what I say, Leandra, just what are you going to do about it?"

She was trembling. She was actually trembling. And there was no way the man could be unaware of it. "I'll give Ted his rein and he and his camera will dog every footstep of yours twenty-four-seven from now until we wrap."

A dimple slashed his hard cheek. His voice dropped a notch. He leaned even closer, until she could feel the whisper of his words on her face. "Why am I not the one shaking in my boots?"

She couldn't respond. Her head was blank.

No, it wasn't blank. It was filled with color. Sapphire-blue color.

Like his eyes.

And her head was filled with scent. Piney and lemony and outdoorsy.

Like him.

And she was filled with want.

For him.

His thick lashes lowered. He was looking at her mouth. She pressed her lips together, wanting to deny everything.

The moment.

The possibilities of what it would feel like to once, just once, have his mouth on hers.

"Whoops. Guess you really didn't hear me come in."

Leandra jumped back from Evan, staring stupidly at Ted, who was standing in the hallway, looking into the kitchen. "What?"

"Your brother was outside. He told me to come on in." Ted was grinning. "Didn't know I was interrupting something."

Her face couldn't possibly get any hotter. "You're not," she assured him blithely. "Have you finished your expense report, yet? I didn't see it in my stuff."

"That's what I came over for." He pulled a slightly crumpled, very folded-up piece of paper from a pocket on the side of his khaki cargo pants and handed it over. "Sorry it's late. To make up for it, I'll take your stuff to the courier when you're finished up to send back to Marian."

That was a particular task that would require a drive

over to Braden, since the local carrier's office was already closed. "Guess you decided hanging around town all weekend wasn't so interesting, after all?"

He looked slightly uncomfortable, but just shrugged. "So, we cool?"

"Yes. We're cool." Leandra unfolded the paper, glanced over it before signing and handed it back to him, along with a thick bundle of papers and several videotapes. "She wants it before tomorrow night."

"No prob." Ted grinned at Evan. "I'll let you two get back to it."

Leandra wanted the earth to open up and swallow her right then and there. Her mind, sadly, had no problem whatsoever conjuring a dozen scenarios involving a very specific "it" and she felt as if that particular fact might as well be tattooed on her forehead in flaming scarlet letters.

She turned blindly to the cupboards, opening and closing them. Dragging down a bowl. Scattering wooden spoons onto the countertop.

"Now what are you doing?" Evan asked.

What *was* she doing? Besides losing her mind and feeling like her body was on the verge of some sinful conflagration? "Baking." In more ways than one. At least in her current frenzy she'd pulled out a boxed cake mix, so the explanation held a modicum of credibility.

"Any particular reason?"

"I need something to do." She resolutely tore open the box, and it ripped right in two. The sealed bag of mix inside tumbled out. She tossed aside the box.

Did he really have to stand there watching her like he was?

Eggs. She needed eggs. And oil. Or something. She tried fitting the two pieces of the box back together. Yes.

There was a picture of three eggs. Thank goodness the instructions were excruciatingly elementary. Her mind was working on only two cylinders.

"Why are you acting weird? Jake also said you never baked."

She yanked open the refrigerator door and pulled out the egg carton. "Maybe I just never baked for Jake. Why are you so preoccupied with him, anyway?" Eduard. Jake. What *was* Evan's problem? She fumbled one of the eggs as she pulled it from the carton and it wobbled across the counter, heading for the edge.

He caught it easily, closing one hand over it. "You're nervous."

"I am not." She pushed her finger at his hand, wanting the egg.

"Yes you are."

"No I'm not! What are we? Five years old and playing in the sandbox?"

His lips quirked and even though she was irritated with him for some truly unfathomable reason, she couldn't help but respond. She gave a half laugh, shaking her head. "Could I please have the egg?"

"I'm not pining for Lucy." He took her wrist in his fingers and turned her hand, placing the egg in her palm. "Talk to her, do whatever." He folded her fingers around the egg, but didn't release her. "There's nothing interesting there."

What was interesting was the way she was suddenly short of breath again. "Why not?"

His thumb slowly stroked over the veins pulsing in her wrist. "Why not...what?"

She swallowed. "Pining?"

"For Lucy," he murmured. His thumb stopped moving, seeming to press directly over her pulse. "I said I wasn't pining for *her*."

She needed to pursue that. Marian would want her to pursue that. Only doing her job was not anything she wanted to be doing just then.

"Evan—"

He seemed to be watching the progress of his hand as it moved up her wrist to her forearm. A sliver of blue between thick black lashes. "Hmm?"

"What are we doing?" Her voice was barely a whisper.

His hand paused at her elbow, palm curling around it.

Her nerves tightened.

He looked at her. "Something I've wanted to do for a long time," he murmured.

And he lowered his head, covering her mouth with his.

# Chapter 6

Evan had kissed her once. A long time ago.

This was nothing like it.

This was not like anything.

His lips grazed hers, barely a whisper. One that sounded through her like a full-bodied orchestra. A soft sound came out of her from nowhere. She felt the egg rolling out of her lax fingers, and wanted to sink into him when his arm closed around her, pulling her close.

He caught her face in his hand, tilting her chin higher, and she dragged in a breath when he lifted his mouth for a moment. She thought she heard him swear, then his mouth was on hers again and the whisper had become a shout.

This was Evan. What was she—what were *they*—doing?

It didn't matter. Reason didn't matter. Her mouth opened under his, her hands dragged through his hair.

She couldn't get enough, couldn't get close enough and he must have felt the same for his hands dragged down her spine, caught her waist and she felt her feet leave the ground as he lifted her higher.

She gasped, and still he kissed her. Deeper. Hotter. Her mind spun as his belt buckle dragged against her belly. Her breasts flattened against his chest until she could feel his heart beating against hers.

"Yo, Evan."

Yes, this *was* Evan. How had she managed to miss this all the years they'd known one another? She wanted to wrap herself around him and absorb him into her very being.

"Yo, oh, *dude*." The voice turned pained. "Get a room, would you, please?"

Protest rose in her as the source of all things wonderful pulled his mouth away from hers. Just as rapidly, she realized that they were no longer alone.

Her forehead hit Evan's shoulder for a nanosecond and then she was scrambling away from him. Eyeing with some shock the way his shirt was half buttoned. The way his hair was disheveled.

Leandra didn't know if she needed to thank Axel for his interruption or strangle him. "What do you want?"

Her little brother was eyeing her with a thoroughly irksome amusement. "Don't shoot the messenger, Leandra. Evan's phone's been ringing for ten minutes, easy. We heard it all the way from his truck. Whoever is calling is pretty persistent."

Phones. What was the significance of all this *phone* business in her life?

Then it hit her. Belatedly, of course. That's the problem when a woman's mind—and body—was fogged with lust. The brain cells starting operating on half time.

*"We heard it,"* Axel had said. *We.*

She managed to focus beyond her brother to the man standing behind him. Ted. Well, it just figured, didn't it? If she were going to be found making a fool of herself, why not be found by a co-worker of hers as well as by her annoying little brother?

Evan wasn't saying much of anything, but he was watching Leandra. She wished she could tell what he was thinking. Feeling. Chagrined? Embarrassed? Thwarted?

She felt all that and more. And she didn't much like having witnesses to it. "Ted, the courier service closes in a few hours. You planning to make it or not?"

"Yeah, it's cool. Just got caught up talking with Axel for a few minutes." He was still holding the paperwork she'd given him. "I'll get going now."

The sooner the better, as far as Leandra was concerned. She looked at her brother. "I thought you'd left, too."

His lips twitched. "Obviously."

The man was enjoying her discomfort far too much. Clearly, their parents hadn't disciplined him enough as a child. "So…why are you still loitering around here?"

"Wanted to talk to Ev about Northern Light."

Leandra lifted her eyebrows. "What about him?"

"Has your name changed to Evan Taggart?"

She made a face. "Fine. Talk away. I have work to do, anyway."

"Leandra."

That was all it took. One utterance of her name in *his* low voice and she was melting all over again.

Yes, she definitely preferred having her libido in cold storage. Being at the mercy of it like this was more than her nerves could take. And having her brother as a witness was more than her pride could take. "I have to run to the grocery. For…um…oil. Sarah doesn't have any oil." She had no way of knowing that, since she hadn't looked, but as an excuse it would do since she was fresh out of imagination.

"Leandra." Evan held out his arm, stopping her dash from the room.

She looked at his hand, suffered an appallingly vivid image of those long, calloused fingers running over her bare flesh, and knew some creative cells were still in treacherous operation.

"I'll see you tomorrow. At Colby's for the party."

His lips twisted. "Don't know why there has to be a damn party just 'cause your show is going to be on television."

"There is a party because everyone in town wants to see *you* on TV for the first time," she countered. "We always do it. Good community spirit and all that. Ted will be filming, too." She skirted his hand, ignoring Axel and trying hard to ignore the narrow-eyed gaze of Evan's that followed her cowardly escape.

She drove her small rental, and instead of hitting the old grocery that had been located in the center of town on Main Street, she drove to the far end of town where all the newer establishments were centered around the sprawling structure that housed CeeVid.

There, the grocery store was nicely impersonal. There were no former schoolmates tending the shelves or parked at the soda fountain counter sharing the latest gossip. There were wide aisles and piped music and she could have been in any supermarket from California to Kansas.

She located the oil and paid for it, and back in her car once again found she was a chicken of such magnitude that she didn't want to go back to Sarah's just yet. It would be just like Axel to hang around waiting. And who knew what would be just like Evan. *He* didn't seem to be the man she remembered, at all.

Who knew he could kiss like that? Or that he could set her skin on fire just from a touch of his hand?

When she drove back through town, she passed Evan's two-story house. The clinic—larger than the house—was behind it, and she could see his dusty pickup truck parked in front of it.

Well, at least *he'd* gone home.

Ninny that *she* was, though, her foot hit the gas a little harder as she sped past. As if he were standing behind the big picture window just waiting to catch her driving by.

The man was probably just amusing himself with her. For no reason that made any sense to her, though.

He and Jake were really good friends, after all.

But Leandra and Jake were finished and had been for a long time.

She turned onto Sarah's street, trying to shut off the ping-pong debate going on inside her head, and coasted to a stop in front of the little house.

Just get through the shoot and move on, she reminded herself. This little detour in Weaver is just that. A detour. Another step on the path where her life couldn't be destroyed again by her own failures.

She nearly jumped out of her skin when someone knocked on the window right beside her head. Sarah looked in at her, concern drawing her eyebrows together as she juggled her book bag. "You okay?"

Her heart slowing again, Leandra nodded. She grabbed up the cooking oil and her purse and left the car. "I was woolgathering, I guess."

Sarah eyed the oil. "I hope that's for mundane purposes and not because *WITS* is heading off into previously unexplored adultlike directions."

"I was baking a cake."

Her cousin stopped in her tracks halfway up the walk. "No kidding. And you didn't see the oil in the cupboard?"

Leandra shrugged, her face warming.

Sarah grinned. "I ran into Axel on my way here. He told me you were here with Evan."

Her fingers flexed around the plastic bottle. "That's all he said?"

Sarah nodded and took the last few steps to the door. "That, and the fact that you had your tongues down each other's throats." She smiled brightly and opened the door.

"I'm going to kill my brother."

Sarah chuckled. Leandra followed her to the kitchen, where she dumped the unnecessary purchase on the counter. The eggs were still resting on the counter, uncracked.

Her cousin looked at the display. "Wow. You really *were* planning to bake a cake."

"Why is everyone so shocked by that fact? I cooked breakfast for Evan just yesterday."

Sarah dumped her satchel on the table. "And a surprise that was, too. Probably because you once vowed that anything to do with a kitchen—other than eating what came out of it—held no interest to you. So, what was it like kissing Evan?"

"Fabulous." The truthful answer came out unexpectedly and she felt her cheeks heat even more.

Sarah laughed softly. "Let's just be glad that *someone*

is kissing someone, okay? God knows I haven't had a reason to touch up my lip gloss in a good long while."

"But he's *Evan!*"

"I know." Sarah's eyes twinkled. She picked up the eggs and deftly cracked them in the bowl. "Six foot something, black-haired, blue-eyed Evan Taggart."

"Six foot two," Leandra murmured. She knew exactly, because they'd asked him for the information for the promotion they were doing for his episodes. "You're not interested in him, are you?" she asked suddenly. Surely her cousin would have said something if she were.

Sarah looked shocked, as if the idea had never once occurred to her.

Leandra kind of knew how that felt. Until recently, the idea had never particularly consumed her, either.

"No," her cousin assured her. "So, it wasn't just a kissing session, then. You're *interested* in the man."

Immediate denial sprung to her lips, only to go unvoiced. "I don't know what to think," she finally admitted. She sank down on one of the kitchen chairs and watched her cousin mix together the rest of the ingredients. "He's a *friend.*"

"Yeah." Sarah measured oil and water into the bowl and handed it to Leandra, along with a wooden spoon. "So try not to break each other's hearts while you're at it."

She snatched the bowl and began stirring. "I've never broken anyone's heart."

"What about Jake?"

The spoon paused for a moment. "No. To be fair, he didn't break mine, either. What broke us both was—" Her voice strangled to a stop. She stirred harder. "Don't we need a cake pan or something?" She pushed the words out, wanting desperately to change the subject.

Sarah pulled out a pan and silently set it in front of her. "What broke you both was losing Emi," she said quietly. "It's more than any person should have to bear. But—"

"I don't want to talk about it." She pushed out of her chair and turned on the oven with an abrupt twist. Talking about kissing Evan was easier than talking about Emi. And she didn't really want to discuss either.

Sarah's gaze was unflinching. "One of these days you're going to need to talk about it, don't you think?"

"You tell me," her voice suddenly shook. "You're the one who took all of her pictures off your refrigerator." She shoved the pan in the oven despite the fact that it was not even close to being preheated, and strode out of the kitchen.

"Leandra!" Sarah called after her, but Leandra just shook her head and kept moving, right out the front door.

She made it across the street and through the park before her anger gave way and she sank down on the grass, watching two girls playing on the swings in the playground.

She pressed her head to her knees, feeling the soft breeze flow over her head. The girls' chatter was indistinct, merely a soothing sound on a quiet afternoon.

What was wrong with her, snapping at Sarah like that? She knew her cousin had only been trying to make things easier for her by removing the pictures.

Coming to Weaver was just making her crazier than ever. Sniping at Sarah. Kissing Evan. What would be next?

She groaned, pressed her head harder to her knees and told herself to just get…a…grip.

"You look like you've lost your best friend."

It wasn't the comment that sent ripples down her

back, but the voice. She couldn't even pretend to be surprised, though. Evan seemed to be everywhere these days. Why not at the park on a Saturday afternoon?

"Are you following me?" She looked up at him, shaking a strand of hair out of her eyes and was startled at the sight of Hannah leaning against his leg. Her head was on a level with Leandra's, and the little girl gave her a long stare before blinking her silky lashes.

"Hannah likes the swings. And since she had a good nap, she gets the swings." He crouched down and turned the child until she was facing the playground. Two of the three swings were still occupied by the older girls. "Go ahead," he encouraged.

Leandra was not entirely surprised when Hannah took about five steps onto the sandy play area, then stopped. She sat down on her rear and began running her toy car up and down her jeans-clad leg. Her tiny tennis shoes tapped against the sand beneath her. Evan didn't coax her any further, though. He just smiled when Hannah cast him a sidelong look, and then sat down next to Leandra.

"Tabby's terrier got loose earlier and licked Hannah's hand. She was upset for an hour. Couldn't tell it looking at her now, though."

"Is she staying all weekend with you?"

"Nah. I'll take her back to Sharon's before supper time. So, what's wrong?"

"Nothing."

"Sure?" He stretched out his legs. They seemed ridiculously long, and she was vaguely surprised to see that he wore white tennis shoes rather than the cowboy boots he typically favored.

"Quite sure."

He plucked a long blade of grass and held it up to

study. "Then why are you hunched down here in the park all alone?"

"Sometimes I *like* being alone," she said pointedly.

He slanted a look her way, then turned it back to the grass. He apparently found it wanting, for he tossed it aside and plucked another. He ran his fingers along it, then carefully positioned his fingers, held it to his lips and blew.

A sharp whistle sounded.

Hannah looked back at him and laughed. The breeze tugged at her hair, making it dance around her narrow shoulders.

A smile creased his face and he whistled through the grass again.

Not even two hours ago, she'd been climbing up the man like he was some tree and she a love-starved monkey. Now, he was whistling through grass to make a little girl laugh. She sighed faintly, smiling a little even though there was a part of her that wanted to cry. "You should have children of your own," she finally said.

He let the grass go and it flitted about in the breeze before settling on the ground. "Then I'd need a wife."

"Well, not technically, though it's the nice way to go about it."

"Only way I'd go about it."

"I don't know, Evan. Accidents happen. Haven't there been women you've—"

"No."

She lifted her eyebrows. "No? Just what does that no mean?"

He leaned back on one arm, his gaze as vivid as the cloud-bejeweled sky above them. "You asking because of the show, Leandra, or because you want to know who or how many women have been warming my bed?"

"I couldn't be the least bit interested, personally," she assured him.

His smile was slow. And it made her twitchy all over, just seeing it. "Right," he drawled.

That's what she got for telling bald-faced lies. She'd never been good at it, not even when she was five years old and in cahoots with her grandfather to sneak away with her mother's brownies. "Well?" She managed the challenge, anyway.

"I'm no saint, but I can assure you, there aren't any unclaimed Taggarts running around. Not from me."

She felt like groaning all over again. Naturally he'd feel that way. It was because his mother had become pregnant with him and abandoned by Darian that she'd ended up married to Darian's half brother, Drew. "I didn't mean—"

His eyebrow lifted, obviously waiting.

She sighed again. Seemed she was in rare form that day for saying the wrong things to people. "I'm sorry."

"Tell me who Eduard is and we'll call it even."

"He owns the production company that produces *WITS*," she informed, her voice abrupt.

"And?"

She tugged her ear. "And nothing. He's seventy years old, if he's a day, all right? I work for him. He's promised me a new show if I can prove myself with *WITS*."

"Yet he taught you how to make fancy eggs."

"So? It wasn't for breakfast after we'd spent a tawdry night together, I assure you. I crewed on a cooking show he produces in Paris. He was always trying out recipes on us that he'd learned from the show."

He looked oddly frustrated. "Why didn't you just say so in the first place?"

"Because you were making such a fuss about it!"

His jaw shifted to one side then slowly centered. "You are one ornery woman, you know that?"

"I'm not a Clay for nothing," she muttered.

"That's for damn sure."

"If you find it so terrible, then why do I keep tripping over you every time I turn around?"

"You're the one who came back to *my* town, Leandra. You left a long time ago."

She stared past Hannah. The two older girls had lost interest in the swings and were skipping away from the playground toward the opposite side of the park. She and Sarah, J.D. and Angeline had played in much the same way when they'd been young.

Leandra had never had a chance to teach Emi to skip. She'd been too young.

She brushed her hand over her eyes and looked back at Evan. "And since I left, I'm not allowed to claim Weaver as my home anymore? Seems pretty harsh."

"Where *do* you call home? California? Jake said you have an apartment a few miles from his but that you never spend any time there because you're always off on location somewhere. You've cut off friends. Hell, you practically cut off your family."

"I never realized that I was such a topic of interest between you and Jake. What does he do? Call you to rehash all of my oddities? Do you check in on me with my folks here, too?"

He shook his head, looking annoyed.

She wasn't sure she believed him.

"Jake wants you to be happy again," Evan said after a moment.

Leandra pressed her lips together for a moment. It was a struggle not to cut and run right then and there. "I want him to be happy, too."

"Have you told *him* that?"

"Of course."

"Are you sure?"

She frowned. "What are you getting at?"

He shrugged, suddenly looking as casual as if they were watching June bugs beside the swimming hole on a summer evening, and she didn't believe the ruse for a second.

"Just seems to me that you might still be more involved than you think," he commented.

"Trust me. We're not."

"You called him to do the show."

"Because he's perfect for the camera, just like you are!" She stretched her legs out, only to draw them back in and cross them. "Criminy, Evan, what does it matter?"

His jaw tightened for a moment. "Because he's trying to move on and so should you."

"I'm not keeping him from moving on."

"Are you so sure?"

She eyed him harder. "What is *with* you?"

"I don't think you want to move on."

"What would you call that bit of *moving* around earlier today in Sarah's kitchen?" She realized her voice had risen and closed her mouth tightly.

"Lust," he said smoothly and even though she'd called it that herself, she still felt stung by the word.

Well, what had she wanted? For him to profess some unspoken adoration of her or something?

This was Evan Taggart here. She knew him too well from days of old. He'd pulled her hair when he'd sat behind her in third grade. He'd put a frog in her lunch box one time. Not that she'd minded all that much—she'd sort of been into frogs when she was ten.

But adoring, he was not.

"I don't *do* lust," she assured him repressively.

He laughed.

Annoyed, she balled her fist and slammed it into his arm, knocking it out from beneath him. He hit the ground flat, and still he laughed.

Harder.

She wanted to pummel him.

Hannah was watching them, a half smile on her pretty face, as if she were equal parts curious and equal parts amused over his behavior.

"Go ahead. Laugh it up, Chuckles." She pushed to her feet, but Evan reached out and grabbed her ankle.

"Don't go getting in a snit. It's too nice an afternoon for it." He was still grinning that wicked, wicked grin. "Besides, who are you kidding?" He made a face and mimicked her. "I don't do lust."

She shook her foot, but dog that he was, he had a hold. "Someone is going to see us," she warned, trying not to smile, herself. How utterly ridiculous they must look. "Look, there are cars driving by right now." She shook her foot yet again and his grip slipped below the hem of her jeans, touching her bare ankle.

It was like he'd touched her with a live wire.

She jumped. He jumped. They stared at each other.

And Hannah suddenly started screaming.

His gaze shuttered and he swore under his breath, pushing to his feet and hurrying over to the girl.

Leandra pressed a hand to her heart that had seemed to have completely stopped for a moment there and took several instinctive steps toward Hannah as well, before she stopped herself and stayed where she was.

Hannah looked perfectly fine. She was still sitting

in the sand, her thumb spinning the wheels of her ever-present car. No tears. Just that high, keening scream.

Evan scooped her up. Leandra couldn't hear what he said to the girl, but after a moment, she stopped screaming just as abruptly as she'd started. She pushed at him and he set her back down, but this time, she didn't sit in the sand. She kept her head against Evan's leg and wrapped her arm proprietarily around his knee. Her blue gaze—so like the man who towered above her—studied Leandra.

Leandra didn't really need the reminder, though.

Hannah was the female who counted in Evan's life. Appealing as Evan could be when he wanted to be, Leandra couldn't afford to forget that she was only there because of *WITS*.

When the job was done, she was gone.

Leandra brushed her hands down the sides of her jeans. "I'd better get back."

"Hannah acts out sometimes. Don't let it bother you."

"You don't have to explain, Evan. I understand."

His eyebrows drew together. "Some people around here don't. Sharon told me they were in the grocery store the other day and something set off Hannah and a woman told Sharon to keep her c-r-a-z-y-blanking kid away from the public." His hand smoothed over Hannah's silky hair.

"Consider the source and let it go. The woman was an idiot. Don't take stock of idiots."

"I don't." He took a step forward only to stop since doing so would have dragged Hannah along a foot, also.

"She has a grip like you do," Leandra observed dryly. "I'll see you tomorrow for your big debut."

Once again, he looked several shades less than

thrilled at the prospect. But it wasn't the show he mentioned, when he spoke again. "Leandra, about Jake."

"What about him?" He had her full attention, yet he was silent and it birthed a kernel of worry inside her. "What about him, Evan? He's all right, isn't he?"

"You two need to talk."

Even more disconcerted, she nodded warily. "Okay."

He nodded. "Good."

"Well." She swallowed. There was only so much yo-yoing her emotions could take, and the day had held plenty already. "See you later."

He silently lifted a hand.

It was Hannah, though, who spoke. "Goodbye, Leandra."

She started. Evan, too, looked just as surprised. "Goodbye, Hannah," she returned.

Then, feeling more off-balance than ever, she retraced her steps back to Sarah's place.

# *Chapter* 7

The moment Leandra opened the door, she smelled chocolate.

"Hey." Sarah barely looked up from her paperback book, which she was reading while sprawled out on the couch. "You're just in time to take the cake out of the oven."

Sure enough, the oven timer went off with a buzz the moment she'd finished speaking.

Leandra went into the kitchen and pulled out the cake, setting it on the cooling rack that Sarah had left out on the counter, and turned off the oven. The chocolate smelled as wonderful as chocolate ever did, but Leandra had no particular appetite for the thing. She tossed the hot pad on the counter and turned away.

But the refrigerator door caught her attention first.

Still a jumble of pictures. Still a mass of images.

Only, Emi's face was back among them. Just a trio

of pictures. Emi at her third birthday party. She'd been wearing a sunny yellow dress.

Leandra closed her eyes for a moment, letting out a long, slow breath.

Sarah came up behind her and pressed her head against Leandra's. "I have dozens more."

"I know." She turned and hugged her cousin. "I'm sorry. I know you were trying to help." She swallowed, and stepped back. "I'm just a crazy person, I think."

"You're not crazy," Sarah dismissed. "We're all trying to take our lead from you, sweetie. You haven't wanted to even mention Emi's name. I thought putting away the pictures was what you'd want."

"Maybe it was." She pushed at her forehead and the pain that seemed to have lodged itself there, and went into the living room. "Evan told me to talk to Jake."

"Was that before you were necking in my kitchen, or after?" Sarah flopped on the couch beside her.

"We weren't necking." Her forehead throbbed harder. Maybe the pain was her version of Pinocchio's wooden nose. For every lie, the pain got worse. "All right, so maybe we were almost necking. Sort of. Maybe."

"Now you're sounding like a politician." Sarah looked amused.

"And it was in the park just now."

"There was more necking there? Wow. Usually the kids wait until after dark for that sort of thing, but you two—"

"Ha-ha. We weren't doing anything there. We just ran into each other. He took Hannah over there to play at the playground. He told me I needed to talk to Jake."

"About what?"

Leandra lifted her shoulders. "It worries me, though. What if something's wrong?"

"Then you'll deal with it," Sarah said simply.

Leandra frowned. "Because I've proven how well I *deal?*" She pulled out her cell phone and dialed her ex-husband. When she got a busy signal, she was relieved, which just proved her point.

She tucked the phone back in her pocket and raked her fingers through her hair. "When was the last time you went riding?"

Sarah started to smile. "Your dad's place or mine?"

"Let's go to the Double-C. I haven't seen the big house since I got here."

"You're on. You bring boots?"

"I figure you probably have a spare pair lying around."

Sarah did, and hours later, Leandra knew that some things hadn't changed over the years, and the pleasure of spending the afternoon on the back of a horse was, thankfully, one of them.

They took their time, plodding over ground that Leandra had once known as well as the back of her hand. There had been few changes at the Double-C since she'd last been there and that was a pleasure, too. A part of her felt guilty for enjoying it so, when she didn't seem to be able to find that easy pleasure at her parents' spread.

By the time they took the horses in, it was evening and Jaimie, Sarah's mother, had the table already set for dinner. Leaving was, of course, out of the question.

The meal was yet another step back in time. Fried chicken, mashed potatoes and gravy. Leandra half expected her aunt to offer her cherry Kool-Aid, which had been pretty much her favorite drink until she was a teenager.

Matthew sat at the head of the big oak table that sat center in the spacious kitchen. His hair was clipped short and his lean, suntanned face made his icy blue eyes look even lighter. Jaimie, an older version of Sarah right down to the long, reddish hair, sat opposite him. And even though Leandra knew they'd been married nearly as long as her own parents had been, she swore they were still giving each other the eye across the table in the same way they had nearly every time Leandra had spent the night with Sarah at the big house.

Not that her parents were any different. Growing up, it had been embarrassing. She wasn't entirely sure that it wasn't embarrassing *now*.

Sarah looked at Leandra over the rim of her iced tea glass, seemed to read her mind and rolled her eyes, smiling and shrugging a little.

"They think we're old coots, Matthew," Jaimie observed, noticing their exchange. Her green eyes danced.

"Maybe I am, Red, but we all know you'll never be old enough to qualify."

Jaimie reached out and patted Sarah's hand humorously. "Your children are your children all their life, darling. You ought to be used to it by now. Some day you'll see." Her smile included Leandra, knowing perfectly well what she'd said. She'd never been afraid of broaching sensitive subjects, and yet she managed to do so without causing pain.

That was her Auntie Jaimie. Bold and loving.

"Now, Leandra. Tell me the truth." Jaimie leaned her elbow on the table. "Were you really making out with Evan in the playground this afternoon?"

Leandra straightened like a shot, nearly spilling her tea down her front. "What?"

"Mom, where did you hear such a thing?"

"Oh, you know Weaver, Sarah. Somebody saw Leandra in the park and they called someone who then called someone and so on and so forth." She smiled a little crookedly, looking much younger than her years. "It was Emily who called me, actually."

Leandra gaped. "My own mother was spreading gossip like that?"

"Well," Jaimie allowed, "she was sort of fact checking, figuring my daughter—" she sent Sarah a pointed look "—would have filled me in on the truth."

"I don't spread gossip," Sarah said loftily.

Matthew snorted softly and picked up his coffee mug, looking highly amused.

"I just said she was looking for *facts,* didn't I?" Jaimie tsked.

"There are no facts to check," Leandra said firmly, sharing a look with Sarah. They'd shared plenty of secrets over the years. She hadn't expected to be doing it again at their age…like this…about Evan.

Had they entered some weird time warp where they were still thirteen and being grilled over why they'd been late coming home from the winter dance? Or were they really sitting there, in their late twenties, fully capable, mostly functioning adults?

Jaimie chuckled suddenly and patted Leandra's hand. "I'm just teasing you, honey. Surely you know that." She pushed away from the table and grabbed a plate of cookies, passing it to Leandra first. "Matthew heard from Squire and Gloria this afternoon."

"Squire's wanting to come back early from their vacation. So far Gloria has kept them on their schedule, touring Europe for two months, but she's not sure how long she can do so," Matthew added. "You know Squire. He's never liked being away from the ranch for too long at a time."

"I think Squire doesn't like being away from the

*family* for too long at a time," Jaimie said dryly. "Still afraid we'll mess things up without his sage advice."

"Interference, you mean." Matthew smiled faintly.

They all chuckled. Squire's interfering ways were known far and wide and though they may have mellowed some in the past few decades, they were by no means extinct.

When Jaimie started to clear the table, Sarah and Leandra tried to take over but to no avail. Then it was good-nights all around and assurances that everyone would be in town for the "do" at Colby's.

And turn out, they did. By the hundreds.

By Happy Hour, there was not a seat to be had inside Colby's Bar & Grill. People spilled outside onto the sidewalk and into the street that her uncle had conveniently closed off to traffic.

*WITS* had arranged the half-dozen large-screen televisions that were situated both inside and out. A local country and western band was cranking out tunes. Those who weren't dancing in the street were sucking down lemonade or beer and filling their bellies with free food.

"If the show about Evan is as popular as this party, you're not going to be associate producer anymore." Ted came up and stopped beside Leandra, where she was doling out *WITS* ball caps and refrigerator magnets to the new arrivals who kept straggling in.

"From your lips," Leandra murmured, her smile never leaving her face as she looked at a young school girl who already had three hats in her hand. "Would you like a bag to hold them all?"

The girl nodded and Leandra handed over a plastic sack with the *WITS* logo prominently featured, but not before she dropped in a few pens and some other doo-dads that brought a huge smile to the girl's face before she ran off.

"Five minutes to showtime," Ted told her.

She appreciated the reminder despite the fact that she was already excruciatingly aware of the time. "Tell Janet—"

"I'm here, I'm here." Janet skidded to a stop behind the table next to Leandra. She had a tall glass of something in her hand and a grin on her face. "Leandra, if your brother could be bottled, we'd never have to work another day in our lives. We'd be rich selling his charm."

"Yeah, he's charming all right, and just as wily." She vacated her chair, making room for Janet. "Evan still inside?"

"Playing pool."

Avoiding the television sets, too, Leandra figured. She left Ted to adjust the sound system he'd tied all of the monitors to, and wound her way through the throng. She saw her parents sitting at a high-top with her uncle Daniel and aunt Maggie, and her father gave her an encouraging thumbs-up. The rest of the family were scattered around, too, all offering their easy support as the evening progressed.

It didn't matter, though. She was still nervous as a cat.

She found Evan at one of the pool tables. "Show time."

He smiled, particularly when her announcement was met with a boisterous round of hoots from those crowded into the bar. But she saw beyond the smile to his discomfort at being the center of all this attention. For some reason, she tucked her arm through his, as if she were going to be capable of alleviating his version of stage fright. "Don't worry," she murmured in his ear when he lowered his head to hear her through the noisy bar. "The network that carries us isn't the *most* popular cable network." It was second, but she didn't figure he needed to hear that just then.

Then the show's theme song blasted out over the sound system, and whatever second or third or tenth thoughts they all might be having were moot.

Somebody grabbed Evan and pulled him closer to one of the large screens, and Leandra found herself falling back, working through the tightly packed bodies until she found a pocket of air and a somewhat removed view of the audience.

Their attention was rapt. As silent as they'd been noisy, as every single person—to a one—craned to see more, to hear every word.

Halfway through the half-hour show, she even allowed herself to believe—just a little—that the interest wasn't entirely owed to Evan. That she might just have had something to do with the engaging pace and content.

Then she stopped watching the audience and watched one of the screens herself.

And her heart nearly stopped in her chest.

In the flesh, Evan was a compelling, impossibly striking man. On the big screen, he was…brilliant.

Beautiful to look at. Wry. Confident.

Single. A state that was played up a little more than Leandra had planned—Marian's doing.

And then, just as quickly as it had begun, the chipper theme song played over the image of Evan and his damnably attractive jeans-clad backside walking away, a beautiful black horse following him along as obediently as a devoted puppy.

Leandra let out a long breath, letting the cheering that had exploded at the notes of the theme song flow over her. She worked her way outside once again, catching a glimpse of Evan, surrounded as people slapped him on the back and called for fresh rounds of drinks.

She went over to the unmanned table where all of the giveaways had been distributed and sank down onto the chair, feeling shaky. But she wasn't allowed much time to collect herself of the nerves that had drained her, because family started descending almost immediately, hugging and laughing and exclaiming that the show was, by far, the most interesting thing they'd ever seen in their entire lives.

Leandra laughed off the exaggeration, but the truth was, she was pleased. And in another blur, the evening wound down until there was just her and Ted still packing away the mess outside while the staff of Colbys finished up inside.

"Wouldn't want to pay that bill out of my pocket," Ted murmured when Leandra signed off on the final bill for the event and bid good-night to the manager.

"Me, either." She waited until the manager left, then stared around at the sidewalk and street. They'd cleaned up all of the trash and broken down all of the boxes that had contained the giveaways. Aside from the stack of cardboard, there was no sign left of the festivities. "Eduard has never been one to stint on promotion."

"Fortunately," Ted added. "Good job tonight, Lee. You want me to give you a lift to your cousin's?"

"Think I'll walk. Work off some of my energy."

He grinned. "Can't see how you'd have any left, but whatever. See you in the morning, then."

"Bright and early at Evan's clinic."

He waved on his way to the van. Her cameraman

knew the schedule as intimately as she did. And in minutes, he was driving away.

She let out a long breath and tugged down the long sleeves of her *WITS* T-shirt as she set off in the direction of Sarah's house. When she heard a car engine come up behind her, she looked back, half expecting Ted to have returned for some reason.

But it was Evan's dusty pickup truck that pulled alongside of her. The windows were down and he had his long arm stretched across the seat as he cocked his head, looking out at her.

"Dontcha know you shouldn't be out alone at this hour?" The tires of his truck slowly turned, keeping time with her pace.

She made an exaggerated perusal of the quiet street, both ways. "In Weaver? Besides, the only one out is you."

"And you."

She heard another car and looked back to see the last of the Colby's crew depart. "And them."

"Want a ride?"

She kept walking. "What for? Nearly to the corner. Another mile after that and I'll be at Sarah's."

Evan eyed her. "Afraid to get in the truck with me?" It was a pretty cheap shot, but accusing her of being afraid of something used to be the surest way of getting under her skin.

And he knew some things hadn't changed when she stopped dead still and gave him an incredulous look. "Excuse me?"

He braked, stopping, as well. "Get in the truck, Leandra." His voice was resigned. "Or I'll just have to follow you the rest of the way."

"You have an overdeveloped sense of responsibility, you know that?" But she reached for the handle and pulled open the truck door.

A rough sound rose in his throat. Right. Responsible.

She joined him in the cab, bringing with her some light fresh scent that teased his nerves in a way he was beginning to get used to.

"I, um, I didn't see when you left earlier." She carefully fastened her seat belt, then pressed her palms together in her lap. "One minute I saw you still in the bar with Axel and Derek and a few other guys, and the next, you were gone."

He didn't kid himself that she would be looking for him for any reason other than *WITS* as he headed down Main Street. "I'd had enough of the freak show."

Her sigh was soft, but still audible. "I really wish you didn't feel that way." Her fingers twined together and she looked out the side window as he turned the corner, heading down Sarah's street.

"Why? Because we used to be friends?"

She looked back at him, her soft lips pressing together for a moment. "That. And the fact that I do have a responsibility to my production. You know, most people have enjoyed their experience once we finish shooting. I, um… Is there something I—we—as a crew can do to make things easier for you? Some way we can get you from feeling like you're a…a sideshow attraction?"

"Keep Ted out of my bedroom."

"Again, I'm sorry for that. It was…unfortunate."

He grimaced. "That's one word for it." He pulled into Sarah's driveway and parked, but when Leandra reached to undo her safety belt, he dropped his hand over hers.

Stupid, but he just couldn't let her go like that. Thinking that his foul mood was because of the show. "Wait."

She blinked and he wondered if she were able to feel

the rumba his pulse had danced into when he touched her. But all she did was look at him, waiting.

He let out a breath. "I didn't leave because of the show," he said abruptly. "Not that I particularly like all that fuss and attention," he added darkly, lest she get her hopes up too much otherwise. "I—"

Her gaze searched his face. "What? If you were just tired, Evan, it's okay. I mean, we were *all* tired, and I know you have to keep some pretty awful hours, sometimes."

He finally let go of her hand, and looked out the windshield. "Yeah, that would be the easy excuse," he muttered.

She frowned. "Look, you don't have to tell me why, Evan. Your reasons are your own. It's fine. You were there for the main event—people got to feel involved in the process of the show. And I wasn't complaining that you'd left—just commenting on the fact that I didn't see you leave. I felt bad about that. As if I'd let you down or something."

He ran his hand around the back of his neck. "Don't. Just…don't." He looked at her. "I left because Darian showed up. He missed the show. Not that he cared."

She looked as surprised as if he'd announced he'd gone into labor. "Then why—" Her expression tightened. "Is Hannah all right?"

"What?" He shook his head a little. "Yeah. Hannah's fine." He supposed he shouldn't feel his own surprise that his niece was her first thought. "Hell, believe me, darlin'. Darian doesn't bother himself over his only grandchild."

She unsnapped her seat belt and shifted in her seat to face him better. "Can I ask you a question?" She didn't exactly wait for his consent as she went right on. "It seems clear to me that you're not completely thrilled with Sharon and Darian taking care of Hannah. Does Katy feel the same way?"

"Sharon and Darian are Katy's parents. Of course she doesn't feel the way I do."

"I didn't mean to stick my nose in."

He sighed again, noisily. "Look, it's not you, okay? For once it's not you," he added in a low voice.

Her too-large eyes looked away, as if he'd insulted her and he felt even worse.

"Sorry," she said. "Look, it's really late. I appreciate the ride—"

"Leandra, I wasn't looking for an apology."

"Fine. Okay. but you need your sleep, too." She shoved open the truck door and smiled brightly at him. "The episode was a hit. *You* were a hit. Better than I could have ever hoped for."

Even better than following Jake around with his celebrity pets? He didn't voice the question. "Leandra!"

But there was no stopping her. "Thanks again." Her voice was deliberately cheerful. "I'll see you in the morning." She shut the door, wincing a little. "Oops. Too loud at this hour. Sorry."

Evan watched Leandra practically jog to the front door, and swore under his breath.

He'd made himself a fine mess of that.

## Chapter 8

Evan still felt like an ass the following morning. So much so, that when Leandra and her crew showed up with their van of cameras and lights and microphones, he invited them into the house where he had breakfast waiting.

Ted took one look at the cinnamon rolls from Ruby's and clapped Evan on the back. "Good man." He grinned and plucked one off the plate, shoving half in his mouth.

"Jeez," Janet muttered, and grabbed a napkin out of the package Evan had thought to toss onto the table alongside the rest of the grub—also scored from Ruby's, thanks to Tabby's connections. "Here." She shoved the napkin into Ted's hands, then picked up a plate, which she handed to Paul, who was nodding and eyeing the food with interest.

Leandra was the last to enter and she closed the door behind her. Her eyebrows raised. "What if we'd already eaten a big breakfast?"

"Did you?" He'd seen what they often ate in the mornings—tortilla chips being a primary favorite as far as he could tell.

She made a face. "No, but we might have."

He lifted his coffee mug and shrugged. "Then I'd have leftovers for the next week. Less cooking. Not a bad deal, either way."

Her eyes narrowed to a slit of chocolate brown, as if she didn't trust a word of it.

Why would she? He hadn't exactly made any of them feel particularly welcome.

He wasn't entirely sure why he was trying to make up for that failure now. Except that his mother would expect him to show some good manners. She and Drew hadn't raised him, after all, to be a complete jerk.

That was just in his genes, courtesy of Darian, who rarely managed to behave with any ethical or moral behavior.

If Evan had needed any more evidence about that, he only had to look at his own behavior the night before when he'd driven Leandra to Sarah's.

"Dig in, Leandra," Janet encouraged. She gestured with her fork before sticking it back into the mound of fluffy eggs she'd added to her plate. "Stop looking a gift horse in the mouth. This is a whole lot better than those granola bars you usually have."

Leandra's cheeks turned a little pink and she avoided looking at Evan. "This really wasn't necessary. But thank you."

He shrugged again. "Consider it returning the favor."

She looked blank.

"The breakfast you fixed me," he prompted.

Her expression cleared. "Oh. Well, for heaven's sake, Evan. That was just eggs and bacon. This—" she waved her hand over the containers he'd put out on the table with something he realized was less than artistry "—is a feast. Eggs, rolls, home fries, sausage, bacon. Sliced fruit. Really—it's too much."

"Shut up, Leandra," Ted told her good-naturedly, "before the guy starts putting the stuff away for someone who appreciates it."

"I *do* appreciate it," she said quickly. Her gaze flickered over Evan again, and the pink was even brighter in her cheeks. "I just…didn't expect it."

"Unexpected doesn't have to mean unpleasant," he said deliberately.

She nodded, a faint smile around the corners of her lips. "Right. You're right. Again."

He picked a paper plate off the stack and handed it to her. "My best china," he drawled.

"Same pattern as mine," Ted said.

"And mine," Paul piped in.

Her fingers brushed against his as she took the plate. "Were you waiting for us, or did you already eat?"

"Yes." He grabbed a plate of his own and added two cinnamon rolls to it. "We'll just consider this seconds."

There weren't enough chairs for all of them to sit, so Evan leaned back against the cupboard and worked his way through the enormous sweet rolls while the others filled their bellies and talked shop.

It was pretty damn surreal.

If anyone would have ever told him there would be a television show filmed in Weaver, much less one about *him,* he'd have laughed his fool head off.

Yet here they all were.

"So she was telling me that on the station she listens to for her morning ride, the deejays were talking about it." Evan focused in to see Janet looking excited.

"Seriously?" Leandra set down her plastic fork. "In Phoenix? That station's number one in their market."

"I know." Janet grinned around a bite of honeydew melon. "They had listeners calling in, all talking about Evan. My friend told me that she wished she had a dog she could bring up here just for an excuse to see him." Her gaze landed on Evan. "Mostly women were calling, of course. Who can blame them?"

The cinnamon roll lost its appeal. "You've got to be kidding."

"Good buzz is important," Paul said.

He'd spoken more than Evan had ever heard before. "Buzz about the show," Evan said warily. He looked at Leandra. "Right? That's what this is all about. So you can get promoted to producer or something."

She nodded. "It works both ways, though. Good word of mouth about you means that more people might tune in next week. It's a win-win situation." She pushed her plate away, even though she'd consumed barely half of what she'd put on it. "So don't you have patients coming in soon?"

"Yeah."

"Then we'd better get set up." She pushed back her chair.

It was evidently the signal her crew needed to do the same, and within minutes, they were trooping out of his kitchen. Ted, Evan noticed, didn't relinquish his plate. He just carried it out with him.

Leandra hung back. "This *was* really nice of you, Evan. I should help you clean up."

"It's just takeout, sport. No big deal. And clean up just means closing the containers and shoving them in the fridge. Think I'm pretty familiar with that particular process."

"Right." Her lashes veiled her eyes. "Is the clinic open already? Or still locked up?"

"I'll be there in a few minutes." He tossed her the key chain.

She caught it and headed toward the door. "Thanks."

Once again, he was letting her walk away without clearing the air.

He really was a slug.

"Leandra, about last night."

She hesitated, her hand on the door latch. "What about it?"

"Darian had his latest squeeze with him. I don't know why Sharon puts up with his infidelities but she does. I got pissed off about it and that's why I left Colby's."

Her lips rounded in a silent O. "You don't have to explain, Evan. I told you that."

Yeah, he didn't have to. For some idiotic reason he still felt compelled to do so, though. "Anyway, about Hannah's guardianship. You were right. I'd take her in a second, but Katy has refused."

She let go of the door knob. "What on earth for?"

"She's got it in her head that I'd use Hannah as an excuse *never* to find a woman to settle down with."

She made a short sound. "Are you serious?"

"As a heart attack."

She blinked, shaking her head a little as if the idea were unfathomable to her. "I can't believe Katy could be so…" She shook her head again.

"Ridiculous?" Evan supplied.

"Well, yes. Actually. My goodness, *she* is a single parent. Does she think she'll never get remarried because of that?"

"Keith left her because of Hannah. Katy's got a bug

in her bonnet about it. And the truth of it is I haven't gone out of my way to convince Katy that I *do* want to settle down. Some day." Admitting it was harder than he would have expected.

She cocked her head slightly. "You wanted to marry once, though. You proposed to Lucy even before we graduated from high school."

"I never proposed."

Her eyebrows shot up into her spiky bangs. "Oh?"

Jesus. He should have just kept his mouth shut about the whole thing. "I didn't. She just brought up the idea of being married somewhere along the way, and everyone assumed that would come to pass sooner or later."

"Everyone? But not you?" She looked skeptical. "Don't pull that on me, Evan. I know you too well. You and Lucy were practically joined at the hip. Are you saying that if she *hadn't* gone to New York, that the two of you wouldn't already be working on your own litter of kids?"

"We were a comfortable habit. I told you before that I wasn't pining for Lucy, and I know she's not longing for the good ol' days with me, either. She's your cousin. Call her yourself if you don't believe me."

"Then why *haven't* you gotten serious about someone since then?"

Because he was Darian's blood, he thought.

"Everyone around here thinks it's because you never got over Lucy."

"Maybe it was convenient," he said flatly. "Believe me, darlin', it hasn't kept me from having female companionship when I've wanted it." Plenty of it, and none from the girl he'd never been able to get out of his head.

She looked as if she'd suddenly sucked on a sour

lemon. "Well, woo-hoo for you." She pulled open the door. "We've got work to do. I'll see you over there."

He watched her stride away and exhaled. There was a reason he worked with animals.

They were a helluva lot easier to get along with.

Despite the promising beginning to the day, Leandra felt grumpy for the rest of the morning.

She didn't have to wonder why.

*Female companionship.*

Though why she should care about the women Evan had in his life, she couldn't begin to fathom. It wasn't as if she wished she were one of the hordes, after all.

She wouldn't *be* one of a horde, in the first place.

She wouldn't share her man with other women; wouldn't want a man who wanted others, anyway.

And just because she was saddled with this inexplicable attraction didn't mean that she intended to do anything about it. She didn't want a relationship.

She'd had that, and had failed on all accounts.

So she was grumpy. She knew she was grumpy and there didn't seem to be a darn thing she could do about it. Except try not to inflict her grumpiness on her crew.

So she let them do their jobs without much interference.

Fortunately, they were good at that.

And then, when Evan's morning of appointments was cut short by a call from a local rancher with a horse who was down, they packed up and followed right along with him. After that was an emergency with a cat stuck in a tree.

Evan's assurances that if the cat were able to get *up* the tree he'd be able to get back down when he was good and ready didn't hold much comfort for the teary six-year-old girl.

So Evan climbed the tree. Retrieved the cat and earned himself a half-dozen scratches as a result.

"Why don't they make guys like that back home?" Janet whispered to Leandra as Ted moved in for a closer shot of Evan returning the now-purring feline to its young owner.

Leandra was saved from answering, though, as her phone vibrated and she moved away from the scene to take Marian's call. As icy as her boss had been a few days earlier, she was now positively gleeful over the results of Evan's first episode, taking full credit for the entire effort, which had been Leandra's idea.

Nothing that Leandra wasn't used to, though. She nevertheless felt a throbbing in her temple by the time Marian's enthused litany wound down.

After hanging up, she followed the crew and Evan to Ruby's and then to the weed-and-feed, where he ordered an assortment of supplies and picked up a package of razors and microwave popcorn.

"Think he's planning on having company for the popcorn?" Ted asked Leandra while they followed Evan. "Considering the razors and soap?"

"If he is, you're not going to catch it on tape," Leandra assured him. "I don't care *what* Marian's been telling you to do."

Ted looked distinctly guilty. "You know Marian."

"Yes, I do. But if Evan does have a date, that's his business. Not ours."

*Liar, liar, pants on fire.*

She mentally drop-kicked the taunting demon into the next county and trailed after Evan and her crew as they continued their parade through Weaver, drawing plenty of attention as they did so.

Not that Evan seemed to notice. Oh, he was still full of plenty of complaints, but Leandra knew enough now to take them in stride.

The man was a natural.

They continued filming as he drove out to his parents' place. It was starting to get dark, which simply meant that Janet and Paul were kept busier ensuring there was enough light for Ted.

Jolie and Drew Taggart came out on the front porch when they heard the commotion of the crew's arrival. If they'd expected their son to drop by, they certainly hadn't expected him to come with the television crew trailing closely behind. Jolie looked distinctly uncomfortable and, as a result, Drew looked distinctly protective.

Unlike their son, natural they were not, but they made the effort for Evan's sake, as they came down off the porch and headed toward the stables behind the main house where Drew kept his string of horses. He was a highly sought-after horse trainer but was also working with Evan on horse breeding. In particular, like Leandra's father, Drew had a pretty mare in mind for Northern Light's foray into daddyland.

By the time the sun went down completely, Leandra called it quits for the day and couldn't help but smile at the relief on Jolie's face when she saw Ted lower his camera and the others begin packing things away in the van.

Leandra went over and thanked them for their patience, having every intention of leaving with them. But Jolie caught Leandra by the hand. "You'll stay and have some coffee and dessert, won't you? Your friends are welcome, too."

Leandra knew her "friends" wanted nothing more than a good night's sleep, since they'd already put in about a fifteen-hour day and had been more than a little vocal about it. And as much as she liked Evan's parents, she wasn't sure she was up to spending more time with their son, particularly in a social setting.

There was definitely something to be said about the security she found behind the camera. Watching lives go on around her, rather than participating in them.

"I'll go ask them," Leandra told Jolie, and the other woman beamed.

As she'd expected, they declined, claiming tiredness. Even Ted, who *rarely* turned down free eats, seemed extremely anxious to get back to the privacy of his motel room. "You stay, though," he encouraged. "These are your people. Chow down."

Leandra's appetite for food wasn't the problem. Her appetite for a certain tall man was. "It's just easier if I drive back in to town with you guys."

Ted snorted a little, shaking his head. "Yeah, right."

"What's *that* supposed to mean?"

Ted lowered his voice. "Look, I've been watching you. You obviously like the guy. Stick around."

She felt her entire body flush. "Evan is a *friend* and that is all."

"Yeah, and my wife loves having me gone all the time," he countered wryly. "But, hey, it's cool. If you're afraid, then—"

"I am not afraid." Admitting the truth to herself was one thing. Admitting it to the cameraman she'd worked with for umpteen episodes was another.

He clearly didn't believe her. "Whatever floats your boat, you know?"

"I'm just as tired as the rest of you," she muttered. "Maybe I want an early night of it."

"Leandra?" Jolie called from the porch. "How would you like your coffee?"

She knew when she was beat. "Fine. Go ahead." She waved at Ted. "I'll see you in the morning." Then she turned back toward the Taggarts' home and raised her voice. "Just black, please, Mrs. Taggart."

"Oh, call me Jolie." The older woman waited until Leandra made it to the porch before turning to go inside. "It's not as if you're still ten years old."

Leandra's gaze fell on Evan the moment they entered the spacious great room. He was standing by the enormous stone fireplace.

Now this was a room that suited him. The thought snuck in without permission.

"Have a seat, honey." Jolie waved toward the leather furniture clustered around the fireplace. "Drew, why don't you start a fire? It's definitely getting chilly in here."

Leandra seated herself on one end of the butter-soft couch. Evan crouched in front of the fireplace himself. "I'll do it, Dad."

Tabby breezed in moments later, not seeming to think a thing of it that Leandra was ensconced in the family's couch. "Hey, there. My mom put on the videotape of Evan's big debut yet? She's watched it like a hundred times."

"Shut up," Evan said, without heat. "Go bug someone else." He set a long match to the kindling he'd packed around the larger logs.

"That show didn't fool me," Tabby told him, grinning. "I know the truth. How bo-oh-ring you really are." But she was grinning as she said it, and before Evan could grab her as he made a move to do, she hustled into the kitchen. "I ate at the café," they heard her tell her mother. "And I gotta finish a report for history tomorrow."

"She puts in a lot of hours at Ruby's, doesn't she? Must make all her homework kind of hard." Leandra looked at Drew.

"Too many hours as far as I'm concerned," he said. "But there's no convincing her of that."

"She keeps her grades up." Evan fitted the fireplace screen in place. "She's stockpiling her earnings so she can see the world when she finishes high school."

"Like your mother is going to allow that," Drew said wryly. "She wants Tabby to stay right here in Weaver."

"And the rest of us don't?" Even though there were plenty of other places to sit, Evan sat next to Leandra on the couch. He propped his boots on the heavy wooden coffee table. "The only one enamored with Tabby's idea is Tabby." He quickly dragged his boots off the table when his mother entered the room.

Leandra bit back a smile. Jolie didn't look fooled for a minute. She probably knew exactly where the scars in that wood—which ironically only increased the rustic-looking charm of the piece—came from.

"Maybe she'll change her mind about leaving for good," Leandra offered.

Evan raised his eyebrows and looked at her. "Did you?" He didn't really wait for the reply she wasn't even sure of herself. "Of course not. You're just as driven as Tabby, only you're further along in the course of it."

"You make ambition sound like a bad thing."

"I didn't say that." He leaned forward and grabbed a

cup of coffee, handing it to her. "And I didn't say I was talking about ambition."

"You think I'm driven." His unfathomable gaze met hers as she took the cup from him.

"Aren't you?"

"What's the difference? You're ambitious, too, Evan. You don't want your veterinary practice to fail, so you work hard at what you do to make sure that doesn't happen."

"But I'm not *driven*." He sat forward again, taking a cup for himself, and a couple of small, perfectly round, golden sugar cookies. He dipped one in his coffee and popped it in his mouth. "And you know there's a difference," he said around the cookie.

"You just leave Leandra alone," Jolie said firmly. "Honestly, it's like you were both still playing in the sandbox together. If you didn't like the way she was building her castle, you just ran over it with your truck."

Leandra couldn't help but smile. Particularly when she noticed the hint of pink creeping above the collar of Evan's blue shirt. "You *were* horrible to me."

"No, I wasn't." He dunked another cookie and polished it off. "Even back then you liked playing director, telling everyone what they should be doing and how they should be acting."

She reached over and pulled his hair—the hair that had grown long enough to curl slightly behind his ears. "I never told you to pull my hair, and that's what you did all through grade school."

"You were the one who always sat in front of me."

"So? If Joey Rasmussen sat in front of you would you have pulled *his* hair?"

Evan smiled faintly. "Joey would be happy to have

someone pull his hair these days. Guy's already lost most of it and he's not even thirty yet."

"You're missing the point."

"You had long blond braids back then," he defended himself. "You always wore red ribbons tied around the ends. What can I say? You might as well have been waving a red flag."

"Well there's no red flag waving now," Jolie told her son. "So you just behave yourself."

"She's the one who just pulled my hair." He sounded so aggrieved that they all laughed, and before Leandra knew it, more than a few quite enjoyable hours had passed before they were finally taking their leave.

"Don't work too hard at making my son famous, now," Jolie ordered as she hugged Leandra.

"Fortunately, folks around here aren't going to let him get much of a swelled head, despite that 'do' over at Colby's," Drew added dryly. "They've seen him sweeping up horse droppings after the Memorial Day parade too many times." He clapped his son on the back, ordering him to drive carefully back to town, and went back inside the house with his wife.

Leandra followed Evan to his pickup truck, wondering what else there was that she no longer knew about the man. "You really *still* work the shovel brigade after the parade?"

He shrugged and opened her door for her. "Somebody's got to."

She climbed up on the high seat, waiting until he came around and was behind the wheel. "Somebody, yes. Like a high school kid. That's about when you started, right?"

"It's a volunteer job," Evan reminded her, pulling away from the house. "High school kids, these days, don't shovel sh—stuff like that unless they get paid to do so."

"So what was your excuse? Why'd you do it?"

"No particular reason."

"Just an affinity for little green apples," Leandra drawled, disbelieving. "Who are you trying to kid?"

"You were in a bunch of those parades yourself."

She'd been the junior rodeo princess for more years than she cared to recall. "Remember when Joey Rasmussen's grandfather's covered wagon caught on fire in the middle of the parade route?"

The light from the dashboard illuminated the grin he flashed. "Yeah. Do you remember why?"

She shook her head. "I never knew. But Joey was always getting into some sort of mischief."

"He was trying to smoke a joint. Only it wasn't pot, it was dried cow chips and when he realized it, he dropped his light on the hay bales stacked in the wagon, and the rest is history."

Leandra chuckled. "Well, the covered wagon was certainly history."

"Joey never tried smoking pot again, either."

"Wonder how he ended up mistaking cow chips for marijuana, anyway? And how did he figure out it wasn't?"

"Somebody switched his little plastic bag of the stuff."

"Obviously." She looked at him suddenly. "No. You?"

"Nah. I just told him the truth after he'd taken a few puffs. Ryan was the one to make the switch. He knew his dad was going to bust Joey for possession. It was just a matter of time before he was caught, considering the way he was bragging about it." He chuckled a little. "Man, the way he worked so hard to roll it, and then he dropped it—and the match—on the hay bale. I thought we'd split a gut laughing, and we were also busy scrambling out of the damn thing before it went up around our ears. Think Joey's parents grounded him for about six months for that one."

"Where is Joey now?"

"Moved to Idaho. Growing potatoes, if you can believe it. He and his wife have about two dozen kids, seems like. Maybe it's really only two or three, though."

Leandra smiled, trying to picture the rowdy kid she'd known settled down as a farmer with a family. "Speaking of Ryan… Have you heard from him lately?"

"Usually he keeps up with email, but he hasn't answered the last few I sent."

"Did you ever consider going into the service?"

"Yeah."

"Seriously? I never really thought of you doing anything other than what you're doing. You're great with animals. Horses, dogs, whatever. You've always been that way. I wasn't at all surprised when you became a vet."

"I was surprised when you ended up doing the television thing."

"Why? I studied production in school."

"You also studied psychology, child development, ceramics and fifth-century literature."

"I didn't study literature."

The corner of his mouth had lifted again. "You did the others."

It occurred to her that he knew a lot of details about her college education. Details she'd never specifically shared with him. They'd been friends, but not particularly close when they'd both been away at different schools. "All right, it's true. I couldn't exactly make up my mind about a degree. It was hard, you know?"

"Finding your niche? You think you've found it now?"

"I'm getting there," she assured, more confidently than she felt.

He didn't reply, and she looked out the window at the passing scenery. There wasn't much to see. No city lights illuminated the country for miles the way they did back in California. There were a few lights, of course. Sparsely situated, marking someone's barn, someone's front porch. The area hardly looked any different now than it had when she was a child. "It was hard because I wanted to make a difference," she mused. "In the world, you know? I just couldn't see doing that by staying here in Weaver."

"People here in Weaver make a difference every day. Maybe not in the global scheme of things, but look at Sarah and the kids she teaches. Or your aunt Rebecca. She was the first doctor in a long while to come to Weaver and stay. The hospital that's been here for most of our lifetime would have probably never existed if not for her, or your uncle Tristan bringing CeeVid to town. Hell, most little towns were dying out back then. Weaver grew. It still grows, for that matter."

He was right. "I just…well, I just grew up knowing the stuff my father used to do. He traveled around the world. Built bridges. Helped impoverished people."

"So you think Jefferson canned it all by coming back to Weaver and starting up Clay Farm?"

"No, of course not." Her parents had married after her father had hung up his traveling boots and had come home to Weaver. "And I'm not saying everyone who is here isn't doing extremely worthwhile things. I just never knew how *I* could contribute. I don't want to follow in my dad's footsteps and breed horses. I don't want to follow in my mom's as an accountant. I don't want to work at CeeVid. Tried that when I was in high school. Remember? I lasted all of three weeks as a clerical assistant. I hated it, and I think everyone was relieved when I quit so that they didn't have to go to the trouble of firing me."

"And now you want to produce your own television shows. You think that'll feed your hunger to make a difference?"

"All of television isn't dreck, you know."

"I never said it was."

"Okay, then." She crossed her arms, not entirely certain why she felt as defensive as she did.

"Okay." His voice was peaceable.

He pulled up on the street outside of Sarah's house. This time he left the engine running.

Suited her just fine. She hopped out of the vehicle. "Thanks for the ride."

"Leandra."

She hesitated. "Yes?"

"I hope you find what you need with this TV stuff."

Her breath eked out. "Thank you."

He nodded once and she watched him pull his truck into a U-turn, heading back home.

But it was a long while before she finally went inside.

# Chapter 9

They started arriving the next week, right after the second episode of *WITS* aired.

Women, that is.

Some old enough to be his mother, Evan thought, some young enough to be illegal.

And all of them with the same thought in mind—that he was their soul mate. If only he'd give them a chance to see it.

He'd tried to be polite, sending the first one who showed up on his doorstep to the hotel before driving back to Missouri, where she'd come from. He'd advised the same of the second, third, fourth and fifth.

By the sixth, he was feeling less polite. Particularly when she didn't seem to realize that camping out on his front porch *wasn't* a trait that would endear her to him.

The deputy who'd come out from the sheriff's office had been mighty amused about the whole thing as he'd finally gotten the woman to move along.

Then there were the phone calls. Messages—friendly and innocent sounding to down-right lurid—left on his answering machine.

When he told Leandra about it, she looked surprised, then sympathetic and suggested he change his phone number. Anyone who really knew him and wanted to reach him used his cell phone, anyway, rather than his home phone, she reasoned.

It was good reasoning, one he'd thought of himself when he wasn't grousing about it. So he called the phone company.

Got a new number.

Too bad moving wasn't a solution as easily accomplished.

By the middle of the week, Sawyer Clay assigned one of his deputies to regular crowd control at Evan's place. "Hotels are getting full up around here," the gray-haired sheriff drawled, standing in the reception area of the clinic and looking out the window at the caution tape his deputy was putting out to corral the crowd—about three dozen women now—from getting closer to the clinic entrance. "Your thing with my niece is turning out to be damn good for tourism this time of year."

"Great." Evan shoved a stack of files to one side of the desk. He needed to hire another receptionist, badly. "Glad to be of assistance."

Sawyer laughed softly, his blue eyes amused. "Don't look so down about it, son. You've got, what? Four more episodes of the show to air? The novelty ought t'wear off soon enough after that."

"You want to put that in writing?" Evan grimaced. "There was a strange woman staring through my living room window when I got up this morning, for God's sake." He wasn't exactly a shy sort, but being caught in his skivvies by a complete stranger had been this side of hard to swallow.

"That's a problem being too eligible," Sawyer said, still grinning. "Might try locking your doors more."

Leandra sailed through the entrance, her clipboard in her hand. "Time to call in reinforcements, I see." She kissed her uncle on the cheek and barely glanced at Evan.

Ever since they'd had dessert that night at his folks' place, she'd been nothing but professional, nothing but work, work, work.

It was almost enough to drive a man insane.

"You never warned me that this might happen," Evan pointed out darkly.

"I never considered that it would." She flipped a page on her clipboard, her pen busy. "Guess there's a first for everything."

Sawyer was still looking out the front window. "You going to put all those women on the next show?"

Evan stifled an oath and eyed Leandra. "Ted's out there filming all of this, isn't he?"

"That's the way it works, Evan."

"Well, my work here is done," Sawyer said. "What you need is a wife, Ev. Scare off all those prospective brides." He let himself out the door, chuckling.

Evan didn't see all that much humor in the situation.

"They're scaring off my regulars," he said to Leandra. "Those *women* out there."

She sighed slightly and her pen finally stopped moving. "I'm sorry. I don't know what more we can do about it, though, aside from cordoning them some distance away like my uncle has done. At least you've got Tommy Potter out there, keeping them all orderly."

Evan crossed the room, dumping magazines on a

side table next to the chairs in the waiting room, and a high-pitched sound rose from outside.

*That* was orderly? He moved back behind the desk and away from the window. "They're out there screaming," he muttered. "What the hell kind of sense does that make? I'm a vet for God's sake, not some rock star."

"Try to ignore them."

"That's a helpful suggestion, Leandra. Thanks."

She pressed her lips together, finally looking up at him. "The attention will die down."

"You didn't know the attention would rise up in the first place." He plucked the clipboard out of her hands and tossed it on the desk alongside his mess of organized disorganization. "Come on. I'm taking Hannah for the afternoon for Sharon. You can come to Braden with me."

"I thought you were doing surgeries this afternoon."

He waved his arm at the empty waiting room. "Can't if there are no customers, can I?"

Her eyebrows knit together. "You're really serious."

"I said so, didn't I?"

"I can't believe this is affecting your business. For pity's sake, the people here in Weaver ought to know better."

"The people here in Weaver don't like walking through a throng of screaming women to get to my clinic door. Who the hell can blame them? They probably figure waiting another month or so for things to get back to normal is better than heading through the gauntlet there."

She stared out the window. "This has never happened before. I don't know what to say. I'm so sorry."

"Sorry enough to call off the rest of the show?"

Her lashes fell. "I can't. You know I can't. I'm bound

by contracts just as surely as you are. It's the way this works."

"Fine." He closed his hand around her arm, and felt the subtle flinch she couldn't quite hide.

"What are you doing?"

"Making sure we're in front of the window so they *all* can see."

She gave him a wary look. "See what?"

He closed his mouth over hers.

Her hands fisted between them. He felt them against his chest.

"Let me go," she said against his lips.

"No damn way," he returned and slid his arms around her back, pulling her up tight against him.

"Evan—"

He was a self-serving bastard, he thought, as the ploy to show the audience outside his clinic that he wasn't quite so available wasn't necessarily his only reason for wanting his hands on her.

*That* came from night after night of dreaming about her.

His friend's wife.

Ex-wife, a voice inside his head reminded.

Her lips softened under his. "Evan—"

He angled his head, going deeper. She tasted of coffee and chocolate and went straight to his head faster than both.

When her hands touched his waist, slowly sliding behind his back, he wanted to pull her away from the window. Wanted to hide her from the intrusive stares, hide her from everything but him.

The office would work. There was a couch here.

Her head fell back and she moaned softly when he

trailed his mouth down her jaw, pulling the collar of her T-shirt aside so he could taste the curve of her neck.

"Ah-hem. Ah-*hem.*" The voice was loud and intrusive. "Giving Ted a lot of fodder out there."

Leandra gulped and yanked out of his arms to stare at Paul. "What?" Her wide gaze followed Paul's nod toward the big, wide window where Ted's camera was pointed squarely in their direction. "Oh, *Lord,*" she muttered, and hustled out the door, giving Evan a look that scorched along the way.

"Sure you know what you're doing?" Paul's voice was mildly curious. "I know that you know Leandra from way back, but she doesn't get too chummy with people these days."

Evan wasn't sure if Paul was warning him away from Leandra for her sake or for Evan's. "I know exactly what I'm doing."

The other man shrugged and seemed to accept it, and followed Evan out the door when he headed after Leandra.

She was busy talking to the crowd; doling out plastic *WITS* bags with one hand and rolled-up T-shirts with the other. The second that Evan came into their view, though, all attention veered his way.

It was damned uncomfortable, is what it was; made him feel like he was some prized monkey at the zoo. And it was definitely time to put a stop to it.

He walked up behind Leandra and wrapped his arms around her from behind. The bags and armload of shirts dropped to the ground when she jumped and let out a soft squeak. Her head reared back and she looked up at him. "What are you *doing?*"

He smiled into her face, but addressed the crowd of women. "Isn't she the prettiest thing you ever saw?"

Despite the myriad desires that had driven all of those women to travel from far and farther, they still gave out a collective "ah-h." Whether it was that sentimental sound or his arms around her that caused the bloom of color in Leandra's face, he'd never know. But he was dead certain that the dark glint in her eyes was owed straight to him.

"What are you doing?"

"Now, now, now. I know you wanted to keep it between us for now, but these folks here have traveled a long way to get to know us."

"They've come to see you." Her voice was so bright, it could have blinded a sunbeam. "Not us."

"Come on, honey," one of the women called out. "If I had *his* arms around me, I wouldn't be complaining much."

Laughter and nods followed the statement. Evan grinned, too. "She's just a little shy. Prefers being behind the camera, instead of in front of it. But I figure you all have earned the right to hear the news straight from me."

The lithe body in his arms was about as malleable as a rod of rebar. She looked up at him again. The glint in her eyes had turned to shards. "News?"

He ignored the shards and dropped a kiss on her lips, also ignoring the hissing sound that was low enough for only his ears.

"You all can be the first to congratulate us since this lovely lady is going to be my wife." He didn't have to turn her around in his arms; she spun like a top to face him and her "are you insane?" comment was drowned out by the even louder "aw-wh-h" that filled the air at his announcement.

He kissed her lips, drowning out any other comments

she cared to add, while applause broke out all around them. "You owe me," he muttered in her ear when she pulled her mouth away from his.

Between their bodies, her fingernails dug into his chest. "Tell them the truth," she said through a clenched smile.

"Dude," Ted said from behind his camera. "Guess there's more going on than even I thought." He finally turned his camera away from them and panned over the crowd, who was acting as if Elvis had just reappeared in the flesh.

Janet and Paul began pulling women forward, getting live comments and Leandra pinched the inside of his arm. "Inside," she said, looking all loverlike.

He was going to be feeling the bruise on his arm for a while, he figured.

He twined his fingers through hers, keeping a good grip just in case she decided to bolt and ruin his charade. "Wither thou goest," he muttered, smiling right back at her. "You all don't mind excusing us for a while, do you?" he asked the crowd at large, and earned them another round of comments and laughter.

The moment they were inside the clinic, Leandra yanked her hand away from Evan's. "Are you *mad?*" She wanted to scream, but managed by some grace of God to keep her tone low. "You can't go around telling people we're getting married!"

"Why not?" Evan leaned back against the reception desk and crossed his arms over his chest. He looked so satisfied with himself that she wanted to kick him.

Or kiss him.

Both choices were completely unacceptable, even though she'd already done the latter. More than once.

And wanted to, again.

Despite his apparent loss of senses.

"Why not?" She propped her hands on her hips. "Why *not?*" Her voice rose and she swallowed hard, taking another deep breath. "Ted was filming all that, you know. Those women are going to expect to see themselves—and us—on the next episode."

"That's the plan."

"The plan. There *is* no plan! And that…that…mockery out there will be edited out. You can count on it."

"You're not going to edit it out," Evan said.

Shock was beginning to gurgle through her nerve endings, overriding the stunned paralysis that had seemed to plague her from the moment he'd put his arms around her. "Of course we are!"

"No, you're not." He grabbed her shoulders and dropped his head close to hers. "Your uncle had a point. If I had a wife, those women out there wouldn't be so damn anxious to throw themselves on my doorstep."

She felt light-headed. "I'm not your wife." She wasn't going to be anyone's wife again.

He looked impatient. "So, they all look pretty happy to me thinking that you are going to be," he said evenly. "I did you a favor doing this show in the first place. Now you do me a favor."

"It wouldn't be honest," she whispered fiercely. "*WITS*—at least when I'm producing it—is not going to be *dis*honest."

"Viewers can draw their own conclusions," he returned, completely unhelpfully, as far as Leandra was concerned. "That's the beauty of it."

The only beauty had been the warmth in her veins caused by Evan's mouth on hers, and even that had obviously been feigned on his part. All for the benefit of his unexpected flock of groupies.

"Find someone else," she said brusquely. "If it is so all-fire important to you. Maybe one of those women who are so ready to be at your beck and call."

She knew her error the moment the words came out, and his blue eyes lit with some unholy amusement. "Now isn't that interesting," he murmured softly. "You almost sound jealous there."

"Not in this lifetime." The words felt like they were ground out between her teeth.

He shrugged. "Doesn't matter. The deed's already done. They think you're going to marry me, and they can go right on thinking it until you pack up your cameras and take your sweet butt right out of town."

"This isn't just about complete strangers, Evan! People you know, *we* know, are watching this show. How are they going to feel if they see that…that…farce you just acted out?"

The corner of his lip lifted. "You think they won't have heard the scoop before then? Honey, this is Weaver, remember? Grapevine here is more effective than the almighty internet. By the time we get out to Braden to get Hannah, your mama will be getting ready to order napkins engraved with our names."

"Exactly." Her arms went up. "That's *exactly* what I mean! They're going to think that there's something between us!"

His lips twisted. "Pretty unbelievable, is that it?"

Her mouth opened, but no words jumped to the fore. "Well, yes," she finally managed. "Why would they believe it?" Her voice gained strength again. "Why would we want them to believe it?"

"Then tell them it's a front. Tell them whatever the hell you want, Leandra." He looked decidedly grim. "But make sure they keep it to themselves, so that they," he nodded toward the window where Ted was thoroughly surrounded by women anxious to get themselves on television, "can move on and find some other oddity to occupy their time."

"I'm not going to ask my family to participate in any sort of deception."

"Sounding a little uptight and prim there," he murmured.

"So what if I do? Are you telling me that you're perfectly content asking your family—even Tabby—to act as if you and I are heading into wedded bliss when they know nothing of the sort is ever going to happen?"

His lips twisted again. "Ever?"

Her stomach danced anxiously, as if she'd shot up an elevator shaft, then plunged right back down again. He was trying to annoy her; the same way he'd tried to annoy her through most of their childhood. All because his life had gone more topsy-turvy than any of them could have expected. She didn't blame him for his reaction, but she wasn't anxious to lay out over the train tracks so he'd feel better. "I'm not even going to discuss this." She'd edit out his outrageous nonsense and that was that.

"Suits me. Arguing's not high on my list of things I want to do today."

The easy capitulation made her even more wary. But she wasn't enamored with arguing, either. "Fine. Good. So I'll tell the crew that we're hitting the road today, instead of taping here."

"No."

She lifted her eyebrows. "Then where?"

"Nowhere. You can tell your crew to pack it in and go on home, because we are done."

Her stomach headed right back into the elevator

shaft. "Evan—" She broke off, not entirely sure what to say. He was leaning easily against the reception desk, but there was nothing easy about his set expression. "You mean done for today, right?"

He slowly shook his head.

The elevator shot down to the sub-sub-basement. "You can't just quit. You signed a contract."

"Sue me."

He didn't realize that the production company could, and would, do just that. "Evan, you can't afford a lawsuit like that." She spread her arms. "You could lose your practice, even!"

"And you'll lose that promotion that's so all-fire important to you."

Her arms lowered. She stared at him. "I swear, there are times I don't know you at all."

He stared back at her, blue eyes as deep and inflexible as a black glacier. "Don't edit it out."

"That's blackmail."

"Consider it a favor for an old friend," he drawled.

She winced. That had been *her* argument when she'd approached him about the show. "Pretending to be engaged to you is not exactly the same thing."

"Ought to be a helluva lot easier." He straightened. "That's the deal, sport. One favor in return for another. If it makes you feel better, tell your folks the truth. I imagine they can keep a secret pretty well." He looked amused for a moment.

"And when the show wraps? What then?"

"Tell the rest of the world that you changed your mind."

As if that would make up for lying to everyone? As if that would salve her conscience? As if that would make working with him as closely as they'd been one whit easier?

"Fine, then," she said, matching his careless tone with an effort. She hated the fact that she felt stung by his attitude. "I guess we'll both be getting what we want."

His gaze didn't waver. "Yes, ma'am. Would seem that way, wouldn't it."

It wasn't a question.

Instead, she had the sinking fear that it was more of a sentence.

## Chapter 10

The news spread like wildfire.

Before the day was over, nearly every member of her family had descended upon Leandra, mostly goggle-eyed and mostly thrilled.

One of the hardest things she'd had to do was tell her parents the truth, and watch her mother's face fall when she realized that Leandra wasn't *really* going to be making her home in Weaver, after all.

They were at Sarah's place, and Leandra's cousin—already cued in to the real scoop—quietly excused herself, leaving Leandra to face her parents alone.

She watched her father slip his palm over Emily's shoulder when she broke the news and felt her throat tighten. "I'm sorry," she said.

Emily waved her hand, but her dark brown eyes were still sad. "Don't be sorry, darling. I just couldn't help... hoping that you'd—" She shook her head and smiled. "Well, it doesn't matter. Has Evan told Jolie and Tag?"

"I suppose he has." She felt inexplicably foolish that she wasn't certain. After all, they *weren't* engaged— why would they confide everything to one another? "He went to Braden earlier. I haven't seen him since."

"What about the rest of the family?" Jefferson asked quietly. "You going to keep up the charade for them?"

"Not if I can help it." She pinched the bridge of her nose. "The problem is, if word gets out that the engagement is a fake, then it could cast a poor light on the integrity of *WITS*." And her future with the production company would be zilch. "There was just no reasoning with Evan, though."

Jefferson made a soft sound. "Peanut, if I had to put up with what that boy's had to put up with, I'd have been damn desperate, too."

Leandra's throat felt tight. "Me, too," she admitted, feeling miserable. The only one to blame was herself, for bringing all the attention onto Evan in the first place. All because she was desperate to prove she could do *something* right. Something worthwhile. Something that did not hurt anyone else.

Emily stepped away from Jefferson and brushed her hands together. "All seems like spilt milk to me," she said briskly. "This is not life and death, here. It's a television show." Leandra was enveloped in a cloud of soft fragrance as her mother gave her a swift hug. "As for anyone who thinks engagements are never broken, they obviously don't understand the reason why people do get engaged, and they can just get over it." Her mother stepped back and Leandra couldn't help but smile.

"I love you, Mom."

Emily's expression softened and she cupped Leandra's cheek for a moment. "Backatcha, sweetheart." Then she angled a look at Jefferson. "Now, I'm trying to get your father to take me to the movies. He only wants to see some action thing."

"She wants to see some kissy thing," he returned, looking amused. "Told her we could have plenty of that at home without paying money for it."

Leandra covered her face. "Too much information, Dad."

Her mother laughed. She kissed Leandra's cheek again, then her dad gave her a tight hug and in minutes, they were out the door.

Leandra watched them from the window. Hand in hand, to the truck parked at the curb. Her dad opened the door for Emily, then lifted her right up inside. She saw her mother's grin flash, and the way she swatted at Jefferson's hands before he closed the door and rounded the vehicle.

"Ever watch your parents and wonder if you'll some day have what they have?" Sarah stopped next to Leandra, watching through the window, too.

"I used to," she murmured.

"Did you think you had it with Jake?"

"When we first married? Sure. But even before—" she swallowed hard "—before we lost Emi, I knew that we didn't."

Sarah sighed faintly. "I thought I came close once, too."

Leandra hugged her cousin. It was rare for Sarah to refer to that. "Couple of sad sacks, aren't we?"

Sarah's lips curved. "And here you are, all engaged and everything."

Leandra rolled her eyes, but inside, she felt shaky. Mostly because she couldn't get out of her head the wondering about what belonging to Evan might really be like. "Let's go to Colby's."

"You want a drink?"

She wanted distraction and that was one place that might provide it. "Pool," she said.

Her cousin didn't look particularly fooled, but she grabbed her purse and they headed out.

At Colby's, however, Leandra was just treated to more well-wishers, and when Sarah got distracted by a few teachers she worked with, Leander excused herself. "I'm going to walk home," she assured Sarah over her protests. "I'll see you later."

Her cousin walked her to the door. "I'd go with you, but I want to get these two on one of my committees and this is the first time they've shown an interest."

"Then you've gotta stay and work your magic."

Sarah rolled her eyes, but headed back to the table and Leandra went outside.

The moon was high, and the air felt cool after the warmth and busyness inside the bar. She walked quickly, for some reason half expecting yet another congratulatory soul to come trotting after her.

A car went careening past, and she made a face after it, glad she'd kept to the sidewalk. Even Weaver wasn't immune to speeding dolts.

At the end of Main, she turned the corner and headed along the row of houses opposite the park. The ever-present breeze drifted over her, chilling her skin into bumps, and she quickened her step. The boots she wore rang out on the sidewalk. A dog barked. She saw the shadow of it racing through the park.

Then she heard the race of a car engine again and turned to see the same car screaming down the street.

She almost expected it to happen before it did. The car. The dog. She was running before the dog went still and the car continued on as if nothing had ever happened.

"Oh, God." The dog lay on its side. She crouched down beside it, gingerly reaching out to touch him. She didn't want to hurt him more, but she also didn't want to earn herself a dog bite, either. "It's okay, puppy." She held the back of her hand near his nose, letting him sniff her before she felt along his neck for a collar.

There was none.

He looked at her, flopping the end of his feathery gold tail a few times, and let out a whine as her fingers touched something wet.

Blood.

Murmuring softly to the animal, she carefully slid her arms under him, wanting to get him out of the street before another car came past or worse, the idiot who'd hit him came back around. She could see the taillights of the vehicle even now driving around the far side of the park. A few more turns and he'd be right back where they were.

The dog whined harder, but didn't struggle. Unfortunately, he also weighed a small ton, and there was no way she could carry him farther than the edge of the sidewalk. She yanked out her cell phone, peering at the dim display as she dialed Evan.

"Taggart." His voice was terse as he answered, but she still felt calmer just hearing it and she managed to relay the situation in a voice that didn't shake quite as much as her body did.

"I'm about five miles out," he said. "Got anything to cover the dog?"

"I could get something."

"Do it. I'll be there in a few minutes."

She shoved the phone back in her pocket and ran her

hand down the dog's head again. "Stay." Stupid command since the dog wasn't going to be going anywhere under his own steam.

She ran back to Colby's, going through the rear door. Nobody even noticed her as she snatched up a stack of cloths that were folded on a shelf in the kitchen. She was tucking them around the dog when Evan's pickup truck pulled up next to her.

He stopped with a lurch, and she ran around the hood of his vehicle going to his side. He was already getting out, his expression dark. His hands grabbed her shoulders. "Is that blood? Are *you* hurt?" Before she could blink, he'd lifted her onto the seat and was leaning in over her. "What exactly happened?"

She tried fielding the hands he was running over her arms and legs, but had little success. She finally caught his fingers in hers and squeezed. "*I'm* not hurt. Just the dog."

He let out a breath, his eyes closing for a moment. Then he straightened. "Give me a freaking heart attack," he muttered and turned to tend to the still dog.

She hovered next to him, feeling useless. "Some fool was speeding. The dog's conscious, but he's bleeding."

"There's a tarp folded up under the seat. Grab it, will you?"

Leandra felt around for the item, scraping her knuckles on the oddball collection of tools and other items before she found the tarp. She pulled it out and joined him on the sidewalk where he was examining the dog.

He was no longer beating the end of his tail. Not even the tiniest bit.

Leandra felt cold inside. She folded her arms around her waist, hovering next to the truck.

"His leg is definitely fractured, and he's going to need stitches for that cut."

"Maybe I shouldn't have moved him from the street."

"Lower the tailgate would you? We're gonna have to lift him up there." He began working the tarp beneath the unconscious dog. "And we've gotta go fast. He's going into shock."

The tail gate fell open with a noisy clang when her fingers slipped. Emi had been in shock when they'd pulled her from the swimming pool.

"Leandra." Evan's voice dragged at her. "I need your help to lift him."

She crouched down beside him, pulling the tarp taut the way he instructed. If she didn't think beyond the moment, she was okay.

Shock.

"On three," Evan said. "One. Two. Three." He lifted the dead weight of the animal far more easily than she did. When he'd carefully slid the injured dog into the truck bed, Evan touched Leandra's shoulder. "You can drive or you can hold the dog. Your choice."

"D-drive."

"Sure?"

She nodded.

He tucked the cloths from Colby's gently around the animal and pulled himself up into the truck bed with an easy motion. "Drive around to the back of the clinic. Park by the rolling door."

Just get to the clinic, she told herself.

*Shock.*

She fumbled with the gear shift, and the truck lurched forward. Her heart was in her throat, making her feel nauseated. Trying to drive more smoothly, she pulled a U-turn, barely managing not to bounce over the curb on the park side of the street, and headed back around the corner and toward the clinic.

She slowed at the red light in the center of town, hurriedly looking over her shoulder at Evan and the dog. He was leaning over the animal and she realized he was administering CPR.

She pressed harder on the gas and sailed through the empty intersection despite the red. Another few blocks and she turned into Evan's drive, going around the house, gravel spitting beneath the tires as she headed for the clinic that was farther back. It was a single story and considerably longer than his house, surrounded by a grassy area and pens on one side, and smooth cement parking on the other. The office and two examining rooms were at the near end—for the folks who brought in their companion animals. Cats. Dogs. Even a ferret or two, Evan had told her when they'd first started filming. Midway down the building, though, was the rolling door. She pulled up so the tail of the truck was closest to it and jumped out of the cab.

He was still giving CPR, only now he was doing chest compressions on the dog. "The code on the door is oh-five-oh-three."

She fumbled open the metal covering for the control panel and rapidly punched in the numbers. With a comforting rumble, the metal door began rolling upward. "Don't you know you're not supposed to use things like your birthday for security codes and passwords and such?" She lowered the tailgate of the truck again.

"If I didn't, I wouldn't remember them. Get a gurney. Should be one by the wall. Lights will come on automatically when you go inside."

And thank goodness for that, she thought as she stepped into the black cavernous opening. A moment later, overhead lights began flicking on in an orderly grid. She grabbed the wheeled cart and ran it out to him, managing to hit the wall and the side of the truck as she did so. "Sorry," she mumbled, scooting it a little more carefully around where he gestured.

He didn't stop his CPR until the last possible second, and then he jumped down from the truck bed and single-handedly lifted the animal onto the gurney. "You're going to have to help me inside," he told her, wheeling the cart around with far more expertise. "He's breathing again, but I don't know if it'll last."

He turned toward the front of the building, rolling the gurney up next to a high, steel table that sat in the center of the surgical area. "Grab that instrument stand. Roll it over here." He moved the dog onto the table, strapped him down and grabbed his stethoscope. "I only saw the one cut on his hind leg. Press the gauze pads—yeah. The large ones."

Leandra blindly ripped open the package that was on the tray along with an array of instruments. Two pads tumbled to the ground.

"Don't worry about them." Evan didn't even seem to be watching her as he filled a needle and shot it into the dog. "Press several pads against the cut. Gently, though. You're not applying a tourniquet or anything."

He dragged a rolling contraption around, and she realized it was some sort of monitor when he began attaching leads to various points of the animal. "Can you tell if the bleeding has stopped?"

She lifted the compress, and smoothed the matted hair away from the cut as best she could, mostly afraid that she would be causing the dog pain. "There's only a small amount of fresh blood."

"Good. There are elastic bandages in that drawer

behind you. You can strap one around the pads on his leg and then help me splint his fracture."

She swallowed and blindly followed his instructions, which seemed to come in an unending flow. She didn't stop to concentrate. Just did what he said. And after what seemed hours, he finally straightened and pulled the stethoscope from around his neck, laying it aside on the tray where the implements no longer lay in such pristine order.

"That's it," he said. "Now, we wait."

Leandra brushed her hand through the dog's luxurious ruff. "What are his chances?"

"Pretty good." Evan crossed to a sink and began washing his hands and forearms. "Haven't done anything in this clinic for days without your pal Ted following me around with that camera of his. Feels a little strange."

Leandra hadn't even given *WITS* a single thought. And now that she did, she knew that Evan's actions would have made great footage.

So why did she feel so glad that Ted *hadn't* been there?

She realized that Evan had asked her a question. "What?"

"Did you see who hit him?"

"The car, yes. But not the driver. He was definitely speeding."

"Judging by the size of our patient there, I imagine the car will be sporting a good-size dent now."

"I hope so." Now that Evan had stopped barking orders at her, she was feeling distinctly woozy. She reached behind her for the counter and locked her knees.

Evan was adjusting a blanket around the dog. "You

did good. Sure you don't want to consider a career change?"

She shook her head, which did nothing to clear her vision. It just seemed to grow hazier and dimmer.

And the last thing she was aware of as her knees turned to liquid was the widening of Evan's blue, blue eyes.

Her pretend fiancé's eyes were bluer than the sky, she thought faintly.

And then she didn't think anything at all.

## Chapter 11

Evan looked up in time to see the remaining color in Leandra's pale face drain away. Her eyes rolled and she pitched forward.

He barely caught her before she knocked herself on the end of the surgery table where the dog still lay. Cursing, he lifted her in his arms and carried her through to a back room that doubled as a break and storage room. There was no expensive lighting system in there. Only a bulb hanging from a forty-year-old fixture in the ceiling.

He settled her on the couch that he'd bought for its comfort rather than its aesthetics, and felt for her pulse, then reached up and yanked the chain for the light.

Already her eyes were fluttering open.

He hunkered down beside her, resting his palm along her neck. Not because he really needed to.

She blinked a few times and he waited, watching the

grogginess clear and clarity take its place. The moment
it did, she was trying to jackknife herself off the sofa.

"Take it easy," he murmured. "You fainted once already. Don't want a second round, do we?"

She subsided. "Don't suppose *we* do," she murmured.
Her eyes were as dark as molasses and he could feel
himself getting sucked into their sticky allure. "Jake
never liked me watching him work. Guess this is probably why."

Evan didn't particularly want to hear about Jake just
then. Particularly after fending off questions about his
sudden engagement to Jake's wife.

Ex-wife.

He straightened and grabbed a paper cup, shoving
it beneath the spout of the water dispenser, and took it
to her. "Here. Drink."

"Sit. Stay." But she did sit up a little and accepted
the cup, drinking it right down. Then she let her head
fall back on the arm of the sofa. "I'm sorry."

Except for the sofa, there were no other places to sit
other than the scarred coffee table that held a healthy
collection of sports magazines and professional jour-
nals. So he sat there. "Sorry for what? Passing out?"

She looked pained. "Yes."

"You're not the first one who has." He propped his
forearms on his thighs and looped his fingers loosely
together between them. Maybe that way he could keep
himself from touching her again. "Don't sweat it. I'm
glad I caught you before you hurt yourself falling."

"Oh. Right. Thank you for that, then, too."

"Too?"

"Well, you helped the dog."

He smiled faintly. "That's what I do. Just part of the
job, ma'am."

"We did a show last year with a single mom in Florida who was trying to break into fashion design. They had a dog needing some treatment and because they couldn't afford the bill, the vet refused to treat the dog. I don't think it's part of the job for *every* veterinarian."

Evan couldn't pretend he was shocked. He'd met plenty of animal care providers who felt the same. He could pretend that he hadn't seen the episodes when they aired, though. Just as he pretended to have rarely seen the show, ever. "It probably wasn't because the vet didn't care, but that he didn't have the resources to keep taking on patients who can't pay."

"Have you ever done that?"

He shook his head. He'd been paid with an assortment of goods and services in the few years since he'd established his practice—from having his house painted to having that fancy lighting system installed out in the main rooms. "I'm the only vet in the area," he dismissed. "Your Florida mom probably had other alternatives."

She made a face and tried sitting up again. This time, she moved more slowly and he kept his infernal hands to himself. "Figures you'd take the high road even on behalf of someone like that."

"I'm not taking any roads. I'm just saying you may not have had the entire story."

"Are you feeling that same understanding for the jerk who hit that dog? I told you the driver was speeding." She swung her legs off the couch. "Or maybe you think the driver had no choice but to hit him."

"I don't think anything of the sort. Would you relax? You've given me heart failure more than once tonight. Can you just stay still for a little bit and give me a break?"

Her chin jutted pugnaciously. "I wasn't trying to give *anyone* heart failure."

"Believe me, darlin'. You appear before anyone with your shirt covered in blood, and you're going to upset a soul or two." He didn't know what he'd thought when he'd seen her that way. He knew what he'd felt, though.

Murderous.

"What did you expect me to do, Evan?" Her voice went so high it nearly squeaked. "Leave him lying there in the street? Act like he's just some piece of roadkill for someone else to deal with?"

He scrubbed his hands down his face. "I'm not suggesting you do anything other than exactly what you did! If the dog makes it through the next few hours, he's going to be fine, so stop getting yourself all worked up."

"That's right! *If.* The dog might not make it. The dog might, might go into shock again, or…get an infection…or have internal injuries that you don't know about yet." Her words were coming so fast, they were practically running on top of each other. "Maybe if I'd been faster, or had stopped the dog from running out in the street, or—"

"Stop." He reached out and caught her face between his hands, making her look at him. Sometimes he was such a bloody idiot it was a wonder he had opposable thumbs. "What happened to this dog was not your fault. If you hadn't gotten help, he would have probably died out there on the street. You cannot blame yourself for this. It wasn't your fault." She tried to look away and he leaned closer. "Losing Emi was *not* your fault, either."

The shudders racking through her slender body stopped as if he'd plunged her into frozen storage. Her brown eyes seemed to grow even darker until they were almost black. They roved over the room, never stopping, never focusing and certainly never looking back at him.

And the pain inside her seemed to blast from her pores in a mushroom cloud.

He moved his hands to her shoulders. "It wasn't your fault," he whispered.

Her restless gaze finally stilled, settling midway down his chest. "You don't know." Her voice was low. Raw.

But he did know. Because Jake had told him. Jake, who'd needed to unburden himself one night after his marriage had fallen apart and Leandra had escaped to Europe to lick her wounds, alone. And it was Jake who'd told Evan—just mere weeks earlier—that he was certain Leandra still had not talked to anyone about what had happened the day Emi died.

"She climbed over the gate in your backyard and fell in the pool."

"And she died because of it," she finished flatly.

"It was not your fault."

"You think if you say that often enough, it's going to magically make it be true? It doesn't work that way, Evan. You don't know. You'll *never* know."

"That doesn't mean I don't know about loss," he said evenly. "Grief."

"Bully for you." She pushed herself off the couch, trying to brush past him, but he caught her around the waist, stopping her cold.

It galled the hell out of him that he was trying to help her and he could still be so easily sidetracked by desire. What did that say about him? That he was more Darian Taggart's son than Drew's?

He let go of her waist. "You need to clean up," he said, moving away from her before his baser instincts gave him the answer he didn't want to acknowledge. "You can take my truck home if you feel like you're steady enough to drive. I can't leave the dog yet."

She plucked at her T-shirt, looking down as if surprised that the bloodstains were still there. "I…I want to wait and see how the dog is."

He could have argued. Could have told her he'd call her, just the way he called any of the other pet owners who'd left their animals in his care for one reason or another. He could have gotten her out of his range by a half-dozen means, yet he just moved to the cupboard in the corner and opened it up. He pulled out a set of scrubs and held them out to her. "They're clean."

She reached out to take them.

Their fingers brushed.

Her lashes lowered, hiding those too-dark eyes of hers. "Thank you."

He shoved his hands in his pockets. He'd manipulated her to suit his own purpose, and as a result had made touching her even more impossible. "You can use the shower if you want. There's one in the bathroom there." He nodded toward the narrow doorway on the other side of the couch. "It's not fancy, but—"

"Thank you."

He nodded again and forced his feet to move out of the office. Thank God for the dog. It gave him something to occupy his mind and his hands as he checked him over again and transferred him to one of his larger kennels. The clinic was deadly silent except for the faint sound of hissing water.

He flipped on the radio and cranked the volume high enough to drown out the sound.

He was mopping up the floor in surgery when she reappeared. The pale green scrubs were meant to fit him, so on Leandra they were a couple million sizes too big. The arms barely stayed up on her shoulders, and she'd rolled up the bottom of the pants so she wouldn't trip on them.

She held a bundle at her waist. Her own clothes. Blue jeans. Blood-stained T-shirt.

He should have looked away when he spotted a hank of white lace bundled together with the rest, but he didn't. He just plagued himself wondering if there was anything between his cotton scrubs and her bare skin.

He flipped the mop back over the floor. "Watch out. Floor's slick."

"You really do handle everything around here, don't you?"

"Pretty much." But he knew the question was rhetorical. After all, she'd been the one asking questions from behind the camera during the second day of filming when she'd had him sitting on a wooden fence rail—as if that were where he spent a good portion of his workday—and wasted hours describing every way from Sunday how his practice worked. She knew that, until recently, he'd employed a part-time bookkeeper. Only Gretchen had left Weaver to be closer to her daughter and grandchildren, who lived in Cheyenne. And she knew he had two rotating assistants who helped with the companion animals.

"Jake only handles surgeries and what he calls the prima donna celebs at the animal hospital." She skirted the center portion of the floor that still gleamed wet. Her ex-husband's real interest was research, though, and the practice he had made enough money to fund it. "I guess you know that, though." She set her bundle on the end of a stainless-steel table. Then she snatched it up again. "That's not sterilized or something is it?"

He shook his head. "It's fine."

She set the clothing back down again. Crossed her arms. Uncrossed them, then crossed them once more.

He shoved the mop in the kick bucket filled with disinfectant. "You can go see the dog. Just around the corner there. He was awake a few minutes ago."

She didn't look at him as she slipped out of the surgery.

He pressed his forehead to the end of the mop handle. What on God's green earth was he doing?

He dumped the mop into the bucket. The floor was as clean as ever. Mopping it again wasn't going to change that any more than reminding himself why Leandra was off-limits changed his wanting her anyway.

He stepped around the wall to see Leandra sitting on the floor in front of the kennel. The dog was slowly licking the small fist she'd pushed between the bars. As he watched, she reached through with her other hand and gently worked her fingertips over his head, crooning softly.

He leaned his shoulder against the empty cage beside him. "I don't suppose you have any pets at home."

She shook her head. Her hair was slightly damp and it stuck out in feathery spikes, reminding him of a bird. The back of her neck looked pale and soft. The shirt had slipped toward her shoulder, baring a trio of freckles.

If he touched those tiny, enticing spots—the only marks on that smooth sweep of velvety skin—would she startle and fly away?

"I'm not home enough for a pet. But when Jake and I were together, he sometimes brought home strays."

"Jake said you were the one to bring home strays."

She was silent for a moment. Then she lifted her shoulder. "Maybe." The V-necked shirt took another run at slipping off the point of her shoulder, but she pulled her hand out of the cage and stopped it. "Why don't you have a pet? Too busy taking care of everyone else's?"

"Yeah."

"When did you and Axel go in together on Northern Light?" She seemed determined to discuss prosaic matters.

"A few months ago. We wanted Ryan to buy in, too, but he's been out of touch. Once we hear from him, if he still wants a share, we'll arrange it."

"I didn't know you were so interested in horse breeding."

"Neither did I." He watched her shirt slip again. There was definitely no bra strap impeding its wayward progress. "I'm in it for the money. Axel's just experimenting around with it. He knows your dad would be pretty happy for him to take a bigger interest in the horse farm."

"I don't think Axel knows *what* he wants to do."

Evan pinched the bridge of his nose. Axel knew exactly what he wanted to do, and the effect it would have on his family if and when he did it. Since the Clays already worried enough about Ryan's naval service, Axel wasn't inclined yet to add to it by revealing he'd pitched his hat into a similar ring. "Maybe," he hedged.

"Besides, what do you need with the money? Isn't this place paying its way? I mean when you don't have your groupies around scaring off the customers."

He grimaced. "There are some other things I'd like to do."

"Expand?"

He shrugged. But even as he was prepared to let her think that, he told her the truth. "I want to help pay for a special school for Hannah."

Her lashes lifted and she looked at him. "Wow."

"It's no big deal," he dismissed. "Just that Katy's a single mom on a serviceman's salary, you know? So if I can help—"

"You will," she finished. "Well," she turned her attention back to the cage. "I know what I want."

He seriously needed to get his mind off those freckles that kept peeking out at him. "What's that?"

"To sleep with you."

He hadn't heard right. "'Scuse me?"

She didn't look at him. Her fingers continued fondling the groggy dog. "I want you to take me to bed," she enunciated clearly as if he were not overly familiar with the English language.

There had been a day when he would have jumped at an offer like that—like a starving man jumped on a morsel of food. But that had been when he was twenty-one and doing anything and everything to forget the fact that the girl he'd never had, had fallen head over heels for his friend. "Why?"

She turned her head at that. But she still didn't manage to meet his gaze and there was a splotch of color riding her cheeks. "Do I have to draw you a picture?"

Unfortunately, no extra effort on her part was required. "Why *now?*" he pushed.

"We are engaged," she reminded him tartly as she faced the kennel once more. "But if you're not interested just say so."

He let out a harsh breath. "You'd try the patience of a saint, you know that? My *interest* is pretty damn evident, as you well know."

"Then what's the problem?"

"The problem is you're going around offering sex like it's a cup of coffee."

"If your percolator is out of commission—"

"Dammit, Leandra!"

Her shoulders moved, and the annoying shirt slipped another inch. "Look, just forget it. I changed my mind, anyway."

"Yeah, that solves it all, doesn't it," he muttered. "Let's just pretend we never had this conversation."

"Exactly."

He grabbed her arms from behind, hauling her to her feet. She let out a gasp, her eyes widening.

"No, not *exactly*." His teeth were clenched. "You don't put something out there like that and then pretend it never happened."

"You're the one who blackmailed me into pretending we're engaged. And you'll want to pretend *that* never happened when this is all over."

"Bugs you, does it? Hasn't even been a full day, yet. You think it's just one big joke, is that it?"

She glared and brushed at his hands, but he had a hold and wasn't remotely close to letting go.

"I know how you used to behave," she said tightly. "Jake told me all about it. Once Lucy was gone, you had a different girl every week."

"Which is it that you prefer, Leandra?" He barely managed not to shake her. "Thinking that I was moping around brokenhearted because Lucy chose New York over me? Or thinking that I was some get-laid-quick guy in college? Which one would make a better story for *WITS*?"

"This isn't about *WITS!*"

There were tears in her eyes. Dammit all to hell.

He let go of her so fast she stumbled, and he felt even more like the front-runner for crumb of the year. "Don't ask me to sleep with you just because you're bored," he snapped.

She managed a reasonable glare that was only slightly mitigated by the shimmer in her eyes. "I thought it was only women who were supposed to act all offended when presented with such a…situation."

"Proposition."

"Don't think that applies, given our affianced state. It doesn't matter, anyway, because like I said, I've changed my mind. In fact, I wouldn't sleep with you now if you begged."

He'd sit, stay and roll over and play dead if he believed she were serious. Though he seriously doubted that a single instance of lovemaking would get her out from beneath his skin. Not when she'd been lodged there as long as she had been. "That's a fact, huh?"

"Yes." She snatched at the shoulder of the shirt, twitching it back up again. "So what do we do about the dog? He has no collar, and you obviously don't recognize him. Do you think he's a stray?"

He barely managed to get his mind off Leandra and him and a bed—or any convenient surface. If he'd needed any confirmation that she really *hadn't* wanted what she'd said, he definitely had it now. "I doubt it. Aside from the injuries from the car, he's in good condition. As for what we do about it, I'll file a complaint over at the sheriff's office, but that probably won't lead to anything, either. All you have is a car description."

"So we just forget about it as if it never happened?"

"What *do* you want to do? Run a door-to-door search for the car? I'd like to see the driver punished, too, but believe me, there's not much more that we can do about it."

She looked even more distressed.

There was one thing he could say about Leandra.

Every emotion she felt was usually broadcast on that expressive face of hers.

She knelt next to the cage again and reached through to pet the dog. "What happens to him, then?"

"We'll post a notice or two, see if someone comes out to claim him. He looks well cared for. Chances are his owners will be looking for him."

"And if they don't?"

"Then I try to find someone to take him."

"And if you can't?"

"You have more questions than Hannah, you know that?" He hunkered down beside her.

"What happens?"

He reached through the bars and gave the dog a gentle scratch. "Animal control will take him."

"No!"

"What do you want me to do? Keep him? If I kept every stray that crosses my path, I'd have my own zoo."

"But you're a vet."

And he'd done plenty of volunteer stints for a host of animal services. "I'm a vet who can't afford his own zoo," he said. His father had attained a certain level of success, but Evan hadn't been born into a family with the kind of resources that she had. "Don't borrow trouble. The owner will probably turn up."

"If he doesn't, I'll take the dog."

"You just said you're not home enough for a pet. And even if you were, this guy won't fit in an apartment. He'll need space to run."

"There are parks." She shot him a look. "Don't you think I can take care of a dog?"

And just that quickly, they were back in quicksand, where everything he said was measured against the death of her daughter. "I think you can do anything you try to do. As long as it's for the right reasons."

Her shoulders sagged, as if she hadn't expected such an admission from him. The shirt slipped yet again. "Thank you," she whispered.

Even though there'd been no begging—other than in his feeble mind—and even though he'd made himself a year's worth of promises otherwise, he touched his finger to that smooth, beckoning trio of freckles.

She froze. He swore he could hear her swallow, and then the slow exhalation that followed.

She reached up and covered his exploring finger with her hand, pressing it against her flesh.

His hand flattened, fingers splayed. He could feel her pulse fluttering beneath his index finger.

"I'm not bored," she said after a moment.

"I know." He moved his thumb over the nape of her neck. Her hair was nearly dry, and it was as silky as anything he'd ever felt. "But we can't sleep together just so you can stop thinking about your daughter."

Her eyes closed. He felt her instinctive wish for flight. But she didn't move. Didn't take her hand from atop his. Didn't do anything but sit there, her pulse beating frantically against his fingers. "And…if I'm not thinking about that?"

"Then I'd still say no out of self-preservation. Can't take being ruined for all other women for the rest of my life."

She made a disbelieving sound. Then she patted his hand briskly and pushed to her feet. "No matter what anyone says, you're a good friend, Evan Taggart."

He grimaced. She thought he was giving her a palatable way out. And maybe he was.

But that didn't mean he hadn't meant every word he'd said.

## *Chapter 12*

Facing Evan when they resumed shooting the next Monday morning took about all the courage that Leandra could muster.

It wasn't just the airing of "the" episode, either. Though she'd gotten calls from friends and coworkers and even Eduard, who'd considered the entire matter *très romantique*.

It was the fact that she'd thrown herself at Evan, and he'd turned her down.

She'd put off going to his clinic until the last possible moment, not until Ted was calling her on her cell phone, wanting to know if she'd had an accident or something because she was *never* late.

She should have known not to worry, though. The minute she joined her already-set-up crew, Evan—who was talking to a girl about her kitten and the shots he needed to give it—barely gave her more than a passing glance.

Having spent every minute since she'd thrown herself at him fretting over this very moment, his lack of reaction was…deflating.

Ted had everything well under control. It was a day of pretty straightforward stuff. Evan had appointments all morning long in the clinic. Clients coming and going, bringing dogs and cats, even a goat. They would shoot continuously and during editing would pull and combine moments for the most effective results.

As Janet termed such days, it was a bit of a snooze.

Leandra sat quietly well behind the cameras, lights and sound equipment, making notes and fielding calls from Marian. When she wasn't doing that, she found herself becoming entirely distracted just watching Evan be Evan.

Even Ted caught Leandra seeming stuck in a daze as she watched the man and teased her about looking lovestruck. Evan caught the comment and Leandra felt herself flushing. Of course, they were *all* watching Evan, but she was in the disquieting position of knowing she wasn't watching him in a professional capacity. Everyone else thought they were engaged—even the crew—but Leandra knew better.

She rose from her chair and gestured silently to her cameraman that she was stepping out.

He nodded and mouthed "cool."

Because the film equipment blocked the area leading toward the rear of the building where the kennel cages were kept, Leandra went out the front door and walked outside the building, re-entering through the door through which they'd brought the injured dog.

He was still in the cage, but he lifted his tawny head and slapped his tail against the blanket beneath him when he spotted her. She crouched next to the bars, tucking her fingers through them. The dog immediately began licking them. "Yeah, you're feeling a whole lot better aren't you," she murmured. "Evan's pretty good at what he does." She rubbed the dog's silky ears and he made a sighing sound. "Wonder what your name is. Where you belong."

"Too bad I'm not Dr. Dolittle so he could tell us."

She bumped her shoulder against the kennel, turning so quickly. Evan stood there, looking very official in his white lab coat. "I didn't hear you come in."

"Sorry." He didn't particularly look it. He crouched beside her and pulled a treat from his pocket, feeding it to the dog, who lapped it up with greedy glee. "I put in a report with the sheriff's office. Just in case something turns up. Maybe the driver'll get stopped for speeding or something. And if anyone reports their dog missing, the county animal control has the info, too."

Leandra focused on Evan's hand, stuck through the cage bars beside hers and tried not to notice how good he smelled. Some combination of fresh air and Taggart that went to her head.

If he moved his thumb even a fraction of an inch, it would brush her hand where it lay, buried in the thick coat of butterscotch-colored dog hair.

She made the mistake of glancing at him, only to notice that his hair was starting to curl a little behind his ear. She made her fingers be satisfied with stroking dog fur, though, since running them through those gleaming black strands was really quite out of the question. Particularly after he'd turned her down. Flat.

She turned and stared again at the dog.

"We okay?" he asked after a moment. "You and me? You know. After the other night."

Her skin started to burn. "Why wouldn't we be?" She hoped she didn't sound like she was bluffing. "We're engaged, aren't we?" Her voice was flippant.

But he sighed and dastardly moved his hand just enough to close over her fingers. She was glad she was sitting on her butt, because she probably would have fallen over had she merely been in a balancing crouch the way he was.

"Then why are you acting so jumpy?"

"Too much caffeine. Don't take any notice of it."

"Easier said than done," he murmured.

She swallowed. *Why* wouldn't he move his hand? For that matter, why hadn't she moved hers? "Don't you have a patient waiting or something?"

"Overweight beagle. Owner's always late."

She moistened her lips, nodding.

He fell silent, too.

To say the air was thick would have been a huge understatement. Yet Leandra couldn't think of a single sensible thing to say. And she couldn't exactly afford to let her tongue run away with her again. It was bad enough that she'd propositioned him once and been turned down.

If she offered herself again she'd have to do something drastic to herself. Like cut out her tongue.

His thumb moved over the back of her hand. "Leandra—"

Couldn't he see that he was destroying her? What on earth was wrong with her that she didn't move away from him? Put some distance between them. Remember that he was just a friend from her home town.

Just Evan Taggart.

Nobody special. Nobody out of the ordinary. Nobody who made her lose track of anything and everything but him.

She swallowed past the vise constricting her throat. "Yes?"

His thumb caressed her hand again. No, he wasn't

caressing her. He was petting the dog. Her hand was simply in the way.

Willpower finally found her and she pulled her hand away from the dog. Ensuring that willpower didn't desert her again just as quickly, she slipped her arm out of the cage, even scooting back a few inches on the floor as she curled her fingers into a fist in her lap.

Evan still hadn't said whatever was on his mind. Her fingernails dug into her palm. "What, Evan?"

He looked at her.

And the expression in those blue, blue eyes reached down inside her and twisted. "What's wrong?"

He made a sound, partly impatient, partly wry and mostly effective in tightening her nerves even more. He pulled his hand from the cage, too, sliding his palm under her fist. "Conscience versus wishful thinking."

For some ridiculous reason, she suddenly felt like crying. But the scrape of a shoe on the floor behind them had Evan's head whipping around just as rapidly as hers. Their hands parted as if they'd been caught doing something naughty.

Ted stood there, his attention on his heavy camera. He'd obviously caught the moment on tape. "Beagle's here."

"What did I tell you? Fifteen minutes, every single time." Evan straightened, brushing his hands down his lab coat. "Coming?" He stuck his hand back out.

She took it, trying to act as if everything were perfectly normal as he pulled her to her feet and quickly released her. She was perfectly aware that Ted was still filming. Not that there was anything unusual in that. It was the way they put together a show, after all. Reality.

And since Evan's big "announcement," she was even more a part of the odd reality.

She moved around behind Ted, and they processed back to the waiting beagle.

For the rest of the afternoon, Leandra kept her nose firmly where it belonged—in the show. They were just packing up the equipment while Evan was cursing over the mess of files and paperwork on the desk when the door to the clinic opened and Darian Taggart stepped in.

Leandra shot a quick look at Evan.

He continued sorting file folders, barely looking at the older man. "What's wrong?"

Darian spread his hands, smiling. "Who says anything is wrong?"

Evan turned to a filing cabinet and dumped a pile inside the drawer. "You're here." His voice was flat.

Leandra saw Ted flip off the cover of his very small, very portable recorder and deliberately stepped in his path, cutting off the view. "Let's head to Colby's. My treat."

Janet and Paul were plenty enthusiastic about that. Ted, however, just eyed her.

She didn't move out of his path.

"This isn't the way we do this." His voice was low. Curious.

"It is today." She lifted the camera out of his hand and fit the cover back over it.

He hesitated, but after a long moment where she dreaded having to pull rank on him, he shrugged and hefted the last bag of equipment on his shoulder and followed the others outside. "We'll be in the van."

She nodded and looked back at Evan. "You're still doing rounds in the morning, right?"

"Yeah." He strode over to her and ignored the stiff surprise in her face as he dropped a kiss on her mouth. "I'll see you later."

She pressed her soft lips together, obviously believing he'd kissed her strictly for the benefit of Darian. She mumbled "later" and headed out the door, her cheeks pink.

For the first time that day, Evan was glad to see the back of Leandra. Whatever had brought Darian around, he figured it wouldn't be pleasant. "And I'm leaving by five in the morning whether your musketeers are here or not," he warned, calling after her.

"We'll be here." Her dark eyes flicked past him to Darian and she smiled as she excused herself.

Evan passed Darian, who was watching her walk toward the van, and reached for more files.

"She's a hot thing, but I can't believe you're going to bother marrying her. Easier to just sleep with 'em, I think," Darian announced.

"Which explains so much about your marriage to Sharon." He stuffed the files into the drawer; there would be hell to pay when he needed to look something up, but the desk needed clearing. The haphazard filing was better than setting a torch to all the paperwork, he figured. Much as getting rid of all the papers appealed. "You still haven't said why you're here."

"Have to be a reason to see my son?"

Evan looked over at the man. "Not your son in any way that matters to me and, yeah, there has to be a reason."

Darian made a face. He stood barely an inch shorter than Evan, and looking at the man, he had a pretty good idea what he, himself, would be like in another twenty years.

Practically carbon copies.

He shoved the last batch of files in the bottom drawer and slammed it shut. "Spit it out, Darian. I've got things to do."

"Picking out china patterns?"

"Maybe." If it got rid of Darian, what was one more lie? Evan had told his folks the truth; it was enough to keep his conscience relatively clear. "China, invitations, the whole bit."

Darian looked suspicious. "Don't fool me, boy. You're not the kind to settle down."

"Like you, you mean?" Darian didn't know what being settled even meant. Marriage sure in hell hadn't stopped him from entertaining himself elsewhere.

"Sharon's all right," Darian said carelessly. "She accepts me the way I am."

Because she's either a saint or a damn fool, Evan thought, not for the first time. And Darian still hadn't said why he'd come; it wasn't as if the man made regular trips to the clinic.

Grabbing the keys, Evan went back to the front door and pushed it open, holding it there.

Outside, the van was just pulling away. He could see Leandra's tousled blond head through the window.

"Katy's coming home next week. We just got an e-mail from her yesterday. Sharon wants to have a party."

He was glad to hear about his cousin's return. "Something wrong with the phone? You didn't have to come here in person."

"I was in Weaver, anyway."

Evan eyed the man. "So you used telling me about it as an excuse to be in Weaver. Pretty thin, don't you think? Maybe Sharon isn't as accepting of your behavior as she used to be. Who is it you're really here to see? The same woman you were with the other week?"

Darian's eyes narrowed and Evan knew he'd hit the nail on the head. Not that it was a particularly tiny nail—given Darian's perpetual behavior, it was about the size of a cow pie.

"A week from Saturday."

Evan had no respect for Darian, but that didn't extend to Katy. "I'll be there."

"Bring your girlfriend."

"Fiancée," Evan drawled.

"We'll see about that. Last fiancée you had didn't want to stick around Weaver, either."

Evan let the jab slide. He and Lucy hadn't been any more engaged than he and Leandra were. "Unless you want to stay locked in with seven dogs, two cats and a ferret for the night…?" He pushed the door wider and Darian finally left.

Evan pulled the door closed and locked it. Two minutes later, his cell rang and with little surprise, he answered Sharon's call. "Yeah, he was here," he told her when she asked if he'd seen Darian.

"Oh, good." Sharon sounded relieved. "We're so thrilled for you, you know. About you and Leandra. So romantic. You know, Darian followed me to Braden way back when. Reminds me a little of you two, now."

The similarity escaped him, but he listened to her prattle on a while about how nice it would be for Katy to be back for the wedding, and speaking of which, when would it be?

"We haven't set a date," he told her.

"Oh, well. Plenty of time for that," she assured him cheerfully and soon rang off.

Evan pocketed the phone and closed the rest of the clinic down, thinking he was as big a fraud as Darian.

The house was quiet when he went across, and even though he'd spent a lot of years telling himself he preferred it that way, it quickly got on his nerves. He showered and found some clean clothes and drove out to Clay Farms.

He didn't go up to the house; just headed around to the stable to check on Northern Light. Not a necessary endeavor; he couldn't trust anyone more than Jefferson Clay when it came to horses.

He turned the stallion out in the corral, then climbed on the fence rail to watch the horse work out his friskies.

"Used to come out here and watch the horses when you were just a boy. Em always said it was when you were chewing on something. Otherwise you went to your folks' place."

Evan was used to Jefferson's silent approaches. He settled his hat lower over his eyes to shade against the setting sun. "Married yourself a bright woman."

"I always thought so." He winced as he swung himself up beside Evan and swore under his breath. "Getting old ain't for sissies." He adjusted his own hat and eyed the horse. "Best-looking stud we've got on the property. Sure you don't want to sell him to me?"

"As sure as I was the last time you asked."

"Stubborn. But smart." Jefferson grinned faintly. "I wouldn't part with him, either."

The sun sank a few inches lower on the horizon, sending long red fingers across the landscape.

"I s'pose I should ask if you wanna talk about it or something."

Evan chuckled humorlessly. "Rather you didn't."

"Suits me. But Emily. She'll ask, you know."

"Nothing to tell. Just finding myself stuck between a rock and a hard place."

Jefferson straightened out one leg, then bent it again, propping his boot heel back on the rail. "Hard wanting someone you think you shouldn't want." He grimaced slightly when Evan shot him a look. "Hell, boy, you think I like talking about this? She's my daughter."

"The engagement isn't real. I know she told you that."

"You wishing it were?"

Evan stared back at the sunset. "It's not. I'm not the marrying kind and she's got her sights set elsewhere."

Jefferson snorted. "You're a vet. Oughta know better than to think that dog's gonna run."

He wasn't going to sit there on the man's fence and debate whether or not he wanted the man's daughter. "Squire coming back soon?"

Jefferson's teeth flashed. "Next weekend."

"Going to be plenty of parties going around. Sharon's throwing one for Katy's return the next weekend."

They sat there and watched the sun take its last dip. "Well, my butt can only take so much these days and Em's got dinner going inside. Welcome to come join us if you'd like." Jefferson climbed off the fence.

"Thanks." He'd shared many meals with them. "I'll take a rain check, if you don't mind."

Jefferson shrugged. "You'll want to be checking with Howard soon. He's got a list of people already interested in Northern's services. You and Ax are going to be neck deep in the business before you know it." He headed off toward the long stone house with a wave.

Evan hoped Jefferson was right about the business. If he were going to pay for Hannah's tuition, he'd be needing funds and the sooner the better, given Katy's impending return.

He climbed off the fence and rounded up the horse and led him back to the state-of-the-art horse barn. He coaxed the animal into his stall with fresh feed, then washed up and headed back to town.

The familiar van was parked outside of Colby's.

He thought about stopping.

Even slowed his truck down to a crawl.

Their engagement was not real. It never would be.

He put his boot harder on the gas and drove past.

# Chapter 13

Leandra sat up with a start, staring around the darkened bedroom at Sarah's, letting her heart settle, trying to get her bearings.

She let out a deep breath and lay back on the bed, bunching the pillow under her cheek.

A noise at her window had her bolting upright again, and she realized it was that same noise that had wakened her.

Then she heard her name. A crackle of something against the glass window. Followed by her name again and a somewhat less-quiet oath.

She threw back the blanket and went to the window, yanking up the shade.

Evan stood on the other side and she gasped, jumping back a foot, nearly tripping over the shoes she'd left lying on the floor.

He lifted his hand in a sketchy wave, as if they were just passing on the street.

She stepped to the window, shoving it upward. "What are you doing?"

He leaned in, smiling harder, and she got a whiff of alcohol through the window screen. "Visiting my fee-on-say."

"Good grief." She looked past him. The bedroom faced the street. Anyone and their mother's brother could drive by and see him tottering outside her window.

Not that there was a lot of traffic at—she glanced at the clock on the nightstand—two in the morning. "You've been drinking."

"Yes, ma'am."

She hadn't seen him drink more than the occasional beer since she'd returned to Weaver. "Why?"

He propped his elbows on the windowsill. "Because I am a parched man," he enunciated, more clearly than she would have expected, given his state. "Living in a desert with no hope of water."

"You're tanked," she muttered. "Just…stay there. I'll get dressed and drive you home."

He smiled again. "Knew you would. Seems like something a fee-on-say would do."

She wished he'd stop calling her that.

She grabbed a sweatshirt from the drawer and dragged it over her head, stuffed her feet in the shoes she'd tripped over and quickly let herself out of the house before he woke up Sarah and the neighbors, too.

He was waiting right where she'd left him. "Well? Come on." She gestured, her keys jangling in her hand. "It's cold out here. You don't even have on a jacket."

"More fee-on-say-uh-lee words." He stepped carefully around a bush, managing to put his boot right in the center of it. "Sorry."

"You can plant Sarah a new one when you're sober." She grabbed his arm and pulled him toward the car, trying hard not to be alarmed. "What's wrong? You don't drink anymore." She knew he'd once done plenty of it in college, right alongside Jake. But those days were long past. "Were you at Colby's or somewhere else?"

"Chaps. Out by CeeVid. Couldn't go to Colby's. You were there."

"Hours ago. Please don't tell me you drove here."

"Do I look that stupid?"

"You look that drunk," she said tartly. But there was no sign of his vehicle on the street.

"I walked."

"Been closer to walk to your house." She opened the passenger door and waited for him to fold himself into the close confines.

He caught her hand when she stepped back to close the door. "I did." He sounded weary. "There's a strange woman sleeping in my bed."

Her lips parted. Since the episode with his announcement had aired, the flocking women had abated considerably. "You picked up a stranger?"

He made a face at her. "Not these days."

His thumb was moving back and forth over her wrist in a very distracting way and she pulled away, only to have him loop his arm around her waist instead. Off balance, she leaned against the car, trying not to fall in his lap. "Evan—"

"Only ones in my bed should be us."

Her mouth ran dry. "Easy for you to say now," she said striving for lightness, "given the way you've already turned me down."

He shook his head and it brushed against her belly. He tightened his arm around her waist, and she hovered, precariously caught with one hand on the opened door and the other on the cold roof of the car. "Had to." His voice sighed against her.

She didn't want to examine that too closely. "Did you call the sheriff? About the woman in your house?"

"Mmm." He turned his head against her abdomen. "Smell good. Always do. Anyone ever tell you that?"

She couldn't say that anyone had. "Evan, what did you do about the woman in your house?"

"Left her there. She was sleeping."

"Thought you'd started locking your doors."

He shrugged. His hand slipped down her waist, cupping her hip, fingers splayed. It was an effort to keep her thoughts controlled. The woman could be robbing Evan blind for all they knew. "You have to call the sheriff's office. Who does the night shift these days?"

"Dunno." His fingers flexed against her hip, and she bit her lip against the rush of sensation he was causing. Then he did it again, and she began wondering if he was doing it deliberately. "Dave Ruiz," he said suddenly.

She grabbed his hand and peeled it away from her hip. "Do you have your cell phone on you?"

He leaned back and spread his arms wide. "Wanna check?"

She did, drat it all, and despite his inebriated state, he seemed well aware of that fact. "I'm going inside to call him." Her voice was prim in the face of the heat ripping through her veins. "Maybe he can meet us at your house. Just wait here." She didn't wait to see if he did so; she just spun on her heel and hurried back inside.

She was dialing the phone in the kitchen trying to be quiet so as not to wake Sarah when she heard a shuffle, and turned to see Evan coming through the small living room. He knocked his shin on the corner of the coffee table and swore softly, hurriedly catching the pretty glass vase of Sarah's that sat on top of it.

The dispatcher answered and she quickly relayed the information before Evan could make even more noise.

"It'll be a while before the deputy can get there," she was told. "He's out on a car accident. We've got a few others on call, though. You say the intruder is sleeping?"

"That's what Evan said."

"Bunch of crazies coming to town lately," the dispatcher said, her voice tart. "Give me a few minutes to raise somebody. Tell the doc not to re-enter his dwelling until we've given the clear. Can he be reached at this number?"

"Yes."

"Right. I'll get on it immediately. Oh, and congratulations on the engagement."

Leandra stared at the phone, feeling a little like she'd fallen down the rabbit hole. She slowly hung up the phone and turned to Evan.

He was leaning against the kitchen doorway. His eyes were narrowed against the kitchen light and his hair was rumpled. His dark T-shirt was coming untucked from the waist of his jeans. Dark stubble shadowed his hard jaw.

He was drunk yet looking at him still jangled every feminine instinct she possessed into shivering attention.

"You're not supposed to go back to the house until they call." She folded her hands together at her waist, feeling uncommonly nervous. "Do you want some coffee or water or something?"

"Something." He lifted his hand. "Come 'ere."

She stood stock still, not taking a single step toward him. "Coffee, I think." But she didn't head toward the coffeepot, either.

"I'm not Jake."

The comment came out of nowhere. She frowned at him. "Shh. Nobody's confusing the two of you. Least of all me."

His lips twisted. "You still love him." His voice was soft, but she still heard him.

Her stomach dipped and swayed. "I divorced him, remember?"

"You haven't replaced him."

"People don't get *replaced*. You haven't ever gotten serious about anyone since Lucy went away, and you insist that isn't because you're still in love with *her*."

"Always'll love her. Just not…love her."

"There you go, then." She crossed her arms. "And keep your voice down or we'll wake up Sarah."

He straightened from his slouching lean and stepped closer. "Say it."

"What?"

"That you're not in love with Jake."

Annoyed, she stretched her arms out, holding him at bay. "I just did." Heavens, there had been two calls just that week from him that she hadn't even returned.

"Not the words." His lips twisted again. "Maybe you can't."

"Oh, for Pete's sake. I am *not* in love with Jake! I'm—" she clamped her lips together, scrambling for the composure that had clearly deserted her. "You're drunk," she said flatly. "If you weren't, you'd be keeping a ten-foot pole between us."

His lips suddenly twitched. "Even I'm not gonna exaggerate about myself that much."

She blinked. What?

Then he closed his hands on her shoulders and yanked her against him, and she realized belatedly just exactly what he'd meant. So much for the theory that inebriation made a man incapable—

Her brain cells scrambled when his hand slid up her ribs, and grazed over her breast. "Evan—"

"Getting right fond of this kitchen." His lips nibbled along her neck.

She tried not to moan and instead, sank her fingers into his hair and pulled.

"Hey!"

"We are *not* doing this. Whoa!" He'd lifted her onto the counter. "Hold it."

He ignored her, stepping between her thighs and tugging her snug against him. "I'm trying to hold you."

Her head fell back against the cupboard behind her. Giving in would be oh, so easy. "This is a pretend engagement," she reminded him a little desperately.

"This—" his hand delved beneath her sweatshirt and camisole and slid wickedly along her spine "— isn't pretend."

She realized her fingertips were kneading his shoulders, and she yanked her hands back. "The other night you wanted nothing to do with *this*. Remember?"

"Shows you I'm not as nice a guy as you thought." He kissed her, almost roughly.

And though she'd expected to taste alcohol, she tasted him; laced with only a hint of coffee and whiskey. Heady.

He sighed against her, his lips softening, coaxing, then sinking deeper into her. She knew there was some reason she should be resisting him; she just couldn't quite put her finger on the reason. Particularly when her fingers were busy smoothing through the thick black locks that they'd so recently pulled.

His arm slid behind her rear and pulled her even

tighter against him. Her legs slid around his hips, ankles looping.

"Too many clothes," he muttered, and worked her sweatshirt up.

She let go of him long enough for him to draw it over her head. "You've got more on than me." Her voice was husky. Raw. A match to the way she felt inside.

The sweatshirt hit the floor and his hands came between them, molding her breasts through the stretchy thin fabric of her camisole.

Desire had been flooding her already. Now it was pushing headily at the dam. She bit back a cry when his fingers teased her nipples into even tighter peaks, and nearly came off the counter when his head dipped and he caught one, fabric and all, between his lips.

He made a low sound, male and satisfied and wanting all in one, and whatever dwindling sense of reason she still possessed fled for good. She just thanked the stars that Sarah was as sound a sleeper as she was. Her hands dragged at his T-shirt, working her hands beneath it, wanting to feel him, more of him, all of him. "Evan—"

"Leave a message." He discovered her other nipple, leaving the first bathed in damp fabric. "I'm busy here."

She traced the waist of his jeans around to the front. Felt the metal button at the top of his fly, and the flesh pushing hard from beneath.

He made that low sound again, the one that sent tingles streaking down her spine, and grabbed her hand, only to slide his between them. Her thin, cotton pajama pants were no protection against his teasing, intimate touch, and she sucked in a hard breath. "Evan—wait."

"Can't." His marauding hand found the thin excuse of a waistband and pulled at it, swirling and delving beneath until he touched only her. "You can't wait. I can't wait." He inhaled on a hiss as he dragged his fingers through the wet desire she couldn't hide, then sank into her. "Just this," he murmured, his mouth hot against her ear. "Just give me this one thing. Come for me."

There was no reason for his demand, his plea, for she was already convulsing against him, her body spinning out of control. She was still trembling when he let go of her and moved away. She reached for him, protesting. She wanted more, so much more than just his hand on her, in her. "No. Where—"

His expression was fierce, his breathing hard. He lifted one hand, calming, and reached for the phone she hadn't even realized had been ringing with the other.

Adjusting her disheveled clothes, her face feeling on fire, she slid off the counter, only to have to grab it again for her knees were barely strong enough to hold her up.

The sheriff's office calling, of course.

Talk about timing.

She pushed her shaking hands through her hair. Where had she left her car keys? In the car? Or had she brought them back inside with her? She'd need to drive Evan back to his place—

"When?" His voice was harsh and she flinched, watching his face turn pale.

Alarm slithered through her and she pushed a kitchen chair toward him when he seemed to reach out, needing something.

He sat down, the phone glued to his ear. "Is Darian there?"

Not the sheriff, then, she thought with even more alarm. Evan's gaze lifted to hers and she mouthed, "Who?"

He just shook his head, but grabbed her hand in his,

practically a death grip. She swallowed. Her head was suddenly pounding and nausea swirled inside her belly.

"I'll find him," he said, his voice flat. Hollow. "I'll get there as soon as I can." Then he dropped the phone on the table. It was an old-fashioned corded kind, affixed to the wall. The cord sprang back, and the receiver clattered off the table, banging the floor.

Moving automatically, Leandra picked it up and placed it on the cradle. "Is it Hannah?" She seemed to hear her voice coming from some long, thin tunnel.

He shoved his hands viciously through his hair. "Katy."

Her knees wavered again and she sank down on the chair opposite him. "What?"

"Her jeep took a grenade yesterday." He ran his hand down his face. "They sent a chaplain to tell Sharon and Darian. But he—" His teeth clenched visibly. "Bastard wasn't even there with his wife. Jesus. Katy must have barely sent off her email about her return before it happened."

Her eyes burned. She reached over and closed her hands over the fist he was pressing against the tabletop. "I'm so sorry," she whispered. Guilt—God, the familiar guilt that she'd tried to erase for so long, clawed at her. But this wasn't about her. It was about Evan. And his family. "What…what can I do?"

There were no vestiges of desire in his eyes now. "I have to find Darian."

"Let me call your parents. Maybe your dad can help find him."

"*Where* Darian is isn't the problem. He's probably with the woman he's currently screwing."

She flinched.

He stood, the chair skidding on the tile floor. "I need your car."

She rose, also. "I'll drive."

He gave her a hard look, one that nearly made her quail. But she hadn't been raised a Clay for nothing, and she kept her gaze steady on his. "*I'll* drive you, Evan."

He exhaled roughly. "Fine."

She swallowed, relieved that it hadn't come down to an argument. There was no question that he was significantly steadier on his feet than he had been when he'd been tapping on her bedroom window, but he'd also been dealt a heavy blow. "It'll take me just a minute to change."

She hurried to her room to do just that. She was buttoning her jeans when Sarah stuck her head in the door, her face sleep-creased. "What's wrong? I thought I heard the phone."

Leandra rapidly filled her in.

Sarah's expression fell, her hand pressing against her chest. "God. That's—" She shook her head, wordless.

"I'm going to drive Evan to Braden," she told her.

Sarah's eyebrows pulled together. "Are you sure you're up to that?" Her voice was cautious.

Leandra felt her eyes burning and resolutely blinked the tears back. "This isn't about Emi." Her voice broke a little. Hannah. That sweet, complicated child would never be reuniting with her mother.

Sarah just pulled Leandra into a swift hug. "Call me if you need me."

Leandra nodded and headed back out to Evan, Sarah trailing behind her. Her cousin didn't say a word. Just put her arms around his wide shoulders and pressed her cheek up against his. There were tears in her eyes when she stepped back to let them leave.

Behind the wheel of the car, Leandra looked at Evan. "Where to?"

He let out a low breath. "The Cozy," he said grimly, referring to a small, aging, out-of-the-way motel. "Darian's favorite home away from home."

She started the engine and silently drove through the dark, still town. When she reached the motel, Evan told her to pull up behind a dark-colored pickup truck.

"Darian's," he said.

She bit her lip. "I'll wait—"

But he shook his head. "Go home, Leandra."

"But—"

"I don't need you here."

The words might as well have been a slap.

She curled her hands tightly around the steering wheel, as if doing so would hold in the hurt.

She didn't say a word. Just nodded.

And when he climbed out of the car, she drove away.

# Chapter 14

The memorial service was two days later.

The church in Braden overflowed with family and friends and strangers, all who'd come to pay their respects to a young woman who'd died in service to her country. There was also a heavy media presence that worked Evan's last nerve down to a nub.

Bad enough that Sharon had insisted on Hannah attending. For any child such an event would be difficult. For Hannah, it was a nightmare.

Too many strangers. Too much activity. Too much confusion. She was in a constant state of terror, but nothing Evan said to her grandmother had any effect. There was no help from Darian's quarter, either. *He*'d spent nearly every minute since Evan had tracked him down at The Cozy in a whiskey-induced stupor.

For once, Evan didn't entirely blame the man.

As for him, he hadn't gone near a bottle since the night in Leandra's kitchen.

"Honey, we're heading back to the house." Evan's parents stopped next to him after the service, when he'd had to escape the cloying smell of too many flowers and haul some fresh air into his lungs. "We have a mountain of food to put out for the people who will be stopping by Sharon's to pay their respects," Jolie said. "Do you think I should take Hannah with us?"

"If you can pry her out of Sharon's grip." He could see them from where he stood outside the church. Sharon standing still and looking fragile, her hand seemingly fused to Hannah's tiny one. Darian had left the church the second the preacher stopped talking. "I haven't had any luck." Sharon had just gotten agitated when he'd tried. "But it's only a matter of time before one of those reporters gets close enough to put her and Hannah on air."

"Speaking of which…" Drew looked curiously over at Leandra, who was standing near her parents not far from them. "How did you keep Leandra's crew away from this?"

"I didn't have to." And Evan had been damned surprised about it, too, since he'd almost gotten used to those cameras following most every one of his moves. "She said they had enough footage for next week's show without intruding here."

His parents' gazes traveled over the news vans that were parked like soldiers shoulder to shoulder down the road. But if they thought it odd that Leandra would turn her crew away from a newsworthy event—painful though it was—they said nothing. "I'll go speak with Sharon," his mother said. "See what I can do."

"Thanks."

She just smiled sadly and patted his arm again before heading over to Sharon.

"Your mother's something, isn't she?" Drew tapped his black cowboy hat against the leg of his dark slacks.

"She doesn't hold Darian's actions against Sharon. They hadn't even met when he and Mom—"

Drew settled his hat on his head. "If it hadn't been for my brother, your mom and I wouldn't have found each other. We wouldn't have you. Or Tabby. Not a day goes by that I don't know that we came out on the high end of that particular stick." He clapped his hand over Evan's shoulder and squeezed. "Things like this happen, makes you even more grateful for what you have."

Someone called his name and he set off.

Evan watched his dad stride through the milling people. It wasn't the first time that Evan had to face the fact that Drew's forgiving nature hadn't rubbed off on him along the way. He wasn't feeling particularly grateful.

Anger? There was a helluva lot of that. Only there didn't seem any place to direct it. Guilt? There was plenty of that, too, and he knew right where to place that.

He was the one who'd encouraged Katy to join the service when she'd first talked about it. Her parents had been horrified and told her she was nuts.

She'd have been safer listening to *them*.

He watched Sharon, who was shaking her head as Jolie spoke with her, even as she was seeming to point Hannah into accepting a hug from one of the people working through the line.

His niece looked petrified.

He yanked at the tie strangling him and strode over to them. He bent down and scooped up Hannah. She felt as stiff as a poker, but her fingers clutched his tie like a life raft. "I'm taking her back to your place," he told Sharon, his voice even. He might have been wrong to encourage Katy, but he damn straight wasn't wrong where Katy's daughter was concerned. "The limo will wait here until you're ready to leave."

"But—"

"I'm taking her."

Sharon blinked. She looked nearly ready to collapse. An argument was clearly beyond her, finally. "All right."

He didn't wait around for her to change her mind; to want to pull Hannah forward to meet and greet every person who passed by them, the way she'd been doing. "See you at the house," he told his mom.

She nodded and he carried Hannah away from the melee, stopping only when Leandra cut across the grass to intercept them. "You heading back to Sharon's?"

"Yeah."

"I should probably go with you." She brushed her hand down the side of her simple black dress. "People keep asking me about the, um, the engagement."

Until she'd entered the church with her parents, he hadn't seen her in person since two nights before, when she'd dropped him at The Cozy. Had only talked to her once on the phone when he'd told her about the memorial service arrangements and she'd floored him by pre-empting his request that she keep her cameras away. But since he'd forced the pretense on her in the first place, he supposed she was right about keeping up appearances as an engaged couple.

"Fine. But all I have is the truck." She wore a black dress and high heels with an elegance that he'd somehow managed to forget she possessed, considering she was almost always in considerably more casual gear.

"Doesn't bother me." She waved slightly to her parents and they headed away from the church.

"Doctor Taggart!" A stiffly coiffed woman jogged across the street toward him. She held a microphone in her hand. "If you could just give us a few moments—"

He lifted his hand, giving her a hard look as he continued down the road. Beside him, Leandra's pace picked up, keeping even with him. Her heels clicked rapidly on the pavement.

"Your cousin died a hero." The reporter's voice followed after him. "Don't you have anything to say about that? What about your newfound celebrity status? Don't you think you owe it to the public to make a statement?"

He swore under his breath and lengthened his stride, grabbing Leandra's elbow with one hand. In his other arm, Hannah started squealing, a high-pitched sound that could have curled hair. "It's okay," he murmured to her.

She took no notice. Just kept up that high, keening sound.

Fifty yards and three more reporters approached before they practically tumbled into the cab of his truck. "Fasten her in," he told Leandra, and gunned the engine.

She was already doing so, and he shot down the street, watching the cameras turned in his direction through the rearview mirror.

Hannah let out a deep sigh and went silent.

He sighed, too. Brushed his hand down her sleek black hair. His gaze met Leandra's for a moment before she looked away.

What did he expect? He'd gotten her nearly naked in her cousin's kitchen, and then pushed her away when she'd only tried to help. He wasn't such a Neanderthal that he didn't realize his actions had been rough.

He *was* Neanderthal enough to have his eyes straying down her slender legs, smoothed in some slightly black nylons, to her ankles and those high, high heels.

Hannah reached past Leandra and opened his glove compartment, and he dragged his attention back where it belonged. He'd learned a long time ago to keep a few spare toy cars around for her, and she pulled out one of the red cars, then sat back again, her finger spinning the wheels.

When they reached Sharon's house, there was another phalanx of trucks waiting.

Hannah, looking out the window, saw, too. A low sound came out of her pursed lips, growing increasingly loud and high. Her knuckles were white around the car she held clenched in her fist.

Leandra carefully touched the little girl's hand. "It's okay, peanut," she murmured. "Don't look at them."

Evan drove right on past the house. Ten minutes later, he was on the highway.

He drummed his thumb against the steering wheel. "You know, you see the news on television. In the papers. You know this happens. Katy knew it could happen when she enlisted. But—"

"But you don't think it will happen to you. To someone you know. Someone you care about." Her voice was soft.

He frowned. "I should have been there for Emi's funeral."

She was silent, absorbing the sudden announcement. "I don't remember her funeral," she admitted huskily. "Who was there. Who wasn't. It's a complete blur to me. Later, after, Jake tried making me go to a grief counselor with him."

"Why didn't you?"

She looked away. "I didn't want to feel better about

losing her." Her voice was husky. "I didn't deserve to feel better. And for a while I hated Jake for not feeling the same way."

"It wasn't your fault, Leandra."

"If not mine, then whose?" She started when Hannah suddenly dumped her car in Leandra's hand and leaned her dark head against her side.

After a taut moment, she slipped her arm around the girl. Before she looked away again, Evan could see that her eyes were damp.

He reached out and turned on the radio, keeping the volume low. They weren't on the road ten minutes before Hannah began snoring softly.

The road hummed beneath the tires and for the first time in days, Evan felt some of his tension ease. The inside of his truck felt quiet and intimate and…familial.

Did Leandra notice the same thing?

He stretched his arm out over the seat, settling a little more comfortably behind the wheel for the drive, and his fingers brushed the back of her head.

She didn't move away.

They finished the trek, with his niece asleep between them, and his fingertips buried in Leandra's soft blond hair.

He headed to his place, but they both noticed the news van parked in front of the clinic. "Dammit."

"Don't stop. We can go out to my parents' farm," Leandra suggested.

If he didn't have Hannah, there was no way he'd let a reporter run him off from his own home. But he did have Hannah to consider. "They might show up out there, too. You being my—"

"Fiancée?" she finished. "It's possible. But Howard

can put a few hands at the gate. Nobody who shouldn't be there will make it past."

This wasn't a case of being inconvenienced by the attention from her show. "This isn't your problem," he said.

She looked pained. "You won't even let me act like a friend now? My parents would offer you the same thing and you know it. Consider it an invitation from them if you have to."

If he put his foot any deeper down his throat, he was going to suffocate on it. "Okay. But just until the attention dies down."

"That might not be as quick as you seem to think."

Leandra's warning turned out to be all too accurate.

If anything, the media attention seemed to increase. Particularly after that week's episode of *WITS* aired.

The footage of the memorial service had been from the news pool, not from Leandra's crew. But it had been part of the show, all the same.

By the next morning, he was getting calls from the major news networks, wanting him to make an appearance.

He tried to be polite as he declined.

The Clays put hands on all the entry points to the property—round the clock, turning away dozens of people each day. Evan stayed in one of the guest suites, and his mother came to stay with Hannah during the day while he breached the persistent looky-loos and reporters and tried to keep his practice from running into the ground.

He'd have been making trips to Braden to check on Sharon, too, but she and Darian had gone to Washington, D.C., for a service there. And though Evan rarely had much good to say about Darian, he was the one who'd convinced Sharon that Hannah should remain in Weaver with Evan.

Evan wished he could believe that Darian was really thinking of Hannah's welfare, but he was cynically aware that the man was happy enough not having to deal with Hannah on a good day.

These were not good days where Hannah was concerned. If anything, she'd withdrawn further into her isolated shell.

"Here." Leandra appeared on the porch beside him where he'd been watching the sun set. "Eat." She pushed a plate toward him. "Or be ready to face my mother's wrath. She saved this for you from dinner."

Her mother had been nothing but gracious.

"Hannah asleep?"

He nodded and took the plate laden with roasted chicken and vegetables even though he wasn't particularly hungry. "She asked about her mom today. Hasn't asked about Katy in months, but today she did."

Leandra sat down on the Adirondack chair beside his. "What did you tell her?"

"I told her she was in heaven."

"Do you think she understands that?"

"As much as she can understand some things."

They fell silent while he managed to make a dent in the food, and when he could stomach no more, he set aside the plate. "Talked to Jake today. Said he hadn't heard from you lately."

She tilted her head, looking at him. "Been sort of busy here."

"Not with filming the show." She'd kept the crew mostly at bay for several days now. He'd been perfectly happy about it, until he'd run into Ted that morning in town, and had learned just what it was costing Leandra.

She didn't reply.

"There was only one reporter at the gate today. So I'm going to take Hannah back home with me tomorrow. Think you can work without getting her on camera?"

"Yes." At that, she didn't hesitate. "Evan—have you thought about what you're going to do about her?"

It had been mostly all he'd thought about. If he wasn't thinking about Hannah, he was thinking about Leandra.

Both pretty impossible situations, as far as he was concerned. One he wanted, but knew her mother had never intended that. The other he wanted, but knew she'd been meant for someone else.

"She has special needs," he finally said. "Her autism is fairly mild, but she still needs special attention. If Katy hadn't—" He cleared his throat. "In North Carolina, there was a program designed for kids like Hannah right in town, where they'd have been living."

"The program that you were prepared to help pay for," she said. She reached over and closed her hand over his. "There's *nothing* in the area here?"

"Sure, if we went to Cheyenne. Gillette." Either option was several hours away. "She should be starting kindergarten next year. The school in Braden will take her, and do their best, but it's not the best for Hannah."

"We did a show once," Leandra said after a while. "On hippotherapy. Have you heard of it?"

"Occupational or physical therapy with horses. Yeah."

"It was geared toward children with varying degrees of autism. We followed one of the therapists for nearly six months. She was incredible with the children. The strides those children made in their daily lives just through the interaction with the therapist and the horse was amazing. This is a horse-filled community. Wouldn't you think something like that would be possible here?"

He'd seen the shows about it. Truth was, he'd watched every show that he'd known Leandra had been involved with. "Closest hippotherapy program is in Cheyenne. It's also too bad there's not a special ed teacher on staff at the school. In fact, there're a lot of things that are too bad." He pushed out of his chair, and Leandra's hand fell away.

"You'll figure it out, Evan."

He looked at her. "How do you know?"

She lifted her shoulders. "I just do."

Why she had faith in him when he didn't, he couldn't fathom. "You need an interview, don't you."

Her expression stilled. She moistened her lips. "No."

"Liar. I know Marian has been hounding you."

She turned her palms up in her lap. "What do you want me to say?"

"You're jeopardizing your job." She made no response and he leaned down, pressing his hands on the arms of her chair. "Why would you do that after you've worked so hard to get where you're at?"

She seemed to sink as far back into the chair as she could go. "Because I don't want to cause you any more grief, okay?"

Silence stretched out, thick and taut.

She moistened her lips.

"God, Leandra." His fingers brushed the nape of her neck.

Her lashes fluttered down. She tilted her head back into his hand. Her breath sighed out of her.

He shifted slightly, leaning closer. He brushed his

thumb against her cheek and it felt as soft and smooth as Hannah's.

"Evan." His name was barely a movement on her lips. "This is getting too complicated. I don't do well with complicated."

"I'm not sure we have much of a choice on that, anymore." He brushed his lips over hers. It was enough to make the world tilt sideways. When he lifted his head, her lips followed his, seeming to cling for a breathtaking moment.

Then she leaned back in the chair again, her lips pressing together. Savoring the kiss, or trying to erase it?

"You can tape whatever you want tomorrow," he told her. "Ask whatever you need. But I have to go to Braden first and pick up some more of Hannah's stuff. Take care of a few things. It'll take me a few hours, probably."

She hesitated for a moment. "Okay."

"Can you stay with her?"

Her eyes widened, alarmed. "With Hannah? Your mom has been pulling that duty."

"She's got a school thing she can't miss with Tabby. Hannah likes you, Leandra. I wouldn't ask otherwise."

"And you can't take her with—" She broke off the question. "Never mind. Of course I—I'll stay with her." She smiled, but it looked forced. "What else are pretend fiancées for?"

# *Chapter 15*

It was raining the next morning when Leandra approached the house where she'd grown up, trying to talk herself out of the trepidation that was assailing her.

She could manage to care for one small girl for a few hours, couldn't she?

She entered through the rear door. She'd run into her father, already, on his way to the horse barn. He'd told her that Emily had her accountant hat on and was meeting with a client over breakfast in town. Aside from Evan and Hannah, the house was empty.

The guest room where Evan had been staying with Hannah was on the second floor, down the hall from Leandra's room when she'd been a child.

She headed up there, and still trying to talk herself out of the odd nervousness that plagued her, she knocked softly on the door.

But there was no answer. Nor to her second knock or

when she spoke his name. She cautiously pushed open the door, peering around it.

The room was spacious. The bed tumbled. "Evan?"

"Hey." He stepped into view and she gulped a little.

He wore nothing but a towel and remnants of steam.

She quickly looked down but his image was already seared in her brain. "I wasn't sure you were in here."

He stepped farther into the room from the connecting bathroom, holding the towel together at his waist. "Hannah's still sleeping."

"Right. Okay. Well, I'll just be downstairs then."

But he lifted his eyebrows a little when she continued standing there like she'd grown roots. "Did you want something else?"

You, she thought, and saw the flush that rose in her face in the mirror over the dresser.

As usual, her libido had disastrous timing.

"No," she assured him quickly, and backed out of the room, shutting the door after her, barely remembering to keep the thing from noisily slamming and waking Hannah.

With the door shut, she raked her fingers through her hair, pressed her palms to her temples and tried to squeeze sensibility back into her brain.

It was a futile effort.

Whether she had her eyes open or closed, she could still see Evan standing there, a minimal amount of white terry cloth barely providing some decency.

But even the vision of that wealth of long, roping muscular legs, a chest sprinkled with black hair and an abdomen the likes of which she'd only seen on the cover of fitness magazines wasn't what disturbed Leandra the most.

No, what disturbed her the most, what shook her

right down to her soul, was the abrupt realization that she didn't just *want* her hometown friend.

She was falling in love with him.

"You trying to memorize the carpet pattern?"

She jerked, looking at Axel as if she'd never seen him before. "Dad didn't say you were still here. Where'd you come from?"

He grinned faintly and gestured with his thumb. "My room." She made a face and brushed past him, but he caught her arm. "What's wrong?"

"Nothing."

He snorted softly. "Yeah, and I'm destined to ride a desk my whole life. You having second thoughts about marrying him?"

How could she forget that not *everyone* knew the truth about that? Not even her own brother? "Sh-should I be?"

"Just figured he'd probably have Hannah with him a lot now."

And Axel assumed that would make a difference to her.

She moistened her lips. The truth was, a month earlier, it might have made a difference.

And now?

Now she was discussing an engagement that wasn't even real as if it *were*.

"Aren't you supposed to be at work or something?" She made a production of looking at her watch.

"Have a meeting."

"For CeeVid?"

"For work," he said, moving down the hall to the stairs. "Later."

She watched his departure. For work. Isn't that what she'd said?

Then she heard a noise behind Evan's bedroom door, and hurriedly escaped down the stairs, too.

She found fresh coffee in the kitchen and poured herself a mug, and within minutes, Evan appeared.

He was safely dressed.

No less distracting, though, in black trousers and a crew-necked ivory sweater. For Evan, the clothing was definitely not the norm.

"Hannah likes Cheerios for breakfast," he told her. "She'll probably sleep another hour, though."

She was plenty curious about his reason for being dressed up, but kept it to herself and just nodded.

He lifted the mug out of her hand and took a long sip, then placed it back in her hand. "Thanks for this."

The coffee? Or watching Hannah?

"Sure." She wriggled her tingling fingers around the mug.

He seemed ready to say something else, but didn't. He just checked his pockets and headed out the door. "I have my cell. Call if you need me."

"It's raining," she stated the obvious. "Drive carefully."

He nodded, and then he was gone.

She had no reason to feel bereft, yet she still did.

The house seemed to loom around her, silent and still except for the rhythmic tick of the grandfather clock standing in the front entry and the sound of raindrops beating against the windows.

She filled her mug to the top again and shut off the coffee maker, then climbed back up the stairs and cautiously looked in on Hannah.

The girl really was sound asleep, sprawled across the narrow bed, her little bow mouth parted softly.

Leandra closed the door and sank down on the hallway floor.

She tilted her head back against the wall behind her and stared blindly at the doorframe, behind which Hannah slept.

She *wasn't* in love with Evan.

How could she be? She'd known him forever and a day.

"Hello?"

She jolted at the completely unexpected voice, and scrambled over to the stairs. "Mom?"

Emily appeared at the bottom of them, looking up at her. "I saw your car parked outside. Come down and sit with me."

"Evan asked me to stay with Hannah while he ran to Braden and took care of some things. Don't worry, though," she added quickly as she descended. "She's sleeping. Safely. I just looked in on her."

"Well," her mother said after a moment, "that's quite a comment, Leandra. Do you actually think I would worry about Hannah being in your care?"

"*I* worry about it. Seems like everyone else should, too."

"Oh, darling." Emily plucked the coffee cup out of her hand and set it atop the wide square newel post. "You're so much like your father sometimes, it boggles the mind." She stood not one inch taller than Leandra, but she still put her hands around Leandra's face and had her looking up at her.

"You were a good mother." Emily's voice was firm, despite its huskiness. "Better than good. You were loving and kind and firm. And I was always, *always* proud of the mother that my own daughter was becoming. You were not careless and you were not thoughtless.

Losing Emi was a terrible tragedy, and it broke all of our hearts. But tragedies are not alleviated by placing blame. They become part of us and we grieve and finally, we accept."

"You don't know." Leandra's voice went thick. "You don't know what it's like to bury your baby."

Emily closed her eyes. "I know what it's like to watch my baby bury hers," she said after a moment. "And know that there's nothing I can do to change that. I don't want to lose my daughter, too, Leandra." She let go and turned away, dashing a hand over her cheeks. "I know what it's like to lose family, darling. I was young, but I still remember when my parents died. I remember going to live with your grandfather, not feeling as if there were anyplace in the world that I belonged."

"Their accident wasn't at all your fault, though. So you don't know what it's like to blame yourself for someone's death." The admission felt raw.

Emily just sighed and shook her head. "I know what it is like to love someone who blames himself for someone else's death," she said quietly. "Leandra, you have to let it go. You have to let Emi go."

"Who are you talking about, because I know it can't have been Dad."

Emily's eyebrows rose a little. "Do you think you know every detail there is to know about your father and me, then? Yes, it is your father I'm talking about. And he'd have let everything that mattered in this life—including *his* life—slide into nothing because he couldn't let go of blaming himself."

"You're talking about my father. The guy who raises horses and used to be in the Peace Corps."

"It was hardly the Peace Corps," Emily said evenly, "but that's for your father to explain if he chooses. Suffice it to say that he felt responsible for an associate's death, just the same way you feel responsible for Emi's."

Leandra gnawed the inside of her cheek. "What changed?"

"He let me love him," Emily said simply.

Leandra's eyes burned.

"Where's my Evan?"

The tiny voice came from the stairwell and nearly made Leandra jump out of her skin. She looked up to see Hannah standing there. Three feet tall, sleep-creased ivory cheeks and lopsided black pigtails, she made Leandra feel like she was sitting on the north side of panic. "He had to go out for a little while and asked me to stay here with you." She looked to her mother, expecting rescue or something, but Emily just smiled calmly at them both.

She swallowed, hard, and faced the child. "Are you hungry?"

Hannah nodded and sat down on the stairs, scooting down the few remaining treads until she was sitting on the kitchen floor. Her pajamas had horses printed on them.

"Do you want some cereal?"

Hannah nodded. She ducked her head, but was clearly watching Emily.

"Well," Emily said. "I have things to attend to, so I'll leave you two ladies to it."

Leandra's lips parted. "You're not going to stay?"

"Nope." She gave Leandra a hug and kissed her cheek. "You'll be fine," she whispered. Then she turned to leave, only to stop short at the door.

Relief swept through Leandra. A reprieve.

"I completely forgot. Gloria called and she and Squire will be back in town tomorrow."

"How are we going to keep him from finding out about the party?"

"By avoiding the man, I suspect. Fortunately there is plenty to keep us all occupied until then." Her gaze went again to Hannah. "Hannah, after you eat, maybe you'd like Leandra to take you to see the horses?"

"I like horses," Hannah replied, looking at the wall beside her.

"There you go, then," Emily said, smiling faintly. "Breakfast, then horses. Plenty to keep you two busy." She opened the door.

"But, Mom—"

"You'll be fine, Leandra. You need to do this. Not just for Evan, but for yourself." She let herself out onto the rear porch and closed the door.

Feeling utterly deserted, Leandra stood there, looking at Hannah.

Hannah just looked back, blinking her beautifully silky black lashes. "Are you sad?"

Leandra started. "No. Are you?"

"I want juice."

Evidently Hannah wasn't sad, either. "Okay." She pulled open the refrigerator and found a bottle of apple juice. She lifted Hannah onto one of the bar stools at the counter and filled a cup for her, then found the cereal and placed it also before her. If she managed each small step, maybe they'd get through the morning without disaster.

Hannah ate quickly, with a minimum of fuss, her attention focused on the food. The moment she was finished, though, she slid off the high stool and faced Leandra. "Horse."

"You need to change out of your pajamas first."

Hannah nodded and held out her hand. "I need shoes."

Leandra stared at Hannah's small palm, extended with the full expectation that it be taken.

The child's mother was lost forever. Did Hannah really understand it? Or did age and autism blunt the painful reality of it?

She stepped forward and took Hannah's hand.

The child's little fingers curled trustingly around hers.

And they went upstairs to find the shoes.

It had been a complete bitch of a morning, as far as Evan was concerned. The only place he wanted to be was back home with Hannah and Leandra, but it seemed as if the world around him kept conspiring to make that task as difficult as possible.

By the time he pulled up at Clay Farm, considerably more than a few hours had passed. Nearly the entire day was gone. He let himself in through the kitchen, expecting Leandra to be at the end of her rope.

There was definitely a rope, he realized.

Only it was spread across the kitchen, one end tied to a table leg, and the other end tied to a barstool. And hanging over the middle portion of the rope was a large sheet, fashioned into a tent.

He shut the door behind him, and set the suitcase full of Hannah's clothes and toys, which he'd picked up in Braden, on the floor out of the way. "Hello?"

There was no answer, but that didn't concern him. Leandra's rental car was parked in plain sight outside.

They weren't in the living room, nor were they upstairs when he went up to check, though he could see that Leandra must have had her cleaning hat on, because the laundry piled on his floor was gone, the beds in both guest rooms were made and the paper that Hannah had methodically shredded into tiny pieces on the floor in her room had been vacuumed.

Frowning a little, he went back down to the kitchen and pulled aside one of the "tent" flaps. Two bed pillows were inside, plus an assortment of papers that had been drawn and colored on. He picked one up. Either Hannah's artistic skills had greatly changed, or Leandra had drawn the picture of his clinic and house.

He left the picture with the others and when he straightened again, he finally saw them. Through the window, outside, two colorful umbrellas bobbing as they headed toward the house.

He opened the door and waited for them. "Nice umbrella," he said when Hannah handed him her umbrella and slipped past him into the house. He shook it off, studying the cartoon dog-angels dancing around amid a bunch of clouds, and folded it.

"Where'd you find these?" He reached for Leandra's. Hers looked like an overinflated beach ball.

She pulled off the slicker that had been drowning her slender form and hung it on the peg next to where he hung Hannah's umbrella. "Dug them out of storage."

She seemed to avoid his eyes as she went over to Hannah, stopping her from climbing in the tent with her wet raincoat still on. "Let's take that off first," she said.

But Hannah shook her head. "I wanna wear it."

"Are you sure? You might get the stuff inside your tent wet and you worked very hard on the pictures you drew."

"I wanna wear it." Hannah looked adamant.

"Okay." Leandra backed away and looked at him. "I suppose the suitcase has more of Hannah's things?"

"Yeah. Looks like you two have been busy in here. Everything go okay?" His voice was careful.

Leandra folded her arms around her chest. "Yes. Actually, everything went fine. What about you? You were gone longer than you expected."

"I saw an attorney."

Her lips parted. She reached back and sat down on the bar stool, the one with the rope attached to its leg. "About?"

"Custody." He waited for her to look shocked, but she didn't. "You're not surprised."

"It makes perfect sense to me. But what about Sharon?"

"She's been hurt enough, I know. But she refuses to see that Hannah has special needs. I don't want to take away her grandchild—or Darian's, for that matter. I just want to make sure Hannah has what she needs, too."

He let out a low breath. "I still feel like a bastard. It's not what Katy wanted."

"Katy expected to be coming home again. There's no way she wouldn't have wanted the very best for Hannah if she could have predicted this."

"I'm not sure I'm cut out to be a parent," he admitted gruffly.

Her expression softened. "Why on earth would you think that?"

"Genetics," he muttered.

Her eyebrows shot up. Then she gave a disbelieving laugh. "You're nothing like Darian, if that's what you're implying."

"Then why'd I show up at your house that night the way I did? The night we learned about Katy?"

A blush hovered over her cheeks. "Why *did* you?"

"Because I wanted you, but you're Jake's, and getting drunk gave me an excuse to pretend it didn't matter."

She hopped off the stool. "I'm *not* Jake's. I don't know why you'd think that even after all we've—" She broke off, flushing harder. "I belong to myself and that's all," she said finally. "Now, shall I call Ted and have him set up somewhere, or do you want to wait until tomorrow?"

He shoved his fingers through his damp hair. "Let's just get it over with."

She nodded. "All right. I'll go call him." Her cheeks still looking rosy, she left the room.

"Goodbye, Leandra." Hannah's soft voice was barely audible above the sound of the rain that had begun pounding harder on the roof.

Evan crouched down on the floor and peeked under the sheet. Hannah was adding her touches to the picture of his house and clinic. "Did you have fun with Leandra today?"

Hannah nodded and resumed her humming. She scratched at the picture with a dark blue crayon. He couldn't quite tell what it was she was drawing, though.

"Where'd you learn the song you're humming?"

The humming ceased. "Leandra." Hannah tucked her tongue between her teeth, added a final flourish to the picture, then dropped the crayon and didn't give the paper another glance. "It's Emi's song," she announced.

Surprise grabbed him. He sat right there on his butt alongside her and picked up the altered drawing. Hannah had added people. Completely out of proportion to the buildings that Leandra had drawn, but they were definitely people. "Leandra told you about Emi?"

"The song is pretty. I want some juice."

"In a minute. Who are the people?" He pointed at the three figures she'd drawn.

"That's my Evan." She rubbed her thumb over the largest figure. The one that was taller than the house. "That's Leandra." She pointed at the middle-sized one. "That's Brandon." She pointed to the smallest figure.

"Who is Brandon?" He'd expected her to say it was *her*.

"Emi's brother."

"Emi didn't have a brother, honey."

"Not yet."

He almost asked what she'd meant by *not yet,* but caught himself. She was just being imaginative. That's what children did. Only Hannah rarely exhibited that kind of imagination. She saw things in extremely practical terms.

"What kind of juice?" he asked after a moment.

"Leandra's juice."

It was pretty clear to him that Hannah had definitely enjoyed Leandra's company.

Like uncle, like niece.

## Chapter 16

The fifth episode aired and the following Monday morning, clips of it were being shown on both local and national talk shows.

Eduard called Leandra to tell her it was the best piece she'd ever done. Even Marian couldn't summon any criticism, though the serious tone of the episode—Katy's death and its effect on Evan and the rest of the town—was hardly her particular style.

Leandra ought to have felt like she'd won a battle.

Instead, she felt as if she were fighting something else entirely.

Her time in Weaver was coming to an end. She'd be staying only through the weekend—long enough to attend Squire's surprise party. The show would wrap several days before that, though, and the crew was scheduled to depart midweek.

They'd been following Evan around on rounds all

morning; had gotten terrific footage of him in the muck and mire as he'd rescued a calf caught in barbed wire while a rain-swollen creek ran wildly at his feet.

He'd looked larger than life, and she'd known as she'd watched the tape that she'd found the final images for the last episode. If the series about Evan didn't inspire a whole new crop of wannabe veterinarians, she'd eat her hat.

Now, it was afternoon, and she'd sent the crew back to the motel to get dry. Evan was meeting in his living room with the attorney who'd come with a package of papers for him to sign, and Hannah was taking her nap.

Feeling restless, she put the pen down on the pad where she'd been drafting a brief, simple press release that would announce the breakup of her and Evan's engagement. She'd send it out in another month or so. She doubted that the news would make much of a headline, but it was an end that still needed to be tied.

Knowing it didn't seem to make her feel any better.

From the living room, she could hear the two men's voices, low and indistinct and she let herself out of the kitchen. She crossed to the clinic and punched in Evan's birthday code. The enormous door obediently rolled up.

She expected the dog they'd rescued to still be in one of the kennels where he'd been just a few days earlier. But he was loose, and the moment she stepped inside and the overhead lights began flicking on, he bounded toward her, all flopping ears and lolling tongue.

She crouched down, grabbing him around the ruff, and trying not to be drowned by dog kisses. She rubbed his silky coat, noticing that he wasn't exactly running free as she'd first thought. He did have a long chain on him, preventing him from exploring too much of the clinic's confines. She nearly fell over when he put his unsplinted paw on her shoulder.

"Ask a girl to dance first, buddy." She sat down and patted her thigh. He scooted down and tried to climb on her lap. She smiled faintly and let him do as he pleased. He finally settled half on, half off.

She was still sitting there, willingly pinned by the dog when she heard footsteps approaching. She looked up at Evan. He'd changed out of his muddy clothes into green scrubs before the attorney had arrived. "Everything with the attorney go okay?"

"Not exactly."

"What's wrong?"

But he just shook his head. "See you found your pal."

She lifted her chin away from the dog's tongue. "You give him a name yet?"

"Start naming animals and they start being your pets."

"That's the same reasoning my dad used with Axel and me when we were kids. We wanted to name this one turkey. He said we couldn't 'cause we wouldn't be wanting to eat him when Thanksgiving rolled around."

"What happened?"

"Mom named him Max and we had roast beef for Thanksgiving that year."

He crouched down beside her. "I've been calling him Fred."

She bit back a smile.

"Owner still hasn't come forward," he continued.

"Are you going to keep him, then?"

"You haven't seen Hannah around dogs, have you? She'd be constantly upset."

"Yet she loves horses."

"Yup. The bigger the better where she's concerned.

She *really* hates birds." He scratched Fred's head. "As long as she's living with me, Fred here's going to have to find another home."

She didn't doubt that Evan remembered her offer to take the dog. Nor did she believe he would have forgotten his response and her overreaction to it. She wasn't going to go down that path again. Defending her life's choices was becoming much too difficult. "So, is Hannah still napping?"

"Yeah."

"She'll be growing out of that pretty soon."

"Expect she will." He nudged the dog off her lap and straightened, holding out his hand to her. "Come on."

"Where?"

"No need to sound so suspicious." He beckoned her with his fingers. "Come on."

She exhaled and let him pull her to her feet.

But he didn't let go of her hand once she was standing. He kept hold, and led her out of the clinic, pushing the button to close the automatic door along the way. He led her back to the house, and her heart beat a little harder when he started up the stairs.

"What are we doing?" She kept her voice low, not wanting to disturb Hannah.

"I want to show you something."

She dug in her heels at the threshold to his bedroom. "What? Your etchings?"

He looked amused. "Maybe I was planning on talking you into playing doctor."

She flushed. "We were ten years old when we played doctor." And they really *had* played doctor, complete with tongue depressors and a stethoscope that Ryan had pinched from his mother's medical supplies.

"Maybe if we tried it now, we'd find it as interesting

as it was supposed to have been back then." He pulled her farther into the bedroom.

She swallowed, more nervous than a cat. "Evan—"

"Shh." He leaned down and caught her lower lip between his teeth, lightly. Tantalizingly.

Shock and pleasure rooted her to the floor. "What are you doing?"

"What I've wanted to do for too damn long." His voice deepened.

"But Hannah—"

He closed his hand over hers and pulled her out into the hall again. Down a few doors, until he silently pushed one open. He waved at his niece.

She was sprawled on the narrow bed, tangled in the sheet, and hadn't so much as stirred when he'd opened the door.

"Told you," he said, closing the door once more.

Leandra trembled. He couldn't possibly know what had been running through her mind. Not unless—

"Jake told you, didn't he? What we were doing when…when Emi got out of the house."

He didn't have to answer. The truth was there in his vivid blue eyes.

Mortified, she turned on her heel, heading for the stairs, but Evan scooped his arm around her waist, hauling her back against him. "Don't run," he said. "Nothing's going to be solved by you always running."

Leandra squirmed out of his hold. "And what's going to be solved by *this?*"

"Maybe more than you think." His voice was low.

"Emi was taking a nap that day," she told him baldly. "She always slept at least an hour and a half every afternoon. And Jake—he was gone so much because of his practice. We hadn't—" She closed her arms around herself. "It had been a, um, a while."

He lowered his head, swearing softly. "You don't have to tell me this, Leandra."

Maybe it wasn't so much that he needed to hear it, but that she suddenly needed to say it. For once and for all. And then he'd understand.

And he would let her run as far and as fast as she wanted to run.

She gave Hannah's closed door a long look, then turned into Evan's bedroom, deliberately keeping her focus away from his rumpled bed. From the pillows that still held an indentation from his head.

"The only thing Jake and I hadn't done with the pool to safety-proof it was install an alarm. We'd done everything else. But Emi—" She shook her head, the memory sharp and painful. "Emi loved climbing. She tried climbing to the top of the refrigerator once. In the blink of an eye, she'd pulled out just the right combination of drawers and cupboard doors and was on top of the counter and looking for the bag of tortilla chips that were on top of the refrigerator. She wanted to play restaurant."

He sat down on the foot of the bed, his gaze hooded. "Resourceful."

"Yeah. When I was a girl, my favorite place to sneak off to was the swimming hole at the C. I guess it makes sense that Emi's favorite place to sneak off to was the pool. We gave her CPR. The fire department was there in record time. But she'd been without oxygen too long." She exhaled, looking at him through painfully dry eyes. "It wasn't planned, you know. Getting pregnant with Emi. Jake wasn't even finished with school. I was still trying to figure out what the heck I wanted to do with my life. But there was never a moment when I didn't want her. Never. And then, almost as quickly as she'd entered our life, she was gone again."

She looked away from Evan, her eyes finally glazing with tears. "It doesn't matter what anyone says. It was my fault."

"There were two of you in the house that day."

"Jake wanted to check on her and I told him she was sleeping. It *was* my fault. I stopped Jake and if I hadn't, Emi wouldn't have gotten out. My daughter died because I wanted to make love with her father."

"Your daughter died because she got past all the barriers protecting her from the pool. You could have been talking on the phone, or any number of other things, when it happened. And even if Jake had checked on her, what's to say she wouldn't have done exactly what she did ten minutes later?"

She shook her head. Why wouldn't he see the point? "Jake never touched me again. Is your friendship so great that he also told you *that?* It's because he blamed me, too."

"Do you think he still does?"

"When we signed the divorce papers, he told me he didn't."

"Did you believe him?"

"I needed to believe he'd forgiven me." She pressed her palms together, staring at her bare fingers. "Our… marriage wasn't working even before the accident. We both knew it, but there was Emi, and neither one of us was ready to do something about it. We never talked. We rarely touched. That afternoon was like a last-ditch effort to…recapture something together…and because of me, we lost the one perfect thing we'd ever done," she finished in a whisper.

He reached out, took her hands and when he pulled her down onto his lap, pressing her head against his shoulder, she didn't resist. "I was the only one who told Katy she was doing the right thing when she enlisted."

She drew in a shuddering breath. "Oh, Evan. Don't. Don't take that guilt on."

"You think you have a corner on it, then?"

She swallowed. "I can't do this. I'm leaving town next week."

"Can't? Or won't? You think by spending the rest of your life without getting involved with someone else, you're going to feel better about what happened that afternoon?"

"Nothing can make me feel better. I don't *want* to feel better!"

"Don't you?" He tilted back her head, staring into her face. "Why the hell are you running around this country the way you do? You're not trying to feel better by watching other people live their lives, instead of living your *own?* You're trying to feel better, all right, you're just not using the right means."

"And you know what *that* might be." Her voice was tight.

He made an impatient sound, and covered her mouth with his.

Sensation exploded through her. Her hands opened and closed over his forearms.

He ripped his mouth away, pressing his forehead against hers. "I have wanted you for *years.*" His voice was grim, as if he weren't any too happy about the fact. "But right now, if you don't want this—if you're bent on convincing yourself you'd rather live like a nun out of some self-imposed punishment—then you'd better go. Because my patience has reached its end."

She shuddered and slid off his lap, yanking the filmy blouse she'd borrowed from Sarah firmly over her hips.

His jaw tightened and his hands closed in fists against his thighs. "Fair enough."

But what was fair?

Certainly not life.

It was full of too many twists and turns and tragedies. They both knew that. Had experienced it.

But when she turned to leave, her feet wouldn't move. Not when everything inside her heart implored her to stay. "Evan—"

He let out a deep breath and stood. "Don't worry. It's okay, Leandra. Everything will be okay."

She sucked in her lip for a second. "Why'd you turn me down that night when you rescued Fred?"

He went still. "It's not the first stupid thing I've done." His lips twisted. "Look how I agreed to do *WITS*."

She pressed her lips together. "You've been a good friend."

"If I was such a good friend I wouldn't have spent the last decade wanting my best friend's woman."

Her lips parted.

"Leave now, Leandra."

She swallowed. "I... No." The words were practically inaudible. Maybe if they finished what they'd started, she could finally, finally move on. She'd leave Weaver and—

Her mind simply refused to contemplate that thought any further.

His eyes closed for a moment and when they opened again, she felt scorched by the heat they contained.

"No," she said a little more clearly. A little more surely. "I don't want to leave."

His jaw shifted to one side. He stepped around her and with a nudge of his hand, pushed the door closed. He stepped closer to her, crowding into her personal space with a steady deliberation that was all the more heady for it.

Desire raced through her veins, doing its best to drown out caution, and she hovered there, tensely anticipating the race of his hands, the crush of his mouth.

But the rush of passion that had licked through them like a wildfire when he'd kissed her before was disconcertingly absent.

Instead, there was only the slow brush of his fingers as he touched her cheek. The glide of his hand down her spine as he closed the inches still between them.

He was slowly, deliberately intoxicating her.

She'd seen him with the animals. And with Hannah. Had experienced firsthand how gifted his long fingers were. But she'd never imagined the deliberate delicacy with which he would touch her.

It wasn't only his hands. It was his entire being.

From her cheekbones, slowly traced by his thumbs, to the point of her chin, slowly nipped by his lips. He found the inside of her wrists, slowly scratched his nails over the tender skin there, and she caught her breath as shivers danced down her spine.

She even felt his smile against her shoulder as he repeated the motion, causing another wave of gooseflesh.

"Like that?" His voice was low, and she had the fanciful wish that she could just swim for a while in that mesmerizing masculine voice.

"Yes." She breathed the word, equally afraid of breaking the spell he was weaving, and afraid she would never break it.

He grazed her arms back up to her shoulders, but not

until he whispered for her to lift her arms did she realize he'd somehow pulled up her blouse, as well.

She lifted her arms, as obedient as a child, yet feeling anything but childlike. She ducked her head, letting
him pull the top free. He let it go, and the filmy blue
garment drifted to the ground.

She could hardly breathe as his gaze locked with hers
and he reached for the hem of the thin blue camisole
she'd worn beneath the blouse. Her skin felt snug and
hot, and she knew her nipples were painfully obvious
beneath the thin clinging fabric.

He was killing her by slow degrees.

She covered his hands with hers and pulled the camisole over her head. And while she was able to exhibit
some mindless bravado, she got rid of her shoes and
jeans, too, until she stood there before him, wearing
nothing but her white lacy panties.

And still his gaze didn't waver from hers.

"Are you sure?"

He would have stopped if she weren't, she realized.
Not because he harbored any uncertainty himself, but
because he was just that kind of man.

She crouched down at his feet and touched the back
of his calf. "Lift."

He lifted one foot then the other as she worked his
tennis shoes off, setting them aside.

Then she rose, standing only inches away from him.
She reached up and touched the collar of his shirt. Followed the V-neck down until she found the hem.

And doubly affirming her answer, she lifted the shirt
and felt the long, slow breath he drew in when she did.
A breath he released when he ducked low enough to let
her pull it off his head.

He wore a T-shirt beneath and the fact that he wore

more underclothes than she did made something inside her lighten.

She ran her hands down his chest, feeling the rigid points of his nipples beneath the soft white cotton, feeling the hard charging beat of his heart, and the way his muscles tightened when she pushed her hands beneath to that corrugated abdomen that had haunted her thoughts.

His breath hissed through his teeth and he grabbed her hands, pressing them flat against his belly. "Tease me next time," he muttered. "Right now, I don't have the patience."

Next time. The thought crowded in with the desire overflowing her veins, leaving her short on patience, herself. She tugged his T-shirt up, revealing more of his torso. Where dark hair swirled over even more hard muscles.

Her fingertips slowed, rubbing upward over the crispy-soft hair until it gave way again to smooth, warm skin stretched over the jut of his collarbone. He finally made a low sound and yanked the shirt off his head and threw it aside with none of the delicacy he'd shown her clothing. His arm slid around her back and he hauled her against him, up on her toes, his chest flush against hers, his mouth on hers.

She felt surrounded by him. His heat. His smell. His taste. Her head spun and she realized he'd lifted her right off her toes. Was carrying her. He didn't stop until she felt the bed behind her calves, and she dragged in a lungful of air when he lifted his head and dropped her on the bed.

The mattress bounced. She automatically reached her arms out to steady herself.

His gaze no longer pinned hers to his. Instead, that

deep blue focus slowly ran over her body, stretched out over the center of his bed.

She chewed her lip, feeling every nerve ending she possessed take notice of his silent perusal. He stood at the side of the bed, his legs planted as he loosened the tie holding the scrubs over his hips. The cotton rustled as he yanked them—and everything else—right off.

Leandra inhaled slowly, unable to pretend she wasn't affected by the sight of him. It was the last, slow breath she managed, for he closed his fingers over her ankles and slowly pulled her back toward him atop the mattress. Pulled steadily, inexorably, until she felt the tantalizing scrape of hair-roughened legs against her smooth ones.

She reached for his shoulders as he leaned over her, threaded her fingers through his thick hair, wanting to touch everywhere, but he gave her no such allowance as his mouth touched her stomach.

She nearly bowed off the bed. "Evan—"

His fingers hooked the narrow band of her panties and he slowly pulled them down her thighs, over her knees, past her calves, his mouth following in their path.

Her hands, bereft, clutched the nubby chenille bedspread as he tarried around her ankles, his breath warm and impossibly arousing. "Thought you said no teasing," she managed.

"No teasing *me*." He kissed her calf. Sliding his hands beneath her knees, bending them as he worked his way back up.

Her eyelids were too heavy. "Sounds unfair to me. Oh—" She pressed her head back into the mattress as he touched her. There.

His marauding fingers slid over her again, tantalizing, taunting and definitely teasing. "Are you complaining?"

She couldn't speak. Just shook her head, her hands twisting in the bedding as his fingers burned along her cleft, rediscovering every secret, every need. Learning just how much she *wasn't* protesting.

Her legs moved restlessly, and he caught them, his big hands holding her as he lowered his mouth and found her.

She cried out, the world shrinking down to exist only of them as she shattered. Abruptly. Completely. And just when she thought he could wring no more desire from her—when she thought her body could not possibly experience more—he kissed his way over her stomach. Reached her breasts and paid such exquisite attention to them that she cried out yet again. She could feel the rigid length of him against her thigh. "Evan." She reached for him and he shifted, finally, *finally* settling against the cradle of her hips.

But still he held back, until she was begging. "Please," she whispered, feeling broken.

His hand tilted her head and he kissed her softly. So softly she felt her heart fall open like a flower bathed in sunlight.

And when he filled her, when she heard him groan her name, when their world shrank even more until the only thing she knew anymore was Evan, so deeply a part of her that she no longer felt like a separate being, until she felt the tide pull them both under an ocean of exquisite perfection that had her gasping and crying out his name, she realized she wasn't broken after all.

She was whole.

Because of Evan.

# *Chapter 17*

Eventually, Leandra figured she had to move. She couldn't lie in Evan's bed all day long. Hannah would be waking eventually.

But every time she shifted, he closed his arm over her and pulled her back against him, and her willpower disintegrated on the thin beams of sunshine that were streaming through his window.

"Looks like it's stopped raining," she murmured.

"Mmm." He slowly ran his hand down her hip. Her thigh.

She could lay there with him like that for the rest of her life.

The realization didn't come with any particular blinding clarity. It was simply there. And because she was deathly afraid the words would come out if she weren't careful, she made herself turn over on the bed and laugh a little. "You *did* want to show me your etchings."

His teeth flashed as he sat up. He pushed aside the tangled bedding and climbed out of bed. "Actually, I was going for something else when you distracted me."

There was plenty there to distract her, too. Like the view of him.

He opened a bottom drawer on his dresser. When he straightened again, he held an oversized book in his hand. He returned to the bed. "Remember this?"

"It's our senior yearbook from high school." She took it when he held it out for her. "You really *are* feeling nostalgic."

He made a face and sat down beside her, pulling her back against his chest. "You said you wanted to make a difference in the world. Remember?"

Her fingers traced over the raised lettering on the cover of the dark blue book. "I don't think I have short-term memory loss. Yes, I remember. What's that got to do with the yearbook?"

"Do you remember what your senior statement was?"

She frowned. "No." She'd forgotten all about the form they'd filled out every year for the yearbook. "It was stupid stuff. Like how rich we wanted to be, how old we'd be before getting married, what ridiculously expensive car we'd drive."

He took the book back from her and flipped it open, paging through until he found what he wanted. "It wasn't all stupid." He handed it back to her, tapping the page.

Her hair had been long back then. Halfway down her back, in fact. Her back that now felt highly sensitized to the man's chest pressed against it. "What do you do? Pull this thing out and read when you're bored?"

"Haven't looked at it in years. I just happen to have an exceptional memory."

She snorted softly. "He who has to write reminder notes to himself that he needs toilet paper."

He covered her hands on the sides of the book, opening it wider and forcing it closer to her nose. "Read it."

She tugged the book out of his grasp. Beneath her senior picture, the statement was printed out in her own then-girlish handwriting. "I want every kid to have the great time growing up in Weaver that I've had." She gave a short laugh. "How incredibly earnest. I don't even remember writing that."

"I remember."

She shrugged, started to hand the book back, wanting just to forget that long-ago child she'd been, but stopped. "What about your statement?" She paged through to the *T*s and found Evan.

Lord, but he'd been a pretty boy. All long black lashes and hair, his eyes looking translucent in the black-and-white photo. No wonder he'd grown into such a striking man.

His handwriting hadn't changed as much as hers had. Even back then, it had been slashing, austere-looking and utterly practical. "One wife. Kids. Truck. Vet practice." She felt ridiculously touched, reading the bullet-like statement. "I'll bet if you looked back, your dad probably had a similar statement. Well, you've got the practice and the truck. And now Hannah. You're nearly there." She handed him back the book. "If you and Luce had gotten married—"

"Lucy and I would never have gotten married, even if she hadn't left for New York. She didn't want to marry me any more than I wanted to marry her."

"That's what Marian found out when she sent a crew to interview her. Otherwise, you would have seen Lucy on *WITS*, too."

"Marian." He closed the yearbook and tossed it to the foot of the bed, his disgust plain. "The woman's a tarantula."

"That may be, but she's also my boss." She climbed off the bed and pulled on the first thing her hand came to—his shirt. She'd always known that Evan had a low opinion of the show—but it had never hurt quite so badly before. "We have all the footage we need for the last episode," she admitted. "I'm going to cancel the rest of the schedule for the week. No more cameras for you."

"Thank God."

She winced. "You've never really told me why you agreed to do it in the first place. You could have simply said no thanks and that would have been the end of it."

"And what would you have done? Gone back to Jake and worked on him some more until he gave in to you?" He rose from the opposite side of the bed.

"Jake wouldn't have given in. *He* had the decency to say no when he meant it."

"Too damn bad he doesn't have the decency to tell you the real reason he wouldn't do the show was because his new fiancée objected!"

"Excuse me?"

Evan swore. He turned away from her, propped his hands on his damnably lean hips and swore again. He snatched up his pants and yanked them over his hips. "Dammit. I *told* him to tell you."

"Jake is…engaged." She gingerly felt around the idea of it and realized it didn't hurt in the least. "Well, good grief. Why on earth didn't *he* tell me?

"I told you to talk to him. How many times has the guy called you lately?"

She felt a stab of guilt, thinking of the number of calls she'd ignored.

Mostly because she'd been too busy with Evan.

"I figured he was just checking up on me, as usual." Annoyance filled her. "And clearly *you've* known all along. Why didn't *you* say something?"

"It wasn't my news to tell." His voice was tight. "Yet here I am. Telling away." He swore again, yanking the tie at his waist.

She pushed her fingers through her hair, refusing to be distracted by the picture he made. "So…you agreed to do the show because you felt sorry for me."

He exhaled. "I didn't say that."

"You didn't have to when it's the only thing that finally makes sense." She turned away. Pity. Pity had motivated him all along.

And not with just the show.

"I've got to go."

"Dammit, wait—"

She kept moving, racing out of his bedroom, down the stairs and out the back door into the cold, his scrub shirt flapping around her bare legs. The gravel cut into her feet, but she still didn't slow as she tumbled into the car seat.

The keys were in the ignition where she'd left them and she gunned the engine, pulling away from the house, tires spinning over the gravel.

Her last sight of Evan was of him standing on the back porch, staring after her.

Before the week was out, her crew had packed up and flown back to California, where they'd take a break for a few weeks before they began shooting their next project.

They didn't know yet that Leandra wouldn't be part of the production team. That Eduard had come through with the promotion.

She would be getting her own show. She was scheduled to meet with him and the development team next week.

There was none of the satisfaction she should have felt, though. None of the anticipation for what lay ahead.

There was only the reality of the flight reservations she had for Monday.

When the rain returned again the day of Squire's party, it suited her mood just fine, though it did make it more challenging for the party preparations.

It took at least half the family coming and going to the old barn at her parents' farm to ready it. Under the efficient eye of Leandra's mother, Axel and a handful of cousins erected the enormous white awning out on the lawn, and Leandra and the rest of her cousins spent the morning clearing the barn of any sign that animals had in fact lived there.

Their efforts definitely were not in vain. By that evening, the rain had calmed to an occasional drizzle and beneath the awning, a wooden dance floor gleamed in the light cast by about a million tiny white lights that had been painstakingly hung around the interior of the awning. There were even portable propane heaters that were guaranteed to keep the chill at bay.

Inside the barn were yet more lights, strung from every rafter. Enormous bunches of wheat stalks, tied with bright red ribbon, stood in the corners and decorated the long tables that were covered with red cloths.

"Think we're going to blow the power grid with all those lights burning?" Sarah stopped next to Leandra and put another tray of hors d'oeuvres on the table.

"It's a possibility. Can you believe we spent half the day sweeping a *dirt* floor?" She was going to be cheerful if it was the last thing she did.

Sarah looked down. "And yet, it still looks like dirt." She grinned. "So, you suppose Squire's still in the dark?"

"He sure didn't say a word to me this past week." The birthday boy was due to arrive in about an hour. She adjusted the edge of one of the tablecloths and repositioned a plastic-covered tray of crab puffs. "Pull that end of the cloth, would you? It's still crooked."

Sarah moved to the end of the long, narrow table and tugged. Leandra readjusted the trays. "So, you want to tell me yet what's happened between you and Evan?"

"No."

"Must have been good," Sarah mused. "Seeing as how people have been talking for the past few days about how they saw you running half-naked around his house."

Leandra refused to be drawn. She hadn't been half-naked. She'd been wearing a shirt that came down to her knees. A shirt she'd pitched in the trash, only to go digging after it again.

Foolishly, she'd taken to sleeping in it.

Sarah just shook her head. "Well, at least tell me you're pleased about the show. The last episode airs tomorrow. Do you think you'll get the promotion you're after?"

"I already did."

Sarah went still. "What?"

Leandra shrugged. "Eduard called yesterday."

"Why didn't you say something?"

"I don't know," she said truthfully. She had a perfect view of the wide-open barn doors behind Sarah and she could see Evan approaching.

He wore black.

All black.

Black leather jacket. Black shirt. Black jeans. Black boots. And as he stepped into the light of the barn, and his gaze focused on Leandra, that sea of black made his blue eyes seem even more startlingly blue. And just looking at him made her catch her breath, even if she did tell herself that she was still furious with him.

She barely noticed the way Sarah did a double-take, looking behind her as if something in Leandra's expression had given her away.

Evan headed toward them, but Leandra turned away, hurrying out the other side of the barn.

He caught up to her before she could make it back to the house, though. "How long are you planning on running?"

She jerked her arm out of his grasp and yanked open the back door to the kitchen. "I have to help set out more food since *guests* are beginning to arrive. And where is Hannah, anyway?"

"Hannah's with my mother at my place. We need to talk about us."

"Us?" Her voice rose over the term. "There is no us, Evan Taggart. There never will be."

"Not while you're burning tracks under those heels of yours." His voice was tight.

Leandra stomped into the kitchen, nearly running smack dab into her aunt Maggie, who was carrying an enormous, empty, crystal punch bowl.

"Watch it there, honey," Maggie said, dancing around Leandra and Evan, and hurrying down the steps.

Her daughters, J.D. and Angeline, were hard on her heels, their own hands full, as well. They'd both arrived by plane the previous day. "Grab what you can," J.D. told her, grinning. "Reports have it that Squire's car is heading this way."

"ETA is about ten minutes," Angeline added.

"So much for the schedule." Leandra was grateful for the excuse to get away from Evan, and she grabbed the nearest tray of sandwiches that waited on the long countertop.

He picked up two more.

"What are you doing?"

"Finishing this crap so you can stop making excuses."

She turned on her heel, ignoring him, which was about as impossible a task as there ever had been and followed her cousins and aunt back to the barn, ducking her head against the fresh sprinkles that had begun falling.

She found a spot for her tray. Then, conscience nipping, she found a place for Evan's two, as well. The family was suddenly descending en masse on the barn, hurrying to get out of sight before Squire appeared.

Not that the man wouldn't know something was up when he saw the awning outside, but some things just couldn't be helped. You couldn't entertain half the town of Weaver without making some accommodations for the crowd.

Evan's hand closed over the back of her neck. She tried to shake him off, but his hold was relentless.

Gentle. But relentless.

He leaned down, his voice in her ear. "I'm not going to let you off the hook this easily, Leandra."

"I'm not stupid enough to get on the hook," she retorted. Someone she didn't recognize standing in front of her turned around and gave her a lock. A moment later, the interior lights were doused.

"You might as well admit that you love me." Evan's voice warmed her ear again.

"Love!" She pinched his arm hard enough to make him curse under his breath. "Get over yourself. We both know what the other day was about and it didn't have *anything* to do with love."

"Shh-h!" The admonishment came from the woman blocking Leandra's view of the barn door.

"S-sorry." Leandra hissed the apology. There was enough rustling of bodies, quiet coughs and murmurs to alert an *unobservant* person, much less her highly observant grandfather.

"You sure about that?" His hand slid down her spine, curved around her waist.

His breath was warm on her neck. Her hands opened, closed, fighting the urge to touch him. To lean back even more against his tall body. "Don't." The command was much too weak, and she pushed his hand away from her hip with renewed vigor. "And I'm quite sure."

"What do you think it was about, then?"

"The same thing that prompted you to agree to do *WITS*. I don't need you feeling sorry for me!"

There was a sudden yell of "Surprise," and the light burst over them again.

His hand slid along her neck, curling around the back. "Jake getting hitched again is something I'm celebrating."

"So why didn't *you* tell me?" She turned and faced him, and the two of them stood there, squared off while all around them, party guests were making their way to the honoree. "Instead, you just kept asking if I'd talked to him!"

"What are you madder about, Leandra? That Jake's getting married again, or that you weren't the first one to know about it?"

Mad didn't begin to describe what she felt, knowing

that what had really rocked her wasn't the fact that Jake was getting married again, but the fact that she'd found herself wishing that she were getting married again.

To Evan.

"I don't care if Jake told a hundred people before he told me! I care that *you* didn't tell me. It's the only reason you…we—" She broke off, flushing. "I should have known better. Friends don't just all of a sudden switch their stripes." It was a pitiful metaphor but no more pitiful than the situation.

She started to turn away, but he grabbed her arm.

She gasped, but it never had a chance to escape because his mouth covered hers and absorbed it.

It was deep. It was hot. It was about as perfect a kiss as she could ever have dreamed.

It was Evan.

He finally dragged his lips from hers. His breath was ragged. "I told you already. It is not *sudden*. It's been years. But once you met Jake, you only had eyes for him."

She felt wobbly. As if she'd sink into a puddle if not for his arms surrounding her. "Wait."

"I've been waiting years," he muttered, his mouth burning across her cheek toward her ear. "Dammit-to-hell, we're standing in the middle of your grandfather's birthday party."

She sprang back from him. What was wrong with her? She looked around, but the only people who seemed to have noticed their clinch was the pinch-lipped woman who'd shushed her and Leandra's father, who was watching them both with a narrow-eyed look.

She flushed. "I have responsibilities here. Mom's expecting my help."

"How long are you going to keep pushing everyone away, Leandra?"

"I don't push people away!"

He held out his arms to his sides. "Is that a fact?" He dropped his arms, took a step closer to her, and when she instinctively sidled an equal step away, he let out a short breath. "Yeah. That's what I thought."

"Just because you don't know how to take no for an answer is—"

He covered her mouth with his hand, muffling her voice. "Don't even go there, Leandra. It's small of you and my patience only goes so far." He pulled his hand away. "Tell your grandfather I'm sorry I didn't get a chance to wish him a happy birthday in person."

Turning on his heel, he strode through the crowd and out the back door.

She followed after him, wanting to stop him, but the words jammed in her throat, threatening to choke her. Which meant that she just stood there watching him disappear into the misty darkness beyond the lights of the awning.

## Chapter 18

"There you are." Sarah was cradling two bags of ice to her chest. "Here. Take one. You look frazzled. What have you and Evan been doing?" She headed toward the enormous barrel in the corner that housed a keg of beer.

"Do I really push people away?"

Sarah stopped in her tracks, but whatever quick comment had sprung to her lips went unsaid. "What's going on?"

"*Do* I?" She searched Sarah's expression. "Never mind. I can see the answer."

Sarah let out a short, puzzled laugh. "What brought this on? Did something happen with Evan? Where'd he go, anyway?"

Nothing was ever going to happen with Evan. Nothing permanent. Nothing lasting. No matter what she thought she felt, there simply was no future. She had her life and he had his. "No. Nothing happened."

Sarah watched her closely. "Is *that* what has you upset?"

"I'm *not* upset."

"Yeah, and I'm not freezing my chest with this bag of ice." She tore it open and dumped it into the barrel. "Do you remember how things used to be with us? I was the only one you told when Joey Rasmussen kissed you on the playground in the second grade. You were the only one I told when I was pregnant in college. We used to share everything. Do you really need me to tell you whether or not you push people away? Leandra, you've been pushing ever since Emi died. I just wish there was some way you'd let us get close enough to be your help!"

"This isn't about Emi!"

"Everything you've done for the past four years has been about Emi."

"Falling in love with Evan isn't." Leandra pressed her lips together, but the admission had already escaped.

Sarah's eyes widened and her lips rounded in a silent "oh."

"Look, it's just a crush. Forget I said anything." She handed her cousin the second bag and headed out of the barn.

"Wait a minute!" Sarah stepped directly in her path. "I can't forget this! How long have you felt this way? I can't believe it. Evan? I mean, I knew you guys had gotten a little cozy, but—"

"Hush! How many people do you want to hear?"

Sarah looked over her shoulder. The closest party guests were a good ten yards away, still trying to greet Squire in person. "I think you're safe," she whispered. "Most everyone here thinks you two are engaged, anyway."

"I'm glad you find this so amusing."

Sarah gave her a look. "Believe me, I'm not laughing. Actually, I sort of thought you were still in love with Jake. And you thought Evan was still hung up on Lucy."

"Half this town thought that," Leandra defended.

"Do you still?"

His voice echoed in her head. *I've been waiting years.* She chewed her lip and shook her head.

"Then what's the problem? Where is he?"

"He left." She looked at the pile of ice inside the barrel. There was nowhere near enough to keep the keg cold. "We need more ice."

"It'll wait." Sarah stepped in her path again. "He left, and you're suddenly wanting to know whether or not you push people away."

"And you just confirmed that I do," Leandra's said flatly.

"Hey there, chickees. You know the beer will fill the glass faster if you actually use the tap." J.D. appeared beside them and studied the keg. "What's up?"

"Leandra realized she's in love with Evan."

"Sarah—" Leandra protested, but it was futile.

"Good thing since they're engaged," J.D. mused. "I'm just surprised it took so long."

Leandra did a double take, not at all certain she'd heard her cousin right. "What are you talking about?"

"The guy had it bad for you in college," J.D. said easily.

"The guy," Leandra countered, "was attached at the hip to Lucy, in case you've forgotten."

"Not in college he wasn't," J.D. drawled. "And then when you went off and fell for Jake, the *guy* was a basket case. Believe me. I saw what he was like."

Angeline joined them. "You know, the birthday boy

is here." Her long brown hair was pulled back in a low ponytail and it swung over her shoulder as she picked up a cup from the stack alongside the keg.

"Leandra's jonesing for Evan," J.D. told her sister.

Leandra groaned. "So much for privacy."

Angeline shot her a sympathetic look. "What does he want to do, wait for the wedding night or something?"

Sarah muffled a laugh.

"That's not the problem," Leandra murmured, feeling her cheeks heat.

Angeline gave her a studied look. "Well, whatever's wrong, if you love him, don't let him go."

"Where are my granddaughters?" The commanding voice rang out, startling them all like they were still children. Leandra looked over to see Squire striding toward them, his arms wide. "Of course. Keeping company with the beer keg."

J.D. and Angeline reached him first, hugging his neck and kissing his cheeks. "Just waiting for you to have the first taste," J.D. assured him brightly. "And being glad that we don't have to hide out from you any longer since we arrived yesterday!"

Squire grinned. Like Evan, he had blue eyes. But beyond the name, there was no similarity in the actual color. While Evan's were as deep and vivid as a sapphire, Squire's were like a pale morning sky and just as piercing as they'd been when Leandra had been a girl. He'd always known when she was up to something, and even before he turned those eyes her way, she knew it was something else that hadn't changed. "Come here, girl," he bid. "You're not excused from hugging an old man, either. Been keeping secrets of your own, haven't you?"

Leandra reached up and hugged her grandfather.

Sudden tears were clogging her head. "Happy birthday, Squire."

He squeezed her hard, practically lifting her off her toes.

Laughter from behind him announced his wife, Gloria's, presence. "Leave some stuffing inside Leandra, Squire," she ordered. "You'd think you hadn't spent the past few days fishing with the girl."

Squire let Leandra back down on her feet. He peered into her face. "You make up your mind about staying or going?"

She just shook her head, keeping her smile in place, though it took a lot of effort. And here she'd thought he was the only one who hadn't been wondering such things about her.

Fortunately, where the birthday boy went, the crowd followed, and Squire was soon distracted again by the rest of the family and the other guests. Leandra kept busy loading and unloading trays of food, freshening drinks and generally trying to hide out in the house as much as she could.

Finally, after what seemed hours, Squire had opened all of the presents that he'd protested receiving, the huge supply of food had amazingly been nearly depleted, the dance floor out under the awning had gotten well-scuffed by dancers despite the wet night, and the last of the guests who didn't have some familial connection to the name of Clay were heading down the highway back to their own homes.

Leandra's parents had departed for the house, along with her aunts and uncles, leaving only the "youngsters" as Squire referred to them, sprawled on a haphazard collection of chairs in the barn.

"You gonna edit together all the videotape Derek

shot tonight for Squire?" Axel stretched his long legs
out. He'd had an assortment of pretty girls on his arm
all night, but for now, he seemed content to hang out
with the family.

Leandra tucked the disks Derek had given her in the
side pocket of her skirt. "That's the plan."

"Tell them about your promotion." Sarah pulled her
feet out of her high-heeled boots and wiggled her toes.

They all looked at her. "What about your engagement?"

She felt her cheeks heat. "Evan and I will work it
out." Her leaving would do that pretty effectively.
*Running.*

The truth of it sat heavily inside of her.

J.D. yawned. "How long do you suppose it'll be before the entire family is back in Weaver at one time
again?"

"Entire family isn't here," Derek pointed out. "Lucy
and Ry didn't make it."

"Last time was Leandra's wedding," Axel said. "Next
time'll probably be another wedding."

Leandra pushed to her feet. She didn't want to think
about weddings. "I'm going to head out. Sarah you want
to come now, or catch a ride later?"

Her cousin kept rubbing her feet. "You go on ahead."

Leandra nodded. She made a tour of goodbyes and
an hour later, she was sitting on the floor in Sarah's
living room surrounded by four years' worth of high
school yearbooks. Trust Sarah to have them all neatly
in order on a bookshelf right there in the living room.

She flipped them all open, finding her picture and
the accompanying statement. As a freshman, she'd still
worn the braids that Evan had often tugged, and she'd
wanted to be a movie star. Of course so had half the

girls in her class, including Sarah. The second year of high school, the braids were gone and mascara had darkened her lashes. She still remembered the argument her father had given against the makeup and the way her mother had stood up for it. That year, she'd simply wanted to travel the world.

She flipped to the third annual. Mascara was there, still, along with shining lip gloss and a million curls down to her shoulders that had taken her and Sarah about two hours with a curling iron to put there. She'd wanted to be either president of the United States, or a psychiatrist. "Crazy," she murmured and pulled the senior book closer to her.

She opened it up, but didn't turn to her page. She turned to Evan's. That was the year that he and Lucy had broken up for a while. When he'd claimed his crush on Leandra. But by the time the senior prom had rolled around near the end of the school year, he and Lucy had once again seemed thick as thieves.

She brushed her fingertips over his image. Even then he'd known what he'd wanted.

She grabbed her cell phone and scrolled through the numbers stored in the memory and despite the ridiculous hour, she dialed. It rang several times before it was answered by a very sleepy, very female voice. "Luce? It's Leandra."

"What's wrong?" Lucy's voice was immediately more alert and alarmed.

"Nothing. Just wanted to hear your voice. Missed you at the party tonight."

She heard rustling, then a faint sigh. "You're calling at this hour because of that? I haven't heard from you since we talked last Christmas."

"I know. I'm sorry about that. And I'm fine. Or getting there, maybe. I'm sorry you had to put up with the *WITS* interview. I tried to stop it."

"Oh, that was nothing. How is Evan, anyway? I heard you two were engaged. Congratulations. He's a great guy. Always has been. Terrible about what happened with Katy, though."

Leandra closed her eyes, feeling like the biggest fraud of the year. "He's going to court to get custody of Hannah," she told her cousin.

Lucy made a soft sound. "Not surprising. Sounds like him. How…how do you feel about that? You going to be okay, I mean? Having a child to raise?"

Longing filled her, making her limbs heavy with it. "I'll be fine," she said huskily. "So, how's life with the ballet?"

"Well, I'm closing in on thirty years of age," Lucy said after a moment. "What do you think?" She let out a breath. "Don't tell anyone yet, because I haven't decided for sure, but I'm thinking about retiring from performing. Maybe open a dance school or something."

"Oh, Luce, that's great."

Her cousin laughed a little. "Yeah. There was a time when I dreamed of nothing but being on stage. But dreams change, don't they. Listen, tell everyone hello for me. I felt horrible not to make it for Squire's party, but we're debuting a new work in two weeks and things are pretty frantic here. If your wandering brings you this way, give me a shout, okay?"

"Will do." The call ended shortly after and Leandra sat there, her hand on the phone.

Wandering. Running.

Is that what her life had become?

She dialed again, this time aiming for the West Coast instead of the East, though Jake's voice was just as sleepy as Lucy's had sounded. "Hey," she greeted, feeling her throat grow a little tight. "Hear congratulations are in order."

"Lee. Yeah. I guess you heard. Evan, huh?" She heard a muffled voice in the background and guessed it was probably the future Mrs. Stallings.

"You could have told me, you know. About—what's her name?"

"Stephanie. She's one of the research lab techs. And I was trying."

She couldn't deny that fact. It had been she who'd been avoiding him. "So, when's the big date?"

"Next month. Lee, it's not just the wedding you need to know about."

She tightened her hand on the phone, something inside her already expecting the news. "Stephanie's pregnant."

"Yeah."

"Well." She let out a breath, expecting pain, but finding none. Just a sweet sadness for what they'd once had. "Congratulations again."

"I wanted to tell you—I just didn't know how. Are you okay?"

Surprisingly, amazingly, she was. "You don't have to worry about me, Jake. I'm going to be fine. I…am fine. Truly. Just…be happy, you know?"

"Yeah. You, too."

She hung up.

"Did you mean it?"

She turned with a jerk, the phone flying out of her hand, hitting the wall.

Evan was standing in the kitchen doorway.

"You scared the life out of me!"

"Kitchen door's always open," he reminded.

"Maybe I should tell Sarah to start locking it." She

crossed her arms, ignoring the yearbook on the coffee table, still open to his photograph. "Where's Hannah?"

"Same place she was a few hours ago. Did you mean it? That *was* Jake, wasn't it?"

She looked at her phone that was now just pieces of black plastic littering the floor. "Yes."

"Yes…what?"

"Yes, it was Jake and yes I meant what I said. I suppose he also told you that he and Stephanie are having a baby?"

He looked startled. "No."

She supposed that was something. That he hadn't felt sorry for her over that fact, as well. "What are you doing here?"

"For some unfathomable reason, I can't seem to stay away from you."

"You don't look any too happy about it."

"Why would I be?" He stepped farther into the room, his gaze roving. "You come here for a few weeks, turn everything upside down and inside out, and will leave again as soon as you can."

She chewed the inside of her lip and nodded. "I… have a job."

"Jobs can be found anywhere, even here in Weaver."

"A career, then."

His lips twisted. No argument to that, she supposed. He nodded toward the yearbooks. "More reminiscing?"

Searching, more like. "Sort of." She pushed back her hair. "Evan, the show isn't turning out quite like I'd planned."

"Not as interesting as Jake would have been."

"There's no comparison." She held up her hand when his expression turned grim. "You're more interesting."

"Yeah." He looked disbelieving. "He deals with poodles owned by girls who are on the cover of gossip rags by day and is curing cancer by night, or something. I'm usually up to my ankles in horse droppings. You remember the weekend I brought Jake back to Weaver?"

The jump took her aback for a moment. "Spring break. We were all home from school."

"I wanted him to meet the girl I couldn't forget."

She looked away, pain spilling through her. "I didn't know. Didn't realize."

"And you never would have. If you'd been happy together, if you hadn't lost Emi, I would have gone on with life, Jake's friend, *your* friend, knowing you had what you wanted. But that didn't happen and I'm not going to keep my mouth shut this time."

"What do you want from me? Another romp in the hay?" She picked up the yearbook and pushed it at him. "I can't be what you want, Evan! I can't give you what you want!"

"You think I don't know that?" His voice rose, too. "You think I wouldn't choose just about anybody else if I *could?* My life is in Weaver, and you—you'd rather have a life anywhere but here. Hannah is a permanent part of my life no matter what happens with the custody suit."

"What do you mean by that? Is Sharon fighting you on it?"

"She hasn't decided." His jaw worked for a moment. "My attorney said I have a good chance of being awarded custody, though, since I'm supposedly getting married."

She stared. "I…see."

"I doubt it. And it doesn't matter because you're leaving Weaver, anyway."

"There you go, then." Her voice was thick. "We're better off as friends. Anything more is simply impossible. You can go find—" her voice broke "—find your-self a *real* fiancée."

He took the book out of her hand, and set it down. "You've been feeling pretty real these days. And it's only impossible if you believe it is." He caught her face between his hands and kissed her.

Her knees went weak. She caught his shoulders. But just when she would have told him anything he wanted to hear, agreed to anything he asked, he lifted his head again.

His eyes were damp. "I am in love with you, Lean-dra. I have been for years. But you have to decide for yourself what you want. I'm not going to beg and I'm not going to use Hannah as an excuse to try to persuade you to stay. With or without you, I'm going to do what's right for her. You were right. Seems I'm more like Drew than I thought.

"I'm finally ready to stop comparing myself to Darian—to stop expecting that I'll follow in his steps. Being like him is *not* what I want and I know it. If what you really want is *WITS* or a show of your own, then so be it. But if that all's just another way of running from the reality of Emi's death, then I hope to God you real-ize it before you spend the rest of your life missing out on the things that you really *do* want."

She opened her mouth, but no words would come.

And after what seemed an eternity, he finally let out a deep sigh. He pressed his lips to her forehead, then stepping over the pieces of broken phone, he walked out the front door.

He didn't look back.

# Chapter 19

"I wish you weren't leaving already." Emily smiled, but it was sad. "Seems like you barely just got here."

Leandra pushed her jacket into her tote, glancing at the big clock on the airport wall. She'd want the jacket for the flight back to California, since she generally froze whenever she flew anywhere. "Time flies and all that," she murmured. Truthfully, it felt as if her trip had lasted eons. Particularly the past two days, during which Evan hadn't so much as made one mention of that night after Squire's party.

It was as if he'd never visited her at Sarah's.

Never told her he loved her.

He couldn't have made things plainer. If anything were to change, it would have to be at her instigation.

"Do you think you'll make it home for Christmas this year?"

Christmas was months away, yet. "Maybe."

"Maybe. That's what you've said for the past four years. Hasn't come to pass, yet."

Her head throbbed. "Mom—"

"Oh, Leandra." Emily sighed and hugged her. "Don't mind me. I'm just missing you already."

Leandra hugged her back, trying not to cry. She hadn't expected leaving to be so difficult. Hadn't expected it to feel as if her heart was being ripped out of her. "I'm sorry I didn't spend more time with you at the farm. I should have."

Emily smoothed her hair, the same way she'd done when she was little. "Next time."

Leandra nodded. Who knew when that would be?

Her father reappeared with a bag of stuff he'd purchased at the small gift shop. "Here." He tucked it in her bulging tote, atop the jacket. "Just some chocolate and a few books."

"Thanks."

He shoved his hands in his pockets and paced the short aisle between the molded plastic seats where they sat. Leandra was aware of the look that kept passing between him and her mother.

She looked at the clock again. Soon she'd have to go through security.

Alone. Alone in life, alone in spirit. Because that was the choice she'd made.

"The stray that—" she had to force his name past her lips "—Evan saved? Fred?"

Her father lifted an eyebrow. "What about him?"

"He needs a home. Evan can't keep him because of Hannah."

"We don't exactly need another dog," Jefferson said dryly. "Given the way your mother keeps bringing them home."

Leandra looked to her mother. Who looked at her husband. "Jefferson?" That was it. That was all Emily said. Just his name.

Her dad smiled, as if that were all he'd been waiting for, and capitulated. "We'll pick him up on the way home."

If only everything were so easily solved.

She brushed her fingers through her hair. The haircut she'd needed a month ago was even more apparent now.

"When do you meet with Montrechet about your new show?" Her dad eyed her, but whatever he was thinking didn't show on his impassive face.

"Tomorrow."

Emily squeezed her hand. "You'll be wonderful, whatever you do."

"You don't look like you're celebrating the idea too much, kid."

"It's what I've been working toward for the past few years. Maybe I can really make a difference, then."

Again, a look passed between Jefferson and Emily. Leandra felt distinctly uneasy when her mother suddenly stood, murmuring something about needing a little walk. Then, even though they were surrounded by dozens of empty seats, her dad took the one that Emily had abandoned.

He stretched out his legs and sighed. "You know, it's okay sometimes to switch gears. Reevaluate what it is you want in this life. Dreams *can* change."

She started a little. Lucy had said the same thing.

"I spent a good part of my life chasing something I believed I wanted because it was easier than facing— and maybe losing—the thing I wanted even more. Are you sure you know what it is you want?"

Living up to her mother's reputation had never been

particularly easy. Living up to her father's had been nigh impossible. "What I *want* is for Emi to be turning seven next year."

He sighed again and took her hand. "And that isn't going to happen, Leandra. No more than Emily wanting her parents to be back made it happen or Katy's parents wanting her back or Squire wanting my mother. But Emily found a home with Squire, and if she hadn't, you wouldn't exist. And Squire found Gloria. If he hadn't, Belle and Nikki and all of theirs wouldn't be part of our family, too. And Evan will have Hannah. It doesn't mean we love the ones who are gone any less."

"I know, Dad. I *know.*" She pushed to her feet. "Knowing doesn't make it any easier."

Her father grimaced. "Anybody who says life is easy is full of crap. But easy or not, you just lift your chin and get to it. *That's* what makes a difference, Leandra. You don't have to go chasing down obscure documentaries the way you've been wanting in order to make a difference in this world. So if, like your mother claims, you're trying somehow to be like I used to be, then get over it. The years before I married your mother are not like *anything* I would want you involved in."

"But—"

"I'm not saying anything more about it. You want to make a difference?" He pushed to his feet, spotting Emily returning. "Make a difference in your own life. Start living it, again, instead of punishing yourself over things that can't be changed."

Her eyes burned. "I'm afraid of ruining it again."

He looked at her. "That's what makes you human, baby. What makes you a Clay—" he held out his hand toward his wife "—is going for it anyway. Seems strange for me to be the one to tell you this, since I know your mom and I have always told you to follow your dreams, but now I'm going to tell you to follow your heart."

Her eyes flooded. She'd never heard her father make an emotional statement like that. She looked at the clock. Less than five minutes to go. Get on the plane and go back to California and grab what she'd been working toward all this time. "What would I do if I stayed?"

"Whatever you want," Jefferson said simply. Then he looked beyond her. "*They* might have something to do with things if you'll let them."

Leandra turned. And there they stood.

Evan. And alongside him, looking just as wary as her uncle, was Hannah.

Leandra's fingers went loose on the tote. "Even if what I want is to use some of your horses," she murmured.

"For what? You want to get into breeding?"

She slowly shook her head, the idea so new and so obvious she wondered why it had taken her so long. "For kids like Hannah."

She missed the faint smile that touched her father's mouth. "Sounds good to me." He moved away with Emily, quietly making themselves scarce.

The tears blurring Leandra's vision didn't blind her to the way Evan held his jaw so tightly or the way Hannah clung to his leg when he started toward her.

"Hannah wanted to say goodbye," he said, his voice gruff when he stopped several feet away. "I wasn't sure we'd make it before your plane left."

Trying not to let disappointment swamp her at the reason for his presence, she crouched down and forced a smile for Hannah's benefit. "I'm glad you came, Hannah." She pointed at the sheet of paper the girl held. "Have you been drawing again?"

Hannah held the paper out. "It's for you."

Leandra's eyes burned even more. She took the paper and immediately recognized her own drawing from the day she'd watched Hannah for Evan. Only Hannah had definitely doctored it. "Thank you." The words were hoarse. "It's beautiful."

"Tell her who the people are, Hannah."

Leandra glanced up at Evan. He wasn't looking at his niece, though. He was watching her, his expression oddly intense.

"That's Evan," Hannah pointed at the picture, though she didn't let go of Evan's leg. "That's you. And that's baby Brandon."

Leandra lifted her eyebrows. "Who's Brandon?"

"The baby you gots to have with my Evan."

Not even a few weeks earlier and she would have winced at the painful idea. Now, she just felt suffocated by longing. She and Evan hadn't used any birth control when they'd made love, but she'd always been as regular as rain and the timing had been all wrong. She pressed her lips together for a moment, trying to make her tight throat work. "It's a very nice drawing, Hannah. Thank you." She stroked her hand down the little girl's head, feeling like she'd won a small victory when Hannah smiled.

Then she stood.

The clock over the gate told her it was time to leave.

She chewed the inside of her lip. Looked up at Evan. "I... Thank you for bringing her."

"I had another reason." Evan knelt down, and spoke to Hannah, clearly trying to extricate himself from her grip, but the girl had no intention of going anywhere.

He straightened again and faced Leandra. "Seems appropriate that she's attached herself," he murmured. "Since it's an indicator of the way it will be for years to come." He stepped forward, carefully moving Hannah right along with him, and the little girl giggled.

Leandra didn't have any laughter in her right then, though. "What other reason?" Her eyes searched his face, wanting to memorize every detail, knowing that no effort was really required there.

He was unforgettable.

He took her hands in his and she nearly started crying all over again at the way his warm hands shook a little. "I know you think you need to get on that plane. That you've worked hard for what's waiting for you at the other end. But I'm selfish. And I'm asking you not to go. I thought I could watch you walk away again, but I was wrong. And if I have to fight with every trick in every book, I'm going to find a way to make you stay. I want you as my wife, Leandra. I want you to have my children. But if all I can have for now is just you, in my life, then that's what I'll take." He dug in his pocket and pulled out a folded piece of paper. "I made a drawing, too."

She did laugh then, just a little, and speechless, she unfolded the paper. It was a mock-up like their yearbook page, she realized. He'd taped a snapshot of himself, which someone had taken during the shoot, onto the top of the paper. And beneath it, he'd written his statement.

*I want to be with Leandra Clay.*

She bit her lip. From the corner of her eye, she could see her parents standing with their arms around each other.

Nothing was impossible unless you believed it was.

She rummaged in the tote that had fallen open near

her feet and found a pen. She flattened the paper on the seat of the chair behind her, wrote a line, then rose and handed it to Evan.

He looked down at it.

"She wants that, too." She whispered the words she'd written.

The page crumpled in his fist. "Are you sure? What about your promotion?"

"It doesn't mean as much as I thought it did." Her tears spilled over. "I'm not sure about a lot of things, actually. But that's not one of them. Not anymore." And for once, admitting it didn't seem so very hard after all.

Follow her dreams. Follow her heart.

How could she not have known until then that doing one meant doing the other?

She stepped toward him, closing the distance between them. And nearly lost her composure when Hannah's arm surrounded her leg just as tightly as it surrounded her uncle's. "I love you, Evan Taggart."

His gaze was fierce. "No more running?"

"Only toward you." She let out a shuddering breath. "You and whatever our life together brings us."

"Is that a proposal?"

She smiled, laughing a little, crying a little. "Aren't we already engaged?" She slid her arms around the man that she loved, the man who'd become so much more to her than a friend. "I don't want you to ever regret this," she whispered.

"Not in this lifetime," he assured her and closed his mouth over hers.

No, she thought, vaguely aware of Hannah squirming out from between them and of the cheers that were coming from the peanut gallery.

Not ever in this lifetime.

Not as long as they were together.

She cupped his face in her hands when he finally lifted his head. "Evan?"

Everything she ever wanted to see in his eyes was there. Naked and bare. "Yeah?"

"Take us home."

His smile was slow and sexy and warmed her right down to her soul. "Finally."

There was no way for anyone to ever truly know what the future would hold.

But she knew, thanks to Evan and Hannah, that she was no longer afraid to find out what *their* future would hold.

She smiled back at them both and held out her hand for Hannah. "Yes. Finally."

\* \* \* \* \*

We hope you enjoyed reading

# HOME ON THE RANCH
and
# JUST FRIENDS?

by *New York Times* bestselling author
**ALLISON LEIGH**

Both were originally **Harlequin®** series stories!

Discover more heartfelt tales of family, friendship and love from the **Harlequin Special Edition** series. Romance is for life, and these stories show that every chapter in a relationship has its challenges and delights and that love can be renewed with each turn of the page!

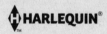

**HARLEQUIN®**

# SPECIAL EDITION

**Life, Love and Family**

**When you're with family, you're home!**

Look for six *new* romances every month
from **Harlequin Special Edition**!

Available wherever books are sold.

www.Harlequin.com

HOTRALBPA0517

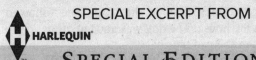
Things had certainly changed around here, he thought as he drove back to his house. Even Maude, who had once seemed as unchangeable as the mountains, had softened up a bit.

A veterans' group meeting. He didn't remember if there'd been one when he was in high school, but he supposed he wouldn't have been interested. His thoughts turned back to those years, and he realized he had some assessing to do.

"Come in?" he asked Ashley as they parked in his driveway.

She didn't hesitate, which relieved him. It meant he hadn't done something to disturb her today. Yet. "Sure," she said and climbed out.

His own exit took a little longer, and Ashley was waiting for him on the porch by the time he rolled up the ramp.

Nell took a quick dash in the yard, then followed eagerly into the house. The dog was good at fitting in her business when she had the chance.

"Stay for a while," he asked Ashley. "I can offer you a soft drink if you'd like."

She held up her latte cup. "Still plenty here."

He rolled into the kitchen and up to the table, where he placed the box holding his extra meal. He didn't go into the living room much. Getting on and off the sofa was a pain, hardly worth the effort most of the time. He supposed he could hang a bar in there like he had over his bed so he could pull himself up and over, but he hadn't felt particularly motivated yet.

But then, almost before he knew what he was doing, he tugged on Ashley's hand until she slid into his lap.

"If I'm outta line, tell me," he said gruffly. "No social skills, like I said."

He watched one corner of her mouth curve upward. "I don't usually like to be manhandled. However, this time I think I'll make an exception. What brought this on?"

"You have any idea how long it's been since I had an attractive woman in my lap?" With those words he felt almost as if he had stripped his psyche bare. Had he gone over some new kind of cliff?

*Don't miss*
*CONARD COUNTY HOMECOMING*
*by Rachel Lee, available June 2017 wherever*
*Harlequin® Special Edition books and ebooks are sold.*

www.Harlequin.com